A whole new way of li[fe]
A chance to escape fr[om]
myself into. A new [...]undings, new
friends, new things to write about. No more lonely
weekends and Augusts when the days lasted forever
because I had nothing to do but work, and no one to see.
No more having to pretend that I was happy living alone,
or that I enjoyed being single. A chance to build a real
life, a real home, a home shared with someone who loved
me. Maybe I might even have children, before it was too
late . . .

I looked at Cecil coldly, and totted up his many defects.
Like my heroines, I'd fantasised about a hero who'd
suddenly appear and fall head over heels in love with me
– but why, oh why, out of all the men in London, did it
have to be *him*?

About the author

Judith Summers is a writer and journalist. Her first two novels, *Dear Sister* and *I, Gloria Gold*, were followed by a prize-winning history of London's Soho. Her third novel, *Crime and Ravishment*, was published in 1996 and is available from Coronet. She lives in North London with her husband and son.

Frogs and Lovers

Judith Summers

CORONET BOOKS
Hodder and Stoughton

First published in Great Britain in 1997 by Hodder and Stoughton
First published in paperback in 1998 by Hodder and Stoughton
A division of Hodder Headline PLC
A Coronet Paperback

10 9 8 7 6 5 4 3 2 1

A CIP catalogue record for this title is available from the
British Library

ISBN 0 340 63820 6

Printed and bound in Great Britain by
Mackays of Chatham PLC, Chatham, Kent

Hodder and Stoughton
A division of Hodder Headline PLC
338 Euston Road
London NW1 3BH

For Jud

Preface

—————◆◆—————

I'm free-falling through the dark sky, nose to nose with my apartment building. My dressing gown flies above me like a parachute, and the night air stings my skin with its cold blast. Living rooms, bedrooms and darkened terraces flicker in front of me like stills from a movie. Far below, the floodlit swimming pool rushes up to meet me like a large aquamarine.

How long does it take for a body to reach the ground when it falls from the thirty-second floor? How long do I have before my bones pulverise to powder and my skull smashes open like a soft-boiled egg?

Oh God, I don't want to die!

Aaaaaaaaaaaah! I don't think I've ever screamed like this before in my life. There's actually something quite liberating about it, particularly when you're stark naked and in the middle of Monte-Carlo, where everyone's normally so well behaved. My throat is open, my body is tensed as if for an orgasm, and terror tingles in every nerve. My stomach's coming out of my mouth and my hands are clutching my water-melon belly protectively – as if that'd do any good.

I mustn't look down! But I can't help it. I'm drawn to see the spot where my destiny lies as surely as someone on a fat-free diet is drawn to a bowl of whipped cream. My head spins as I squint into the abyss.

Down.

Down.

Down to the tastefully floodlit palm trees and the swimming pool and the glowing marquee where my upstairs neighbour and self-appointed mentor Zuzu Lamarre is currently entertaining one hundred and fifty of her most intimate friends.

Goodbye world! All fairy tales come to an end, and they aren't usually happy ones.

Is this it? Is my life really over?

How I wish I could talk to Elena!

Why was I such an idiot?

None of this would ever have happened if I hadn't married that frog!

One

It all started a year ago, with Lorelei's bad timing.

Less than two minutes after Andy had stormed out of my flat muttering, 'See you sometime, then!' the buzzer rang, and my rock-bottom spirits soared skywards. 'I knew it!' I cried as I jumped out of bed. He'd had a change of heart already! Our relationship wasn't over after all!

I didn't bother to talk to Andy over the intercom, but simply pushed the release button to let him back into the block of flats. Throwing on a cotton kimono, I flung open my front door, and ran barefoot down the corridor to meet the lift.

'Darling, I just knew you'd come back!' I sobbed, throwing my arms wide in forgiveness as the steel lift doors slid apart.

Then I said, 'Oh, shit!'

For standing in the lift was a petite, middle-aged woman with skin drawn tightly over her prominent cheekbones and a pile of stiff, black candy floss atop her head. Her over-chiselled, peach-powdered nose wrinkled with distaste when she saw me standing there half-naked, and her small, hard, unforgiving mouth twisted into a jaded sneer.

I knew it was useless to try to bluff my way out of the situation – I really wasn't up to it at that moment – so, pulling the flapping sides of my kimono together, I fled back into my flat. The determined clack-clack of high heels followed close behind me. 'Who the hell is the bastard?' rasped a harsh New York voice over my shoulder. 'More to the point – why won't he marry you?'

I should have slammed the front door on her, but I didn't have the courage. Coward that I am, I ran into my bedroom and threw myself face down on the bed. The front door slammed, trapping me with the finality of a cell door, and the clack-clack of steel-tipped stilettos continued to stalk me across the wood-strip floor.

A moment later, without looking up, I sensed a disapproving presence in the doorway. 'Jesus, Lisa,' said my mother after a short pause. 'What a fucking mess!'

Like a pig in search of truffles, she sniffed the air for the giveaway odour of illicit sex. Having caught it, she gave a dramatic sigh of resignation, dropped the shiny envelope of her black-patent handbag onto the chair where Andy had thrown my bra and pants an hour earlier, and flung open the sash window, letting the chill evening air blow in.

'Lisa, Lisa, Lisa!' she sighed as despairingly as if I'd just been convicted of first degree murder.

'Will you please shut that window, Mummy?'

My mother eyed the rumpled sheets with revulsion, then her dainty hands – the nails carefully lacquered in vermillion, the swollen-knuckled fingers ringed with imitation rubies – smoothed out a corner of the duvet with a cat-like, feminine gesture. She sat down beside me. 'Look at me, baby.'

I pulled a pillow over my head. The pillowslip smelled of Andy's shampoo. 'Mummy,' I said as calmly as I could, 'will you please go away?'

As if I hadn't spoken, my mother, Lorelei Higgins, undid the line of gold buttons marching down her tightly upholstered chest, and her red M&S jacket split open to reveal a weight of gilt chains and necklaces better suited to a lord mayor. 'Sit up, Lisa,' she commanded in her bossiest voice. 'Don't behave like a kid. You're a young . . .' After a moment's hesitation, temptation overcame her, and she added a pointed 'ish' to the adjective, 'youngish woman. You're free to do what you choose. I suppose screwing around's nothing to be ashamed of – at your age.'

2

'I don't *screw around*,' I said in strangulated voice. 'And anyway, I'm *not* ashamed!'

'It's not as if you're married, and cheating on a *husband*.' As usual, she pronounced the *h* word in a sour tone. Doing her best to eradicate this, she cleared her throat and added, coaxingly, 'Why don't you tell Mommy all about it?'

I knew from the past that this proposition was about as inviting as being asked to plunge my hand into the whirring blades of a Magimix. 'I don't want to. Thank you.'

'OK.' She sniffed again. 'As far as I'm concerned, the subject's closed.' After a brief but painful struggle, Lorelei's lips, glued together by the tacky glue of blood-red lipstick, fought free of each other, and she continued, 'Yet again, we'll sweep all talk of your personal life under the rug. Strange, I'd have thought the subject of love would have interested you, Lisa, if only professionally. But then, no one can tell you anything about it, because you know all about it, don't you?' She gave a bitter laugh. 'My daughter, alias *Mahonia Medmenham* – the bestselling romantic novelist!'

Mahonia Medmenham – that was me. OK, so I'd never won the Booker. But I'd scooped the Romantic Novelist of the Year Award (1987), and the Fragrant Rose Award (1990), and the Pink Peony Award (1992), and the Sugar Almond Award (1994), and even the Guild of Romance Writers Prize (1995, and again, Highly Commended, in 1996). After ten years in the romantic fiction business, Mahonia – or rather I – seemed to have the recipe for love stories down to a T: take three pages of flowers and add a good deflowering; stir in a dollop of heartless heroes for every heroine with a heart of gold; mix in thirty pages of fraught misunderstandings to every one of reconciliation; sprinkle on adjectives *ad lib*, and seduction scenes *ad nauseam*, and garnish with a generous portion of lust, redolent with unfulfilled longing and heavy with dot-dot-dots. And let's not forget that ubiquitous happy ending.

So much for fiction. As my present situation showed, I should have stuck to writing about love and not chanced my arm with it in real life. 'Please, Mum!' I shouted into the pillow. 'Do you have to go on at me? Can't you see that I'm upset?'

'Of course I can, baby.' After a short pause, during which her hand tentatively patted the back of my head in a half-hearted attempt at expressing sympathy, Lorelei said in a tone of accusation, 'And can't you see how seeing you like this – wasting your tears on some worthless jerk – upsets me?'

Suddenly, out of the blue, I remembered the afternoon of my tenth birthday, when I'd broken my leg at Queen's Ice Rink. It had been Lorelei, not I, who'd had to be treated for shock by the ambulance crew. What was it about my mother, I wondered now with a spurt of anger, that she had to appropriate whatever pain or pleasure I happened to be feeling? Didn't she have enough feelings of her own?

'Then go away!' I snapped. 'I didn't invite you here!'

'So that's the score, is it? OK. I know when I'm not wanted.' Though she got to her feet and plucked her handbag from the knicker-chair, my mother made no move to leave the room. Instead, she opened my wardrobe, and widened her eyes at the reflection in the mirror inside the door. At fifty-six, and thanks to a lifetime of self-devotion and two recent face-lifts, my mother is still almost as youthful looking and pretty as she was in 1958 when Horace, my English father, fell in love with her while on a business trip to the States. Everything about Lorelei – from her hair through to her high, pointed bosom and down to her tiny arched feet – is petite, pert and feminine. Apart from her dark hair – tinted black and tortured with a comb every week by her hairdresser Stanley – she's the image of the Anita Loos heroine she renamed herself after when she was a teenager, and quite the opposite of tall, strong-looking, big-boned me. However, under Lorelei's fluffy exterior lies a will of granite that can, if given half a chance, crush any resistance it meets. She's ready at a moment's notice to squeeze the life out of any potential victim – especially me.

She pulled back her lips in a baboon-like grimace, and wiped

4

a smear of lipstick from her Persil-white teeth. 'Wanna know something, Lisa?' she remarked to my reflection. 'You're . . . very . . . hard on me.' Her voice was now quavering with the melodramatic quality of an actor in one of the daytime soaps she's addicted to. 'I'm . . . only . . . trying to help you, sweetheart. To be a comfort . . . to my only daughter . . . in her hour of need.'

No matter that I know all her tricks by now, I still fall for them hook, line and sinker. After a lifetime of practice, Lorelei's become an expert at turning the guilt tables on me. 'Look, I'm sorry,' I apologised, rolling over and reaching for the box of tissues on the bedside table. 'It's just that you . . .'

'You're my daughter, Lisa. You don't have to make excuses for yourself.'

I gritted my teeth. 'I wasn't going to. I was just trying to explain that . . .'

'There's no need to explain anything!' The wardrobe door shut with a decisive click as she turned towards me. 'My poor baby, you're thirty-five and childless and you haven't even got a man! What more is there to say?'

There was plenty more, but Lorelei wasn't interested in any of it. That I, her daughter, had written and published ten romantic novels during the last eight years was, to Lorelei, an incidental and unimportant fact of my life. That people say I'm kind, and have a gift for friendship; that some call my gangly body graceful – if in the manner of a giraffe – and say that my long, rather mournful face and shoulder-length chestnut hair has an unusual, Modiglianiesque beauty; these things counted for nothing compared to the fact that I had failed to get married and produce a grandchild for her to criticise. For me to be still single and childless was, as she saw it, a damning indictment not of my upbringing but of the selfishness of my chosen way of life. For it wasn't by chance that I was – at that blessed time – still a single woman. It was – yes, it had to be said, and as often as possible by Lorelei – my own damned fault. Because I hadn't missed the boat by bad luck or accident. In her opinion, I'd done it by standing passively on the quayside while, one by one, all the eligible men in London strolled up the gangplank with my friends and contemporaries. Any offers to take me aboard – of which there had been two or three along the way – had been firmly, and in Lorelei's opinion, foolishly declined. Now that I'd turned thirty-five, the boat had pulled anchor and sailed away; it was little more than a dot on the horizon, and I had only a one-in-a-million chance of catching it.

Usually I'm hardened to my mother's attacks. But in the aftermath of splitting up with Andy, I was reduced to tears. Sensing a rare moment of weakness in me, and thus a chance for her to breach my hitherto impenetrable defences and finally take charge of my life, Lorelei sat down beside me again, and engulfed me in a suffocating *Georgio of Beverly Hills* embrace. 'So the bastard's walked out on you, has he?' she wheedled. 'What's his name? Huh? Mmm? Tell Mommy! Do you love him very much, baby? C'mon, honey, don't be shy! I guess he's a married man, isn't he? Huh? Isn't he, Lisa? What's the matter, sweetheart – won't he leave his wife?'

Here, I made a fatal mistake by admitting, 'He doesn't have a wife.'

The highly perfumed clinch ended abruptly as Lorelei drew away in a state of bewildered shock. 'Whadyamean?'

I should have known that any attempt to explain the odd situation with Andy was doomed to failure. Still, having started, I blundered on. 'He's got a . . . well, a sort of old girlfriend he shares a flat with.'

'A *girlfriend*?' My mother pronounced this word as if it were something offensive she had stepped in on the street. Her small nose wrinkled disdainfully between the taut drums of her over-stretched cheeks. 'So what's the big problem? Why doesn't he ditch her?'

'Because . . .' I tried to remember all the plausible, and laudible, reasons Andy had given over the past two years why he couldn't leave his old girlfriend Francesca at that precise time: Francesca's recurrent bouts of depression; Francesca's

6

latest failed suicide attempt; Francesca's redundancy; the torn ligament which had left Francesca on crutches, and helpless, for several months; Francesca's terrible fear at being alone at night in their rented Shepherd's Bush flat after she'd been mugged in a nearby street; the erroneous result of Francesca's cervical smear which had resulted in a short-lived, but understandably traumatic, cancer scare. 'It's complicated.'

'Bullshit.' Mommy Dearest raised the two darts of her sharply plucked eyebrows. 'That kinda situation's never complicated, Lisa – not if a man really loves you.'

'You don't understand . . .' My protest petered out as I realised something shocking: for once, my mother was right. I'd tried for a long time to persuade myself that there were genuine reasons why Andy had to carry on sharing a flat with Francesca, but . . . There'd always been that *but*, right from the beginning. Whatever Andy professed to feel for me – and, during the two years we'd been seeing each other he'd professed a lot, very convincingly: true love, kinship of the soul, a life time's worth of commitment, unending and earth-shattering passion, etcetera etcetera – if he'd really loved me, he would have told Francesca about our relationship long ago. His excuses had been nothing but – well, yes, excuses, designed to keep me where I liked to keep my mother – at emotional arm's length, and to ensure the continuation of the current and, for him, comfortable, status quo.

Just an hour ago, after we'd made love in this very bed, he'd told me that he and Francesca were now thinking of buying a flat together. Actually, it was more than thinking: they'd found a place, and made an offer on it. 'It's not what you think, Puss darling,' he'd said, leaning over my naked body, and running his index finger around my much-kissed mouth. 'It's just a matter of practicality. It just kind of makes financial sense. Our lease is up where we are, and the landlord's planning to triple the rent. A grand a month for that Shepherd's Bush hovel! It's fucking outrageous, isn't it?'

'I wouldn't know,' I said. 'I've never seen the place.' I

pulled the duvet up over my breasts, and looked away from him.

Andy sighed. 'Look, Lisa, you know that I don't really want to buy a place with Francesca.'

'Don't you?' I said quietly.

'Are you crazy? But, well, if it wasn't for me, she'd be homeless. On the street.' He rolled over onto his belly, treating me to a view of his long naked back. Then, propping himself up on an elbow, he pushed his unruly black curls behind his ears, and gave a helpless grimace. 'I just can't do that to Francesca – not after so long, not at this moment, when she's in such a bloody awful state. You know, she'd never be able to afford to rent a place by herself. She earns such a fucking pittance.'

For once, this plea for sympathy cut no ice with me. 'Does she have to do freelance telephone research for that PR company? Couldn't she look for a full-time job?' I asked with straining patience.

Andy laughed. 'Where?'

'Maybe you could help her find one.'

'Darling!' His full lips twisted into a patronising smile. 'I'm a television producer!'

'Well, you know lots of people. Surely you could pull a few strings.'

'Lisa! Come off it! You know it doesn't work like that. Besides, even if Francesca found a proper job, how'd she ever get to work every day? She's got to work at home because of her claustrophobia. I mean, you know what a problem she has with taking buses or the tube.'

'It's funny how she seems to manage to get to Soho whenever she's meeting you at the Groucho Club.'

Andy pulled the duvet down and nuzzled one of my nipples. 'Do cheer up, darling!' he murmured. 'It's not like you to sound so bitter!'

Despite the stab of desire between my legs, I pushed him away and, fighting the pride and reserve which had kept me silent for the last two years, I forced myself to go on, 'I'm not bitter, Andy. I'm just fed up with playing second fiddle to Francesca all the time – no, don't interrupt me! Of having to organise *my* life so as not to upset *her*. I'm the one you're meant to be going out with. I wish you were a quarter as concerned about what upsets me.'

'Of course I am! You *know* I hate this situation as much as you do.'

I looked at him with a feeling of sadness. Why did he have to be so good-looking and so disarmingly charming? Why did I have to love everything about him: his true-blue English eyes; the Eton accent in which he swore so freely; his Peter Pan-ish attitude to life; his formidable intelligence; his self-deprecating sense of humour and his schoolboy grin; the buoyant self-confidence which seemed to flow, as if by birthright, through his impoverished, aristocratic veins? I wanted so much to believe what he was saying; and, I supposed, there was a slim chance it could be true. And yet there was that seed of doubt, nagging me as surely as a stone caught in my shoe ... 'I wonder,' I sighed.

'Jesus, Lisa!' Andy said impatiently. 'Don't you think I'd much rather be living with you? Francesca's like a bloody millstone round my neck! It's just – well, she depends on me. She's so pathetic, and weedy, and vulnerable and ...'

'I'm vulnerable, too,' I protested.

'You? No, Puss, you're strong, and independent, and self-sufficient.' He squeezed my hand. 'That's why I love you so much.'

'Maybe I'm not as self-sufficient as you think.' I watched with growing apprehension as a shadow of fear fell across my lover's face. Still, having gone so far, I carried on, 'You told me when we first started going out that you and Francesca weren't lovers any more, and that you just happened to share the same flat, and that it was only a matter of time until one of you moved out. That was two years ago, Andy, and you still haven't even told her you're seeing me. Now you tell me you're buying a flat with her. What the hell am I supposed to think?'

He bristled like a cornered skunk. 'Why can't you understand that it just makes financial sense? The flat's a bloody good bargain – I mean a two-bedroom flat in Hammersmith Grove for 110 grand!' When I failed to look impressed, he reached for the pack of cigarettes on the bedside table. 'I don't understand why you're making such heavy weather of this. I thought this kind of relationship suited you.'

'I don't know what made you think that. You've never asked me if it did.'

'You don't really want to settle down, do you? Writers aren't supposed to be so bourgeois.'

'How can you be so disingenuous, Andy? Buying a house with someone means something. It's a commitment.' A match flared angrily in the semi-darkness of the winter afternoon as he lit a cigarette. For once, he seemed lost for words. With a flick of his wrist, he sent the spent matchstick flying across the room. Despite a growing feeling of doom, I continued, 'You've told me time and again how much you love me, and that you'd like us to be together. So, if you're making a commitment, why isn't it to me?'

'Because . . .' Smoke billowed from his nose, and he turned towards me angrily. 'Look, I've got no choice in the matter!'

'Why?'

'Because if I leave Francesca at the moment, she'll probably take another overdose!'

How many times had I heard this one before? How many times had I chastised myself for the retort which sprang to mind – *I hope she bloody well succeeds.*

'Well, when will you be able to leave her?' I persisted. 'I'm not going to wait for ever. I want a proper relationship. I don't always want to live by myself. I'm getting to the point when I want someone who puts me first.'

Andy sighed with profound boredom. 'In another minute you'll be telling me you want to have babies and things!'

The words had been on the tip of my tongue. Stung by his derisive tone, I bit them back.

Andy sucked hard on his cigarette. 'Look, Puss, please don't lay this trip on me today. Can't you just accept that buying this place with Francesca is simply a matter of convenience?'

'No, Andy, it's more than that to me.' I'd swallowed so much over the years, but this stuck in my throat like a lump of dry bread. If I didn't make a stand about Francesca now, I knew I never would. Fighting my natural reticence, I forced myself to make the only demand I'd ever made on him. 'If you go ahead and buy this flat with her, well, then I won't see you any more.'

He laughed. 'You can't be serious!'

Couldn't I be? Maybe he was right. After all, how many times in the past had I sworn to myself that I'd end our relationship and then gone back on my word? I forced myself to say, 'I am.' He pulled a funny face at me, but I wasn't amused. 'I don't want to go on like this.'

'Like what?'

'Like never being able to phone you when you're at home. Like having to spend every holiday by myself because you've promised to spend time with Francesca. I've had enough of it. Don't smile – I'm serious.'

There was a long pause. Andy looked as if he didn't know what to say. Then he stood up, and started to get dressed, pulling on his trousers angrily. 'I'm sorry, Lisa, but there's nothing I can do about the flat.'

'Of course there is – if you want to.'

His hands punched through the arms of his shirt. 'Want's got nothing to do with it. We've already exchanged contracts.'

So that was it. The man I'd adored for the last two years had already signed the death warrant on our relationship. I suppose I ought to have felt grateful for seeing him in his true light at long last, but I just felt devastated. The rest of my life seemed to stretch ahead of me like a bleak, lonely Bank Holiday weekend. Maybe my mother was right after all and I'd left it too late to build a proper relationship. I wasn't getting any younger. In fact, I was dangerously approaching the crunch-time when my hormones would turn against me. From now on until doomsday, every time I looked in the mirror my face would look that much more wrinkled and careworn than the time before. Why, that very morning, I'd found three grey hairs in my comb . . .

'Lisa? Are you listening to me?'

With tears dripping down my cheeks, I looked up into my mother's face and made the fatal mistake of admitting how I felt. 'Oh, Mummy, I'm so miserable!'

'I'm not surprised!' Lorelei's voice oozed with *schadenfreude*. 'You've got a hell of a lot to be miserable about!'

I should have known better than to cry on her shoulder-pads but, lethal as I knew it was, there was nevertheless something comforting in her over-perfumed embrace. 'Oh God,' I muttered, 'what am I going to do?'

Her silicone-injected bosoms heaved beneath the silky blouse. 'Listen to me, kid – it's high time you got married.'

'Who to?' I wept. 'There aren't any single men!'

Lorelei's lips smacked together smugly. 'Leave it to me, honey. I'll find you a husband.'

This brought me to my senses in the nick of time. 'No thanks!' I said as I pulled away. 'If I want one, I'll find one myself.'

Lorelei narrowed her eyes. 'Pardon me if I speak frankly for a change, dear, but if you don't mind me saying so, you're not doing very well in the love stakes. May I remind you that when I was your age I'd been married for – what? – fourteen years, and you were in your teens. My, when I think of all the opportunities you've wasted. All those men you've turned down in the past!'

'Mummy, please don't do this now!'

But she was away like a greyhound out of the slips, charging through my ex-partners on her bejewelled fingers. 'There was David, and Mark, and Simon, and Howard . . .'

'I never went out with Howard . . .'

'You could've dated him, if you'd wanted to! There was Ian, and that nice Martin. And What's-his-name – you

12

know, the one with the big ears and glasses? And Guy. And Phil.'

'Phil was just a friend. He's gay. Did you hear me?'

I might as well have saved my breath, because, as usual, Lorelei ignored me. 'And Alan. Oh yeah, and that other fellow, Graham, who you shacked up with a while back? As I remember, he was very keen on you! And for a time you seemed keen too. So what happened?'

I hung my head. 'Things just didn't work out.'

'That's what you always say, Lisa. But I'll tell you what really happened: Miss Clever clogs Mahonia Medmenham here decided she was too good for him. So, like the rest of them, Graham – a perfectly regular kind of guy as I recall – got married to someone else. And Miss Clever Clogs here ends up wasting years of her life locked up in a room writing love stories, and screwing a man who doesn't even want her!' Lorelei's tongue lay still for a moment before lashing out for a grande finale: 'And now, Miss Clever Clogs here is too proud to admit that she's on the shelf!'

'I'm not!'

Lorelei licked her lips, and threw down the gauntlet. 'Then prove it to me, Lisa!' Instead of wasting your time at that desk in the other room, writing all that schmaltz about love, find yourself a man – an ordinary single man – and have a proper relationship! And, if you can find anyone who wants to date you – and frankly, I must admit I have my doubts – take my advice and get your hooks into him fast. You're far too old to turn down any more opportunities. It's time to get married and get a real life!'

Two

Once my mother sinks her teeth into something, she never lets go of it. So it was no surprise to me when she rang up three days later and said that she'd fixed up a blind date for me.

'How dare you?' I seethed. 'Why did you do that when I expressly told you not to do anything of the sort?'

'You *did*?'

'You know that I did.'

'Strange, I can't remember.' She attempted to sound bewildered. But I wasn't fooled, particularly as she continued in a cheerful voice, 'Still, what the heck? I knew you'd be pleased.'

I gritted my teeth. 'No. You knew I'd be livid.'

'Oh no, I didn't!'

'Oh yes, you did!'

'Oh no, I did not!'

'You did!'

'For Chrissake, Lisa, you sound like a six-year-old at a Punch and Judy show.'

'I'm not six. I'm thirty-five,' I said without thinking. Which was precisely what my mother had wanted me to say.

'Exactly!' I could almost see Lorelei smacking her Lancôme'd lips together with satisfaction. 'A single woman of your age needs all the help she can get. I was only trying to cheer you up, honey,' she wheedled on when I remained silent. 'You seemed so unhappy the other night.'

'Well, I'm all right now,' I lied.

'You are? Why? Has *that man* broken up with his *girlfriend*?'

To my dismay, I hadn't even heard from Andy since he'd charged out of my flat. It was one thing for me to give him the push, another for him to accept it without a struggle. I'd lain awake at night expecting him to turn up unannounced, or at least for an impassioned phone call begging me to take him back. But no phone call had come, and neither had he.

'Lisa? I asked you a question,' barked Lorelei when I didn't answer.

'Yes, I heard you.'

'Well? Hmm? Really, can't you be straight about this and give me an answer? At least, tell Mommy if you're back together with him? Aw, c'mon, then, honey! Take the risk of seeing this guy! What have you got to lose?'

I sighed with resignation. 'Who is he?'

'He's forty-three. And a doctor. What could be better?'

'Where'd you dig him up?'

'I didn't dig him up anywhere. He happens to be a nephew of Marjorie Barcham.'

'Who on earth's she?'

'You know Marjorie – our next door neighbour. Number 14.'

'*Her*? God! What did you do, discuss me over the fence while you were hanging out the washing?'

'I don't *hang out the washing*. There's not much point, in this godforsaken climate. No, as it happens, I ran into Marjorie at the supermarket and . . .'

'And, as you were pushing your trollies past the nappies section, the subject of your single, childless daughter just happened to flash into your mind.'

A long pause indicated that I'd scored a bull's-eye. At last, my mother said, 'So what if it did?'

'So you told Marjorie that I'd just been ditched by my boyfriend, and did she know any single male, however pathetic and awful he might be, who might be inveigled into taking me out.' My mother's silence indicated that I'd

16

scored another direct hit. 'How could you, Mum? I'm so embarrassed I could die!'

'How do you think I felt, having to tell Marjorie the whole story?'

'You didn't *have* to tell her anything! I could really kill you, you know.'

At this, my mother slipped into her daytime soap mode: 'You're killing me already, Lisa,' she said in a trembly voice. 'Some part of me dies every time I think what a mess you've made of your life!'

In the end, the guilt got to me, and when Dr Michael Forenham rang me the next day, I arranged to meet him for a meal at Quaglino's restaurant on the following Saturday night. Against my better judgement. What good could possibly come of it? He sounded quite acceptable on the telephone, but I knew that there had to be something substantially wrong with a man who accepted a blind date cooked up by his aunt in the nappy aisle of Tesco's.

To my surprise, Dr Forenham didn't look like the Quasimodo I'd been expecting. Dressed in a checked tweed jacket with leather patched elbows, he sat alone at a table in the upstairs bar at Quaglino's stooped over the copy of the *Lancet* he'd said he'd be carrying, his long, outstretched legs encased in pristine jeans. His salt-and-pepper hair might have been thinning at the top, but what remained of it was well cut and glossy. He looked – yes – quite presentable, and for a brief moment when I saw him, my heart leaped with the vain hope that, for once, my mother could have got things right.

'Excuse me, but are you Michael?'

'Lisa?' He smiled up at me with bright green eyes which were not unfriendly, then uncurled his body to its full, six foot two height. 'Sit down. We'll have a drink before we go down and dine. Waiter – bring the lady a glass of Chardonnay!'

I hadn't wanted any wine, but I soon realised I'd need it in order to get through the evening. For I ran out of things I wanted to say to Dr Michael Forenham even before I'd

17

worked my way through the bowl of designer olives on the designer table. Unfortunately, he had plenty to say to me – all of it about himself. By the time we'd gone downstairs to eat, I'd learned more about him than I knew about my parents: his age, to the hour of day; his star sign – Capricorn; how many squash medals he'd won; and the model number and year of manufacture of his BMW. I also knew that he played the guitar so well that a professional had once told him he played as well as Julian Bream and that he could, had he wanted to, have turned professional. And I knew how much he earned, before and after tax. Oh yes, and the size, position and price of his Chelsea flat; and the number and relative fame of the women who queued up for an appointment at his private practice in Harley Street.

'What exactly do you do specialise in, Michael?' I said, forcing my features into an interested smile.

At which my date said something that sounded like, 'I examine cunts.'

Sure I'd misheard, I leaned forward across the table. 'Sorry?'

'I examine cunts,' he repeated with a grin. 'Thought that'd make you sit up! It's true, you know. I'm a gynaecologist.'

I stared at him with a blank expression, secretly astonished that, in this day and age when everything is acceptable, I was still capable of being shocked. My date took full advantage of my silence to list his many professional qualifications, and to tell me in detail about his life-long fascination with female genitalia – or twats, as he described them with relish.

He paused for a moment to eat a breadstick, then, long nose twitching, looked me up and down, as if I was a cow in a cattle market. 'You're very thin. You're not bulimic or anorexic by any chance, are you?'

I cleared my throat. 'This is just how I am.'

'Good. I can't stand women with eating disorders. I like my food too much.'

After we'd ordered, he said – so loudly that the people at the next table turned round – 'So, Lisa, what's your trip? How come a woman of your age isn't married yet?'

If I'd have had more courage, I'd have thrown my drink at him. Instead, being me, I bowed my humiliated head, fought back the retort that came to mind, and murmured lamely, 'I suppose that's just how it's worked out.'

Dr Forenham's thin mouth stretched into a patronising smile. 'Nothing's ever that simple, Lisa. You learn that in my line of work. There's always a reason for everything. For instance, if a woman can't conceive, there's a blocked tube somewhere or a leaky womb. Or the poor cow's husband can't get it up because he's screwing around with someone else.' He laughed as if this was the funniest thing he'd ever heard, then clicked his fingers at the waiter. 'Hey, man, where's our hors d'oeuvres? Believe me, I could tell you some stories,' he continued. 'About women, women just like you. Girls who've fucked around and put off having kids till their mid-thirties because of their careers. I see them come into my surgery every day, begging for fertility treatment. Poor, desperate cows. They just can't accept that they've left it too late.'

'Excuse me for a moment, will you?' Cheeks on fire, I stood up, picked up my bag and headed for the ladies' lavatory. I had a feeling I was about to be sick. At the last minute, I swerved to the left and ran up the stairs. Pausing at the top, I looked down over the glass and steel banister: my date was scanning his copy of the *Lancet*, and hadn't seen me. Turning on my heels, I headed for the door.

Outside, I trudged towards Piccadilly Circus through the cold steady March drizzle, feeling tearful and humiliated. How I wanted to see Andy! I wanted to smell his smell, and feel the comfort of his arms around me. But Andy wasn't on offer, not tonight or any other night. What awaited me at the other end of the Northern Line was an empty flat, an empty fridge, an empty bed, and an answering machine with no messages on it – except, no doubt, one from Lorelei, demanding that I phone her up and tell her how the evening went.

Had the gynaecologist been a sick joke on her part, I

wondered, a form of punishment for my not having fulfilled my duty and supplied her with grandchildren? Or was he really the cream of the remaining unmarried crop? If so, I'd happily stay single for the rest of my life.

Desperate to salvage some sanity from the evening, I took shelter in a telephone booth and dialled Elena's number.

'The madhouse,' crackled a dry, cheerful voice at the other end of the line.

'It's me,' I said.

'Lisa? What on earth's wrong?'

That's what I like about Elena – she always knows exactly what I'm feeling. Since I first went to work at Pink Peony Publishing as her secretary eleven years ago, her intuition about me has never once failed. Tonight, it reduced me to tears. 'Oh, Elena,' I sniffed. 'How can you tell?'

'Your voice. It goes all high and squeaky when you're upset. Like a strangulated chihuahua. So what's up?'

'You know that blind date my mother arranged for me . . .'

'It was tonight! What . . . Oh, damn, hold on a moment, will you?' Her gravelly voice shot up two octaves. '*Don't play with it, eat it, sweetie*!' she crooned off telephone. 'Sorry. Go on, Lisa. *Did you hear me, Rupert? Eat*! Sorry, Lisa. You were saying. So?'

'I walked out on him.'

Elena whooped with delight. 'Fabulous! Lorelei won't like that! What happened? And where are you now?'

'In a phone box off Jermyn Street. Standing in the rain.'

Elena sighed. 'I wish you'd stop being such a Luddite, and get yourself a mobile phone. I thought you were having supper with him at Quag's.'

'I was. I did. I mean, I got as far as ordering – or rather he did. Oh, Elena, I've never felt so humiliated in my life.'

'Why? *Don't throw those chips on the floor, children! For God's sake, Sophie, why are you crying?*'

'Rupert stole my fish finger!'

'*I did not!*'

'*Well, stab him with your fork or steal it back*. Sorry, Lisa. Go on.'

'He was just so . . .'

'*Mum, can I have a Coke?*'

'*Get it yourself! Can't you see I'm busy? Really, can't I ever get five minutes' peace?* Jesus Christ! Carry on, Lisa.'

'He was so rude, Elena, so insulting . . .'

From the other end of the phone came a terrible crash, followed after a short pause by a heart-rending wail. 'Damn! I'd better go,' Elena said sulkily. 'Suppertime and all that.'

'*Mum!*'

'*One minute, Sophie.* Sorry, Lisa.'

'It's all right,' I sighed. This kind of interruption happens whenever I called Elena at home. If I call her at work, she's always dashing off to lunch, or some crucial meeting. She never seems to have more than five minutes free. Whereas I – I had all the time in the world, and nothing but work to fill it.

'*Mummy!*'

'*Yes, yes!* Look, Lisa, why don't you come over? I'll slip them a couple of Mogadons for pudding, and with any luck they'll be asleep by the time you get here.'

'What, come over now? To *Clapham*?'

'Don't sound so shocked. It's not the South Pole.'

'But it's past nine o'clock!'

'Lisa! You're such a stick-in-the-mud! It's Saturday night! Even my brats are still up. Going to bed late for once won't kill you.'

'No. No, I couldn't possibly.'

'Please! Peter's out at the pub, playing in some bloody darts championship, and I'm all alone. In a manner of speaking. I could do with someone to get legless with, and some grown-up conversation. Besides, there's something I need to talk to you about.'

'What?'

'Well, work. Mmm. Actually, it's a bit delicate. On second thoughts, maybe tonight's not the right time.'

'Why?' I asked suspiciously, but Elena refused to be drawn.

'Oh, do come over,' she said. 'Live dangerously for once.'

I contemplated the dangers of the late-night Tube back from Clapham, and decided against it. As I put down the phone, a black depression settled over my shoulders. Head lowered, I trudged towards the tube. I imagined Elena at home in her cramped, untidy house filled with muddy dogs and moulting cat, squabbling, snotty-nosed kids, piles of Disney videos and Lego scattered across the floor. I could see her standing in her cluttered kitchen which always smelled faintly of curry powder and scorched fish fingers, wiping her hands on her stained apron and shrieking at the kids to go to bed. Elena was only one year older than I, but she'd already built herself a real, grown-up existence, with a husband, kids, and a semidetached house. Whereas I was still detached – and I couldn't help feeling inadequate and envious of her. It was strange: in the past I'd relished my solitude, but now I suddenly I felt like the little match girl – a perpetual outsider, gazing through brightly lit windows at other people's happy lives.

The icy rain dripped down my neck and face as I crossed Lower Regent Street and headed towards the Haymarket. Wiping my tears away with the back of my hand, I stepped off the pavement and into the flooded road . . .

A car's hooter sounded loudly to my left. I looked up with a start to see a pair of headlights flashing in the dark. As the car swerved to avoid me, I jumped back and felt myself tumbling sideways. The next moment, I was lying on the kerb with my feet in the overflowing gutter. My left ankle felt like a shard of hot, jagged steel had been jammed through it.

The car – a red Ford Escort – screeched to a halt several metres down the road. The driver's door swung open, and a figure jumped out and ran towards me. High up on his huge head, a pair of bulging eyes stared down at me with terror. 'Oh, G-god,' he stammered. 'Are you all r-r-right?'

'Couldn't you have looked where you were going?' I yelled.

The driver recoiled, and his full lower lip jutted forward. 'I'm sorry. I'm terribly sorry. You see, you – you – you just stepped out into the road. I . . . I had a g-green light. I s-stopped as soon as I saw you – but . . .' His short arms flapped up and down like penguin flippers. At their tips, tiny webbed fingers grasped at the air. 'Did I h-hit you?'

I rubbed my ankle. 'I don't think so.'

'Oh God!' he said again. 'Look, shall I call an ambulance?' He swivelled round, scanning the street in desperation. 'There m-must be a phone box near here somewhere.'

I glared at him. 'Don't bother.'

'Please!'

'I'll be all right.'

He spread his arms again. 'B-but – what can I do?'

'Just help me up, will you?'

The driver hooked his fingers under my arm and pulled me into a vertical position. Once I was on my feet, I towered over him and had a clear view of the rain-drenched strands of hair plastered in a spiral on top of his balding pate. I yanked my arm free, put my injured foot on the pavement, and tried to take a step away from him. 'Oh Lord! Let me have a look!' he cried when I yelped with pain. And before I could stop him, he squatted down beside me like the frog he so resembled. 'Oh dear! Your feet! They're s-soaking wet,' he murmured.

'Yes, I do know that.'

He caressed my ankle with a clammy fingertip. 'I don't think it's b-broken. But m-maybe you should get it . . .' There was a long pause before the next word came out, '. . . X-rayed. Where's the nearest c-casualty department nowadays?'

'God knows! Probably in Birmingham.' He grinned up at me for a second. Then his gaze returned to my ankle, which he stroked again. 'Please stop doing that!' I snapped. 'Really, I'm all right. I just want to go home. I'm getting very wet standing here.'

23

'Of course!' He jumped to his feet, glanced at me for a split second, then looked away. 'Can I help you to your c-c-car?'

'I don't have a car. I was on my way to the Tube.'

'But . . .' His high forehead furrowed like a crinkle-cut chip. When his stutter next allowed him to speak, he sounded horrified: 'You can't possibly take the Tube! Not with that ankle!'

'Of course I can. I'll be fine.'

'No, you won't, you won't!' He sounded so sure that I began to believe him. In order to disprove him, I took a step away from him, but a sharp pain shot up my leg. 'Please . . . Look . . . Look . . . Can I . . .? Could I . . .?'

Impatient to get away, I pulled my coat collar up against the rain and glared down at him. 'What is it now?'

A long, thin tongue flicked out and moistened his lips. 'Would you allow me to d-drop you home?'

'No.'

'Or at least, let me get you a taxi? I'll p-pay for it. Please! After what's happened, it's the least I can do.'

'No. OK, yes. You can find me a taxi. Only I'll pay for it.'

'But . . .'

'I insist!' Hunched over my folded arms, I waited on the kerb, shivering, while the frog stood out in the road, gazing into the headlights of the oncoming traffic which roared around the corner from Piccadilly Circus. At long last he spotted a taxi, and raised his arms to wave at it wildly. When it failed to slow down, he put two fingers between his lips and let out a piercing whistle. 'Can't you see that its light's off?' I shouted above the traffic noise. 'It's not for hire!'

'Sorry!'

Another ten minutes passed without a single free taxi having driven down the Haymarket. By now, my coat was damp through, and my soaking trousers clung to my calves like a wetsuit. My hair – carefully washed and dried in preparation for the blind date – had turned into a soggy waterfall, from which a steady flow of cold water dripped down my neck. What an evening! I thought, shivering miserably. Things couldn't get much worse.

At long last, a free taxi rounded the corner. The frog semaphored violently, but if the cabbie saw him he ignored him, for he pulled up on the opposite side of the road, where a couple of women were also flagging him down. Dodging out through the traffic, my self-appointed saviour engaged the cabbie and the women in a fruitless argument. A minute later, the two women climbed inside, the cab drove off, and the frog leaped back across the Haymarket, a humiliated, dejected specimen.

'I'm so sorry,' he croaked. 'I don't know where all the taxis have gone! I suppose it must b-be the rain.'

'This is ridiculous!' I spat through chattering teeth. 'I'm absolutely freezing! If I'd only taken the Tube in the first place, I would have been home by now!'

'Look ...' He attempted to blot dry his wet fore- head with his soaking sleeve. 'Let me drive you there. Please.'

'No, thanks.'

'Yes. You must let me. Really, I in ... insist. It wouldn't be any trouble.'

I weighed up the advantages of being spared the late-night Tube and delivered to my door post haste with the potential dangers of accepting a lift from a stranger. This one looked safe enough – not that one could necessarily tell by appearances. But he was certainly small enough for me to overpower him if I needed to.

'Well, OK. Thank you,' I added begrudgingly. 'As long as I'm not taking you out of your way.'

He shook his head, showering me with raindrops. 'No, no! Not at all.'

I squinted down at him suspiciously. 'How can you know that when I haven't told you where I live yet?'

'Oh, it doesn't matter. I've nothing else to do.' He must have realised how pathetic that sounded, for he quickly added, 'I mean, I'm not in a hurry right now.'

I limped to his car. The frog opened the passenger door for me like an old-fashioned gentleman. Inside, the Ford Escort smelled of pine disinfectant, the source of which was a plastic fir tree dangling from the back-view mirror. On the driver's seat, which was pulled right forward, lay a thick wedge of foam covered by a crocheted blanket. The frog climbed onto this and adjusted his buttocks with care. Collapsing forwards through his open jacket, his paunch pushed against the steering wheel like a built-in airbag.

On the dashboard was a packet of Fruit Gums, and the remains of a bar of Cadbury's Dairy Milk, which he now handed to me like a sacrificial offering. 'Help yourself. Though I don't know if there's much left. Oh, dear! You're shivering. Sh-shall I put on the heating?' He reached out and fumbled with the dashboard controls, then, when he'd found the right button, bunched his fingers around the wheel. 'Where do you live?'

'Belsize Park.'

The frog grunted knowingly. After several glances in the mirror, plus another over his shoulder, he crunched the gear stick into first and pulled out from the kerb. The windscreen wipers swept the screen clear with a frenetic action which was in stark contrast to his driving. I resigned myself to being killed in a collision. Though he couldn't have been older than forty-five, he drove as slowly, as badly and as deliberately as an elderly Sunday driver. As he tootled down Pall Mall, the bus only inches behind us hooted at him in frustration. When he turned from St James's Street into Piccadilly, a battered 2CV overtook him on the inside. The frog ground his teeth anxiously. Driving seemed to take all his concentration. His skill with the gears seemed as jerky as his speech.

'It's ... It's h-horrible weather, isn't it?' he spat out as the Escort crawled towards Hyde Park Corner at 10 mph. 'I'd forgotten how ghastly the English w-winter can be.'

I couldn't be bothered to answer. Sunk in self-absorbed

misery, I gazed through the windscreen, and wondered why it was that, unlike Elena, I'd never managed to make any relationship last. Maybe my mother was right, and it was my own fault. Why, even my ex-boyfriend Graham, whom I'd chucked because he was so unbearable to live with, was now happily married, with one child of two years old and a baby on the way. Last time I'd seen him, I'd felt quite nostalgic about him . . .

The frog's splayed digits drummed against the wheel as we circled Hyde Park Corner for a second time. 'Why are you going round and round?' I barked at him.

'There was a car on the outside lane . . . It . . . it cut me up . . . I couldn't turn off.'

Yet again, we crept round Hyde Park Corner, then, with a sudden jerk, the frog yanked the steering wheel to the left. Tyres screeching, we skidded into Park Lane and jolted north towards Marble Arch. I gritted my teeth and stared out into the bottle-green darkness of Hyde Park. Lips fused together by passion, limbs entwined, a man and woman were embracing in a pool of white light under a streetlamp. A lump of longing formed in my throat.

My chauffeur glanced in the same direction. After a short pause he said, 'Do you . . . Are you . . . Have you always lived in London?'

I muttered yes, then bit my lips shut. How could I carry on a conversation when the road to our left led towards Shepherd's Bush, where Andy and Francesca were no doubt curled up together in their cosy bed?

'Are . . . Are you warm enough?'

'Mmm.' Holding back my tears, I wiped the condensation off the side window. The frog must have realised I didn't want to talk, because he didn't say anything else until we reached Swiss Cottage and he asked me for directions. A few minutes later, he drew up outside my block of flats.

'Oh dear, there's nowhere to park!' he wailed.

'There never is. Just pull up here.'

'But . . . Wouldn't you like me to help you upstairs?'

27

'No!' My hand was on the door handle even before the car had stopped. I forced myself to turn and thank him for dropping me home. 'What's the matter?' I added, seeing the alarmed expression on his face.

'You're . . . you're crying!' he murmured in amazement.

'No, I'm not,' I retorted. But when I touched my cheek, I found that he was right.

'Oh dear, oh dear! Poor thing! Your ankle must really be hurting you.'

At this, I suddenly broke down and began to sob uncontrollably. For a minute, the frog watched me weeping, then without saying a word, he reached across my knees, opened the glove compartment and took out a box of Man-sized Kleenex.

In an attempt to regain my composure, I blew my nose. 'I'm sorry to make such a scene,' I sniffed. 'Whatever must you be thinking?'

There was a long pause. Then the frog cleared his throat. 'Actually,' he stuttered, 'I was just w-wondering what you were doing tomorrow night.'

Three

‹His name's Cecil Brown. He's short, bald and fat,' I moaned into the telephone receiver the following evening.

'You make him sound irresistible,' drawled Elena.

I sank down onto my battered velvet sofa, folded one leg under my body, then carefully lifted my sprained and swollen ankle onto the seat cushion. 'The poor thing has this terrible stutter. Oh, yes – and he drives a red Ford Escort.'

Elena snorted. 'That's not an arrestable offence, you old snob. Some of my best friends drive red Ford Escorts.' There was a short pause, then she giggled. 'At least, our window cleaner does. Does it have a nodding daschund in the back, and dingly-dangly mascots hanging from the mirror?'

'No. But there *is* a thick cushion thing on the driver's seat, so that he can see out of the windows.' Both Elena and I hooted. 'Oh, God, how can I be such a bitch?'

'You are a bitch, Lisa. You don't deserve to go out with anyone.'

'I'm sure he's very nice,' I added damningly. 'If only he didn't look like a frog!'

'Ah! Maybe he'll turn into a prince if you kiss him.'

I shuddered. 'Believe me, I'm not going to find out.'

'Poor bastard!' Despite the adjective, Elena didn't sound at all sympathetic. 'One's got to admire him, though, if only for thinking he's in with a chance. What does he do?'

'God knows. We never got that far.'

There was a melodramatic gasp. 'Good God, Lisa! You mean, he might not work in publishing or the media? What's come over you?'

Annoyed, I bit my lip. Usually I relished my friend's barbed-wire tongue. But at that moment, the lacerations cut wide and deep. 'That's unfair. You know I've never picked my boyfriends by their jobs! Please don't be horrid to me, Elena. He'll be here soon and then I'll be stuck with him all evening. Oh God, I feel like a real heel! I wish I hadn't agreed to go out with him.'

'So why did you?'

'I don't know.' I stared at the Hockney landscape poster above my fireplace, and wished I was in a car, driving away from reality through its colourful canyons. 'I suppose, because he asked me. And because I wasn't up to saying no.'

'You don't usually have any difficulty in doing that. In fact, you're unbelievably choosey.'

'I was. I've changed.'

'Since when?'

'Since last week. Besides . . .' I thought of the poor man's stutter, and the frightened, Mad Cow-like rolling of his eyes. 'He seemed so pathetic.'

'Now, there's a novel reason for going out with someone! And talking of novels . . .'

'Yes?' I prompted when her voice petered out.

'No, no, it's nothing,' Elena said hurriedly.

'Uhhuh. And what does that mean?'

'Oh . . . Forget it. It's just something about your next book we need to discuss.'

As it's not like Elena to be coy, I began to worry. 'Tell me now, Elena.'

'It can wait, darling. Now's not the right time.'

'Elena!'

She drew in her breath slowly. 'OK, OK. About that new three-book deal we've been negotiating . . .'

'Yes?'

'Well . . .' She paused, then blurted out, 'I'm afraid I can only offer you a contract for one novel this time.'

'But . . .' I felt like a football had just smacked into my solar plexus. 'Why?'

'Frankly, darling, the Mahonia Medmenham titles haven't been selling as well as they used to. The sales department is having kittens, and the reps are up in arms – and you know how much power *they* wield. They're moaning that your stuff is too conventional. Too middle-of-the-road. Too . . . too old hat.'

'My books are old hat?'

'Don't take it personally, Lisa. It's not just your books. We're making cuts across the board. The thing is, darling, when Pink Peony started out thirty years ago, there was romantic fiction on one hand, and real literature on the other. So if readers wanted a bit of escapism, they had to come to us. But nowadays, there's so much bloody competition from mainstream fiction that we're hard pressed to survive. Publishing's become such a rat race. Things have changed so much in the three years since you gave up working here that you simply wouldn't recognise the market. All that eighties boom stuff is dead as a dodo. The Jackie Collinses and Barbara Taylor Bradfords and Danielle Steeles of this world have got the bonkbuster and sex-and-shopping market sewn up, and even the bloody Aga sagas have probably had their day. According to the reps, what the nineties readership wants are more up-to-date themes. Younger themes with a darker edge. Techno stuff, and streetwise thrillers, and Lager sagas . . .'

'What the hell's a Lager saga?' I muttered.

'Don't ask. An Aga saga about the New Man. You know – house-husbands navel-gazing down the pub. As for the romance lists – well, things have got to be harder edged there, too. More explicitly erotic. Today's romance reader wants stories with a contemporary twist – like a sci-fi or a fantasy element. Cyberspace instead of sighs. Love on the Internet, instead of in the office. S&M and body piercing instead of bodice rippers. So, darling, the company's having to modernise its image, and I'm having to modernise my list. And titles like your last book, *Cry No More, Moira* – though it was a brilliant book, honestly, a real weepy – frankly, it's just too bloody nice. And nice doesn't sell, Lisa.'

'I see.'

'So Simon decided – and I'm afraid I've had to agree – to take it one book at a time from you in future.'

'I see.'

'And . . . oh God, you're going to hate me for this! There's something else.'

'What?'

'Shit, this is difficult! Look, I know you wanted a bigger advance for your next book than we paid you for the last. But . . . well, I just can't go up, Lisa. In fact, I've got to come down. The maximum I can offer you this time is £5,000.'

Five thousand pounds. That was half of what I'd got paid for my last two novels. Five thousand pounds might sound a lot to get paid for a book, but it wasn't exactly a living when that book took you nine months or a year to write. 'But I can barely afford to pay my mortgage as it is!' I wailed.

Elena sighed. 'Lisa, I'm really sorry to spring this on you. I know you're hurt, but please don't take it against me. Personally, I love what you write. If I had my way, I'd give you a ten-book contract and triple your advance. But I'm not the boss round here – Simon is. I'm only a paid-up member of the Gestapo. Obeying orders.'

'Sure.'

'I've depressed you, haven't I? I'm such an idiot. I knew this wasn't the right time to bring the subject up. Just when you're going out on your date with the frog prince.'

'I'm not going to go,' I said. 'What's the point? Besides, after what you've just told me, I can't face it.'

'Oh, you must go! Getting out in the world will do you good.'

'You sound like my mother. Oh well, I suppose I've got nothing else to do. If I stay in, I'll just sit around brooding about what you just told me, or being depressed about Andy. I've *got* to get over him, Elena. I've got to make a proper relationship with someone else soon or I'll never get married and have a baby.'

I could almost see Elena's sardonic expression. 'Now

who's sounding like Lorelei? Really, being married's not that fabulous. In fact, it's one big compromise.'

'You seem to enjoy it.'

She paused. 'I'm good at making compromises. I mean, Peter's jolly nice, but he's not exactly Keanu Reeves, is he?'

I thought of Elena's husband, a thin-faced, mild-mannered schoolteacher with an endearing smile, a bronchial chest and a neck permanently wrapped in a long woolly scarf. 'He's lovely!' I said protectively.

'Do you think so? In that case, I'll divorce him, and you can have him second time around. Ha!'

'It's not funny, Elena! I really am desperate. The singles scene's a jungle, and I've had enough of it. More than enough. I've thrown away too many opportunities to settle down, and I haven't got any more time to waste. If you can compromise, so can I.'

'You?' Elena guffawed. 'Miss High Standards herself?'

'Yes. I bet you anything you like that I'll marry the next man who asks me.'

'Whatever he's like?'

'Yes. Anyone.'

'Really? OK, you're on. A crate of champagne for the wedding if you win.'

I giggled. 'It's a safe bet. Since there aren't any single, straight men of marriageable age around.'

'And Cecil is, at least, single?'

'Oh!' I giggled again. 'Actually, I forgot to ask. I'm sure he must be. I can't see who'd have him. Anyway, I've decided that I've got to give everyone a chance.'

'So pathetic old Cecil is in with a chance after all?'

'Don't be ridiculous!'

'Then why ... Damn! Hold on a mo. *What is it, Sophie?*'

'*Mum, what does ...*'

'*Can't you see I'm busy, poppet?* Go on, Lisa.'

'Anyway, it seemed kind of rude to say no after he'd brought me all the way home.'

'*Mum, what does boil . . .*'

'I thought he ran you over first?'

'Not really. I stepped out into the street without looking.'

'*What does boil wash . . .*'

'Hold on a sec, Lisa, will you?' Muffled by her hand, Elena's voice climbed an octave '*Poppet, I've told you lots and lots of times not to disturb Mummy when she's working on the phone.*'

'*But you're not working, you're talking to Lisa!*'

'*Can't it wait?*'

'*What does "boil wash" mean?*'

'*Oh, for goodness' sake! Go and ask your father!* Sorry, Lisa, go on.'

'There's nothing more to say, really. I'm absolutely dreading the whole evening. Cecil and I are on different planets. We've got absolutely nothing in common and . . .'

'*Mum!*'

'*Go away!*'

'*Please! Look, I said please! Please, please, please, Mum! What does "boil wash" mean?*'

'Are you sure you want children?' Elena muttered into the receiver. Over-strained with sweetness and patience, her voice continued, '*Why do you want to know, Sophie?*'

'*Because, because that's what it says above the red button on the washing machine. Boil wash.*'

'Really! You see what I have to deal with, Lisa?'

'*And Rupert's just put Kitkat in and pressed it and . . .*'

There was a strangulated 'Shit!' from the other end of the line. Then the phone went dead. I hurled down the receiver, faintly annoyed that Elena never managed to finish off a conversation. Actually, I was more than faintly annoyed with her. There was, after all, the business of my advance. I knew that it wasn't her fault that my books weren't selling, and I knew that a writer has to be able to take criticism. Still . . . Did she really expect me to live for nine months on a measly £5,000 advance?

The clock on the mantelpiece ticked slowly on, marking

the barren passage of my life. Without Elena to distract me, my thoughts drifted back to Andy. My fingers traced his phone number on the key-pad. I *could* ring him up. I *could* ask him to come over. What I would only give to spend the evening at home with him, curled up in front of the television or, alternately and preferably, nestled up in bed. But Andy wasn't there for me. When I thought about it, he'd never really been there for me when I needed him, and he certainly wasn't there for me now.

I limped over to the window, flicked open the slats of the venetian blind and looked out into the rain-drenched street. A red Ford Escort was already parked across the road, its side-lights on, its windows steamed up. In the light of the streetlamp I could glimpse a furtive figure seated behind the wheel. My heart sank. A full five minutes passed before the driver's door opened and the figure slid out and splashed across the road under a huge golfing umbrella.

When the intercom buzzer sounded, I limped into the hall and picked up the receiver. There was a eerie silence while the man downstairs attempted to speak. 'I'll come down,' I said eventually. Bracing myself for an awful evening, I threw on a coat, and limped out to the lift.

The frog was waiting outside in the rain, dressed in a beige, hooded anorak and clutching a limp bunch of freesias. His face lit up when he saw me, sending my stomach into a nauseous spin. I could tell he was already smitten, and the responsibility of it weighed heavily on me. Maybe he knew that his crush on me was doomed, because his very stance spoke of pathos and failure: the downward slope of his shoulders; the nervous look in his eyes; the quivering of his full, fleshy lips. Even his clothes seemed to have given up all hope of impressing me, for his socks were falling down and his grey serge trousers flapped loosely beneath his knees, ending a full inch above his thin and surprisingly hirsute ankles.

Arranging my face into a smile which I hoped disguised my revulsion, I greeted this vision as brightly as I could.

'Hello, Lisa,' he croaked back. 'How's your f-f . . .'

'Foot?' I finished for him. Cheeks burning, Cecil nodded. 'It's fine. Still a bit painful, but I'll survive.'

He nodded again. His fingers glowed with a bone-like pallor as he clutched the open umbrella and, stretching up on tiptoes, held it above my head. Laying his other hand lightly on my coat sleeve, he steered me across the road and opened the passenger door. Trapped, I sank back into the deep soft seat and waited while Cecil climbed in the other side – no mean mountaineering feat for a man of his size.

'I've b—' He stopped. 'I've b—' he began again. His stutter was crucifying. If he hadn't have been staring at me in that awestruck way which made me think he fancied me like mad, I would have felt sorry for him. As it was, his impediment was already beginning to provoke an irrational and uncharacteristically nasty annoyance in me – almost as nasty and irrational as that caused by the foam wedge upon which he was rearranging his buttocks, and without which he would probably not have been able to see above the steering wheel. 'I hope you don't mind but I've booked a table at the Caprice,' he said as he started the engine.

'*What?*'

Cecil shot me an anxious look. 'Isn't that OK?'

No, it wasn't OK. The Caprice happens to be one of my favourite restaurants. Andy and I had shared many a romantic tryst there on his expenses, whenever expenses had allowed. What made it worse was that Andy knew the people who owned and ran the Caprice, and because we'd been there so often together, most of the staff now knew me by name. The thought of being seen there with a man like Cecil – perhaps by Andy himself! – was too awful to contemplate. Crossing my fingers in the dark, I said, 'Well, if I'm honest, Cecil, I hate the Caprice.'

The frog looked at me curiously with his bulging eyes. 'Why?'

'Oh . . .' I cast around my imagination for a feasible reason. 'Well, it's so crowded and . . . and noisy and . . . and I don't like the food,' I lied again. And then I dreamed up an inspired and libellous embellishment: 'I once got food poisoning from their salmon fishcakes.'

Cecil's eyes widened in sympathy. 'How awful! I'm so sorry! W—' His voice stuck on the consonant like a cracked record.

'Would I rather we went somewhere else? Yes, please. If you don't mind.'

'Not at all. How about Langans or M—' He took a deep breath 'Mezzo's – if we can get a table? No? Pont de la Tour? Or . . . or . . .'

'Or?' I chimed in helpfully.

Cecil spat it out: 'Orso's?'

'Let's just go somewhere more local,' I suggested. 'I know a lovely, quiet, old-fashioned bistro off the Finchley Road.'

Fifteen minutes later we were sitting opposite each other on pink plush banquettes, the only two people in an otherwise deserted restaurant. A candle in a Chianti bottle sputtered between us, dripping a stalactite of wax onto the worn gingham cloth. Behind us, and suspended across the walls, large fishnets held a flotsam of plastic crabs, bunches of purple rubber grapes and dried seaweed. Flickering candle-bulbs set in black lanterns cast a funereal glow over the table. Two waiters, leaning against a mosaic bar, stared at us as if we were aliens – which was exactly what I felt like. Dreary, empty and silent – if you didn't count the low-level hotel-lobby muzac and the occasional coughs of the bored, tubercular waiters – this was a restaurant to commit suicide in, a place to string oneself up from the dim wrought-iron chandelier or overdose on aspirin; on second thoughts, a double helping of the collapsed, age-encrusted and, no doubt, salmonella-rich, Tiramisu on the dessert trolley would probably see one off just as soon.

'Tell me about yourself, Cecil,' I said, feigning interest in the batrachian figure opposite me.

My date shrugged. 'I'm afraid there's not a lot to tell. What can I say? I was born in Bradford, but when I was ten my parents moved to London . . .' Because of his stutter, his progress through the years was painfully slow. I tilted my head to one side and nodded encouragement, though my mind was elsewhere – drifting back to my favourite table at the Caprice where, one night, Andy had slipped a hand under the thick white tablecloth and walked his fingers up under my skirt . . .

'But that's enough about me, Lisa, I don't want to b-bore you.'

'No, do go on.'

'Really? Well I . . .'

And then I remembered when Andy and I had first met, at the country hotel in Yorkshire where Pink Peony Publishing were holding their annual sales conference. I was there to talk to the sales reps about my seventh romantic novel, *A Man of Intrigue*, and Andy was making a documentary about the romantic fiction market for Channel 4 – a snide, tongue-in-cheek job, as I later found out. During the formal dinner, our eyes had met, and locked, over a bottle of Cava, and later on, when he'd finished filming for the night, we'd talked for an hour in the hotel bar. Then he'd walked me to my bedroom, and we'd kissed in the corridor, and then we'd heard Elena coming and, giggling, hysterically, we'd run inside and closed the door. And then we'd kissed again, this time more passionately, and gradually, item by item, pulled off each other's clothes. And then . . . And then . . .

'It's rather warm and sour, isn't it?'

'Sorry?'

'This wine.' Cecil winced as he took another sip. 'I think it's corked. Shall I order something else?'

'No, no. It's fine. Really. Oh, good, look, our food's coming! Mmm! My crespellini look delicious!'

Cecil stared doubtfully at his hors d'oeuvres. 'What do you suppose *this* is?' he said, prodding his fork into a long brown desiccated object nestling next to the hard green melon balls in the centre of his plate.

I leaned forward and inspected it. 'I don't know. It looks

like a dog-chew. Perhaps it's a slice of Parma ham. A very ancient one.'

Cecil beamed back at me. 'I'm so glad you told me. I was about to send it back. I thought it was the sole of a shoe.'

I tried to laugh, at this and his other jokes, but whenever I did the cheese sauce coating the crespellini congealed in my mouth. Hoping that Cecil wouldn't notice I wasn't eating much, I pushed the food around my plate and shovelled it under my knife, just as I'd done with semolina during school lunches.

'So, what do you do, Cecil?'

'I . . . I'm in business, Lisa. It's just a small thing, really – import, exporting. I deal in . . .'

My eyes glazed over as I recalled the first time Andy had mentioned Francesca to me, late one night after we'd made love – this being, as I was to learn, his favourite time for confessions. Out the story poured, convoluted and messy, like the blood-coloured contents of an upturned can of beans: how he shared a flat with an old girlfriend, with whom he'd recently broken up; how she was still unnaturally attached to him, and extraordinarily jealous; and how she was just recovering from her second near-fatal overdose that year.

Far away from me, on the other side of the table, Cecil droned on: 'The thing is, I haven't lived in . . .'

In hindsight, I know I should have realised right away that the can of beans stank to high heaven. But what's hindsight if not an instrument of self-torture? The truth is that I wanted to believe Andy because I'd fallen in love with him. I was happy to be deceived. Happy to deceive myself . . .

'If you don't mind me asking, Lisa, what do you d-do?'

I looked up blankly into Cecil's shining face. 'Oh. Well, actually . . .'

'Yes?'

'I'm a novelist.'

Cecil looked suitably impressed. 'How marvellous!'

'Not really.' I wasn't being modest. *Alone Once More*, *Touch a Shattered Heart*, *A Woman of Vagrant Charm*,

39

and let's not forget *Roses for Rhona* – you only have to read through the titles of my books to realise that they're not literary fiction. In fact, they're the kind of stories that make everyone think, Oh, I could do that! Which is exactly what I'd said to Elena ten years ago when I joined Pink Peony as her secretary. And Elena'd said to me, 'Well, go on then, Lisa, have a try.' So I did. And I found that I could. And since then, that's how I'd been earning my living, by writing escapist love stories about timid heroines – women rather like myself, in fact – who, in a bid to escape a tragedy in their past, embark on adventures during which they meet handsome heroes who are the very opposite of Cecil Brown. Men with improbable names like Brett St John or Madden Sellafield. Men with pectorals as hard as the Matterhorn and hearts as hard to conquer as the north face of K2. And, of course, rough facial stubble, piercing eyes, strong jaws and, in these more explicit times, a penis as long as a banana and as thick as a wrist. Not to forget the ubiquitous cleft chin. For some strange reason, cleft-chinned heroes are very important to the readers – who, research shows, are predominantly poverty-stricken single mothers living in tower blocks, just the kind of women who ought to know better than to believe that love conquers all. As Elena said to the reps at the last sales conference, despite the soaring divorce rate and breakdown in family values, romance still holds millions of readers in exactly the same way my heroes hold my heroines – i.e., in a vice-like, enthralling grip.

Or, so it had. Till now. I suddenly remembered my conversation with Elena – my falling sales figures, and that £5,000 advance. I knocked back a glass of wine. Perhaps it was a glass too many for, unusually for me, I began to talk garrulously about what I do, and in a rather horrible, self-important manner, even going so far as to tell Cecil my pseudonym.

His mouth dropped open to reveal a mouthful of uneven, crooked teeth. 'You're not really Mahonia Medmenham!' he exclaimed. 'Why, my mother and sister read your books all the time!'

After that, I gabbled on like a plane speeding ahead on automatic pilot: the controls were functioning, the engine throbbing, but the captain's mind was elsewhere. If it wasn't for bloody Francesca I thought, Andy and I could have had a perfect relationship. Because the truth was that we got along so well. Never in a million years would I meet anyone I liked half as much. Why, I worshipped him: worshipped his sick sense of humour, and his wild, impulsive streak, and his large pale, slender feet, encased in shoes which were always, endearingly, worn down at the heels.

'How fascinating!' said Cecil.

'Well, not really. I mean, it's hardly a glamorous life, Cecil. I mean, most of the time I'm sitting at home, by myself, day after day . . .'

Oh, Andy! The more I thought about him now, the more I wanted to see him. I *had* to see him. I needed him. The moment I got home tonight, I'd phone him up and tell him to come over. We'd make up. We'd make love. If he wouldn't break up with Francesca, I'd learn to live with the status quo. Because the thought of being without him for the rest of my life was simply unbearable . . .

As if from far away, I heard myself say 'really marvellous because it's . . .' and I suddenly realised that I had no idea what I was talking to Cecil about. My words trickled to a halt in the middle of the sentence.

Cecil looked confused. After a short silence, he cleared his throat. 'W-would you like some d-d—' he stuttered.

'Dessert? No, thanks. Actually, I'm a little tired. If you don't mind, I think I'd like to go home now.'

He signed the air with a nervous flourish, and the tubercular waiter leaned against the bar, totting up the bill. After a short search in his inside pockets, Cecil produced a credit card. So did I.

'Let's split it, Cecil.'

'No, no! Let me!' He grabbed the bill as the waiter put it down. Quick off the mark, I snatched it away. Cecil flinched as if I had hit him.

'I insist we split it,' I said. 'Honestly, I'd much rather.' Rather not be beholden. Rather not feel that I owed him anything, especially not another date.

After a show of reluctance, Cecil agreed. He looked hurt, almost insulted. I tried not to feel too bad about it. After all, this was the late twentieth century; and if my little show of independence put him off me, all well and good.

He drove me home in silence, and with much backing in and out, parked his car outside my block of flats. Even before he'd put the handbrake on, my fingers were hooked around the doorhandle.

'Thanks for a lovely evening,' I said, turning towards him.

'No – thank *you*.' I was about to make a run for it, when his hand brushed my shoulder. 'Lisa . . .'

Please, please, I prayed as I swivelled round, let him not try to kiss me!

'I really have enjoyed tonight.'

I swallowed hard. It seemed so rude not to respond, so I said, over-cheerfully, 'So have I.'

'Really? Do you . . . Could we . . . Might I . . .?' Cecil faltered. With a despairing gesture, he wiped a bead of sweat from his brow. 'You see, I . . . I'm only here for another few days. I'm sure someone like you m-must be very busy but . . . Is there any chance that we might get together again?'

Four

Somehow, despite my intention never to clap eyes on Cecil Brown again, I found myself agreeing to go out with him the following evening. And the next evening. And the night after that.

Even though I couldn't stand the sight of him, I had to admit that, as a date, Cecil was faultless. Unlike Andy, who'd only ever bought me the occasional bunch of roses – the kind with lethal thorns which ripped my fingers to ribbons and heads which invariably drooped on their stalks – Cecil sent me flowers every morning by special delivery: huge bunches of orange and red ranunculi, white lilies which filled my flat with their heavy perfume, and purple anemones with long, curvaceous stems. Due, perhaps, to his terrible stammer, Cecil's phone calls were mercifully brief, and he never once rang during the hours when I wrote – something that Andy had done all the time. Neither, after our first date, did Cecil bore me with his jokes; in fact, he said very little, encouraging me instead to talk about myself. He even phoned up Pink Peony's sales department, ordered a complete set of my novels, and had them biked over to him without delay. After reading them all in a marathon overnight stint, he declared that they were 'simply marvellous', an opinion which, though flattering on the one hand, confirmed my suspicion that he was man of execrable taste.

And yet . . . Cecil's taste wasn't all bad. Somehow that large-pored nose of his managed to sniff out the best cultural events in London, such as Placido Domingo singing *Otello* at the Royal Opera House, and the latest Tom Stoppard play, for which he magically obtained the best stalls tickets, even though it was completely sold out. Though he didn't object on Monday night when I grabbed our restaurant bill and insisted on paying my share again, when we had a Chinese meal after the opera on Tuesday he asked if I'd mind if he paid for everything in future. 'B-business expenses,' he explained with a nervous giggle. 'You see, I need the receipts.' After a moment's thought, I agreed. There seemed no great danger in letting him pick up the tab, for Cecil didn't seem to expect anything in return. On the contrary, he kept at a comfortably safe distance all the time we were together, he never once hinted that he'd like to come up for coffee when he dropped me home and, to my profound relief, he never attempted to kiss me goodnight.

In fact, throughout that week Cecil's behaviour was impeccable – until I made the mistake of taking him with me to Pink Peony's anniversary party on Friday night.

'Join us to Celebrate 30 Years of Romance!' gushed the invitation on my mantelpiece – a rose-coloured card decorated in inimitable Pink Peony style with hearts, flowers and embossed gold swags. Though I'd already RSVP'd to say I would be going, after hearing about my new contract I'd had a change of heart. I wasn't schlepping up to their offices in Soho Square just to be humiliated, as I told Elena when I rang her up at work on Wednesday night.

'But you must come!' she insisted. 'All our other authors will be there, Lisa. It'll look bad if you're not.'

'I don't care what it looks like.'

Elena grunted her disapproval. 'Well, darling, you should care. These things matter. If you don't show your face, people here will think you can't be bothered with them.'

'They'd be right. I mean, if they can't be bothered to pay me properly, then . . .'

'Careful Lisa!' she interrupted me. 'You're sounding rather bitter. I know it's hard to accept, but the sad fact is that you – and I, for that matter – are only worth what we're worth. Market forces, and all that. Look, if you feel that badly about it, you could take your next novel to another publisher and try your luck there. Not that I'm recommending that, of course,' she added when I gave a shocked gasp. 'I'd be devastated to lose you from my list. Look, why don't we have lunch next week? I'm free on Tuesday. We can talk the whole thing over then, and think of ways of bumping up your sales figures next time around. Ok? And do come to the party. Really, I insist on it. Hey – why don't you bring what's-his-name with you?'

'Cecil? Are you kidding!'

'Oh, go on! Why not? He can protect you from the unwanted attentions of the drunken sales reps. And besides,' Elena added with a malicious giggle, 'it'll give me a chance to see if you're exaggerating or if he really does look like a frog.'

'You're right, he does,' she muttered into my ear as she planted a noisy hello kiss on both my cheeks when Cecil and I arrived at the party. 'And you must be Cecil!' she said out loud, turning her smile on him. Her large blue eyes skimmed up his face to the thin swirl of hair which topped his huge skull, and her long mouth, smeared clumsily with frosted lipstick, gave an almost imperceptible twitch. 'I'm so pleased to meet you at last!'

'My pleasure,' Cecil stammered back, gawping at her. As usual, Elena looked extraordinary. She isn't so much pretty as striking – all angles and chisels and pale skin, like a marble bust from the 1930s English school. She teeters on the brink of looking either fabulously chic or totally wrecked, that particular night in a sleeveless black jersey Jean Muir dress, the stunning simplicity of which was offset by food stains on her shoulder and the hint of a grey bra-strap showing in the V neck.

'Lisa's told me so much about you!' Ignoring my glare, Elena hooked her straight blonde bob of hair behind her left ear, from which dangled a silver skull-and-crossbones and three county-looking pearls, and continued, 'You know, it's really quite rare I get to meet her friends.'

'Really?' Cecil smiled at me in the same pleased, adoring way he'd smiled when I'd asked him to the party, and my heart plummeted. Like some Jane Austen heroine, I berated myself for leading him on when I had no intention of getting involved with him. Why had I let Elena talk me into inviting him tonight? A quick look around the crowded room was enough to make me realise that he was the least attractive man there. Why was I seeing him at all? I asked myself. Was I really that hard up for male company that I had to settle for someone like him? More to the point, did I really want him hanging around my neck all evening when I could have been having a good time alone?

Well, perhaps *good time* was an exaggeration. Pink Peony was not known for its lavish entertainment budget, and its thirtieth birthday shindig was being held in its usual, inimitable style: in a basement office, with cheap wine, cheap publicity in the shape of a plethora of tabloid paparazzi, and a single bowl of twiglets. This time, they had gone further than usual and even skimped on elbow room. There'd been a time when I'd known most of the staff in the company, but now I barely recognised anyone – and, to my chagrin, no one seemed to recognise me. With Cecil trailing behind me like a stone on a chain, I struggled through the densely packed crowd in search of someone to talk to, and gasped for oxygen in the much-breathed, tobacco-thick air.

'Mahonia!' At last, a silver-haired man in a tweed jacket and a pair of metal-rimmed glasses pushed towards me. It was Simon Partridge, the managing director of Pink Peony. The man responsible for my one-book contract and the fifty per cent cut in my next advance.

'Hello, Simon.'

I pulled my lips into a smile as, cigarette dangling from his lips, he lunged forward to kiss me. 'Marvellous to see you, darling,' he drawled in his Boston accent. 'You're looking wonderful as usual!' No thanks to you, I thought. 'So very glad you made it here on this, this historic occasion.' His eyes flickered down to the gnome who'd pushed into view beside me. 'And who's this?'

'A *friend*,' I said with deliberate emphasis. 'Simon Partridge, Cecil Brown.'

'How do you do?' Cecil held out his hand, but Simon couldn't take it, for his right hand was wrapped around a wine glass and his left was wrapped around a tall, lank-haired anorexic dressed in hipster PVC trousers and a shrivelled-up nylon shirt which skimmed her thrice-pierced navel.

'Have you met Flora?' Simon asked me, giving her waist a squeeze.

'No.'

'Darling, you must! Mahonia Medmenham, Flora MacNalty.' The anorexic smiled at me. I smiled back. 'Mahonia's one of our stable of old writers, darling,' Simon continued, then turned to me. 'Flora's just won the Betty Trask Award with her first novel.'

My smile froze. So did my voice. 'Congratulations,' I spat out.

'We're bringing it out in paperback next week.' Simon indicated a huge poster of Flora's face on a nearby wall, and a pile of books on a table. 'It took a stiff auction to get her, bless her, and we're all thrilled to bits that we managed to sign her up.'

'Oh, didn't I read something about that in the *Sunday Times* last week?' Cecil stuttered. 'Wasn't the auction rumoured to be for a six-figure advance?'

I guess my expression must have given my shock away, for the anorexic's smile changed to a smug simper, and Simon Partridge blanched. 'My dear chap,' he bellowed, 'you can't believe everything you read in the papers! Oh look, do forgive me – there's Auberon over there! I must just say hello.'

The moment Simon and Flora were out of sight, I elbowed my way to the display table and picked up a copy of Flora MacNalty's book. Superimposed on the cover photograph of a condom lying on a computer keyboard was the novel's title, embossed in gold letters – *Cyberfuck*.

Cyberfuck?

Marla and Klaus were thousands of miles apart,' read the blurb on the back cover – '*he in Sydney, she in Paris. But, from the first day he hacked into her files, they were both caught up in an emotional Web. Were they doomed to remain on-screen addresses to each other, or were they destined to link up?* Cyberfuck *bristles with the electricity of their mutual lust. For Internet, read Intercourse. For E-mail, read Erotica. After you've surfed through the pages of* Cyberfuck, *turning on your computer will never be the same again . . .*'

I flipped open the cover and glanced at the page entitled About the Author. The first three words were enough for me: Born in 1976 . . .

1976. Flora MacNalty, the bitch, was barely out of nappies. Barely out of nappies, with a six-figure advance up her sleeve. Whereas I was thirty-five, earning a scant £5,000 for my eleventh novel.

'Now, that's a subtle title!' Cecil muttered in my ear.

I slammed *Cyberfuck* shut and threw it back on the pile.

'Are you all right, Lisa?'

I swung round and smiled into my date's ugly face. 'Fine. Perfect. But I've had enough of this party. Do you mind if we leave?'

We escaped out into Soho. Cecil wanted to take me out to Mezzo's for dinner, but I told him I didn't feel like it. We crossed the street and got into his Ford Escort, and while he drove me back to Belsize Park, I brooded silently on my own failures and Flora MacNalty's success. Flora MacNalty, with her youth and her thrice-pierced navel, was the future of the world, and the future of romantic fiction. And I? I was a has-been – no, worse, an almost-was. Either way, I was the past.

Cecil parked outside my block of flats, and I said goodnight and lunged for the door handle. But just as I was about to make my getaway, he grabbed my wrist with his tiny webbed hand.

'Lisa?'

'Yes?'

'Um . . . Thank you so much for inviting me to the party tonight.'

'It was nothing, Cecil,' I said quickly.

'Well, I really appreciated it.'

'I'm so glad. Well then, goodnight.' I tried to wrench my hand away, but Cecil's clammy fingers continued to encircle my wrist like a manacle.

'Lisa?'

'Yes?'

He cleared his throat. 'Do you think we could talk for a moment?'

'Of course.'

With growing apprehension, I watched Cecil's lips attempt to form his next word. The air grew still and tense. Oh God, he was going to make a pass at me! I glanced longingly at the entrance of the block, wishing that I could escape before he tried anything. Unaware of what I was feeling, Cecil struggled on.

'You see,' he said, 'the thing is, Lisa, the thing is I'm going home on Monday.'

'Home?' I repeated vaguely. I'd never imagined Cecil having a home, or friends, or a family. So minimal was my curiosity about him that I'd never once imagined him anywhere outside his car.

'Yes. You know, back to Monte-Carlo.'

'Monte-Carlo?' Astonishment made my voice soar. 'Goodness, Cecil! That's not where you live, is it?'

Cecil blinked with equal astonishment, and at last he let go of my wrist. 'But I told you it was!' he cried in a hurt voice.

'Really?'

'Yes! On our first date!'

Had he really? Then how was it that I had absolutely no memory of it? Cecil Brown lived in Monte-Carlo. How extraordinary! The thought of him living in a tax haven on the Côte d'Azur seemed even less likely than

49

him living on the moon. 'Sorry. Of course you did!' I lied.

He nodded doubtfully. As he gazed at me with a hint of suspicion, he seemed to hesitate, and with a feeling of glee I prayed that he'd changed his mind. Alas, a moment later he cleared his throat and continued: 'Well, before I go back . . . You see, Lisa, I'd like to get things settled. You see . . . The . . . The . . . The thing is . . . I . . . You see . . .' His sentence staggered to a halt. If his previous conversation had been lightly peppered with helpless pauses, he seemed now to have bitten into a tough steak au poivre. In deep distress, he stared down at his hands and spread his fingers on the wheel. After a full minute, his eyes swivelled round towards me, brimming with fear. 'You see, I've fallen in love with you, Lisa,' he mumbled.

A premonition came to me that something too terrible for words was about to happen. This wasn't a simple pass. I knew I had to stop Cecil before he made a complete fool of himself. I tried to speak, but found that my tongue had lost its power.

Then, like a damp squib, Cecil sputtered, 'I love you.'

I turned away from him and stared out of the car window. I knew I ought to be grateful that he felt so deeply for me, but it seemed like a horrible imposition. Inside me a cold voice screamed, *Shut up, shut up!* Unaware of this, Cecil continued.

'I can't tell you how much I've enjoyed spending time with you. You're . . . You're really the m . . . the most . . .' His stutter was worse than ever. He took a deep breath, and began again: 'The most marvellous woman I've ever met. You're so clever, so talented, so . . . so kind . . .' Kind? What a joke! If only he knew! 'So w . . . Sorry. So warm. And intelligent. And . . . and of course so very funny sometimes. What I'm trying to say, Lisa, is . . .' During the long pause that followed, I turned to look at him as, red in the face, he struggled valiantly to get the words out. But his stutter got the better of him, and he covered his face with his hands. 'Shit!' he breathed.

Even though I didn't want him to go on, his distress was unbearable to witness. 'Cecil . . .' I began. He shook his head violently. 'Look, it doesn't matter . . .' I started.

'No! It does!'

For a moment I forgot the situation, and my hand stretched across the huge chasm between us and touched his arm. 'I know it's frustrating for you . . . Take your time. Honestly, there's no rush.'

He smiled at me gratefully through his miserable eyes. There was a long pause, then he suddenly blurted, 'Lisa, will you marry me?'

I smiled back at him, relieved for him that he'd managed at last to get the words out. But, a moment later, the full horror of what he'd asked me began to sink in.

Cecil Brown had proposed to me.

I thought suddenly of my bet with Elena that I'd marry the first man who asked me. Anyone, I'd said. At the time I'd meant it. I still did. But somehow that *anyone* hadn't included Cecil. Because Cecil wasn't anyone. Cecil was a frog.

'Lisa?'

Cecil stared at me expectantly as I struggled to find the least painful way to let him down. All I could manage at first was, 'Oh, Cecil!' With a sad sigh, I stared intently at my clenched fingers, as if in the dark valleys between them I'd find the kindest way to convey to him the complete impossibility, the bizarre incongruity, the ridiculous impropriety of his shocking proposal. But before the words came to me, Cecil carried on.

'I'm sorry to spring this on you. I know it's all a bit sudden. I mean, I know we only m—' He struggled, and defeated, the consonant, 'met last Sunday. But . . . well . . . it's . . . well, frankly, it's been the best week of my life.' He was looking straight ahead now, staring out through the rain-spattered windscreen. 'And I don't want to risk losing you, Lisa.'

This was so pathetic that I began to feel annoyed with him again. Lose me? How could he lose me? Didn't he have the sense to realise that I'd never been his to lose? 'Look, Cecil, the thing is . . .'

Unhooking his left hand from the steering wheel, around which it had been tightly entwined, the frog turned towards me and asked in an alarmed voice, 'There's no one else, is there?' When I said nothing, he continued in a rush, 'I mean, I'm s-sure you must have lots of suitors—' The old-fashioned word, worthy of a character in a Mahonia Medmenham novel, brought a smile to my lips. 'A woman like you . . . But you, well, you haven't mentioned anyone, so I just presumed there wasn't. Is there, Lisa?'

I didn't have the heart to explain the messy truth – that there was, and yet at the same time there wasn't. Instead, I muttered, 'Not at the moment, no.'

The anxious creases on his brow unfurrowed, and his eyes glittered with unspoken relief. 'So . . . there is a chance then?'

Here was my opportunity to escape. So why didn't I just say 'No?' and be done with it? In the long run, it would have saved us so much pain! But I wasn't courageous enough to utter that short, simple word. What I did was smile sadly in what I hoped was an offputting way.

Mistaking this for encouragement, Cecil blundered on across the emotional minefield he'd entered: 'Not that I can think of a single reason why someone like you should marry someone like me.'

This was not fishing for compliments, but stated matter-of-factly, echoing my sentiments exactly; at last Cecil had said something with which I wholeheartedly agreed. Looking away, I said, 'Don't be silly, Cecil.'

'After all, I'd be asking you to come and live in Monaco with me. You'd be giving up a lot – your flat, your family, your friends . . . It'd be a whole new way of life for you.'

A whole new way of life? Something shifted inside me. A chance to escape from Andy, and the rut I'd dug myself into. A new place, new surroundings, new friends. No more struggling to pay the mortgage on a meagre income. No more queuing for buses in the rain, and no more lonely weekends and holidays when the days lasted forever because I had no one to see, and nothing to do but work. No more having to pretend that I was happy living alone, or that I enjoyed being single. A chance to build a real life, a real home, a home shared with someone who loved me. Maybe I might even have a baby, before it was too late . . .

No, no! What was I thinking of? I looked at Cecil coldly, and totted up his many defects. Like my heroines, I'd fantasised about a hero who'd suddenly appear out of nowhere and fall head over heels in love with me – but why, oh why, out of all the men in London, did it have to be *him*? So small and so bald, so fat and – yes, it had to be said – so horrendously ugly? So devoid of style, intelligence, charm, personality, wit and humour – in fact of every quality that made a man attractive to me? I had nothing whatsoever in common with him. Even his name, Cecil Brown – for which he could in no way be held responsible – grated on me like sandpaper rubbed against raw skin.

Perhaps Cecil sensed what I was thinking, because his sagging cheeks turned a dark shade of puce, and he stuttered humbly, 'I may not deserve you, Lisa, but I promise you one thing.' Grabbing my hand with his sweaty fingers, he looked searchingly into my eyes. 'I'll do anything in my power to win your love. *Anything.* I'll stop at nothing to make you happy. I mean that from the bottom of my heart.'

'Oh, Cecil!' I extricated my hand from his, aware that there was one answer I could give him. Still, I hesitated, aware that I'd reached an important crossroads in my life. I could stick to my decision to marry the first man who asked me, win my bet with Elena and take a step forward, or I could remain where I'd been stuck for years: in a rut, in love with a man who didn't really want me.

Andy, Andy! Why did I still love him so much? I hadn't even admitted it to myself before, but I'd been nursing a secret hope that he might have a change of heart and give up Francesca. After three weeks without a single phone call from him, it was time I realised that this wasn't going to happen. Any passionate reunion between us was doomed to remain my fantasy. So, since I couldn't have the man I adored, I might as well marry anyone. Wouldn't weak, boring and malleable Cecil do as well as anyone else?

I was thirty-five years old. Thirty-five, as opposed to Flora MacNalty's scant twenty. Time was running out for me to find a father for my putative children. Before too long, the ticking time bomb of my biology would explode in my face. I'd have missed the reproductive boat, and, the way things seemed to be going, I wouldn't even have the lifebelt of a career to cling on to. Maybe I couldn't afford to dismiss Cecil's proposal lightly. After all, it could be my last chance.

I watched Cecil watching me, his eyes wide, vulnerable and expectant. He looked like a dog who expected to be kicked by his vicious brute of an owner. The tip of his tongue protruded nervously between his crooked teeth. It was unfair to keep comparing him with Andy, but I just couldn't stop myself. There it was, a fact as bare as the fleshy pate upon which Cecil's hair was plastered in that awful spiral: Cecil didn't in any way come up to scratch.

In vain, I tried to imagine waking up in bed beside him in the mornings. My mouth stretched into a bemused and weary smile which Cecil, interpreting as acceptance of his offer, returned with a full-bodied beam. As he lunged towards me, I turned my face away, and the two wet cushions of his lips landed smack on my lower cheek.

Five

And so, lacking the necessary strength of mind to either commit myself to, or extract myself from, the situation in which I found myself, I drifted passively towards marrying Cecil, without quite realising what a terrible thing I was doing.

The experience wasn't all unpleasant. Apart from enjoying my father's delight at my engagement, I derived a certain satisfaction in having proved my mother wrong with such speed. I wasn't on the shelf after all; nor was I, as she'd believed, incapable of finding myself a husband. In fact, the task had taken me less than two weeks.

With poignant relish, I tasted the sweet milk of maternal approbation for the first time in my life. At last I'd done something right in Lorelei's eyes! My fiancé might look as if he'd just crawled out of a pond – '*I* always liked handsome guys,' she remarked to me pointedly after their first meeting, the day after Cecil's proposal – but he possessed three vital attributes which made him faultless as husband material for her prodigal 35-year-old daughter: he was solvent, he was willing, and he was alive.

On top of this, I was greeted with adoration by Cecil's widowed mother, Rita, and his married sister Jackie, two diminutive, mouse-grey women who lived less than a mile away from my own parents in two intercommunicating semi-detached houses behind Willesden Green. In Edna's front room, festooned with Austrian blinds, plastic doilies and Draylon sofas, I was clutched by tender hands, pronounced 'absolutely beautiful!' and dragged down to the floor to play Cluedo with my two future nieces – nine-year-old Claudia

and eleven-year-old Harriet, giggling girls with straining
waistbands, flat brown hair and bitten nails.

The approbation I received that weekend – from my
parents, from Cecil's family and, of course, from Cecil
himself – affected me like a shot of Prozac, taking the
edge off my negative feelings and numbing the emotional
bruises inflicted by Andy. I could even begin to think of my
former lover with something verging on equanimity – or at
least, with the smug, angry satisfaction of knowing that I'd
broken away from him for good.

That Cecil flew back to the South of France on Monday
morning only added to the unreality of the situation. I was
engaged to be married, but there was no fiancé in sight. My
intended's absence, marred only by his short, faltering phone
calls – telephone conversations were not his forte, for obvious
reasons – enabled me to convince myself that what I was
doing was right.

Elena, however, proved a little harder to persuade than I.
'*You're what?*' she said, when I broke the news to her during
our working lunch at the Marshall Street Cranks restaurant
on Tuesday.

I repeated the word with great solemnity: 'Engaged.'

Perplexed, Elena shook her head. Her hair danced above
the salt-cellar hollows visible inside the stretched boat-neck
of an old, bobbly Joseph jumper. 'What do you mean, Lisa?
Engaged on the telephone?'

I gritted my teeth. 'Don't be stupid. Engaged to be
married.'

There was a loud guffaw from the other side of the table, and
a grain of brown rice flew out of Elena's mouth and across the
table, and landed beside my wholemeal roll. 'Darling, no one
gets *engaged* any more except juniors at the hairdresser!'

I stared at her grimly, my forkful of grated carrot salad
frozen halfway to my lips. 'Do keep your voice down.'

Her chin jerked forward. 'You're not serious?' she said in
her breathy voice. When I nodded, she picked up her glass
of wine and drained the contents in one gulp. Her eyes rolled

with the exaggerated gesture of an actress in a silent film. 'Bloody hell!'

With a sinking heart, I felt a chasm open up between us. 'Is that all you've got to say?' After all, as well as being my editor and my ex-boss, Elena is supposed to be my best friend. 'Aren't you going to congratulate me?'

'Of course!' She cleared her throat with a dry rasp. 'Congratulations!'

'Thank you.'

'Sorry! It's brilliant news. Really! Hey, who knows, we might even get some sales out of it. I can just see it in your next publicity promo: *Mahonia Medmenham Gets Married*. It certainly sounds a lot more catchy than *Mahonia Medmenham Gets Laid*.' She guffawed again. 'I'm just, well, incredibly surprised that's all. I must be getting cynical in my old age, because, I don't mind telling you now, I never thought Andy'd ever dump old Francesca!'

I bristled. 'He hasn't. I'm not engaged to Andy.'

Her high brow wrinkled in confusion. 'But then . . .?'

I steeled myself, and said: 'I'm engaged to Cecil.'

'*Who?*'

'You know – the man I brought to the party.'

Her lip trembled. '*Him?*' The thin wash of beige that was Elena's habitual colour suddenly drained back into her cheeks. 'Beast! You nearly had me believing you then! You told me you despised him!'

'Well,' I snapped, 'I've obviously changed my mind since then.'

There was a long pause during which Elena chewed and swallowed a mouthful of her leek savoury. Then she put down her fork and said, 'I'm sorry, darling. Forgive me if I'm being thick, but I don't quite understand. You're actually going to marry Cecil? Is that right?'

'Yes.' And, ignoring her gasp, I added, 'And I'm going to live in Monaco.'

'*What?*' Her jaw dropped. 'Is that where he lives? Do you mean he's a tax exile?'

I shrugged. Until that moment, I'd honestly never thought about it. 'I suppose so.'

'Christ, he must be loaded! No wonder you . . . No, sorry, I didn't mean that. Really I didn't. Actually, I really liked him,' she added quickly. Too quickly.

'*Did* you?'

'Mmm! I thought he was terrific. Really interesting. I mean, I didn't have much chance to talk to him, but . . . well, I'm sure he's the sort of man who has hidden depths. Honestly, Lisa, I'm really, really thrilled for you!' To convince herself, as well as me, she repeated the *really* a couple of extra times. 'I only hope that now you're going to be rich, you won't stop writing novels.'

'Don't be stupid.'

'Well, well! Gosh! That *was* quick work, Lisa. Um, what does he do?'

'Cecil? He's in . . .' Loathe to admit that I hadn't a clue, I blustered on in a vague way. 'He's in business. Kind of import-export.'

'Really?' She sounded as if I'd just said *child molester*. Never before, during the ten years I'd known her, had I seen Elena so lost for words. 'Gosh. Wow! Brilliant. When did this all happen?'

'On Friday.'

'You sly old dog – you never even told me you'd slept with him!'

A hot flush rose up the back of my neck, and I snapped, 'I don't have to tell you everything I do.'

Elena recoiled. 'Pardon me for presuming! Point taken. Only you're not usually this reticent about telling me that sort of thing. I guess it must be true love. Unless . . .' Suddenly her limpid blue eyes narrowed into X-ray slits which bored into my conscience like laser beams. 'You have slept with him, haven't you?' she said in the same tone in which my mother used to ask me whether or not I'd done my homework. Try as I might to control it, a blush spread like a flash fire across my face. 'Haven't you?' Elena persisted. I turned away from her gaze, just as I'd turned away from Cecil on the four occasions he'd tried to kiss me over the weekend. Taking my reluctance to meet his lips as the old-fashioned modesty of a blushing bride-to-be, he had, with characteristic humility, not pushed the matter any further. Elena, however, was not so easily put off. 'Lisa? You haven't, have you? Why ever not?'

Like a child caught out fibbing, I clutched at the most obvious excuse. 'If you must know, we've decided to wait till after the wedding!'

'But *why*? What's the matter? Don't you fancy him?'

'Of course I do!' I lied again.

'Then . . .' She threw her hands up. 'I'm sorry, darling, I don't understand.'

'Look, this isn't just some cheap affair!' I exploded, sounding as sanctimonious as one of my heroines. 'Cecil and I are getting *married*, for God's sake! We'll be together for the rest of our lives!'

'Precisely! So don't you think you ought to check out the bonking situation first?' Elena asked with faultless logic. When I didn't reply, she grabbed my hand across the scrubbed pine table and leaned towards me. 'Listen, Lisa, I don't mean to be negative or anything, but are you sure you know what you're doing? I mean, you're not marrying this man on the rebound from Andy, are you?'

'For heaven's sake, Elena! Do you really think I'd do something as stupid as that?'

So it was that I, who had in the past fallen into bed with men at the slightest stirrings of love or lust, now reached the eve of my wedding day two months later without having once so much as snogged with my fiancé. Dragged back to my parents' house to sleep my last single night, and doped up to the eyeballs on Lorelei's Valium, I gazed numbly at my huge cellophane-wrapped mushroom of a wedding dress hanging on the back of the dining-room door. The accessories were all there, too, neatly laid out on the sideboard – satin court shoes, satin underwear, satin handbag and satin-effect white stockings, even a veil. Was this complete Wedding Barbie outfit really mine? I wondered suddenly. Was I really going to put it on the following morning? Or was the whole thing just a weird dream?

'Try it on, baby,' my mother said as she shuffled into the dining room in her new white velour M&S dressing gown and high-heeled velvet Dolcis slippers, doubles of the ones she'd bought for me when we'd gone out shopping for my trousseau.

I looked at the mushroom doubtfully. 'I think I'll wait till tomorrow.'

'Go on! Just put on the veil, at least. To please me.'

'No thanks, Mum. I don't really feel like it.'

My mother's smile froze. Before I could protest again, she picked up the headdress and jammed it onto my head. 'Ah! You look great! That stupid shop assistant didn't know what she was talking about when she said that style was too young for you. You don't look a bit like mutton dressed as lamb!'

Horrified, I ripped the veil off. 'You never told me she'd said that! Honestly, Mum, I wished I'd never let you talk me into it!'

'Be careful, Lisa! You'll ruin it! You can't show up in a torn veil in front of a hundred and twenty guests.'

I froze. 'How many did you say?'

My mother sniffed. 'Lisa, a hundred and twenty guests is nothing.'

'It's not nothing – it's about a hundred more than I wanted to come! You haven't really invited that many people, have you?'

'Really, Lisa! Why are you kicking up such a fuss? After all, you said you were happy to leave all the wedding arrangements to me.'

'But . . . you know I only wanted a handful of people to come! Just close family, and Elena. I mean, who are they all? And how'll they all fit into the registry office?'

'Uh huh.' Lorelei cleared her throat. 'The church.'

'*Church?*' My jaw dropped. 'What *church*?'

'The one where you and Cecil are getting married tomorrow. Now don't start making trouble, Lisa, because . . .'

'But . . .'

'Oh heck! There's the phone again!' Escaping into the hall, Lorelie conducted a conversation with the receiver. 'Oh, hi, gorgeous! Yes. Ye-es! Mmm – no. Of course! And you'll bring everything you need with you, just as we agreed? See you at nine tomorrow. Kissey kissey. That was Stanley,' she said as she shuffled back into the dining room. 'He'll be here at nine o'clock sharp tomorrow. He'll style your hair first.'

I stared at her, shocked. Stanley was the maestro of Lorelei's back-combed candy floss. Never would I let him near my hair. 'I'm perfectly capable of doing my own hair!'

'Don't be crazy, honey! No one styles their own hair on their wedding day! Believe me, I know what I'm talking about! You're having Stanley, and that's that!'

I turned away, gritted my teeth, and comforted myself with the thought that, as from the following night, I'd be living in Monaco, well out of Lorelei's reach. 'You said you'd do exactly as I wanted,' I muttered. 'I can't believe that you've arranged all this behind my back!'

'I don't understand you, Lisa,' my mother retaliated. 'After all, you've waited long enough to get married. Why all this cloak-and-dagger nonsense? I'd have thought you'd have wanted everyone to see how lucky you are to find a man like Cecil at your age. C'mon, we'll have a ball tomorrow! Jesus, I think I'm more excited about it than you are!'

'Well, there's a surprise.'

The gap between my mother's false eyelashes narrowed. 'You may be my daughter, but . . . You're a cold fish, Lisa. So bloody British, like your father. All that stiff-upper-lip crap. You just can't let go and enjoy yourself. Nothing's ever good enough for you. Wanna know something? When I think back, you've always been the same. When you saw something you wanted, nothing could stop you getting it. But the moment you had it – pah!' Her long fingernails flicked skywards in a blood-red shower. 'Suddenly, you weren't interested any more.'

61

Before I had time to contemplate the uncomfortable truth of this or think of a ripost, the doorbell rang. 'I'll get it,' I snapped, pleased to have an excuse to slam out of the room. What could it be but yet another delivery of flowers, bearing the message, *love from Cecil*?

Scowling, I flung open the front door. Andy was slouched in the porch, dressed in a pair of worn jeans, the black cashmere polo-neck sweater I'd bought him for his last birthday, and his old, torn flying jacket. His face was unshaven and haggard, and his hair was standing on end. He looked as if he'd been tossing and turning all night and had just rolled out of bed.

'I ran into Elena yesterday,' he said abruptly. 'You're not really thinking of getting married, are you?'

Dizzy with shock, I clutched the doorframe. 'Not thinking about it,' I said. 'Doing it.'

'When?'

'Tomorrow.'

'Shit!' Andy's face went white. He shook his head. 'How bloody, bloody stupid of you, Lisa!'

Out of control and pounding audibly, my traitorous heart crashed against my ribs. 'I'll tell you what was stupid, Andy – ever getting mixed up with you.'

Reaching into the back pocket of his jeans, he pulled out his cigarettes. 'You can't get married, Lisa,' he said as he lit up.

'Can't I?' Why, oh why, did seeing him make me feel so lightheaded? 'Why not?'

The cobalt of his irises flashed at me from under his thick eyelashes. 'Because you love me. Because we belong together.'

Thrilled, and at the same time furious, I glared back at him. 'God, you're arrogant! How the hell do you know what I feel?' He raised his eyebrows knowingly, and my cheeks began to flush red. 'Anyway,' I hurried on, 'even if I did still feel something for you – which I don't – what would follow from that?'

Smoke billowed from his nostrils like steam from a boiling kettle. 'Come on, Lisa! What's the point of involving another poor fucker in our crazy triangle?'

'Lisa?' Through the drumming of blood in my ears, I could hear Lorelei's footsteps shuffle down the hall. 'Who is it?'

I quickly pulled the door to. 'It's no one, Mum.'

'Whadya mean?'

'It's just a man. For me. Go away, will you? Please? Look, it's just a man I used to know.'

My mother bristled. Before I could stop her, she pushed past me, wormed her head through the open crack, and wrinkled her nose at the untidy loafer littering her doorstep. 'What's he want?' Before Andy could incriminate himself, I grabbed my mother by the arm, yanked her back inside, and pushed the door to. 'It's that man, isn't it?' she hissed in a stage whisper.

I shook my head, in a lame attempt at bluffing. 'What man? What are you talking about?'

'You can't lie to me, Lisa. It's him! The one with the *girlfriend*.'

'*Please!*'

'Tell him to get the hell out of here!'

'I'm going to!'

'Go on then!'

'Look, I will! In my own time! If you leave me alone.'

Slowly, with many a reluctant backward glance, Lorelei shuffled back to the kitchen, muttering a string of insults under her breath. The moment she was out of earshot, I opened the door again.

'May I remind you, Andy, that the triangle was never of my making? Anyway, it doesn't exist any more. It's all over between us. Finished.'

He turned and walked halfway down the garden path, then, to my relief, sauntered back again, his hands deep in jacket pockets, cigarette dangling from his lips. 'Look, I know it was all my fault, Puss. Believe me, I've been doing a lot of thinking lately.' With an absent-minded gesture, he plucked a handful of buds from one of my father's prize rose bushes. 'Look, I feel fucking ridiculous standing out here. Can't we go somewhere and talk?'

'What about?'

'Our future.'

'We don't have a future, Andy. We scarcely have a past.'

'For Christ's sake, Lisa! I need to talk to you!' Desperately, he ran a hand through his hair, raking it into untidy clumps. 'I'm in such a fucking mess. Come on! Just come and sit in the car with me for a moment. For old time's sake.'

I knew I shouldn't go with him, but the scent of danger was irresistible. 'OK. For five minutes. That's all.'

Leaving the front door on the latch, I followed him down the garden path, and climbed into the passenger seat of his battered Saab. The interior smelled painfully familiar. Andy jumped in beside me and started the engine, and the Saab shot off down the road. 'Where the hell are you going?' I shouted. 'I haven't even shut the front door! My mother will think I've been kidnapped!'

He grinned sheepishly. 'You have.'

Though a reckless hysteria flooded through me, I said, 'This isn't funny, Andy.'

'I know. I'm not being funny.'

'Turn the car round immediately and drop me home!'

'Look, relax, will you? I don't know why you're so uptight. This whole business is obviously a lot more fucking painful for me than it is for you. You're obviously very happy about getting married.'

'Yes, I am.'

'Then what have you got to lose, for Christ's sake?'

Gripping the wheel with white knuckles, he raced through the neat suburban terraces and headed away from Cricklewood towards the West End. I glanced at the set, determined line of his mouth and the anxious pulse that throbbed in his temple, and I smiled to myself, elated by a sudden feeling of power.

'So,' I said in a cheerful voice, 'how's Francesca?'

'A pain in the neck.'

'She must be feeding you well.' I leaned across the gear lever and prodded his waistline. 'You'll have to watch it – you're getting a paunch.'

He caught hold of my fingers, kissed them, then pushed them into the hot tight crack between his thighs. I let them linger there for a delicious moment before roughly fishing them out. Andy turned to me with a vulnerable expression. 'Don't be horrid to me, Puss. It doesn't suit you. Shit!' He slammed on the brakes as the traffic came to a standstill. He turned the wheel violently to the right, pulled out into the oncoming traffic, and shot down the wrong side of the road. A lorry coming towards us hooted and flashed its lights. As the traffic on the left started to move again, Andy jerked the wheel round and cut back in. After a long pause, he said, 'So who's this bloke you're marrying? Elena was very secretive. She wouldn't tell me anything – except to say that he's fucking loaded. You're not marrying him for his money, are you?' he added after a moment, putting his hand on my knee.

I swatted it off, as if it were a cockroach. 'How dare you say that!'

'Sorry. So, who is he?'

I tapped my fingertips together and buttoned my lip. When Andy lit another cigarette, I grabbed it from him, took a long drag, and handed it back. The Saab sped down Maida Vale and into the Edgware Road without either of us saying a word. At long last I said, 'What's the point of this, Andy? Why are we sitting here snarling at each other?'

'I don't know. Sorry.' He reached for my hand, kissed the palm, and placed it high up on his thigh. This time I didn't take it away. 'I didn't mean it to be like this. Quite the opposite. I . . . I just wanted to apologise.'

My heart began to pound again. 'What for?'

'For being such a shit.'

At these words, a thaw started in my ice-hard resolve.

'I've been a selfish bastard, Lisa.'

Drip-drip went the ice. Drip-drip.

'I want you back.'

Drip-drip. Drip- drip.

'I need you, darling.'

The last of my defences melted. My resolve was no more substantial than a handful of water.

'I miss you,' Andy went on. 'All the fucking time. I can't sleep. I can't eat. I can't work. I can't concentrate. I don't want to see anyone or talk to anyone. I just can't bear being without you. It's you I love, Puss, not Francesca. I've made a terrible mistake. I fucked up. Just like you're about to fuck up by marrying – what the hell *is* his name?'

By now we'd reached Marble Arch. To the right was the place where I'd seen the couple kissing on the night I'd met Cecil. Now I was here with Andy, and he was saying all the things I'd been longing for him to say for the last two and a half years. But it was too late. At that very moment, Cecil was on a London-bound plane from Nice, the florists were putting the final touches to the table decorations, and the caterers were baking hundreds of mini vol-au-vents. By this time tomorrow, I'd be Mrs Cecil Brown. It was all so tragic and sad . . .

The Saab swung into Park Lane then careered left into Upper Brook Street. 'Where are we going?' I muttered through my tears. Andy glanced at his watch, then accelerated through a red light, whizzed round Grosvenor Square, past the Connaught and down into Berkeley Square. 'It's three o'clock, Andy. Too late for the Caprice.'

'We're not going to the Caprice.' As we entered Piccadilly, Andy did a sharp U-turn and pulled up on a double yellow line outside the Ritz Hotel.

'You can't stop here. You'll get clamped!' I protested.

Andy shrugged. He leaped out, walked round to my side of the car and, in an unprecedented chivalrous gesture, opened the door for me. When the doorman rushed towards him, ready to wave on the battered wreck, Andy pressed a £20 note into his hand. 'Look after this, will you?' he said in his poshest Eton accent. The doorman touched the peak of his cap. Andy propelled me into the hotel lobby, a hand pressed firmly into the small of my back.

'Oh, Puss, I want to fuck you so much!' he murmured.

So that was it! I pulled free and stopped. 'Forget it. Because I don't want to fuck you.' It was a lie of course, and he knew it. I did want to fuck him. Very very much. The thought of it made my knees buckle. In fact, I was finding it hard to stand up. 'I don't,' I repeated, trailing behind him as, ignoring my protests, he strode up to the reception desk.

'Yes, sir?'

'Andy Hetherington. Power TV. I phoned this morning and booked a suite for an interview.'

Oh, the presumption of it! Blinded by tears of fury, I turned on my heels and walked away from him, but he caught up with me as I was about to speed through the revolving door.

I swung round to face him. 'How could you do this?'

'Lisa . . .'

'No! Take me home. Now.'

'But . . .' He placed his hands on my shoulders. 'Look, I just wanted somewhere private where we could talk things over. Honestly. That's all.'

'Sure. *Read my lips.* And?'

'And nothing.'

'Bullshit!'

He looked away for a moment, and gave a deep sigh. Then, turning back towards me, he gazed deeply into my eyes. 'I know you're angry with me, but . . . Christ, darling, this is important! I'm trying to save you from making a complete fuck-up. We're talking about the rest of our lives! Look, if it's really over between us, if you don't feel anything for me – nothing at all – if you're really sure about what-ever-his-name-is, then, OK, go home now. Otherwise . . .' His thick dark brows drew together in a brooding frown. 'Just give me half an hour of your time, darling. Half an hour. That's all I'm asking for. Then I'll drop you home. It's not much to ask for, is it? After all,' he added in a bitter voice, 'you'll be with *him* for a lifetime.'

I knew I ought to leave, but . . . I looked up into Andy's earnest, convincing face, and the last drips of my resolve drained away. 'OK, Andy, I'll give you half an hour. At most. I'll come up to the room with you. But let me make one thing clear – you're mistaken if you think I'm going to do anything other than talk.'

Once in the bedroom, with the Please Do Not Disturb sign hooked up outside, we talked.

'Oh, Puss!'

'Oh, Andy!'

'Oh, Puss! Your mouth tastes so gorgeous!'

'Oh, Andy!'

'Oh God, I've missed you! I've . . . Mmm! Oh, I love you!'

'Oh . . .'

'Ooh!'

'Ah! Hey, don't rip off all my buttons! I've got to be able to leave here looking *vaguely* respectable!'

As I undid his belt buckle, he pressed me up against the closed door. 'We'll never leave here. Never. I'll . . . yes!' He pushed up my bra, fastened his lips around my left nipple and sucked it roughly. 'I'll cancel my six o'clock meeting and we'll stay here all night, and all tomorrow, and all the next day and all the next and . . . Oh, yes!' For my hand had fought its way into his jeans, and released his penis from the constriction of his boxer shorts. He shivered as my fingers tightened around the thick, ridged column and slid upwards to the engorged head. 'Oh, yes, yes!' As his legs collapsed under him, he fell sprawling across the double bed, taking me with him. 'Oh, darling!' With the instinct of a homing pigeon returning to its perch, his hand flew into the warm darkness underneath my skirt. Yanking down the top of my thick black tights, he ran a finger over my clitoris, then slipped it deep inside me. 'Oh, you juicy, darling, wet, wonderful Pussy!' he sighed.

Maybe I shouldn't have been such a pushover. But before I knew it, the act was a *fait accompli*. After a momentary pang of guilt about betraying Cecil, I forgot all about him. Who *was* this shadowy figure I was supposed to marry? Nothing to do with me! As the oxygen of passion filled my lungs again, reviving my whole body, I realised that, far from being able to forget Andy, I couldn't live without him. I needed him, and I belonged with him. Our lips had been made to devour each other's, just as our hands had been made to caress each other's skin. While we wrestled our mutual passion into submission, lust blotted out all my thoughts. Only afterwards – when I caught sight of the bruise-like smudges of mascara on my cheeks in the bathroom mirror, and my flushed chin, and my mussed-up hair – did I stop to consider what I'd just done. Through the open door, I heard Andy phoning room service and ordering a bottle of Veuve Clicquot champagne, and I suddenly thought of the planned wedding reception, and how hurt and humiliated Cecil would be when I told him that our marriage was off.

'Hey, you!' Beyond the reflection of my face, Andy appeared in the doorway, his body glistening, his mouth twisted into an irresistible lopsided smile. 'You're looking horribly pensive,' he murmured as he slid his hands under my arms and caressed my breasts. When I smiled back at his reflection, he nuzzled my ear. 'What are you thinking about?'

I didn't have time to tell him, because before I could say anything he pulled me round to face him and silenced me with a kiss. Then he yanked me into the shower, where he soaped the creases of my body with a gentleness that surprised me, and then made love to me all over again.

Later, wrapped up in a thick white bath sheet, I stood beside the window and looked out onto Piccadilly. It was dark now; collars drawn up, a steady stream of miserable-looking commuters were scurrying along the wet pavements and disappearing down into the Tube. I felt at peace, and apart from the world. The hotel room was a paradisaical tropical island suspended in a cold unwelcoming sea.

Draped in a bath sheet, Andy ambled over to me and refilled my glass of champagne. As he kissed my bare shoulder, a tremor of fear passed through me: did anyone deserve to be as happy as I was? 'To us, darling!' I murmured.

He raised his glass to me and drank. 'To you, Puss.'

'And the future.'

'To our future!'

Our future. As he said it, my last fears dissolved into a feeling of profound relief. I lay down on the bed and stretched out my toes, luxuriating in the last-minute, fairy-tale reprieve that had saved me from marrying a frog. 'Oh, darling,' I sighed. 'I'm so glad that we found each other in time. Though I do feel awful about Cecil.'

Andy's eyebrows shot up. 'Is that what he's called?' He laughed. 'What a fucking awful name!'

'Don't be bitchy. He's really sweet, and he's really marvellous to me. And,' I slid my hand under the rumpled blanket and crossed my fingers, 'I do love him very, very much. But I guess it was a mistake to think that I could marry him.' At this, Andy didn't smile so much as smirk. 'Heaven knows what he's going to say when I tell him about us. Oh God, and then there's my mother! By now she probably thinks you've dragged me off to some dark alley and murdered me!' I swigged another mouthful of champagne. 'Pour me some more of this, will you? I think I'm going to need it when I speak to her.'

Andy glanced at the watch on his thick, hair-flecked wrist. 'Shit, it's six-thirty!'

'Is it? Oh no, I really ought to go home now and face the music.'

'Oh, do you have to go, Puss?' He threw himself down next to me, and kissed my hand. 'I'm meant to be meeting someone, but I can always cancel it. Then we could stay here all night.'

'But I've got to explain all this to . . .' I hesitated. My own arrangements for that night – drinks with Cecil's parents, followed by an intimate hen night with Elena at Ken Lo's

– suddenly seemed as expendable as Cecil. 'Yes, that'd be wonderful,' I said. 'I can always phone and explain, can't I?' I sighed with relief. The nightmare of tomorrow was over, cancelled before it had begun. Once the rumpus had died down, I'd marry Andy and live happily ever after. In a few months, Cecil would meet someone else and do the same . . . 'Darling,' I murmured as I kissed Andy's shoulder, 'what'll you tell Francesca?'

'I dunno.' He slid his hand under the bath towel and up between my legs. 'I'll say that I've got to go up and see someone in Manchester tonight.'

'No, no! I meant about us.'

He drew away. An anxious shadow fell across his face. 'I don't know, Puss. The truth, I suppose. If only . . .'

'Yes?' My high voice betrayed my pang of anxiety.

'If only we weren't in the middle of doing up the bloody flat!'

I began to feel uneasy. I turfed Andy off me, and rolled over onto my side. 'So you've moved in already, have you?'

'Yeah. Last week. It's Cardboard City there. Fucking turmoil. The cooker's in the bedroom and the bath's in the hall. The roof leaks, and my shirts are strung up from the lavatory cistern. I don't see how we'll ever get straight. I'm so pushed at work that I've hardly got any time off. And when I do get an hour off, Fran drags me down to fucking Ikea to look at bathroom fittings and laminated flooring and shelving units. I'm afraid I'm not cut out for this DIY shit. Frankly, this whole thing couldn't have come at a worse time. We'll have to fix the place up now, because we'll never get rid of it as it is.' He shook his head. 'I wonder what Francesca'll do if I move out?' I noted the 'if' with alarm. 'I mean, she'll never be able to afford the mortgage by herself.'

How many suggestions had I made in the past concerning Francesca and her many problems? Oh well, what was one more? I spoke as dispassionately as I could: 'She could always take in a lodger.'

'How can she, when there's only one bedroom? Besides,

you know how paranoid she is, she'd never trust a stranger to . . .'

I sat up. I felt like a cold dagger had just been thrust through my ribs. 'What did you say?'

'That she'd never trust a . . .'

'Not that. Before. You said there's only one bedroom in the flat.'

'Yeah? So?'

'You told me before that it had two bedrooms.'

He laughed. 'No, I didn't!'

'Yes, you did. Surely you remember, Andy? That night . . . when you first told me . . . You said that buying the flat together was a matter of convenience, and you were going to carry on having separate lives. People who share bedrooms don't live separate lives, Andy!' The mounting crescendo of my anger began to spill over as it dawned on me that, yet again, I'd been had. 'I thought that you and Francesca hadn't slept together for years!'

'We haven't!' he squealed. 'I mean, we never fuck. Well, not often. But, well, we've always shared a bed. We only had one bed, so there wasn't much alternative. Hey, what are you doing, Puss?' he added as I jumped up.

'What does it look like?' Falling to my knees, I searched for my clothes in the pile of tangled garments beside the bed.

He frowned at me. 'I thought we were going to stay here all night?'

'And I thought everything had changed!' I shouted as I disentangled my bra strap from the legs of his trousers. 'That you really meant what you said this time.'

'But I do, darling!'

Did he really believe that? If so, he was the only one. Close to tears, I knelt up on the floor, and shook my head incredulously. 'You just didn't want to lose me, did you? You just wanted to make sure I was still there. Still your puppet. That I'd still jerk into action if you pulled the strings.'

'Lisa . . .'

'I don't think you've got any intention of ever splitting up with Francesca. In fact, I don't even think you've got any intention of telling her about me.'

'That's really unfair! I will!'

'When?'

He wiped the back of his hand across his forehead, an anxious gesture. 'Just as soon as I can! Honestly! You know – as soon as everything's settled down and I've sorted out the flat problem.'

Speechless with rage, I jammed my arms into my shirt, and, with shaking fingers, did up the buttons. Then I pulled on my tights, and stumbled into my skirt. I was about to leave, when I changed my mind, went back to the bed and poured the remaining contents of the champagne bottle over him.

'Forget it, Andy,' I said bitterly. 'Because I won't be there.'

Six

The torture began. A blinding light burned into my face. When I tried to turn away from it, a hand yanked my chin forward. Something sharp pierced my scalp, and I winced with pain.

'Hold still!' a voice commanded.

My armpits prickled with fear as the sharp object stabbed my scalp again. Then the interrogation started:

'Well? How do you feel?'

How did my interrogator think? Terrified. But there was a lump in my throat which made it impossible for me to answer him. Silent as the grave I felt like crawling into, I squinted painfully into the light.

'Eh, Lisa?' persisted my invisible questioner. 'How do you feel on this, the happiest day of your life?'

I managed a single word: 'Thirsty!' and, with great effort, drew my lips back into a grimace which I hoped might pass as a grin. I'd smiled so much already this morning that my facial muscles were aching like thighs after an aerobics class. Only three more hours, I told myself, and my cheeks could sag back into the mournful expression I'd cranked them up from earlier. Till then, I had to keep up this marathon effort. Everyone was expecting it. I had to suppress my inclination to go berserk and go for the burn instead.

The white light atop the video camera swayed dangerously in front of me. 'Thirsty?' repeated my father's voice from behind it. 'Is that all you can say? Aren't you excited, Lisa? After all, this is the greatest day of your life!'

The greatest mistake, perhaps. The lump in my throat had

now swollen so much that it was threatening to choke me. To tell the truth, it would have been a blessed relief if it had. But no such luck. I'd made my choice, and I wasn't going to escape a minute of suffering. Still grimacing into the black Cyclops in front of me, I nodded several times.

'You're getting married today!' my father persisted.

Through gritted teeth, I mustered a cheery, 'Yes!' Now a pain shot through my neck. The pearl choker – the traditional something 'old' and 'borrowed', lent to me for the occasion by my future mother-in-law – was threatening to garotte me. Maybe that's what Rita had intended. Maybe she'd lied about liking my novels. Maybe she'd had me followed yesterday, and knew what I'd been up to in the Ritz.

Hysteria churned in my stomach like a bad case of gastro-enteritis. The acid taste of vomit began slowly but inexorably to rise up in my throat. Desperate to hold it down, I tried to remember the words of the stress relief tape I'd played to myself during the sleepless hours of the night: *You are alone, floating on a white cloud in a blue sky. Everything around you is soft and peaceful. Your mind is like a deep lake, its surface is as flat and still as a mirror. Nothing disturbs you. Breathe deeply, deeply . . .* As I gasped for breath, my ribs strained against the bodice of my shantung wedding dress. Virginal white – what a joke! If only the guests knew what I'd been doing with Andy less than twenty-four hours ago!

The zip dug into my back, the sleeves gripped my arms like boa constrictors, and the beaded neckline scratched at my throat. 'It's a dream dress!' Cecil's sister Jackie had exclaimed when I'd arrived at the church. To me it felt more like a shroud, a shroud in which my old self, my real self, was about to be buried. How did that speech from *Hamlet* go? *White his shroud as the mountain snow/Larded with sweet flowers;/which bewept to the grave did go/With true-love showers*. Jesus, what the hell was I doing? A woman of thirty-five years old dressed up like the Sugar Plum Fairy, with flowers woven Ophelia-like into my hair. *There's rosemary, that's for remembrance; pray, love, remember. And there is pansies, that's for thoughts* . . . Oh, clever Ophelia! Compared to the ordeal of getting married, drowning oneself in a stream seemed infinitely easier.

'Horace!' rasped my mother's voice behind me. 'The music's started! Everyone's waiting. For Chrissake, give that goddam video camera to someone else and take Lisa's arm! Hey – where's the bouquet? Where the hell's the goddam bouquet?'

A bouquet of pepper-scented freesias was thrust between my clammy fingers. I swung round, desperate to escape, but two giggling yellow canaries in lemon frills and beaded headbands had closed off the exit route behind me. Why on earth had I let my mother arrange this farcical church wedding, with Claudia and Harriet as bridesmaids? I didn't need them. I didn't need *any* of this.

Why had I agreed to get married at all?

With a cluck of his tongue, Stanley, my mother's hairdresser, secured my headdress with a final hairpin. Now my mother moved into focus, and smirking victoriously, drew the veil over my face. Though I wasn't married yet, I was already locked up in a domestic prison, peering out through my own personal net curtain at the free world. I was trapped, trapped, trapped . . .

The blinding light clicked off, leaving me blinking into a fuzzy yellow haze. My father took my arm, and I stumbled forwards. Dank, dark, and lined with staring eyes, a birth canal lay before me, at the end of which – in the frog-like shape of Cecil – a new, grown-up life awaited me. The safe, if unadventurous *modus vivendi* I'd created during my adulthood ended here.

'Good luck, love,' my father muttered, squeezing my hand.

I tried in vain to make my feet move forwards, but the soles of my white satin shoes seemed to have been super-glued to the floor. In an act of rebellion, my whole body shrank from what had to be done. Now that the actual moment of commitment had arrived, my hysteria gushed up like a faucet on full power.

I couldn't go through with this wedding. I had to escape. But how? How? Not knowing what to do, I turned to the man who had been my saviour up till now.

'Daddy?'

My father's eyes twinkled at me. 'Yes, darling?' And before I could croak another word, he shook his head and added softly, 'Lisa, you look a picture. Beautiful! Just beautiful!' He wiped a tear away from under his glasses and went on, tremulously, 'I can't tell you how proud you've made me today! So, love, are you ready?'

Realising I was beaten, I gave up fighting fate. 'Yes, Dad,' I muttered with resignation. 'I'm ready.'

And ready I was – ready to turn around, run down the church steps, and never come back again.

Later that afternoon, exhausted and hung over – that was me, I couldn't speak for Cecil who was so overcome by the day's events that he scarcely uttered a word – I stepped out onto the tarmac at Nice airport, confetti spilling from my passport and my wrist manacled by Cecil's clutch. As I dozed, semiconscious, in the deep leather seats of the Mercedes taxi that sped us along the *moyenne corniche* to Monaco, where, at my own insistence ('No, no, Cecil, I really don't want a honeymoon,') we were to spend our first night in Cecil's flat, I became uncomfortably aware of a hot, soft, moist, unfamiliar hand fondling my knee.

Side by side, yet a million miles away from each other, we stopped off to eat a champagne dinner in the gilded splendour of the Hôtel de Paris' *Salle Empire*, our conversation as stilted as that of mismatched strangers on a first date. Ravenously hungry all of a sudden, I wolfed down a large helping of pâté de fois gras, a sizeable sole meunière, and a double portion of crème brûlée – while Cecil toyed with a small plate of mushroom risotto, his bulbous eyes staring at me fearfully, as if he guessed that I was unconsciously putting off the moment when we finally went home, and so to bed.

* * *

Later, the Mercedes jerked to a halt beneath a large mosaic-covered canopy on the sea front. Cecil opened the door for me, and I crawled out. Above me loomed a thirty-six-storey concrete corn-on-the-cob. Of the eight or nine tower blocks I'd glimpsed as we'd driven along the Avenue Princesse Grace, the Bellavista Tower was by far the ugliest, thrusting rudely up into the night sky with all the subtlety of a giant, floodlit erection.

I followed Cecil through the glass doors and into a lobby the size of a hotel ballroom. Huge upturned crystal pyramids dangled from the ceiling, and acres of snow-blindingly white marble unrolled under our feet. Jumping up from his perch behind a large granite reception desk, a uniformed concierge looked me up and down suspiciously. But when he saw Cecil, he nodded at him and sat down again.

'Bonsoir, M. Brown.'

'Bonsoir, M. Georges.'

I held my breath as a mirror-lined lift rocketed us up to the thirty-second floor, leaving my stomach on the ground. We stepped out into a small, dimly lit lobby. Cecil fumbled in his jacket pocket for a key. When he'd found it, he unlocked one of two wooden front doors in front of us and, picking me up with a gargantuan effort, scooped me over the threshold and into my new home.

'Well, darling, this is it!'

'Ouch, Cecil! You're hurting me!'

'Sorry. Umph!' Straining loudly, Cecil put me down, then reached for a light switch. I screwed up my eyes as a chandelier exploded overhead, highlighting the beads of sweat on my husband's forehead in a particularly unattractive way. As my eyes grew accustomed to the football-pitch brightness, I took in the thick pink Chinese rug on the white marble floor, and the four sets of ornate white double doors around me – doors offset with large ormolu knobs, and panelled in dark green flock velvet wallpaper, the kind that local Indian restaurants used to be decorated in when I was young.

'Come and see the rest of the flat, darling!'

Cecil flung open the nearest double doors, switched on a bank of spotlights and, taking my hand, dragged me into a large rectangular living room where, it seemed, the contents of a high-class brothel had been mixed haphazardly into the set of a Jane Austen film: there was Regency-striped paper hung with Tretchikoff-style oil paintings of half-naked women, and ornate gilt furniture upholstered in scarlet velvet, and a vast, ormolu-trimmed shelving unit on which were arranged books, Staffordshire figurines, lava lamps, cut-glass vases, and a garish collection of weeping china clowns.

Cecil smiled, proud as a lord mayor showing off his newly decorated council chamber. 'Well, darling. What do you think of it?'

I thought, *I want to back to London on the next plane.* I thought, *What can I possibly have in common with a man with such dreadful taste?* 'It's ...' I swallowed. '... very nice, Cecil.'

'Do you think so? You don't have to say that, you know. Come and look at our b-b-bedroom!' Before I could protest, he grabbed my hand and led me back through the hall to a large square room where highly lacquered black walls fought for dominance with a king-size, circular bed. Behind the bed rose a high gold velvet headboard set with more loudspeakers and control buttons than the dashboard of a Lamborghini.

I began to feel faint. 'What are all those knobs for, Cecil?' I murmured.

He pointed them out to me proudly. 'Radio. Clock. TV – that comes out of the wall opposite when you press this button. Cassette recorder. Video recorder. This one here's for the built-in CD unit – I think. That one tilts the mattress up and down at either end. And this red switch sets off the *pièce de résistance*. See?'

Cecil flicked the switch. Feeling distinctly queasy, I watched the circular bed revolve through a full 360 degrees. 'Wow!' I said. 'That's useful.'

Cecil gave me a curious look and turned the motor off. I wandered over to the Louis XV-style dressing table set in front of a wall of thick, floor-length gold velvet curtains. On it, an enormous bunch of white roses was arranged in a simple glass vase. I picked up the handwritten card propped up beside the vase and deciphered Cecil's tiny handwriting: *Welcome home to my darling wife.*

I thought with unbearable melancholy of my cheap and cheerfully furnished flat in Belsize Park – now in the process of being sold – and my eyes suddenly brimmed with tears. Unable to control them, I sank down on the bed, crying quietly.

'Lisa?' Short legs apart, Cecil sat down beside me, and squeezed my unresponsive, fish-cold hand. 'W-what's the matter, darling?'

'Nothing,' I sobbed.

He frowned at me for a long moment, then glanced around the bedroom. 'Oh dear, it's this place, isn't it?' he stammered. 'I'm so sorry, darling. It's not very pretty, is it? I should have thought . . . You see, I bought all the furniture from the previous tenants, and I guess I've just lived with it. There didn't seem much point changing anything or doing the place up. Not just for me. Well, not until now, that is,' he added, smiling at me with stifling sentimentality. 'Look, I'd like you to feel free to change anything you want to.'

'Really?' I sniffed.

'Really!' He gazed up at me with adoration. 'In fact, I'd love it. It'll give you something to do in your spare time. While I'm working, I mean, and when you're not writing. And, well, it badly needs a woman's touch.' His heavy eyelids blinked at me meaningfully, as if hinting that, perhaps, he did too. When I looked away, he hurried on, 'My own furniture and paintings have been in storage ever since I moved to Monaco. We could get it out and see if you like any of it. But don't feel you have to keep it – not if you don't want it. I'm sure you've got much better taste than I have.'

I began to sob even louder. Perplexed, Cecil sucked on his protruding lower lip. 'Poor darling!' he murmured. His arm slid around my shoulder, and I relaxed against his solid, almost motherly, bulk. 'Poor, poor darling! This is such a lot for you to take on, isn't it? All these changes, I mean. Giving up your home. Getting married. Moving here. All at the same time. I wish there was something I could do to m-make it all easier for you. Is there?'

There was something. But how could I tell him what it was? Because, frankly, the only way Cecil could have made me feel better at that moment was by dropping dead. 'I'll be all right. Really I will,' I muttered in a martyred voice I recognised as my mother's, and blew my nose in the handkerchief he now handed me.

'I know you will!' Cecil gave my ribs a comforting squeeze. I became aware that his arm was still around my shoulder, and that his lips were getting much too close. A moment later his dewy eyes met mine, and he touched my chin and began to draw it down, down towards his . . .

'Oh gosh!' I exclaimed, jumping up – and accidentally hurling Cecil back across the mattress. 'I'm simply *dying* to go to the loo!'

Awkwardly, circling each without touching, as wary as two wild weasels imprisoned in a cage, we unpacked a few of our things and prepared for bed. Alone in the marble ensuite bathroom, I scrubbed myself manically under a hot shower, but the odour of Andy still clung to my skin.

At last, teeth cleaned, make-up removed, negligée sash double-knotted for extra safety at my waist, I came out of the bathroom and Cecil went in, brushing past me with a whispered, 'Sorry!' From behind the closed door came the sound of gargling, then of the shower running, and, as an undertone, the splash of urine hitting the lavatory bowl.

Revolted by these intimacies, I parted the gold velvet curtains, slid opened the french windows and escaped onto a wide, terracotta-tiled balcony. The crisp night air bit through my night clothes. I shivered with cold. Clutching the balcony rail, I gazed out across the Mediterranean. A full moon hung like a large pale bauble in the inky sky, sending a firework trail across the jet-black sea. A dizzying thirty-two floors below Cecil's flat, a ruff of white surf bordered the slate-grey beach. I'd written countless love scenes in my time, and imagined countless romantic situations. But never had I seen or imagined anything quite as romantic as this . . .

Far below, someone laughed wildly. With a loud roar, a motorbike revved down the street. I heard someone whisper my name, turned and saw Cecil, standing by the open french window. Combed carefully over the top of his balding scalp, his freshly washed hair gleamed like an oil-slick in the moonlight. His bathrobe was tied loosely under his paunch, and his hairy legs protruded under the hemline like two short matchsticks. In turn, these descended sharply into a pair of large, bunioned feet.

This vision in black-and-red striped towelling repeated my name again, and then, smiling amorously, held out its arms to me.

For a moment I froze in horror, not knowing what to do. Then the gargantuan supper I'd eaten earlier made a decision for me. Retching, I dodged past Cecil and lurched for the bathroom. 'Sorry,' I mumbled into my cupped fingers. 'I think I'm going to be sick.'

After Cecil had sponged the stains from the carpet and gone inside to watch television, I fell asleep, weeping and alone, in the vast circular bed. In a dream that seemed far more real than my wedding, Andy came to my flat, promising that he'd stay with me forever if I forgave him just this one more time. He said that we belonged together. And to prove it, he took me in his arms and slid his warm, moist tongue deep into my mouth . . .

I awoke with a start to the sound of soft, unfamiliar snoring. A hot hand lay on my hip, and a pillow of naked flesh was pressed into my back. Careful not to wake my husband, I prised his hands from my body, slid out of bed and padded into the bordello of a living room. Out on the balcony I sank wearily down on one of the two wooden sunbeds and gulped thirstily at the crisp early morning air. Gradually, the night sky gave way to purple clouds, through which a red ball of sun rose slowly over the sea.

That I'd made a dreadful mistake in marrying Cecil went without saying. The thing was, what was I going to do about it? Soldier on with the farcical situation, in the hope that I'd overcome my aversion to him? Or pack up my few possessions and get the hell out before even more harm was done? With our marriage annulled on the grounds of non-consummation, I'd be able to pick up the pieces of my old life, devote myself to writing, and resign myself to being childless and alone for the rest of my life. It was a tempting thought – but oh, the humiliation of admitting I'd been so stupid! I tried to imagine what acerbic comment Elena would make if I fled back to London on the day after my wedding, but my imagination failed me. How Andy would gloat when he found out! My father would be broken-hearted with disappointment. My mother would never let me live it down. What had she said on the fateful day she'd found me crying over Andy? '*No one can tell you anything about love, because you know it all, don't you? My daughter, the romantic novelist!*' Once again, Lorelei had been been right. I was a hopeless case.

Helpless with indecision, I paced the balcony. At last, clutching the balcony rail, I gazed out to sea.

Then I heard the crash on the balcony above me.

It sounded like splintering glass.

A voice called out, '*Non!*' – or was that my imagination? Maybe it was just that grating noise – like the sound of a metal chair being dragged across ceramic tiles.

Then, suddenly, a pair of men's crocodile shoes dropped down in front of me. Protruding from them, two legs clad in black crêpe evening trousers, the kind with black satin stripes up the side.

A white evening jacket, studded with gold buttons. The flash of a white shirt collar. The slash of a bow-tie . . .

The falling man seemed to hang suspended in the air for a split second, his eyes bulging with terror, his hands stretched towards me as if he expected me to save him. Then he plummeted silently out of my sight, swiftly followed by a taupe toupee.

Too shocked even to scream, I recoiled towards the windows. An eternity later there came a dull thud from far below me. Then – nothing. An eerie silence descended over Monaco; no traffic; no birdsong; even the waves seemed to stop breaking on the shore.

Paralysed with fear, I waited for something else to happen. When nothing did, I stood up and moved slowly back towards the balcony rail.

Perhaps I'd imagined it.

I forced myself to look down.

Far, far below, a broken black and white doll lay prostrate in the Bellavista Tower's back garden, leaking a bright, scarlet streak into the swimming pool.

Seven

———✦———

The principality of Monaco, famed for its casinos, its ruling family, and the Monte-Carlo Grand Prix. A slither of land, smaller in area than Hyde Park, sited in a natural amphitheatre between the mountains and the Mediterranean in the southeast corner of France. Population: just under 30,000, a sixth of whom are native Monégasques. The rest, like my husband Cecil, are either British, French, Italians or other foreign nationals who either live there for business reasons or because, under the local laws, they don't have to pay any tax.

For seven hundred years, the ruling Grimaldi family has survived bloody wars and equally bloody scandals and surveyed its pocket-sized domain from its ancient palace at the end of the rocky promontory of Monacoville town, two hundred feet above the sea. If he turns to the left, today's ruler, Prince Rainier, has a perfect view of the brand new Olympic-standard football stadium down in the district of Fontvieille, a new town built in the eighties on thirty-one hectares of land reclaimed from the sea. If he turns to the right, he can look down across the old port, where millionaires' yachts bob like small toys next to the vast super-yachts of multi-billionaires and ex-arms dealers, and from there he can glance up to the fabulous Hôtel de Paris, the fountain-filled Casino Gardens and the green-roofed wedding cake of the Casino itself, Monaco's main attraction and the first port of call for the hundreds of thousands of tourists who pour through the principality each year.

Climbing up the steep hills behind the Casino, and bordering the manmade Larvotto beach, is the district of Monte-Carlo, an area almost entirely rebuilt since the war. Every now and then, tucked between a cantilevered road and another building sight, one can still glimpse some small reminder of its faded past – a lone palm tree, for instance, or an old, cream stucco house complete with red-tiled roof, painted shutters and rococo balconies overgrown with pelargoniums. But, for the most part, Monte-Carlo is made up of a plethora of faceless concrete apartment buildings which have turned Rainier's once-picturesque principality into a miniature, but nondescript Hong Kong.

The thirty-six-storey Bellavista Tower, where Cecil lived, was just such one of these buildings. Within it, the first weeks of my marriage flew by with the speed of a punctured Zeppelin. Left alone all day while Cecil went off to his office somewhere near the port, I wandered restlessly from room to room, rearranging Cecil's furniture in a vain attempt to make it look more tasteful, and wishing I was back home. I spent hours on the balcony, staring blankly at the fabulous view – down the French coast to Nice, or across to Italy. With a stone lodged where my stomach had once been, I sat miserably in the huge kitchen, trying in vain to think of something vaguely healthy to give Cecil to eat when he came back from work. For myself, I had no appetite for the delicious charcuterie on sale in the food markets, or the fabulous crusty breads, or the pungent cheeses. I had no appetite for anything, not even life.

When Cecil wasn't working, he and I drove into the hinterland in his black convertible Carerra – not for nothing had that old red Ford Escort he kept at his mother's house to use when he was in London born a sticker which said, 'My other car's a Porsche.' Green Michelin guide in one hand, Cecil's webbed fingers in the other, I trotted dutifully through scores of cobbled hill villages, mountain gorges and river ravines. At Cecil's side, I soaked up twentieth-century culture in the form of the Picasso museum on the ramparts at Antibes, and the Léger museum at Biot, and the Gallery of

Modern Art in Nice. At the Fondation Maeght, a dramatic art gallery set on a hillside outside Saint-Paul de Vence, I marvelled at the Miró sculptures, cooed at the Calder mobiles, and even managed a forced giggle when my corpulent companion tried to conceal himself, for my amusement, behind an anorexic Giacometti bronze.

There I was, a newly-wed living in one of the most glamorous places in Europe. I knew I should have been happy. But despite my best effort to put a brave face on it, neither Cecil nor I were fooled. It was never more than half an hour before misery dragged down the corners of my mouth. Wherever we went and whatever we did, there was no escaping the fact that I found my husband both unattractive and deeply annoying. Or, that I felt embarrassed to be seen in public with him. Or, that when we sat across a table, we had absolutely nothing to say to each other – at least, I had nothing to say to Cecil; if he had anything to say to me, he never managed to spit it out.

Minute by minute, hour by hour, the silences between us grew more uncomfortable, and the more uncomfortable they became, the harder they were to break. This downwards spiral turned into a vicious circle: as my face grew longer, so Cecil grew more desperate; and the more desperate he became, the more I despised him; and the more I despised him, the more I'd catch him gazing at me in a confused yet adoring fashion, like some doting, abused dog.

This pathetic devotion of Cecil's made me extremely angry. I was angry with him for loving me. I was angry with him for looking like he did. I was angry with him for stuttering, and for not being Andy, and angry with him simply for being himself. Most of all, I was angry with myself for having drifted into marrying a man I neither loved, liked nor fancied, and – on days when I wasn't so busy feeling sorry for myself that I couldn't feel sorry for Cecil – for being such an unreasonable, unfeeling bitch.

What was Cecil's opinion of our misalliance? For a misalliance it undeniably was. We had so little in common that we were scarcely of the same species: I, naturally, was a human being; but Cecil – well, Cecil, with his moist skin and his triple chin, his sticking-out eyes and his short, plump thighs, Cecil was a frog.

Was his amphibian brain complex or sensitive enough to guess the dark thoughts which, before a fortnight of married life had elapsed, began to trickle in a poisonous stream through the backwaters of my mind? Thoughts that started with a simple *If only I hadn't married him* and graduated through *If only he'd go away for a few days* to the more dubious *If only he'd disappear!* From then on, it was a short, downhill slope to thoughts of heart attacks, fatal car crashes and freak pedalo accidents – events which would neatly dispose of Cecil while leaving me free to return to my old life in London without the shame of admitting my mistake.

Thankfully, after our catastrophic wedding night, Cecil didn't try to make make a pass at me again. In fact, he seldom came close enough to touch me, but skirted around me as warily as a goldfish circumnavigating a crocodile, only rarely daring to dart forward to snatch a quick peck on the cheek. Perhaps my vomiting on the bedroom carpet had put him off me, or maybe it was the period cramps I complained of week in, week out (luckily for me, Cecil's knowledge of female biology seemed on a par with his ability to talk).

Even so, my husband and I continued to share one bed, though our bedtime ritual was choreographed more carefully than a West End farce to ensure that we never saw each other naked, or accidentally touched. While Cecil stayed in the living room, I locked myself in our ensuite bathroom, where I shrouded myself in a pair of cotton pyjamas I'd picked up for 60 francs in the supermarket at Fontvieille (the enticing satin nightdresses from my trousseau having been confined to the back of a drawer). Double-wrapped like a Spangle in a towelling bathrobe, I'd dash for bed just as Cecil made his humble entrance. Then, mumbling something about being exhausted, I'd throw off the robe, jump into bed and pull the covers up to my neck. Twenty seconds later, I'd hear the bathroom door click shut, and the whirring vibrations of Cecil's electric toothbrush would drill through my head. By the time he emerged after his ablutions – a quick wash, a long pee, followed by another quick wash for good measure – my head was covered by a pillow, and I was breathing slowly and rythmically, as if deeply asleep.

'Goodnight, darling,' he'd whisper as, careful neither to disturb nor touch me, he slipped between the sheets. And I'd remain silent, curled up like the foetus I was beginning to realise I'd never have inside me now.

'Pregnant yet?' Elena asked with crass insensitivity whenever we spoke on the telephone.

'Not yet,' I'd mumble. For how could I admit to her that my marriage had yet to be consummated?

No wonder I was so angry with myself: desperately seeking sperm, I'd married a man I couldn't bear to touch me.

Had she only known about it, my mother would have crowed.

That I didn't return home within a month was due to the surprise free gift which came with marrying Cecil.

'What's this?' I shouted when he slipped the grey plastic card into my hand over breakfast one morning during our third week together. I say shouted, because we were eating on our balcony, and it was the week of the Monte-Carlo Grand Prix. Half the roads in the principality had been boarded up with steel safety barriers, and the air was rent by ear-splitting *neeaows*.

My husband shrugged, and began to munch intently on a croissant. His cheeks were flushed an embarrassed puce. I looked down at the name embossed on the platinum American Express card: Madame Lisa Brown. It took me a moment to realise that meant me. 'Where did this come from, Cecil?'

Cecil's tongue flicked out and licked a crumb from his upper lip. 'I . . . er, I took the liberty of ordering it for you,' he croaked. With a nervous gesture, he adjusted the collar of his dressing gown. 'I thought it might be useful for you to have one, darling,' he shouted as another racing car vroomed around a nearby corner. 'For paying for things for the flat when we get round to redecorating. And buying food for us. And other household expenses,' he added in his normal voice. 'Oh yes – and for buying yourself some clothes and things. I mean, I'm sure you must need a completely different wardrobe, now that you're going to be living in such a hot climate.'

I thought of the astronomical price tags I'd seen in the windows of the local clothes shops. 'I can't afford a different wardrobe, Cecil,' I said in an exasperated voice. 'In fact, judging from the prices I've seen here, I can't even afford to buy a pair of knickers on the pittance I earn from my books.'

'Precisely,' he stuttered. 'And the last thing I want is for you to use up all your money. I mean, it's I who asked you to come and live here, isn't it? So why should you be put to any expense? No, darling, the bill for this card will be paid out of our joint bank account.'

'Our joint account?' I echoed over the next *neeaow*. 'You mean, you want us to pool our incomes?'

Cecil looked shocked. 'No, no, no, Lisa! You must keep all your own income separately! After all, you work so hard for it! No, no, the money in our joint account will all come from my income.'

'Yours?' I repeated like an idiot. 'You mean, you want me to spend your money?'

'You may as well, darling.' His face creased into an apologetic smile. 'You see, I may not be a billionaire, and I'm certainly not wealthy compared to most of the people who live here. But, well, I do actually have quite a lot of money. In fact, I never know quite what to do with it. So if you don't spend some of it for me, it'll just sit in the bank, gathering interest with the rest. Besides,' he added, reaching across the table and taking my hand, 'it's not *my* money any more, is it?'

92

Neeaow. Neeaow.

'What are you talking about?' I shouted.

Cecil blinked at me tenderly, and mouthed the words, 'It's *ours*.'

Later that morning, during a temporary lull in the racing, I slipped the Amex card into my old British Home Stores handbag, strolled along the promenade and, crossing the road at the huge scar of a building site which dominated the sea front, I took the public lift up to the Boulevard des Moulins. As I wandered past the shops, staring at the goods on display in the windows, a shameful elation overcame me. My God, I realised, I'm rich. Rich! Not only didn't I have to pay my mortgage or telephone bills any more, I could actually walk into any of these shops and buy myself whatever I wanted. Whenever I wanted. Without having to think about the cost!

Could it really be true? Biting my lip, I rushed into the nearest clothes shop, chose a T-shirt at random, and handed over my credit card. Clutching my purchase, I reeled back out onto the street and dashed into the interior design shop next door, where a small, plain silver picture frame caught my eye. Seven hundred francs. I did a quick calculation. That was almost £100! I was about to leave without it, when I remembered what Cecil had said: '*If you don't spend some of it for me, it'll just sit in the bank, gathering interest with the rest.*'

Armed with these two purchases, I then entered the Charles Jourdan shoe shop, where I bought a pair of white-patent strappy sandals with impossibly high spikey heels. And a matching belt. And matching handbag. Gathering courage along with each extra carrier bag, I worked my way down the street to the Casino Square, sauntered past the fountains and strode confidently into the premises of Chanel.

Which was where I met the woman who was to become both my mentor and my ruin.

She was standing in the middle of the shop admiring herself in a mirror, a petite, bird-like, middle-aged woman in a sleeveless black linen dress. Her eyes were hidden by a huge pair of black sunglasses, and a heavily fringed, sleek black wig fell over her face. 'Black! Remember, I most haff everything black!' she called out in a voice which sounded part Dutch, part Hungarian, and part extra in a New York film.

'Oui, Madame Lamarre!' The assistant serving her bustled forward, a jacket in her arms. The woman called Madame Lamarre held out two scrawny arms, and slipped into it, and the assistant did up the buttons for her. 'Mais, c'est parfait, Madame!'

'Vous pensez?' Madame Lamarre said in slow French thick with Middle European overtones. Taking off her sunglasses to reveal a short chiselled nose with flared nostrils and a pair of eyelids lifted to tearing point, she examined her reflection in a mirror.

'That looks lovely on you,' I said when she noticed me looking at her.

She pouted at herself. 'You think so?'

'Black suits you.'

'Dahlink, everything suits me.' Her voice was dry, but not unfriendly. 'But I have to wear black at the moment because I'm in mourning.'

'Oh! I'm so sorry!'

Madame Lamarre waved a skeletal, dismissive hand. 'It's not important. My husband died two weeks ago.'

'Oh, how dreadful!' I gasped. 'That's awful. You must be devastated.'

She smiled at me briskly. 'Naturally I'm devastated,' she repeated as she turned to the side and continued examining her reflection from this new angle. 'I mean, to have to dress in black, during the summer! With all these lovely bright colours in the boutiques this season! And with those handsome young racing drivers everywhere! Mademoiselle!'

'Madame?'

'I've just remembered! I need *un chapeau*! No, not that one! It's quite wrong! Something for *ce soir*. *Pour dîner à la Salle Empire*. My dear, everyone will be there tonight, so I must have something stunning.' She gazed round at the shelves, then pointed to a black, wide-brimmed hat crowned with a ring of ostrich feathers – the kind of style my mother might have worn for a wedding. 'That one, there!'

'Celui-ci?'

'Oui!' She allowed the assistant to place it on her head. 'Not bad. But so dark for May! If only Boris had killed himself in September it wouldn't have been so bad!'

'Your husband killed himself?' I breathed. 'How terrible!'

'Of course, it was terrible!' the woman snapped back at me. 'He threw himself off our balcony – so messy – without leaving so much as a goodbye note. Luckily, like my last three late husbands, Boris was well insured.'

I suddenly felt faint. 'Wh . . . where do you live?'

'In the Bellavista, of course. Why are you looking at me like that, Madame? Believe me, the Bellavista's the only place in Monaco to live.'

The ground slipped away beneath me. I sank down on a nearby chair, feeling sick. 'It's just that – well, I live there, too. And, oh God, you see I think I saw your husband jump!'

Two pencilled-in eyebrows rose a couple of millimetres on her otherwise immobile face. 'Really? Then that's more than I did! In fact, I was only saying to him last night – I still talk to him, you know – *Boris, you should have told me you were jumping, I'd have come and given you a push!* Hah! But of course, I never get up until at least eleven, and Boris knew better than to disturb my beauty sleep. So, we're neighbours, are we, dahlink?' she continued without a moment's pause. 'And you live . . .?'

'On the thirty-second floor.'

'You're new here?'

'I . . . I've just got married to someone who lives here.'

Parting her lips, into which was etched a thick smear of Chanel Rouge Noir, she tapped her teeth thoughtfully with an index finger ringed with one of the largest diamonds I had ever seen. 'Not what's-his-name? The Englishman? Cecil Brown?'

95

'Well, yes!' I mumbled in an ashamed voice. 'Do you know him?'

'Of course I know him! I know everyone. This is a small place, dahlink, and the English-speaking community is even smaller. Why, there are only about a thousand of us here, and most of those aren't worth bothering with, believe me. I'm not English myself by birth, of course, but Boris, when he was alive, was a pillar of the British Society here. Of course I know Cecil! That is, I know him by sight. He's not the most social of creatures, is he? But I heard he's very successful in business. And let's be frank, dahlink, that's what counts in a husband, isn't it? Well, well, so you live underneath me? And,' she added, glancing at my carrier bags, 'I see you've been shopping? We should get to know each other – we seem to have so much in common, and I'm going to need some cheering up, now that Boris isn't around. Now, where did that girl disappear to? I need something for going out to dinner tomorrow, too – I'm dining at the Chèvre d'Or with the Marksons – you do know the Marksons? No? Oh. Yes, and I must have a new black *maillot* and swimming hat for the Beach Club. Then how about if you and I pop across to the Café de Paris and get ourselves a coffee? If we can get across the square without being run over by those dreadful racing cars? Meanwhile, what are you going to try on while you're waiting for me? How about that lovely little strapless white dress over there?'

Half an hour later, with my very first purchase from Chanel – a pair of gilt double-C earrings – I was initiated into the world in which I now lived. A world where the rich and idle idled away their riches in endless shopping expeditions and restaurant meals. A world where casual dress meant wearing only two diamond bracelets and three diamond rings to go to the swimming pool, and changing your designer bathing costume only three times a day. A world where nothing, not even a bra, was worth wearing unless it was embossed with at least two initials – and I'm not talking M&S. A world where the only cruelty associated with fur coats was in not having enough of them. A world where appearances were so all-important that to use the communal pool in your block of flats was simply not done – not because someone had recently killed himself beside it, but because to use the communal pool might give people the impression that you didn't own a boat and swim from that. A world where, if you had money you flaunted it, and if you didn't have it – well, you had no right to be there.

Shallow, vain, complacent, selfish, bossy and outrageously snobbish as she was, I grew to be fond of my new neighbour Zuzu Lamarre over the next few weeks, much as one grows fond of a tune on the radio one loathes on first hearing but gets hooked on in time. Her self-obsession reminded me of my mother's, though it was on a much grander scale. Zuzu Lamarre's body was her temple, plastic surgery her religion; she had been stitched up, silicone-injected, liposucked and lifted in all the places these things were possible, and in many places they were not. If each operation could have made her look younger, Zuzu Lamarre would by rights have looked about five years old. As it was, she looked exactly like she was – a rich, vain woman in her mid-sixties who was desperate to be young again.

Zuzu's daily life, like that of her friends', was a constant fight against the inevitability of ageing – a long and punishing round of massage, exercise regimes and manicures, interspersed with tri-weekly sessions at the hairdresser's, bi-monthly trips to Swiss health spas, and daily shopping expeditions – 'too tiresome, dahlink!' – for expensive clothes. Three bedrooms in her penthouse flat were lined with walk-in closets: one for suits; one for coats; one for cocktail dresses; and so on right down to her underwear; there was even a closet containing nothing but Zuzu's furs. She dressed up as if she was going to Ascot even when she was only popping across the road for a baguette – an expedition which inevitably required a designer suit with matching shoes, sunglasses and UVA-shielding wide-brimmed hat, as well as the company of Margherita, her flat-footed Philippino housekeeper, who always trudged mournfully behind her in the same loose black slacks and baggy green shirt with the express purpose of carrying home Zuzu's bags.

Presuming that, being a writer, I was worth lionising, Zuzu immediately took me under her wing. If she was a bully, I presented the perfect victim: the new girl, otherwise friendless, easily impressable and unschooled in the local ways. After one look at my meagre wardrobe, she declared all of it fit for the bin. And after a cursory and horrified glance around Cecil's apartment, she insisted on introducing me to her interior decorator, a suave, handsome Frenchman called Alexandre who oozed Gallic charm much as a chocolate eclair oozes whipped cream and who, on Zuzu's insistence, took on the considerable task of helping me transform the flat from a Saudi-inspired bordello into something approaching a fashionable home.

Zuzu and her women friends, Pandora, Tamara and Marina – The Spoiled Wives Club, as Cecil once referred to them with a rare flash of wit – introduced me to life in the principality, and showed me everything it was essential to know – viz: at which salon one should get one's hair cut; where one could buy the best smoked salmon; at which café on the marble esplanade it was *de rigueur* to take one's morning coffee; where to swim – at the Hôtel de Paris or the Monte-Carlo Beach Club, never from the public beach; and how to get a decent table in Rampoldi's, the cramped, popular restaurant which, according to Zuzu, *was* really the only place for anyone who *was* anyone to eat.

Under Zuzu's tutelage, I jettisoned my Belsize Park wardrobe of black tracksuits, black jumpers and shabby black leggings, and, suitably attired in white Armani jeans, white Kenzo shirt and white diamanté-encrusted trainers, joined her and her friends for a daily swim at the Monte-Carlo Beach Club, where the person swimming beside me up and down the Olympic-sized swimming pool might well be a Russian gangster, or an American film director, or even a member of the ruling Grimaldi family. Afterwards, we'd smother ourselves in Factor 30 and recline on the sunbeds to gossip while, draped in a designer robe, matching hat and gold high-heeled mules, Zuzu would take up her favourite position slap bang in the middle of the terracotta-tiled terrace, a vantage point where she could ogle all the young and hunky lifeguards, greet the few people whom she thought worth greeting, and make a point of cutting dead those whom she did not.

My life changed under Zuzu's influence. I took to having my nails manicured twice a week, and gave up reading my imported copy of the *Guardian* in favour of the local paper, *Nice-Matin*. My horizons shrank. Was there a Government crisis in Britain? A major flood in India? Had poverty reached new levels in the US? Did I know or care? Were any of these things at all important compared to the French Franc/Deutschmark exchange rate, or the price of cappuccino at the Negresco Hotel in Nice, or having to decide whether I'd rather go water-skiing before or after lunch?

And so, instead of leaving Cecil, as I should have done if I'd had any integrity, I spent and idled my way through June and July. Membership of the Beach Club, the beautiful weather and my American Express card were some compensation for the pain of being married to a man one hated, but they weren't quite enough. There was no such thing as a free lunch – or, in my case, a free dozen pairs of Versace trousers. The price tag was Cecil. And it was a price which I found hard to pay.

With a sinking heart which pined for cold, grey, rainy England, I awoke every morning to temperatures in the high eighties, displeased to see the sky so relentlessly blue. I ached to go home, and I ached for Andy. I ached for sex. Sex? I'd almost forgotten what it was. In the past, it'd had never been that important to me, but after three months of abstinence, I seemed to be on perma-nent heat. Wherever I looked, I saw reminders of the inadequacy of my relationship with Cecil: a man and a woman with their arms around each other in the Casino gardens; a smiling pregnant woman paddling hand in hand with a toddler; a young couple kissing passionately in the sea.

At the Beach Club, where I now passed a good part of each aimless day, handsome Italian aristocrats and their glamorous wives lounged on the mattresses beside the pool, laughing, kissing, playing with their beautiful children, and making endless phone calls on their mobile phones. I listened enviously to their easy, happy laughter, and watched their warm embraces with longing. What I would have given to be the mother of those beautiful children, or the wife of this or that witty, good-looking man! But that kind of fulfilment obviously wasn't for me. I'd chosen my sunbed, now I had to lie on it. I was condemned to a life of frustration and misery in Monaco. And no one in the world, apart from yours truly, would ever feel sorry for me.

'Mmm! That looks wonderful!'

Turning his paunch sideways, my husband squeezed out through the balcony doors, and sat down at our new glass and steel table on one of the stylish though hellishly uncomfortable wrought-iron terrace chairs chosen by Alexandre. Smiling delightedly at the dinner I'd prepared for him, Cecil licked his lips and tucked his napkin into the open neck of his shirt.

'Must you do that, Cecil?' I snarled before I could stop myself.

'Oh. Sorry, darling.' Obedient to my every command, he pulled the offending item down onto his lap. 'Mmm, chops! Lovely!'

'They're high in calories, so don't take too many.' Looking disappointed, Cecil put one back. 'So, did you have a good day at work?'

There was a long pause while he chewed and swallowed his mouthful. 'So-so, thank you. And what did you do today? Did you manage to get down to work at last?'

This was a sore point with me. In fact, Elena had asked me the very same question when she'd phoned me up earlier that day. The truth was that, after three months in my new home, I hadn't even got round to unpacking my computer yet. Trying to psyche myself up to write a sexy romance while married to a frog like Cecil was, in my opinion, an impossibility. Especially when the motivation for doing it was only £5,000 – about the same amount I now regularly clocked up on my credit card every couple of weeks. 'How could I get down to work?' I snapped. 'I'd much too much to do.'

My husband blinked at me with mild curiosity. 'Really, Lisa?'

'Why do you say it like that? Do you think this flat runs itself? Besides, this morning I had to go to the Beach Club with Zuzu. And my hair looked such an awful mess after I'd been swimming that I had to go and get it done . . .' A knot of annoyance formed in my stomach as I watched Cecil pile his plate high with new potatoes. 'No, don't have so many of those! Why don't you have some salad instead?'

'But the potatoes look so d . . .' Cecil stammered to a halt, as he saw my disapproving expression.

I reached across the table, and scooped half the tiny tubers off his plate. 'If you want to get thinner, you'll just have to eat less. And you do want to lose weight, don't you, Cecil? I thought we'd agreed on that.'

Cecil saw my eyes skim over his protruding belly. 'Yes. Of course. It's just . . .'

'What?'

He gave me a pathetic look. 'I'm so terribly hungry.' When he got no response, he speared one of the three tiny potatoes I'd left him, and sucked it into his mouth. 'So how was the hairdresser, darling?'

'Awful! You wouldn't believe how long Jacques kept me waiting for! I was there for hours!'

'Poor Lisa! How ghastly!'

'At least it meant I had time for a pedicure while I was waiting. Then, on the way home, I popped into Bennetton and bought a couple more T-shirts. Then I met Alexandre, and we drove into Nice to look at some curtain fabrics.'

'Did you find anything nice, darling?'

I sighed. 'Nothing definite. One or two maybes. But there's such a lot to choose. By the way, Alexandre says we'll have to replace everything in the entire flat if we want the new stuff to look any good. Zuzu thinks so too. And I must say, I agree with them.'

Cecil's lips parted to reveal a mouthful of half-chewed salad. Beneath their tint of a light suntan, his podgy jowls turned white. 'Replace everything?' he whispered.

'Yes. Not just the furniture, but all the bathroom fixtures, and the kitchen fitments – and all the rugs and carpets, of course. Don't look so surprised, Cecil. If we're changing the look completely, we can't just keep some of it.'

'C-can't we?'

'Of course not!'

'But . . . Why not?'

'Because the old stuff won't go with the new stuff, of course!' I put down my knife and fork, and tried to control the tidal wave of resentment which was welling up inside me. 'Do you have a problem with this, Cecil?'

'No! No, not at all!' He cleared his throat. 'It's just that . . . well . . .'

'What?' My voice rose. 'For heaven's sake! You asked me to redecorate this dump when we first came here! I've been working really hard on the plans.' This was a slight exaggeration. Pouring over sample books with a sophisticated, handsome and flirtatious Frenchman was not exactly gruelling work. In fact, I'd begun to look forward to my meetings with Alexandre. Our time together was now the only romantic excitement I had. When he drew close over a sample book and murmured, 'What colour sheets do we want on our bed?' I almost forgot it wasn't *our* bed we were choosing them for. 'You don't seem very enthusiastic about any of it, Cecil.'

My husband's eyes filled with dismay. 'But I am, darling! It's just that . . . well . . . I mean, won't it cost . . .? Oh, forget it. Sorry.' He reached over the table and squeezed my hand. After a respectable interval, I withdrew it and carried on eating. 'Will there be any room for my own paintings and things when they come out of storage?' he asked in a tentative voice.

I'd grown to dread the arrival of Cecil's oft-talked-about possessions much as I dreaded his daily return from the office. 'I don't know. Perhaps.'

He nodded glumly. 'Only, I've got some rather nice things . . . I think you might like them,' he ventured. And seeing the set line of my mouth, went on, 'Though I can't guarantee it.'

'Well, I suppose I'll have a look at them.'

'Thanks, darling. You're so kind. What are you planning for the b . . . b . . .?' His voice tripped on the unmentionable word, and his pale cheeks flushed scarlet.

'The bedroom?' I said with a brazenness I didn't feel. 'Well, we're getting rid of that vulgar round bed, of course, and those ghastly wardrobes, and all that black lacquer. Alexandre says it's pure seventies *Playboy* style. Instead, it'll all be white and yellow, with special paint effects on the walls and a whole bank of built-in cupboards opposite the window, in a sort of Provençal style. With distressed doors.'

Cecil choked on a rocket leaf. His red jowls turned even redder, and I was forced to thump him on the back. 'What, might I ask, are distressed doors?' he said when he'd recovered.

'Honestly, Cecil! Distressed! It's a paint finish! You know – roughed up and sanded down. Made to look like it's old.'

'But we've got old wardrobes already! I thought the whole point was to have everything new!' He saw me wince, and winced himself. 'Only joking, Lisa!'

In vain, I tried to control my murderous anger. Why was it that the more I determined to be nice to Cecil, the harder it became? 'Alexandre's our interior decorator, Cecil. You agreed we should hire him to help me, and I'm only telling you what he said. If you don't want me to change anything in the flat, I won't. We'll leave this . . .' I waved my hand in the direction of the living room, 'this mausoleum of bad taste as it is. Frankly, I don't care either way.'

I listened to my complaining voice with horror. What had happened to me? I'd never been like this in the past. It seemed that marriage to Cecil and three months of living in Monaco had turned me into a shallow, spoiled, nagging shrew. Why didn't I just leave Cecil if I hated him so much? All I had to do was utter the simple words, 'Cecil, I don't love you' and I'd be free to cut and run. Yet every time I tried to say them, they stuck in my throat.

Had Cecil noticed how nasty and materialistic I'd become during the last few weeks? He seemed to accept my manic purchases and my outpourings of vulcanic anger with the same equanimity, almost passivity, with which he accepted my continuing cold shoulder in the bedroom department. He didn't demand anything of me, nor did he seem to expect anything. He seemed content merely to exist at my side like some kind of battered handbag. From time to time, as now, I admit that it occurred to me that I had married an idiot. In which case, I really ought to feel sorry for him, and be nicer to him.

Ashamed of myself, I put down my cutlery, pushed my plate aside and smiled at Cecil. 'You've got some lettuce on your chin,' I remarked as gently as I could.

'Oops! Sorry.' He wiped it off with a corner of his napkin.

'Anyway,' I went on, determined to be more positive. 'Alexandre and I chose some wallpaper swatches for the hall, and some paint swatches for the living room. Look, I'll get them and show you.'

I pushed back my chair, but with a sudden, impulsive gesture Cecil clutched my hand. 'No, don't go!'

'Why?'

'I like you sitting here.'

'But . . .' My throat constricted. I felt like I was being strangled. 'I'm only going next door to get the swatches. I'm coming back!'

'No, sit down,' Cecil said. And added urgently, 'Please. I don't want to see the swatches, darling. You're the boss now. And whatever you say goes. I'm sure my taste is nothing to write home about. And you're right, you know – everything in this flat really should go.'

I sighed with relief at this small victory. 'It is pretty horrible, Cecil. I don't know how you could have lived here for so long without doing anything to it.'

'There didn't seem much point when I was living by myself. This flat wasn't a home. In those days.' My husband smiled at me meaningfully, the implication being that now it was, and his love washed over me in a cloying wave. I tried to smile back at him, but only managed a grimace. Taking this for encouragement, Cecil leaned towards me, and puckered his heavy lips. I wanted to scream. Instead, I turned my head away, and the kiss landed safely on my cheek.

Cecil pulled back, frowning. He didn't look angry, just thoroughly confused. 'Look, Lisa,' he stuttered. 'You know . . . I mean, I know this is difficult but . . . Shouldn't we really talk about . . .?'

I jumped up and began to clear the dishes with a loud clatter. 'Sorry?'

Cecil's lips clamped shut. Lost in thought, he gazed up into space. After a short pause, he glanced at me again. 'Darling . . .' he began.

'What?'

'Well, I've sort of invited a friend of mine to come and stay here. Next week.'

'A friend?' I said incredulously, never having heard him use the word before. 'Who?'

'Oh . . . Just someone. You know. Someone I used to know. From school. I um, I hope that's all right with you.'

I emitted a long-suffering sigh that indicated that it wasn't. 'I suppose so, Cecil. Only, I wish you'd asked me first. I mean, how can we invite someone to stay when the place is such a pigsty and we're about to be invaded by the decorators?'

Cecil bit his lip. 'This may not be your taste, Lisa, but it's

105

hardly a pigsty,' he said with a half-laugh. 'Besides, I . . . I'm sure Robert won't mind. He's used to roughing it.'

Furious with him for taking the initiative without asking my permission, I stomped into the kitchen. Putting up with Cecil was bad enough. Now I'd have to put up with his friend, too. How would we continue our farcical marriage under the scrutiny of a stranger?

Bloody, bloody Cecil! And bloody, bloody Robert! If he was a good friend of Cecil's, I dreaded to think what he'd be like.

Eight

He swept through the Arrivals doors straight out of the pages of a romantic novel, and strode forwards into the airport on a pair of endless, slender legs. Stopping for a moment, he ran a hand through his mane of mahogany, shoulder-length curls while his eyes searched the waiting crowd. Above a stubbly, deeply cleft chin, his lips – full, sensuous and achingly kissable – twitched with expectation.

And so did mine.

When Cecil suddenly pointed in the direction of this Adonis and said, 'There's Robert!' I thought he must mean the pasty-faced wimp near him. But when Cecil threw his hands in the air and shouted in an over-loud voice, 'Robert! Robert! We're over here!' it was the Adonis who swung round.

'Cecil!' he exclaimed in a voice so deep it made my whole body vibrate. Red linen jacket swinging like a matador's cloak from shoulders which would have done a body-builder proud, he glided towards us, and clasped Cecil's little paws in his large, elegant hands. 'Good to see you, my friend!' A moment later, two dark-fringed navy blue eyes turned their beam on me, and I was transfixed as surely as a rabbit in the headlights of an oncoming car. 'And you – you must be Lisa!'

The way he said my name made it sound as delectable as Chantilly cream. For the first time since the eve of my wedding, a spontaneous smile lit up my face. 'I guess I must be.'

Robert clasped my hand, and kept hold of it for a very long while as if he, too, felt the wave of electricity tingling between our fingers. 'Cecil told me you were attractive,' he

107

said with a slight, perplexed shake of his head. 'But he didn't let on you were as beautiful as this!'

At that moment I forgot where I was, and why Robert and I were meeting, and everything but his mesmerising face was blotted out. Had I been balancing on one foot on the edge of Beachy Head, I could have felt no dizzier.

Without losing eye-contact with me, Robert murmured, 'Am I allowed to kiss the wife, Cecil?'

From somewhere a million miles away from us came the sound of nervous laughter, and a high voice stuttered, 'I think that's up to Lisa, isn't it?'

The well-defined brushstroke of Robert's right eyebrow rose in a quizzical gesture, and my face started to burn like hot strawberry jam. 'Permission granted,' I said as calmly as I could.

Robert's hand slid slowly up my left arm, setting my skin on fire. With a firm, confident gesture, he drew me towards him till our bodies were almost touching and our faces were only inches apart. As the gap closed, and my breasts pressed gently against his chest, the fire in my arm shot through my body, turning the disused space between my legs into a furnace. With a slight, almost imperceptible catch of his breath, Robert touched my cheek with his lips, and I breathed in a sweet, earthy smell something between the scent of wild mushrooms and the perfume of ripe, sun-warmed Muscat grapes.

Then, with a painful wrench which left me reeling, he drew away and dropped my hand. Now, turning to Cecil, he clapped him on the shoulder. 'You lucky bastard!' he said. 'I wish I could say that you don't deserve her!' And Cecil blushed and grabbed my hand, and the world came back again with a horrid crash.

Arm in arm, Cecil and Robert pushed through the luggage hall's glass doors to collect Robert's bags, while I remained outside, rooted to the spot, trembling with the as yet undigested knowledge that, during the last thirty seconds, the course of my life had irrevocably changed. If falling in love is a virus, I'd just picked up a highly contagious strain. It was coursing through my blood cells, invading my lymph glands and replicating at the speed of light. It was destroying all remaining trace-cells of Andy, and turning them into Robert clones. It was making me wish I'd never been born, and, on the other hand, producing delusions that I'd never been happier. A mere sixty seconds after infection, I was totally in the virus's grip, and exhibiting an alarming array of symptoms: palpitations, shivering, euphoria, nausea, freezing extremities, feverishness, and weakness in the knees.

In short, by the time my husband and his friend had retrieved Robert's suitcase from the baggage carousel, love had made me extremely ill.

'I can't tell you how sorry I was to miss the wedding,' his voice boomed as, crammed into the Porsche, the three of us sped back to Monte-Carlo through the dramatic mountain backdrop that bordered the *péage*.

With a pounding heart, I turned around and smiled at him – he was squeezed into the space behind the front seats, within kissing distance of me, his long limbs collapsed together like the spokes of an umbrella. 'What kept you away?'

'My dear Lisa, I'm sorry to say it was termites.'

Cecil spluttered over the steering wheel. 'What?'

''Fraid so, Cess.' Robert's hand – a hand of classical perfection, I now noticed, marred only by one well-chewed fingernail – raked through his long hair. 'Believe it or not, I was somewhere between Woolabongalonga and Alice Springs, studying the reproductive habits of *termitidœ bellicosus*.'

I heard myself say, 'How absolutely fascinating!' And while I stared resolutely through the windscreen at the motorway viaduct ahead of us, I had a split-second vision of my future self trekking through some leech-infested swamp, kitted out in khaki and explorer's hat, merrily rooting for termites with Robert among the fallen leaves . . .

'Termites? Ugh!' Cecil shuddered. 'Sooner you than me. Both Lisa and I h-hate creepy crawlies, don't we, darling?'

That *we* sounded like the clink of handcuffs. 'No, I don't, Cecil!' I snapped. 'I can't imagine what gave you that idea.'

'I don't just study termites, Lisa,' Robert went on, as Cecil shot me a confused look – after all, had he not come to my rescue the other day, when I'd found a tiny spider in our bath? 'I'm an observer of everything that moves: animals, fish, the birds and the bees. Even human beings from time to time.' Accidentally – or was it on purpose? – his hand brushed my hair as he shifted in his seat. 'Though, yes, I admit termites are my speciality. At least, that's what my books are about.'

'Oh, so you write about insects?'

Cecil's sternum puffed with pride behind the steering wheel. 'Lisa's a writer, too, you know.'

'*Are* you?'

Before I could say a word, Cecil answered for me: 'Yes. She's very successful, as it happens.'

'Cecil!' I protested. 'Really, Robert, I don't write anything very important – just romantic fiction.'

'Love stories? Mmm!' Robert made the kind of appreciative noise one usually makes when one's been offered a huge plate of chocolate truffles. 'I *devour* love stories when I'm out in the bush. I hope yours are awfully slushy, Lisa, with lots of steamy sex.'

With difficulty, I managed a strangulated, 'Some.'

'I bet your books are a bloody sight more readable than the academic dust I write. Though, I have to say, the love-life of the termite *is* very steamy in its own way. Did you know, for example, that after mating, certain species of female imprison the male in their love-nest, and even eat them alive? And let me tell you, they have very powerful jaws.'

'That sounds rather sexy to me,' Cecil piped up.

What had got into him suddenly? I forced the kind of laugh which I felt might be appropriate to a liberated, late twentieth-century woman who was at ease talking about such intimacies with her spouse. 'Cecil didn't tell me you were a naturist, Robert.'

Cecil choked back a laugh. 'Darling, I think the word you want's *naturalist*.'

'Don't take any notice of the old pedant, Lisa. As it happens, you're not far out – in fact, it often amounts to the same thing. I don't usually wear clothes when I'm working. It's really so much more comfortable to do what the Aborigines do – or did, before they discovered the joy of Levis and drip-dry shirts – and go around starkers except for a few daubs of paint.'

I closed my eyes to a vision of Robert crawling naked through the bush, and I shivered violently. 'Are you feeling all right, darling?' Cecil asked.

'What? Of course!'

'Only you look . . .'

'For goodness' sake, Cecil, watch the road! You nearly hit that tourist coach!'

'Sorry, darling.'

'Don't kill me on my first day here, Cess!' Robert laughed. 'At least, not before I've taken you both out to dinner at the Hôtel de Paris tonight! And, tomorrow, I think tomorrow I'll treat you to lunch at the Colombe d'Or in Saint-Paul, if that's all right by you. I dreamed of their hors d'oeuvres trolley every time I chewed my way through an armadillo steak!'

'You don't really eat armadillos, do you?' Turning around, I caught another glimpse of those dark blue eyes, which now crinkled into a wicked grin.

'Only for Sunday lunch.'

'Seriously? What do they taste like?'

'Hard to describe. A bit like like boiled pork, mixed with very ancient venison. And I mean ancient. Off-off ancient. Like a slab of meat that's been hung in a fly-blown outhouse for half a year or so. Imagine adding fifty-odd cloves of garlic to that, then boiling it up with some old fish stew and a couple of Big Macs.' He grinned again, this time revealing a mouthful of perfectly shaped, brilliant-white teeth. 'There you have it, Lisa. Armadillo smells high as a Himalayan mountain, and it's about as tough to bite into.'

By this time, the love virus had made its way down my

aorta, back up my jugular and into my lungs, where it was doing its best to stop me breathing. Multiplying out of control, it infiltrated my spinal fluid, shot up my spinal cord with the speed of an Exorcet missile and exploded inside my head. I felt literally high, as if I was no longer in the car, but floating three feet above it. I was in love, in love, in love . . .

We reached the Monaco exit, and turned off the *péage*. With his usual, annoying hesitancy, Cecil paid the toll at the toll both, then steered the Porsche into the smoky orange gloom of the exit tunnel. As we came out into the sunlight at the other end, a feeling of pure joy flooded through my veins and I experienced a total rebirth. Gone was the nasty bitch who'd berated Cecil for eating three croissants and jam for breakfast that morning. Suddenly I was Mother Teresa, benevolent to the whole of humanity – yes, even to Cecil! I was Pollyanna, in love with everything and everyone. I was emotionally exfoliated – it was as if the top layers of my skin had been sloughed away, leaving my feelings quivering like dragonflies underneath the raw surface. I wanted to laugh and cry at the same time, and throw my hands up in the air and scream at the sheer brilliance of being. How simple, exciting and beautiful life was now that Robert had entered the bleak darkness of my soul and switched on the light!

I smiled beatifically to myself. I turned around and smiled beatifically at Robert. I even managed to flash a smile at poor old Cecil.

And poor old Cecil – well, Cecil smiled back at me, and in a daring and possessive gesture, put his hand on my knee.

And, in a flash, Mother Teresa was no more. I was just Cecil's wife again.

And, so help me, I wanted to murder him.

Back at the Bellavista Tower, we sat on the balcony while Cecil and Robert reminisced about their days at Brondesbury and Kilburn Grammar School over a glass of wine.

'Do you remember Noakes, Cess? The guy who stapled

his nose with the burser's stapler, and had to be rushed to hospital to have them taken out?'

'Oh, yes!'

'I ran into him in London the other day. Would you believe the bloody fellow's a QC now?'

'No! Well, I b-bumped into Barnaby just before Christmas!'

'Who?'

'You know, the red-haired nerd who shut himself in a games locker and had to be rescued by the fire brigade? Wasn't it his mother who ran off with the caretaker's wife?'

'And the caretaker – Fred, wasn't it? – took up with the school nurse! If I remember, Fred got a divorce on some ludicrous grounds. Wasn't it because his wife had never made a decent homemade soup for him, or something?'

'Granted a decree absolute on the grounds that their marriage was never consommé,' Cecil quipped.

I jumped up from the table, and walked over to the balcony railing, knowing all too well who this dig was meant for. Unaware of the unspoken antagonism between Cecil and me, Robert rocked with laughter. 'Oh dear, oh dear! The same old witty Cecil, I see! But we mustn't bore Lisa with all this talk about the old days, Cess! Tell me about you two. How did you meet?'

'Oh, we . . .' Cecil stood up and came over to me, his eyes brimming with sentiment. 'You tell Robert, d-darling,' he said as he slung the harness of his arm around my waist.

I inched away. 'You tell him if you want to.'

'Well, Rob, I'm afraid, you see that I . . . Actually, I was driving along and I . . . I ran Lisa over.'

'Good Lord!'

'In the Haymarket. It was raining, and – well, I'm not used to driving in London any more. And when Lisa stepped off the kerb, I just couldn't seem to stop in time so . . .'

'It was my fault,' I interrupted. 'I crossed the road without looking.'

Robert winked at me. 'Naughty girl! You must have been

running away from something to forget your Highway Code. Now, I wonder what it was?'

'Oh, I . . .' Out of the corner of my eye, I saw Cecil watching me curiously, as if this was a question he too had wanted to ask me for a long time. 'A blind date with a mad gynaecologist, actually!' I said with a smile. And added for good measure, 'Arranged by my mother.'

Cecil's jaw dropped 'Really, darling?'

Robert slapped his knees and roared with laughter. 'C'mon, Cess! Lisa's got to be having us on. Why, if she needed her mother to arrange a blind date for her – why then, I'm an actor with the RSC!'

The following morning, to my horror, Cecil announced that, in honour of his friend's visit, he'd decided to take the whole week off work. So, day by day, the week passed without my having an opportunity to be alone with Robert. For wherever Robert and I went, Cecil made sure he went, too. In fact, he seemed to possess an uncanny instinct for ruining any chance of us being alone.

On Monday, when Robert and I happened to wake simultaneously at 6 a.m. and found ourselves together in the kitchen, it was only seconds later that Cecil bounced out of bed and pottered in to join us, his red-and-black striped bathrobe knotted decisively over his paunch. On Tuesday, when Robert expressed a desire to jog along the beach before breakfast and, at the last minute, I said I'd like to go, too, Cecil insisted on stumbling along between us, red faced, sweaty and out of breath, his flabby belly bouncing beneath a skin-tight T-shirt.

Later that day, over at the Beach Club, Cecil shadowed Robert in and out of the sea and up and down the pool, his short, hairless arms thrashing the water in a desperate bid to keep up with Robert's sleek, shark-like crawl.

'Dahlink,' Zuzu drawled when she saw Cecil and Robert walking up from the beach in their bathing trunks, towels draped over their shoulders. 'Is that really Cecil's friend? My

God, what a body! Look at that chest! And you say he's here alone? Now, you simply mustn't be selfish and keep him all to yourself! You really must think of your poor widowed friend!'

I didn't stand a chance after that. For as soon as we sat down to eat in the restaurant beside the pool, Zuzu swooped down on our table to join us. And it was only a matter of minutes before Marina, Pandora and Tamara followed suit. While I crunched frustratedly through the breadsticks, they buzzed around Robert like flies around a mango, and flirted with him outrageously.

And so the week went on. Whenever Robert, Cecil and I were at the Beach Club, the Spoiled Wives Club descended on us. If we managed to shake them off for a few moments, it was only to resume our old *pas de trois*. When we went out sightseeing, Cecil made sure to walk between Robert and me, just as he made sure to wedge himself between us at every restaurant or café table. At home, Cecil followed Robert from room to room like a warden escorting a maximum security prisoner: he even accompanied him to the bathroom door, as if to kill off any possibility that Robert and I might bump into each other in the hall.

In the early hours of Thursday morning, seething with frustration and restless as a cat on heat on amphetamines, I tossed and turned in my marital bed, while the prison warden snored peacefully beside me. What should I do? Time was running out fast. Every second that passed was another lost opportunity. In the vain hope that the cause of my frustration might be seeking me out, I slipped out of bed and prowled the flat in my satin negligée (unearthed from my underwear drawer for the duration of Robert's visit). When there was no sign of Robert, I plucked up courage to enter our spare room, where I found Robert sprawled half-naked on the bed, his head thrown back against the pillow, the sheet twisted modestly between his muscular legs. I longed so much to fall on him and kiss him awake, but I didn't dare. What if Cecil came in and found us? Even worse, what if Robert didn't return my feelings? I had no hard evidence that he liked me; for all I knew it was pure accident that had caused our eyes to collide with such electric consequences over our pizzas at the African Queen restaurant in Beaulieu the night before.

Back in bed, wracked with lust, I lay awake and listened with growing annoyance to Cecil's intermittent snores. Evil thoughts chased circles in my mind. If only I could temporarily dispose of him! Lock him in the broom cupboard, for instance, to stop him from getting under our feet ... If only he'd fall ill or something! Or, even better, fall under a car ... No, no, how could I think such a dreadful thing? I didn't want anything awful to happen to Cecil. Of course I didn't. Just something small. Like a bout of serious food poisoning, the kind of thing that would keep him at home and in bed, so that Robert and I could go out just once by ourselves.

How *was* I going to prevent Cecil from becoming a spoke in the wheel of good fortune that had unexpectedly rolled my way? And what good fortune it was! For Robert was remarkable in every way. Warm, witty and charming, even to Zuzu when she draped herself like a fur stole around his shoulders, he was one of those rare, special people with a real gift for enjoying life. When one was with him, ordinary things seemed extraordinary, mundane things magnificent. He transformed boring chores into brilliant fun, and fun into euphoric frolics. He knew how to tell a joke, and when to be serious. Whenever he turned his attention on me, I felt like the most wonderful, intelligent, beautiful and fascinating person alive.

I knew I wasn't, of course. Because the most wonderful, intelligent, beautiful and fascinating person alive was Robert. He was also, to my astonishment, single and not in any relationship, his brief marriage ('A big mistake. She was an arachnophobe, and I was finishing my thesis on the black widow spider,' he confided in me with his wonderfully dry sense of humour) having ended in divorce ten years before. What about girlfriends? I ventured. Robert shrugged. 'Some chance! The only females I meet nowadays have six legs and lay 80,000 eggs a day.'

Poor, hapless Cecil! It wasn't his fault that, beside Robert, he faded into insignificance. Well, not quite insignificance, because everything he did, said or *was* that week aggravated me that little bit more than it usually did. His flab looked flabbier, his hair thinner. His conversation was duller, and his awful jokes fell even flatter on the floor. Compared to Robert's swallow-dives, perfectly executed from the Beach Club's top board, Cecil's belly flops made that much more wash and noise. By some strange optical illusion, every time he stood next to Robert, he seemed to shrink by half a dozen inches – in height, that was; his girth expanded by double that amount. The sound of Cecil's pee hitting the lavatory bowl in our ensuite bathroom grew louder every evening; by Thursday it felt like a pile-driver being driven through my head.

Did Cecil notice that I gritted my teeth whenever he called me *darling*? That I glowed with happiness whenever Robert was nearby, but scowled the moment he walked away? Or that I spent every waking minute that week vascillating between euphoria and tears? If he did, he never said anything. But from time to time, I caught him looking at me with a pained expression, as if he knew that I felt for Robert all the emotion that was due to him.

On Friday, the last full day of Robert's stay with us, a miracle happened. We were breakfasting on the balcony when the telephone rang, and a clipped, masculine French voice I'd never heard before demanded to speak to *Monsieur Brown*.

I brought the cordless phone out to the table and handed it to Cecil. '*Oui?*' he said, in the accurate but hopelessly accented French that made me both jealous of his ability and, at the same time, so grated on my nerves. '*Oui?*' Mouthing the words *sorry* and *work* at us, he pushed back his chair with a terrible screech that set my teeth on edge. '*Oui,*

Jean-Claude, j'écoute. Non. Non, pas aujourd'hui. Je suis désolé, mais c'est pas possible. Oui?' He frowned. *'Tu sais, je suis en vacance cette semaine. Peut-être . . .?'* As he listened to the fast volley of words issuing from the receiver, Cecil sighed deeply, and rubbed his furrowed brow with his hand. *'Oui?'* he repeated curiously. *'Vraiment? C'est combien? Et ce n'est pas possible qu'on attendre jusqu'à lundi?'* He sighed again, this time with resignation, then he glanced at his watch and muttered, *'D'accord. OK. Non, ça va. Oui, il y a un vol à midi. Oui. D'accord. A bientôt.* Oh, bugger!' he swore as he put down the receiver.

'What's up, Cess?'

'Bloody business!' he stuttered. 'Would you believe it, I've got to fly up to Paris today!'

My heart high-jumped to heights previously only reached by Olympic gold medallists. 'Oh, no, Cecil! That's too bad!' I struggled to control the elation that was threatening to split my aching face into a grin. 'What a shame! And on Robert's last day, too! Are you sure you can't put it off till next week?' I added out of guilt.

Cecil blinked at me miserably. 'I would if I could, Lisa, but . . . Oh, bugger it!' he stammered, turning to Robert with a distressed look. 'I'm so sorry, Rob. I'd do anything to get out of going, you know I would. But, well, I'm afraid I'm going to have to set off for the airport immediately. Isn't it just my luck to miss the last day of your visit?'

Robert patted him on the back. 'Never mind, Cess. I'll see you tomorrow morning, before I set off for the airport.'

'I'm afraid you won't,' Cecil muttered angrily. 'I've got a meeting in Paris this evening, so I'm going to have to stay the night.'

Nine

With a solicitude I'd never shown him before, I packed Cecil an overnight case and even insisted that, instead of him taking a taxi or the helicopter, Robert and I drive him to the airport without delay.

I pulled up in the narrow road outside the departures terminal and, already at one with each other in shorts and T-shirts, Robert and I got out of the car to say goodbye to Cecil. He looked so woebegone in his buttoned-up suit that I actually put my arms around him and gave him a quick hug. 'Are you sure that you'll be all right by yourself in Paris?' I asked as if he was a child going off alone for the first time. 'Will you manage to find something to eat?'

'In Paris?' His bulbous eyes rolled. 'I might manage to, Lisa. Besides, as I said, I'm going to be tied up in meetings till late tonight.'

'Oh, poor you!'

Grateful for this crumb of concern, my about-to-be cuckolded husband smiled at me wanly, then clasped Robert's hand. 'I'm only sorry to be leaving on your last day, Rob. It's not as if we see each other that often.'

Robert clapped him on the back. 'Don't worry, old friend. There's always a next time. Maybe you and Lisa will get down under for a visit one of these years.'

'Yes, that'd be marvellous, wouldn't it, Lisa?'

I smiled brightly. Though Cecil didn't yet know it, after tonight he and I would never be going anywhere together again. 'Do take care of yourself, Cecil.'

'I will.' He gave a wistful sigh, and looked up at Robert. 'I really wish I didn't have to go. But I know that Lisa'll look after you. Won't you, darling?'

'Don't worry, of course I will!'

Cecil glanced from me to Robert anxiously, as if he guessed what that implied, and for an awful moment I thought he was going to burst into tears. 'I'd better go,' he said in a choked voice. 'Or I'll miss my plane.'

Robert and I got back into the car. This time we were sitting side by side, our legs close together, our knees separated by a mere gear-stick. With a pang of remorse, as if I'd just sent my husband off to his death, I glanced in the driver's mirror, and watched his squat shape grow smaller as I drove away. But as he disappeared into the terminal, so did my guilt. Putting my foot down on the accelerator, I swung the car onto the N7 towards Nice. Out of the corner of my left eye, I could see Robert looking at me, a small, quizzical smile playing on his face.

'Well, Lisa!' he sighed at last.

'*Well!*' I purred in my most husky voice. 'Here we are, Robert!' And refrained from adding, *by ourselves*.

There was a long pause. A first move needed to be made, but I lacked the confidence to make it. Did Robert? A quick glance showed me that his gaze had shifted to my lap where my shorts had ridden up, revealing practically every inch of my bare suntanned thighs . . .

Robert cleared his throat. 'Cecil told you to look after me,' he said in an amused voice.

I swallowed hard as my excitement mounted. 'Yes. Yes, he did.' With incredible recklessness, I pulled out into the middle lane, overtaking a sleek blue Mercedes on the inside. 'Well, it's your last day in the South of France,' I said over the throb of the engine. 'And I'm at your disposal.'

'*Really?*'

'So, you call the shots and I'll follow, Robert. Just tell me what'd you like to do.'

And so Robert told me.

To be honest, it wasn't quite what I'd had in mind. I'd

had in mind – yes! – driving straight back to the flat, ripping each other's clothes off, and spending the next twenty-four hours exercising the rusting, hitherto unused springs of Cecil's revolving remote-controlled bed.

But Robert ... Robert said he'd like to seek out some quiet, secluded beach and have a picnic.

To which I answered, 'Oh! What a great idea!'

I think my vocal chords must have betrayed my disappointment, because my passenger turned sideways in his seat and frowned at me. 'Is that OK with you?' he asked in a curious voice.

'Mmm!' I attempted to inject a little enthusiasm in my tone. 'Of course it is! Finding a *quiet* beach on the Côte d'Azur in August may not be very easy, but, well, I'm sure we'll manage. And having a picnic's a brilliant idea.'

'Do you really think so?'

'*Oh, yes!*'

'Ah!' Was I imagining things, or did Robert sound disappointed? After a moment, he went on, 'Only I'm getting rather peckish ...'

'Me too!'

'... but I really couldn't stomach another big restaurant meal. I haven't stopped eating since I got here.' He patted his stomach. 'I'm getting so fat.'

I laughed. 'Hardly! But I know what you mean. Eating out's an occupational hazard of living in France. Everything tastes so delicious. I must've put on half a stone in the three months I've been here.'

His long legs shifted as he turned towards me, and swung his arm over the back of my seat. As his eyes travelled swiftly up my thighs to the flat stomach and full breasts outlined by my tight white T-shirt, I felt as if I was being tickled by a swarm of bees. 'But, Lisa, your body's absolutely fabulous!' he exclaimed. A deep blush flooded into my cheeks, and my absolutely fabulous body prickled with heat. 'Which is more than I can say for poor old Cess,' Robert added. 'He's certainly put on a bit since I last saw him!'

121

This was the first disloyal remark Robert had made all week, and I noted it gleefully. 'When *was* the last time you saw Cecil?' I asked in a casual tone.

'Yonks ago. Must've been before I started researching termites – yes, probably when I came back from that mountain cat expedition to darkest Peru.' He paused, then said. 'Is it really only three months ago?'

'What?'

'That you and Cess got married?'

My heart began to bang against my rib cage like a wild chimpanzee thumping on the bars of its cage. 'Mmm. Why do you ask?'

'No reason. Only that . . . Well, in that case I feel very honoured that you invited me to stay with you.'

I cleared my throat and said, 'Cecil's very fond of you.' Though not half as fond as I am, I wanted to add.

'Yes, but . . . After all, you're still practically on your honeymoon. I'd have thought you'd want to be alone.'

I took a deep breath and plunged along the murky road to ditching my husband. 'Well . . . not really.'

'Oh?' Robert's rich voice made the single syllable undulate with curiosity.

'I mean, er . . . You see . . .' I took a deep breath. 'I suppose Cecil and I don't have that sort of relationship.'

There was a short pause. Then Robert said, 'What's *that sort of relationship*?'

I blundered on: 'Well, the sort that's, well, you know, sort of exclusive. I mean, it's not the sort of relationship where we need to be by ourselves all the time. Oh, shit!' I swerved towards the neatly planted central reservation of the eight-lane Promenade des Anglais as a battered 2CV cut me up on the inside. 'God, they're really the worst drivers here!'

'Maniacs. But you're coping wonderfully.'

My skin suddenly turned to goosebumps. I reached across Robert, dangerously close to his thighs, and turned the air conditioning down. Sunk in a thoughtful silence,

Robert stared ahead. 'So, what sort of relationship *do* you and Cecil have?' he continued at last.

'Well, we . . .' Oh God, oh God, oh God! What should I tell him? That Cecil and I had a platonic relationship? Or, more accurately, no relationship? That any relationship that we appeared to have was a sham? That Cecil adored me and that, in return, I despised him? If I admitted all this to Robert, what on earth would he think of me? 'Well . . . You see . . . it's sort of . . . Oh, look! There's a parking space!' I swung the car to the right, cutting up two lanes of traffic, and pulled in alongside the sea. 'And it's just across the road from the open-air market! Brilliant! We can go and buy some food for the picnic!'

As we wandered from stall to stall, gathering goodies, Robert touched me lightly on the shoulder in order to bring my attention to this or that. We bought food, lots of it: crusty *baguettes a l'ancienne*, dusted with flour; slices of dark Italian salami and pale *mortadello* speckled with peppercorns; local black olives, marinated in oil and Provençal herbs; a huge triangle of runny Brie; fuzzy, fragrant white-fleshed peaches; a *tarte aux pommes* and huge, sticky *pains au raisins*; ice-cold Perrier, and warm red wine.

Robert frowned at the bulging plastic bags hanging from his arm. 'Do you think this is enough, Lisa? Oh look, sweets!' he suddenly yelped, bounding across the market place to a stall of brightly coloured jelly gums. 'We've got to have some of these!' I couldn't stop laughing as, like a child in paradise, he leaned over the open plastic tubs and, with great deliberation, picked out a large, gaudy selection of fried eggs, caterpillars and wiggly worms. 'What, no termites?' I joked, and he turned and smiled at me so warmly that I thought I was going to melt.

On nearby Cap Ferrat, at the end of a narrow, winding lane crowded with cars and lined with expensive villas, we found a small beach overlooking Villefranche bay, where we spread out our purchases on the sun-warmed stones. Now that we were by ourselves, Robert and I got on better than ever: we talked at length, about our families and our work; we skimmed stones across the water, and, as the day got hotter, stripped to our underwear and swam; we even built a silly sculpture from the flotsam and jetsam washed up on the beach, and generally larked about like two kids let out of school.

After we'd eaten nearly everything we'd bought, we swam again, then lay down side by side on the large travelling rug which Cecil, with premature middle-aged forethought, always kept in the car boot, and let the sun dry us. Languid and sleepy from the wine, I closed my eyes on the brilliant sky, and listened to the soft lapping of the waves. A ship's horn hooted on the other side of the bay. A seagull cried overhead. I wondered with a sick hope whether Cecil's plane might have crashed on its way to Paris . . . All the time, I was aware of Robert's hard, muscular body next to me, so close yet still so far away . . .

After a long time, he murmured in a deep, melodic voice, *'Under the greenwood tree, who loves to lie with me and turn his merry note unto the sweet bird's throat, Come hither, come hither, come hither . . .'*

I turned my head and squinted at him through my sunglasses, only to find him propped up on one elbow, staring down at me. 'Where's that from?' I asked.

'As You Like It. Act Five. Scene One.'

I smiled. 'You're very cultured for a man who spends his days on his hands and knees, crawling after insects.'

'I do *not crawl*!' Bristling with mock indignation, he picked up a minute pebble and aimed it at my feet. 'No, I . . . I *scramble*.'

I giggled. Once again, we lapsed into a sleepy silence. I rolled over onto my stomach and rested my head on my hands. The sun beat into my back, making me feel hot and sexy. Robert rolled over, too, and seemed to inch closer. My blood pulsed through my body with a slow, regular beat. At long last, I felt a large hand settle lightly on my arm.

'Lisa?'

I turned over to face him. Slowly, cautiously, he stretched out a hand and stroked my cheek. My lips parted with desire, and so did his. He began to say something, but then stopped, as if he'd thought better of it, and before I could make a move, he scrambled quickly to his feet.

'Come on,' he said briskly, as he started to gather up the debris of our picnic. 'Let's drive back to Monte-Carlo before we fall asleep.'

Back at the flat, I waited for Robert to pounce on me. But he locked himself in his bathroom, showered and then fell asleep, leaving me teetering on a knife-edge of uncertainty which was both agonizing and exquisite – like being on the point of orgasm for hour after hour without quite reaching it. Ill with longing, I lay down alone on my bed and wondered when – or if – the moment would come when Robert would wake up, come in and kiss me. Curling up under the covers, I tried in vain to sleep. But how could I relax when we had so little time? In less than twenty-four hours, Cecil would be back home, and Robert would be London-bound on an Air France plane. After a few days there, he'd head off to Australia again. Unless something drastic happened between us pronto, I'd never see him again.

But how could I precipitate some action? As far as he knew, I was happily married to Cecil, and unless I made it pretty obvious that I was available, he'd naturally hold back because Robert, I realised, was a loyal friend to Cecil, and a principled, ethical, honest man.

Five o'clock. Six o'clock. Seven. Measuring my loss with every blink of the digital clock face, I watched the precious time pass. At last, Robert woke up. Side by side but at a respectable distance from each other, we demolished the contents of the fridge in front of the huge TV. Then, at Robert's suggestion, we walked along to Loews Hotel, where we window-shopped for outrageously vulgar jewellery then mingled with the crowds of American tourists and, big spenders that we were, played the two-franc one-armed bandits in the casino. I didn't care when I lost 100 francs in five minutes flat, because I already felt like I'd won the jackpot: I was having fun, for the first time in months.

When we'd lost all our money, we walked back along the marble esplanade, dodging the speeding rollerbladers, and stopped for a drink at the Festival Café. Afterwards, we ran down the slope to the dark beach, where we took off our shoes and crunched across the stones towards the sea. Relaxed as a child, Robert rolled up his trouser legs and splashed along the thin necklace of white surf which bordered the black water. 'Monaco's an amazing place,' he mused as he turned to look back at the mosaic of lighted windows in the buildings.

'Amazing's the word,' I agreed. 'Actually, I find living here rather strange. I mean, I haven't been here long enough to judge, but . . .'

'But what?' he prompted.

I thought about it for a moment. For the first time in weeks, I realised that I was thinking like my old self. 'It's a bit like living in Disneyland,' I started to explain. 'Except that it's a Disneyland for grown-ups. Life's so easy – at least, it is for the tax exile community. We've all got lots of money, and there's no crime here to speak of. And there's no unemployment. You never see anyone sleeping rough in the streets. In fact it's perfect. Almost too perfect. Even the weather's perfect! Do you know, sometimes I wake up in the morning, and look out the window, and I'm longing for it to rain . . .'

He picked up a stone and hurled it into the water. 'Maybe you're homesick.'

I smiled at him. 'Homesick for bad weather, and litter, and muggers, and urban decay. I know this probably sounds silly, and incredibly spoiled of me,' I went on when he stopped laughing, 'but life's just too well-ordered here. No one ever has rows in the street, and no one ever looks untidy or messy. You never even see a plant or a palm tree with a leaf out of place.' We both turned to look across at the line of faceless concrete tower blocks which bordered the Avenue Princesse Grace. 'It must have been beautiful here, before they built all those. But then, the whole coastline's beautiful, isn't it?'

I stared out to sea. A large, three-quarter moon floated low over the horizon, casting a phosphorescent snail's track across the flat black mirror of the water. 'Beautiful,' Robert repeated. And added, after a long pause, 'Just like you.'

I held my breath. I knew that if he was going to make a move, it was now or never. Frightened that the moment would pass, I said his name, and at the same time he said mine. We smiled at each other shyly.

'You first,' Robert insisted.

'No, you,'

After a short pause, he said, 'Oh Lisa, I've enjoyed staying here so much. So very much. It's been great seeing Cecil again. And . . .' He hesitated. 'And . . . meeting you.' My stomach did a double somersault. 'You're a fantastic person, you know. You . . . you've made me so welcome.'

I swallowed. 'I've enjoyed you being here.'

'Have you? You know, Lisa, it's strange but . . .'

'What?' I prompted.

'Forgive the cliché but I kind of feel I've known you forever. When Cecil rang me up and told me about you, I never expected this.'

I looked at him quizzically. 'This?'

'That I'd like you so much.' Robert wasn't smiling any more. He reached over and took my hand. Tiny rivulets of water lapped at my feet, but I felt as if I was standing underneath a huge wave which had been gathering all day, and was now cresting. Any second now it would break over my head.

'Oh, Lisa!' Robert murmured as, slowly and surely, he slipped his arms around me and gathered me to him. 'You're trembling! Don't be afraid.' With a feeling of great relief, I leaned against his chest. I raised my face to his, and our lips met in an electric kiss.

At the same moment, there was a loud explosion, and the sky lit up in a shower of pink and green sparks.

We looked up at the huge, ephemeral dahlias bursting above us, and both started to laugh. 'What do you know, the earth moved – on cue!' Robert said.

'Sorry to disappoint you, but it's only the Sporting Club.' I pointed to the floodlit circular nightclub that stood out like a small spaceship on the peninsula beside the beach. 'They let off fireworks every Friday night!'

Faster and faster, rockets continued to explode overhead while Robert's kisses exploded in my mouth, turning my damp squib of a body into an incandescent Roman Candle.

'Lisa, Lisa, Lisa!' Robert ran his hands through my hair, and gently tilting my chin back, kissed my neck. 'What *are* we doing?'

'I don't know,' I gasped. 'But . . . Oh, let's not think about it now!'

The fireworks stopped, but we carried on kissing. After a long while, Robert drew away, and stared into my face. '*Oh, coz, coz, coz, my pretty little coz, that thou didst know how many fathom deep I am in love . . .*' he murmured.

I attempted to swallow the lump that had suddenly swollen in my throat. 'Where's that from?'

'*As You Like It.*' He sighed deeply, sadly almost, then kissed me again with extraordinary tenderness. 'And how *do* you like it, Lisa?' he asked, with unmistakable meaning. 'Well? Shall I tell you how *I'd* like it? With you?'

Ten

Back in the flat, with the bedroom curtains drawn, I lay fully clothed on Cecil's bed whilst Robert knelt on the floor, methodically sorting through the contents of my chest of drawers. It wasn't just the air conditioning which was making me shiver so violently; there was a cold, uneasy feeling seeping into my heart.

'So,' I squeaked, hoping that I sounded more relaxed than I felt. 'Um, just how long have you . . . you know . . . been into this sort of thing?'

Robert wound a pair of my old black tights around his hands and stretched them taut, just like a strangler in a silent film. 'As long as I can remember, Lisa.' He dropped the tights to the floor along with two other pairs he'd selected, then turned away from me and opened the next drawer down. 'It all started with my mother.'

Visions of *Psycho* flashed before my eyes. 'Really?'

'Yes.' His hands – murderer's hands, I now realised – rummaged through my bras and pants. 'You see, she used to tie my wrists together when I was naughty, and lock me in the cupboard under the stairs.'

'How awful!'

He shot me a grateful look. 'It sounds silly now, Lisa, but at the time . . . Frankly, I was fucking terrified.'

'You poor thing! How could anyone do that to a child?' Robert shrugged. 'Did she . . . Did it happen a lot?'

'A hell of a lot, darling. Because, you see, I was a bloody naughty kid. And being locked up like that only made me worse. Because, well – God, I've never told this to anyone before! – you see, in a funny way, darling, after the fear wore off, I started to enjoy the punishment. Very much. The thing was, see, the cupboard under the stairs was where Mum threw all her dirty laundry. You know – her underwear and things. Silky vests. Stiff cotton brassières with straps as wide as bandages and pointy cups big enough to stick your head in. Huge pairs of soft, thermal knickers. Mmm!' He lifted a long chiffon leopard-print scarf from the drawer – an old, unworn present from my own mother – and drew it through his fingers, then crushed up a pair of my lacy pants and buried his nose in them. 'And so,' he continued, glancing at me shyly through the velvet curtains of his eyelashes, 'Naughty little Robert became even naughtier. I used . . . Now, this is embarrassing! You see, when I was locked up like that, I used to work my hands free and . . . well, I used to jerk off in her underwear.' He flashed me a schoolboyish grin that reminded me uncannily of Andy. 'I suppose it was then that I began to associate sex with bondage. Or so my shrink says.'

I thought about this for a moment, then said, 'I didn't know there were any shrinks out in the Australian bush.'

Robert turned away. 'Unfortunately, there aren't. I make up for it by having megadoses of mine whenever I'm in London. I'm a five times a week man.'

I looked at him with new eyes. 'You're the last person I'd have imagined going to see a psychoanalyst. You seem so, well, normal. And uncomplicated.'

Gathering up the pile of garments he'd selected, Robert carried them over to the bed and dumped them down next to me. 'There's a lot about me you don't know yet, darling,' he murmured as he knotted a pair of tights around my right wrist. 'Perhaps you never will know.' A tremor of fear passed through me. Was I imagining it, or was there something ominous in those words? 'But oh, I haven't undressed you yet!' Robert added, after we'd kissed.

Quickly and efficiently he removed my T-shirt and shorts, and then, after another passionate clinch, my bra and pants. There was something impersonal, almost clinical about his actions, and I couldn't help wondering how many times he'd performed them before, and with whom. As I stretched out stark naked on the bed, I wondered what the hell I was letting myself in for. Maybe Robert sensed what I was feeling, because, in the middle of tethering my wrist to the right bed leg with the tights, he paused and looked down at me with concern. 'Darling! You're trembling! You're not frightened, are you?'

'No, no. Not really.' Who was I kidding? 'Well, OK, I suppose I am kind of scared. I mean, I've never done anything like this before.'

'Good.' Robert gave a pleased smile, and kissed me again. 'Relax!' Now he knotted the leg of another pair of tights around my left wrist, then walked round to the left side of the bed, got down on his knees and secured the free end. 'Believe me, you'll enjoy it.'

Would I? I already had my doubts – grave, tremendous ones which were making my emotions wobble like aspic during an earthquake. 'You . . . er . . .' I blushed.

'Yes?'

'Um . . . do you . . . Gosh, why is this so embarrassing? Look, do you have a condom?'

Robert patted the back pocket of his jeans. 'Not that I was planning on this, you understand . . .' he said, rather shame-faced. 'Only . . . You know the Boy Scout motto: Be Prepared.' Another tights leg was knotted expertly around my left ankle, then Robert dropped to the floor again, lifted the pelmet and, bottom in the air, began to search under it. 'There must be another bed leg under here somewhere,' said his muffled voice. 'Ah, there it is!' Something yanked on my ankle, and my hip wrenched painfully in its socket. 'Oh, have I tied it too tightly, darling?' he said when he heard me wince. 'Sorry. Got carried away. Is that better?'

I shook my loosened leg. 'Much better, thanks.'

'Won't be long now till we're ready. And do try to relax,' he urged from his knees as he grabbed the fourth pair of tights. 'You look like you're about to take some terrible exam. This'll be good fun! I'm sure you'll like it. Remember, once you're all tied up, I'll be your slave for the rest of the night.'

I raised my head and looked at him. 'I thought the whole idea of bondage was that I'd be your slave.'

'No! Not with me. I'm the enslaved one. Obligated to pleasure you. And I will pleasure you, Lisa. Believe me, I will. And I'll stop, the moment you want me to. *If* you want me to. It's all a question of trust. And you do trust me, don't you?'

Did I? I had, down on the beach half an hour earlier, but now that I was pinioned to the bed, I wasn't so sure. Frankly, I didn't like all this bondage stuff one little bit. I wanted to get up and put my clothes on, and get the hell out of there. I wanted to telephone Elena, and ask her what I ought to do. I could already hear her outraged scream deafening my ears: *'Are you out of your fucking mind, Lisa? Have you spent the last thirty years avoiding rapists and murderers only to offer yourself up to some potential maniac like a joint of meat on a plate?'*

But it was too late to ask for Elena's advice, for I was spreadeagled over the bed like one of those dripping, steamrollered ducks you see hanging in the windows of the Chinese restaurants in Soho. And if Robert intended to chop me up with a machete and eat me with pancakes and hoi sin sauce, there was nothing I could do to stop him.

'Now all we need's the blindfold,' Robert purred in my ear.

A blindfold? Oh God, he really was going to murder me after all! The gory scene unfolded on the Cinerama screen of my closed eyelids: the violent stab of the knife, my shrieks of terror, Cecil's horrified face when he returned from Paris the following afternoon and found me reduced to a pool of congealed Bolognese sauce on the blood-sodden frying pan of the circular mattress. I twisted my head up in alarm. 'No, Robert, don't blindfold me, please!'

'But it's essential.'

'Why?'

'I just have to, darling. Now, where did I put that sensational chiffon scarf?'

Just then, the room plunged into total darkness.

'Robert?' I cried out. 'What's happening? Please, I beg you, turn the lights back on!'

'But I didn't turn them off! It must be a power cut. Christ, I can't see a thing! Where are you?'

'Over here.'

'Where's here? Keep talking, then I can find my way over to the bed.'

'OK. I'm over here ... here. *Come to me. Come to meeee ...*'

There was a crash and he let out a terrible yell. 'Oh shit!'

'What?'

'Fuck! I stubbed my big toe on something! I think I've broken it! And I'm lost! I'm bloody lost, Lisa! I can't find the bed.'

'I'd get up and help you find it. Only ...' My unfinished sentence hung in the air between us. I started to laugh hysterically, and so did he.

'Well, this is some great seduction scene!' he roared, and began to quote, "*Come, thick night, And pall thee in the dunnest smoke of hell, that* – Ow! – *that my keen knife see not the wound it makes, Nor* – Damn it! what was that? – *Nor Heaven peep through the blanket of the dark, to cry, "Hold, hold!"* Aaah!' The mattress gave way as he fell fowards and crash-landed beside me. 'Gottcha!' I felt his breath on my neck, then my left nipple was sucked into a warm, moist mouth. I sighed with pleasure as his hand settled halfway down my naked thighs. 'God, your skin's so soft!' he murmured. 'I wish I could feast on you forever! Oh, Lisa, Lisa! I feel like a blind man in paradise!' I felt him slip down towards my feet and slide his tongue between two of my toes. 'Mmm! You taste of the sea – all salty and gritty. And what lovely, slim ankles you have. And – Ooh! what's this bit here?'

I melted with pleasure as his tongue caressed my instep, and licked a slow, lazy path back up to my thigh. Suddenly he seemed to freeze. 'Oh shit!'

'Robert? What's the matter?' I asked as he threw himself down beside me, his head settled into the crook of my outspread arm. 'What's wrong?'

'How I wish I didn't have to do this, Lisa!' he murmured sadly into the blackout. Do *what*? I wondered. 'If only things were less complicated!' he went on.

I let out my breath. 'You mean, because of Cecil?'

'Mmmm. This really is bloody appalling. He'd kill me if he knew how I felt about you.'

We both sighed in unison. 'Look, Robert, we really need to talk. About Cecil and I.'

'Yes, yes. But not now. Not now. We haven't got much time.' He seemed to regain his spirits suddenly, because he rolled over again and began to rain a shower of kisses onto my naked belly. 'Now I'm going to blindfold you, darling,' he whispered between kisses. 'Just . . . in case . . . the lights come back on. Then . . . mmm! . . . then I'm going to . . . aah! . . . get undressed and . . . oh! . . . fuck you senseless.'

'Not quite senseless, I hope,' I muttered breathlessly.

'Now, where the hell's that scarf? Ahha!' An invisible hand raised my head, and with one quick, expert movement, bound the chiffon at the back. I felt him stand up, and heard the unmistakable clunk of an unbuckling belt and the zap of an unzipping fly. Wet with desire, I imagined Robert's lean, naked body towering over me in the dark: his flat, hard chest, his slender hips, his powerful thighs, his thick penis lolling forward, heavy with longing.

The bed creaked as Robert lay down beside me, and for a short, delicious moment, I felt the hard bulk of him pressed against my thighs. Then, with a sudden wrench, he pulled away.

'Bugger!' he moaned. 'Wouldn't you just know it? I'm desperate for a slash.'

'Don't be long!' Bereft, I heard him stumble through the

darkness and into the ensuite bathroom, cursing as he stubbed his toe yet again. After a moment, his pee hit the pan in a tinkling musical symphony. A moment later the door creaked and he was back.

There was a long pause, pregnant with excitement. 'Robert?' I called. 'I'm over here.' I could hear his heavy, regular breathing as he came over and sat down beside me, and placed one hand on either side of my body. 'Oh, Robert!' I sighed as his breath tickled my ear. When he didn't answer, I whispered, 'You won't hurt me, will you?'

In lieu of an answer, Robert bent over and, very gently, began to nuzzle my left wrist. From the wrist, his lips travelled up my arm, past my elbow and to my armpit, working his way up slowly but thoroughly, until not a single square centimetre of my skin remained unkissed.

As he caressed my ribs and suckled at my breasts again, I began to relax and enjoy the strange, thrilling sensation of abandoning myself to being pleasured by an invisible presence. 'Oh yes, oh yes!' I sighed as his lips changed direction and kissed a path down past my belly button to the small triangle of my pubic hair. 'Oh, darling Robert, that feels just wonderful!'

My invisible lover sighed, and sank down between my legs to feast on me. 'Oh, Lisa!' he mumbled between mouthfuls. 'You've got no idea how long I've wanted to do this!'

Much, much later, after a fathomless time of being kissed and fucked and licked and loved more tenderly and unselfishly than I'd ever been loved in my life, I fell asleep.

I was alone when I woke up, and the bedside light was on. Robert had obviously untied me while I was sleeping, for I was underneath the covers, and the tights and scarf lay in an untidy heap at the foot of the bed.

I rolled over and stretched out luxuriously between the cool cotton sheets, and listened to the sound of cheerful whistling coming from out in the hall. A moment later, naked but for Cecil's frilly kitchen apron, Robert came into the bedroom clutching an open bottle of Cecil's best champagne.

'You look ridiculous!' I giggled, smiling at him shyly.

'That's a fine way to greet me!' Upending the bottle, he took a big swig, then sat down beside me on the bed and gave me a brief, but tender, kiss on the lips. 'So, how was it for you?' he said, drawing back and looking at me with concern.

'Wonderful.' I squeezed his hand. 'You must know it was. And, since we're asking, how was it for you?'

'Indescribable.' Robert threw back his head and took another gulp of Bollinger. 'I'll remember this night for as long as I live.'

'Seriously!' I laughed.

He wiped his mouth with the back of his hand, and, unsmiling and anxious, his eyes bore down on me from a dead-pan face. 'I am being serious, Lisa. In fact, I don't remember ever having been so serious in all my life.'

Dizzy with elation, I took his hand. 'Robert, I need to tell you something. Something important about Cecil.'

At the mention of his friend's name, his face broke into a tortured frown. 'Please, don't talk about him, Lisa,' he almost spat. 'I just can't bear to think of him ever making love to you again!'

'But that's just it, darling! You see, Cecil and I never have . . .' But before I could say another word, he leapt up with a howl.

'Shit! I completely forgot about your eggs!'

'My *what*?'

'Your boiled eggs! I was making you some! But they've been on for at least fifteen minutes! Christ, I hope they haven't boiled dry! Hang on! If they're still extant, I'll bring them in!'

'Hurry back!' I called as he bounded from the room, leaving me helpless with laughter.

'I'll put a girdle round the earth in forty minutes!'

'Even I know where that quote's from!' I shouted out after him. 'It's Puck, in *A Midsummer Night's Dream*!'

I lay back on the pillows, smiling to myself, toes curled contentedly like the cat which got the cream. The sounds of Robert crashing about in the kitchen gave me a warm, hopeful feeling I hadn't experienced in ages. Picking up the champagne bottle, I kissed the moist neck where he had put his lips, then took another swig and dared to let myself contemplate the future. Once my marriage to Cecil was annulled, and Robert and I were married, this would be my life – lying in bed, being tended by this funny, darling, handsome, cultured man! But I was forgetting – there'd be no bed, for I'd be living in the outback then, sleeping in a hammock strung from a eucalyptus tree, and the sound of kookaburras would be ringing in my ears, and Robert would be cooking our meals in a billycan over an open fire . . .

'Burnt the buggers, so I'm making you new ones!' he called out from the hallway. 'Stay in bed, darling! I won't be a tick!'

'Don't worry!' I yelled back. 'I'm not going anywhere!'

Oh, wonderful future, sleeping al fresco under the Antipodean stars, writing in the shade of a gum tree, with a cuddly little tame koala bear – yes, I was sure Robert would tame me a koala – asleep on my knee. Just the two of us, miles from civilisation! No more prying phone calls from Lorelei or ascerbic comments from Elena to plague me, because we wouldn't have a phone. No more need for me to churn out romantic novels for the money! I'd be free to live my own life, and free to write a real book – fact, this time, not fiction. It'd be good – no, better than that, brilliant. In next to no time, worldwide sales of *A Year in Woolabongalonga* would rival those of *A Year in Provence* . . .

Somewhere in the distance, I heard a key rattling in a lock, but I was so deeply entrenched in my fantasy that I didn't take in what it meant.

'Lisa?'

'I'm still here!' I called out cheerfully. Of course, the truth was that Cecil was right, and I couldn't stand insects, and the only time I'd ever slept under canvas was when I'd fallen asleep in a marquee at a posh twenty-first birthday party. But I was sure I'd get used to the outdoor life. I'd have hypnotherapy to help me over my insect phobia. And Robert would teach me to love nature with the same passion with which I already loved him. I'd learn to adore all the animals – kangaroos and dingos, anteaters and scorpions, platypuses – or was it platipi? – capybarras, vipers and lizards, snakes and frogs . . .

'Lisa?'

Frogs . . . As a bloated face topped by two protruding eyes popped around the bedroom door, fantasy and reality collided head-on. For a moment I was confused. Then my jaw dropped, and I gasped out, 'Cecil!'

A lovelorn smile spread across the frog's face. 'Hello, darling. Still awake?'

'But . . .' I glared at him incredulously, while my blood pounded guiltily in my ears. 'W-what on earth are you doing here?' I stuttered. 'You're meant to be in Paris!'

'I finished work early, and managed to get the last flight home. Pleased to see me?'

Sure I was – as pleased as I'd have been to see Adolf Hitler or the Yorkshire Ripper. 'Of course I'm pleased!' I snarled. As he walked towards me, his lips puckering for our usual peck-on-the-cheek, I pulled the sheet up to my chin and shrank back against the pillows. 'You could have at least rung from the airport to let me know you were coming!'

'S-sorry, darling. I never thought to do that.' He looked so innocent, but I couldn't quite believe him. I was certain he'd come home in the hope of finding Robert and me in just the kind of compromising situation we were in.

'How was your day?'

'Fine, thanks.' Slipping out of his suit jacket, Cecil sat down on the end of the bed, beside the telltale pile of tights. 'Tiring, though. I can't wait to have a shower, and come to bed. Did . . . did you and Robert have a good time?'

'What? Yes. Great. Fine. Well, I suppose it was OK.'

OK till you walked in, I wanted to yell. For now that I'd recovered from the shock of Cecil's untimely appearance, I felt like throttling him. For what right did he have to return unannounced and spoil my precious night with Robert? Talking of Robert, where the hell *was* he? I strained my ears for the sound of whistling or saucepan-crashing, but heard nothing. Had he heard Cecil come in, or would he prance through the bedroom door any second now, stark naked but for two egg cups balanced on his nipples and an erection the size of a rolling pin poking out beneath the apron frills?

'What did you get up to?' Cecil said with a leer.

I froze. 'What's that supposed to mean?'

Perhaps I'd imagined the leer, for now it seemed to have turned into a rather bewildered smile. 'Well – just . . . what did you do all day?'

'For God's sake, Cecil, we didn't *do* anything!'

'B-but . . .' Cecil's forehead crinkled into a frown. 'You must have done something.'

'Not much,' I said, blushing to the roots of my pubic hair. 'This and that. You know. Gosh, it's hot in here. Open the window will you? Thanks. Actually,' I said to his back, 'we had a picnic.'

Cecil slid the window open. 'That's nice, darling.' Still smiling, he came back to the bed and sat down again. This time, he looked curiously at the pile of tights, and the open, well-rummaged drawers of the chest. 'What's been going on here?'

'Nothing! I was just . . . having a sort out,' I lied with shocking ease. 'Getting rid of all the stuff I don't need.'

He picked up my mangled, sweaty bonds, and examined them curiously. 'What a good idea. Are these to throw out? Shall I put them in the wastepaper basket for you?'

'Thanks.'

Cecil carried the sordid garments over to the bin. Could he not smell the scent of sex on them? I wondered. Was he so sexless himself that he couldn't smell the scent of sex on me? 'Where's Robert?'

Yes, where *was* he? 'How should I know?' I snapped. 'He's probably asleep.'

'It's a bit early to go to bed, isn't it?' He glanced at his watch. 'Oh, no, it's half past twelve.'

'Is it?'

My husband perused my face. 'Look, I'm so sorry to have landed you with Robert all day. Was it an awful bind?'

I went cold when I heard that word. 'Why on earth should it have been a *bind*, Cecil?'

'Having to look after him, darling.' I breathed again. 'After all, he's *my* friend.'

That's what you think! I screamed inside. And, like a six-year-old child having a jealous squabble in the school playground, I couldn't stop myself from saying, 'He's my friend, too!'

'Is he?' Cecil frowned. 'Lisa, are you sure everything's all right?'

'Yes. Why shouldn't it be?'

'Only you seem a little, well, tense.'

'I wasn't! I mean, I'm not. I'm just tired, that's all. I probably had too much ...' I hesitated. What was the word? *Sex*? '... sun,' I finished off firmly. 'I was about to go to sleep when you came in.'

'And I disturbed you? Sorry, darling.'

What a louse I was, making him feel guilty, when Robert and I were the ones at fault! 'It doesn't matter, Cecil. It's nice to see you.'

'Is it?' He beamed. 'Well, it's nice to see you, too.' His hand slithered across the lust-rumpled linen, and covered mine. 'Very nice. I missed you.' Head tilted, he gazed at me with a besotted look which made me feel more trapped than all Robert's bondage had.

'But, Cecil, you've only been away for a few hours!'

'Still ...' His fingers – little stumps, compared to the elegant ones which had recently been delving inside me – gave my hand a squeeze. On the pretence of raking my hair, I pulled mine free. Ever insensitive to my feelings, Cecil continued to smile. Didn't he notice my coldness? How dumb could he be? But just then, his right eyebrow shot up as he noticed the half-drunk bottle on the bedside table. 'I see you've been drinking.'

I gulped. 'Not *drinking*, Cecil. Just having a drink. I . . . I was thirsty.'

He nodded slowly. 'Champagne.' His flat tone transformed the word into an accusation that would have done any prosecuting barrister proud.

'Why not? I happen to like champagne. Surely I don't have to ask your permission every time I want to open a bottle?'

He looked shocked. 'Not at all, darling. What makes you think that?'

'Because . . . Because . . .' I blundered on. 'You look so . . . so suspicious!'

He spread his hands wide. 'What of?'

'Anyone would think . . .' My strident voice cut out as I noticed Robert's tousled head peep around the open door.

'Knock knock!' he said coyly. Cecil swung round. 'Thought I heard you come in, Cess!'

'Robert!' All smiles, Cecil stood up to greet him. 'Come in!'

'Into your private boudoir? No, no, I couldn't!'

'Please! Lisa won't mind. You don't, do you, darling?'

'Feel free.' I smoothed down my hair. 'Just call this Euston station.'

As my lover entered, parcelled up to the neck in an old tartan dressing gown, I shot him a helpless look. In return, he yawned with exaggerated tiredness. 'The doorbell woke me up,' he lied with amazing stupidity. I grimaced at him behind Cecil's back, for Cecil hadn't rung the bell. Luckily for us, Cecil didn't seem to notice. 'Er . . . I thought you weren't going to be back till tomorrow, Cess.'

'I managed to catch the late flight.'

'Great! Brilliant!' Need he have sounded so enthusiastic? 'Have a good day?'

'Not bad, thanks.'

Robert yawned again, so ostentatiously wide that I glimpsed two gold-capped molars at the back of his mouth. 'How was *gai Paree*?'

'Not very *gai*, as a matter of fact. Cold and damp. More like April than August. Except that it was overflowing with tourists. I'd much rather have been here.'

'I bet. The weather here's been fantastic. Hasn't it, Lisa?' I managed a faint *mmm* of agreement. 'Lisa and I had a picnic.'

'Yes. Lisa told me.'

'Ah, did she?' Robert's head nodded inanely, like one of those plaster dachshunds that sit in the back windows of cars.

Cecil smiled at his friend for a moment, then back at me. 'I gather you both had a good time?'

'Yes,' Robert and I said in unison. In the pause that followed, we glanced at each other complicitly.

'It was OK,' Robert said.

'*Quite* good,' I added in modification.

Robert shrugged. 'Very enjoyable. Well,' he added, after seeing my dismayed expression, 'Let me put it this way, Cess: we had as good a time as we could've had, seeing that you weren't here.'

Eleven

———◆———

Robert left the next morning, without us being able to snatch a single private moment. Maybe on purpose, or perhaps out of insensitivity – didn't he realise that he wasn't wanted? – Cecil hovered around us as persistently as a mosquito, so that, from the time we all got up to the time Robert departed, he and I were never alone.

Since there was no room in the Porsche for the three of us plus Robert's extra luggage – on a shopping expedition to Italy earlier that week, he'd bought himself three new suits and six shirts, which he'd packed in a fake Louis Vuitton suitcase he'd picked up for a song in Ventimiglia market – I offered to drive Robert to the airport myself. 'You must be tired after all that travelling you did yesterday, Cecil. Why don't you take things easy today?' But Cecil, damn him, wouldn't hear of it. Which meant that I was forced to kiss my lover goodbye in the lobby outside our apartment, while Cecil waited in the lift, his finger welded to the Open Door button.

'Goodbye, Robert. It was so nice to meet you.'

'Bye, Lisa.' His eyes gazed soulfully into mine. 'Thanks so much for having me.'

'My pleasure. You're welcome back any time.'

He put his arms around me and drew me towards him for a quick, chaste, goodbye kiss. 'I'll be in touch. Promise,' he breathed as his lips gently brushed both my cheeks.

'Hurry up, Rob!' croaked a voice behind the high pile of suitcases in the lift. 'I can't hold the lift much longer, my thumb's gone numb.'

143

'Just coming, Cess.' Robert winked at me as he walked backwards into the lift. Out of sight of Cecil, he blew me a kiss. A moment later, the lift door slid shut, wiping his beautiful smile from my sight.

I shivered with grief in the windowless lobby. What had seemed unimaginable last night had now actually happened: the light which had burned so incandescently and briefly had gone out of my life.

Rushing back into the flat, I tore through the kitchen to the back balcony, from where I watched the car emerge from the underground garage thirty-two storeys below me and head down the Avenue Princesse Grace. Then, bursting into tears, I ran into the spare bedroom, threw myself on the bed – the bed Robert had slept in – and buried my head in the pillows, searching in vain for his smell.

Paroxysms of sobs tore through my body. Robert had been gone for less than ten minutes, but it already felt like ten days. How could I bear to be apart from the man with whom all my hopes, my happiness and my future were now inextricably bound up? How could I carry on the ridiculous charade which Cecil and I had been playing for the past three months?

I couldn't, of course. And why should I? I had to leave Cecil straight away and return to London, where I'd be reunited with Robert, the man with whom I wanted to be for the rest of my life!

Oh joyful realisation! I'd start packing now, so that by the time Cecil returned from dropping Robert at the airport, I'd be ready to set off there myself. But first things first – I just had to tell to Elena. I grabbed the telephone, and dialled her number.

'Yes?'

'Elena? Hi! It's me.'

'Can't talk now,' she growled back. 'Just leaving the house. Got to take the kids to school.'

'But darling,' I laughed, 'it's Saturday morning! And the summer holidays!'

'Summer school.'

I laughed. 'Don't Rupert and Sophie ever just spend time at home?'

'Not if I can help it,' Elena said crossly. 'You wouldn't understand that, not having children. Besides, it so happens that I've got a manuscript to edit by Monday. Some of us do have to earn a living still, you know.'

'Sorry.'

'*Plus* I've got a ghastly hangover.'

'Oh. Sorry.'

'Ring me later. I might be in.'

I managed a tremulous 'OK,' which Elena picked up on immediately.

'What's the matter?'

'Nothing. Nothing at all.'

'*Lisa!*'

'No. No, really. You're busy. You've got more important things to do than listen to me. It can wait.'

Elena sighed. 'Look, hold on a tick. *Sophie?*' she yelled into the distance.

'*What?*'

'*Get your shoes on and find the car keys, will you? And get Rupert ready!*'

'*But Mum . . .*'

'*And don't argue! And make sure you've both got your swimming togs. And towels. We'll be leaving here in five minutes flat!* So?' Elena uncupped her hand from the receiver, and beamed me her undivided attention.

'Well, Elena,' I said solemnly, 'I've decided to leave Cecil.'

This news was greeted by an ominous silence from the London end. Then, 'Are you trying to get into the *Guinness Book of Records* or something?' my supposed friend snapped. 'You've only been married to him for a couple of weeks!'

'It's been nearly three months, actually.'

She paused again. 'That's not exactly what I'd call giving it a chance.'

'I have given it a chance!' I protested. 'Honestly, I have, Elena! Look, I know what you're saying but . . . Oh, God, the whole thing's a disaster!' I listened in vain for the sympathetic reaction I so wanted, but there came only an impatient, weary sigh from the London end. 'A complete disaster,' I added for good measure.

'How?'

'I . . . I can't explain. It's . . . well, it's too embarrassing.'

'To tell me? Come off it!'

'It's just . . .' Suddenly it all seemed too much to explain, and I burst into tears.

Now Elena sounded worried. 'Christ, is it really that awful? What's the matter, darling? Is Cecil violent or something? Does he beat you up?'

'No, no!'

'Then is it the bonking? Is he a sadist in bed?'

'It's nothing like that,' I sniffed. 'Cecil's very sweet to me. In fact, he couldn't be nicer. He's so bloody nice that I want to kill him half the time. But . . . Oh, it's just me, Elena! It's all my fault!'

'What do you mean? Are you having some sort of breakdown?'

I reached for a tissue on the bedside table, and blew my streaming nose. 'I don't think so. The awful truth is that I . . . oh, Elena, I just don't love him!'

Elena emitted a long hiss, like the sound of a puncturing tyre. 'Surprise, surprise! *Honestly*, Lisa!'

'Oh, Elena, what have I done?'

She sighed again. 'For God's sake, whatever induced you to marry the poor bastard?'

'I don't know. I suppose I was upset about Andy . . . and . . . and I wanted to get married . . . to have kids and things . . . like you . . . I mean, you seem so happy . . . And I was afraid I wouldn't ever find anyone after Andy . . . and so . . . and so . . .'

'And so you married Cecil on the rebound.' By now, I could almost see a hologram of Elena's sardonic expression materialise in front of my eyes. 'Brilliant, Lisa! You know, I knew that you didn't love him.'

'Did you? Oh God!' I wailed. 'I've really fucked up this time, haven't I?'

Elena considered this for a moment. 'I wouldn't say no. How're you managing to write through all this?'

For the first time in weeks, I remembered that the deadline for handing in my new Mahonia Medmenham manuscript was less than six weeks away, at the end of October, and I hadn't written a word of it yet. 'Not very well,' I muttered. 'I'm being a bit slow.'

'Shit! I suppose we can always put back publication if we have to. What a nuisance! I've just persuaded Simon to make it our title of the month for next April.'

'I'm sorry!'

'Oh, Lisa, you are a twerp! Really, I hate to say I told you so about Cecil, but . . .'

'Go on. I deserve it.'

'He's just not your type, is he? You like them handsome, selfish and nasty . . .'

'I don't!'

'. . . and Cecil's – well, let's be frank, Cecil's very plain and very kind. Look, much as I'd like to rub your nose in it now, I really haven't got time. I'll phone you as soon as I can. But cheer up, OK? Getting divorced isn't the end of the world.'

'Isn't it? OK. Thanks, Elena, you're such a wonderful friend to me.'

'True.'

'Honestly, I don't know what I'd do without you.'

'Sure.'

'And Elena?'

'Yup?'

'There's . . . Well, there's something else.'

'What?'

'You see, an old schoolfriend of Cecil's has been staying with us this last week. A . . . a male friend. His name's Robert.'

There was a long silence at the end of which my friend said curtly, 'And?'

'The thing is . . . well, the thing is, I've . . . oh, I might as well tell you . . . You see, I've fallen in love with him. And, well, I think he's in love with me.' These words seemed to fall into a black hole. 'Elena?' I said at last. 'Are you still there? Look, this time I really mean it, darling. I really know that Robert's the man I want to be with for the rest of my life.'

To my astonishment, this marvellous news didn't elicit the congratulations it merited. Instead, before slamming the phone down on me, Elena yelled, '*Jesus, Lisa! It's about time you grew up!*'

Upset by this uncalled-for comment, I lay on the bed, my hand clutching the telephone, and waited for Robert to ring me from Nice airport. The minutes passed so slowly that the hands of my watch barely seemed to move. When, after an hour, Robert still hadn't phoned, I began to visualise tragic scenarios which might have taken place en route: the car had driven off a viaduct and crashed down into a ravine, and the love of my life and my husband were both dead; Cecil, damn him, had put the car in the short-term car park and accompanied Robert into the departures terminal, and was sticking to him like a limpet until the moment the flight was called; Robert, unable to stop himself, had told Cecil all about us on the journey, and Cecil had decided to take the flight to London, while Robert was currently winging his way back to me at the wheel of Cecil's Porsche . . .

At last, the telephone rang. 'Hello, gorgeous.'

My heart soared like a helium balloon. 'Robert! Where are you?'

'In the departure lounge. Standing in front of the duty free shop and wishing I could buy you some perfume. What sort do you wear?'

'Oh, I don't know!' I giggled. 'Allure by Chanel. Opium, sometimes.'

'I'll remember that. Though I think I prefer you when you're not wearing anything.' A shiver of desire passed down my spine. 'Christ, that was some close shave last night,' he went on.

'It certainly was!'

'It made me feel bloody awful.'

'Me, too.'

'My first thought was – what if Cecil had come home an hour earlier?'

'God, that would have been terrible, wouldn't it?'

'And then,' Robert said, 'then I thought, wouldn't it have been marvellous if he hadn't come home at all?' At this, my body melted like a knob of butter thrown into a hot wok. 'And that made me feel even more horrible. I mean, how could I think that?' Easily, I said to myself. And kept to myself. 'Goddam it, Lisa, this is such a weird situation. I don't think I've felt like this since I was fifteen and in love with Beverly Miller.'

'Who on earth was Beverly Miller?' I giggled again.

'She lived two doors down from us. She was twenty-one, and looked like a cross between Ursula Undress – as we used to call her – and Cilla Black, and she wore the shortest miniskirts I've ever seen. I used to clean her father's car on Saturdays for nothing, just for the thrill of sitting where she'd sat in the back seat. Oh darling, what are we going to do?'

'I don't know . . . We really need to talk, Robert. There's something I've just got to tell you . . .'

'But when? Hold on a sec, they're mumbling some announcement over the tannoy . . . That's the last call for my flight, darling. I'm afraid I've got to run. Look, I'll call you from London.'

'When?'

'As soon as I get there. Love you, darling!'

'Love you, too!' I whispered. But the phone was already dead.

A moment later, it rang again.

'Darling?'

'*Yes?*'

'It's only me,' croaked a horribly familiar voice. My heart

149

sank. 'I'm in the car. Sorry I'm late. I stopped and had a coffee with Robert when I dropped him off. I'm on my way home now.' When I didn't reply, Cecil hesitated for a moment, before saying, 'Are you OK?'

I bristled. 'Why shouldn't I be?'

'I j-just thought . . .' The phone cut out for a moment, then Cecil said, '. . . fancy doing anything special today? I thought perhaps we might go out to lunch. Say, to Mougins, or . . .'

'No thanks. I don't feel like it.' I had no intention of going anywhere. What if I was out when Robert called?

And so I stayed in all day, in a state of high expectation.

And all the next day.

And all the next.

I'd have presumed that the telephone was out of order, only my mother phoned every morning as usual, and dropped her usual hints about wanting to be a grandmother. Cecil's mother rang several times, too, with veiled concern about how I was looking after her precious son. Cecil's sister rang. A man rang several times for Cecil. Oh yes, and there was even a begrudging call from Elena, who made a curt, unconvincing apology for her rude outburst, then asked briskly – more out of form than genuine feeling – 'Have you made up your mind what you're going to do?'

'Not yet,' I replied coldly.

'Oh well,' she added with a sniff, 'let me know when you do. And Lisa?'

'Yes?'

'About your next book . . . Can you give me *any* idea when I can expect to see that manuscript? You are working on it, aren't you?'

'Of course,' I lied.

'Good. Because, you see, I've promised the sales team that it's going to be a real hot property. A winner. And one has to be professional about this, doesn't one? I mean, we're not teenagers any more, are we? We can't just drop everything and fall to pieces because some new man appears on the scene.'

Stung into action, I unearthed an old shorthand pad from my as-yet-to-be-unpacked belongings, and sat in front of it at the balcony table, the cordless phone at my side. But, like a love-sick adolescent, the only thing I succeeded in writing down was Robert's name: Robert . . . **Robert** . . . *Robert* . . . Roberto . . . *I love Robert* . . . *Trebor* (that was Robert spelled backwards) – all obliterated by a scrawl of Biro marks in case Cecil found it when he came home from work.

I thought about jumping on a plane to London, and turning up unannounced on the doorstep of Robert's Camberwell pied-à-terre. If I waited too long, he'd have flown back to Australia . . . But my pride wouldn't allow it. I needed a sign – just a single sign from him – that he wanted me.

But no sign came. Why, oh why, didn't Robert phone me? Had he changed his mind about us? Or had he decided to hold back out of some misguided sense of loyalty to Cecil? If so, where did I fit into the picture? After what had happened between us, where was his loyalty to me?

A week passed. Two weeks. The love bug clung on and turned into a bad case of post-viral syndrome. In record time, I'd reached the inevitable ME end of my love affair. I no longer prowled the flat feverishly like a cat on a hot-tin roof; instead I slumped around in an unwashed dressing gown, tired, listless, sick at heart and on the edge of hysteria.

Monaco was indifferent to my silent suffering. Coach parties of tourists filed behind the raised umbrellas of guides through the Place de la Casino, and oggled the Ferraris, Rolls-Royces and Mercedes parked outside the Hôtel de Paris. Sleek speedboats and vast millionaires' yachts cut white swathes across the turquoise sea. The beach was packed with sunworshippers who, it appeared, had never heard of skin cancer. Firework displays lit up the port every other evening; each explosion of ephemeral light and colour served only as a painful reminder of Robert's first kiss.

I tried not to snap too much at Cecil. But it was a hard task when everyone except the two of us seemed to be having the time of their lives. Sensitivity may not have been Cecil's strongest emotional characteristic but, after a few weeks of having to put up with my black moods and long silences, even he began to realise that something was seriously wrong.

'Is anything the matter, Lisa?' he asked one morning about three weeks after Robert's departure as we walked along the Avenue Princesse Grace towards the Beach Club.

'No.'

'Are you sure?' He stopped outside the open-air cinema, and put down the basket of towels he was carrying.

'Quite sure, thank you. Why on earth are you stopping, Cecil? I can't stand out here in the sun. This heat's making me dizzy. I want to get to the Beach Club and have a swim.'

I started to walk on, but he grabbed my hands in both of his.

'Just a minute, Lisa . . .' His anxious eyes scanned my face. 'The thing is, you look so . . .' His chin jerked involuntarily in the air as his stutter got the better of him.

'For heaven's sake, Cecil!' I snapped before I could stop myself. 'Spit it out!'

He dropped my hands as quickly as if they were made of red-hot metal, then his lower lip jutted out, and the loose folds of his jowls quivered with hurt.

'I'm sorry,' I muttered, shame-faced. 'I'm really sorry, Cecil. I don't know why I said that. Really. What were you going to say?'

He looked at me sadly for a moment, then muttered, 'It wasn't important.'

'Cecil, please . . .' I watched him stomp off down the road in his baggy shorts and Hawaiian-style shirt, his pudgy shoulders slumped, his head lowered, the oil slick of his plastered-down hair ruffled by the breeze. Poor Cecil! How vile I was to him! It wasn't his fault that I loathed him, or that I'd fallen in love with his best friend. What right had I to take out my misery on him?

I ran along the sea front, and caught up with him just as he entered the luxury car showroom that was the Beach Club's car park. When I touched his shoulder, he neither stopped nor turned around. 'Cecil? I'm sorry,' I said quietly, linking my arm through his. 'Please believe me, I really didn't mean to say that. I don't know what came over me. I just don't know what's the matter with me nowadays.'

'Don't you?' he said, angrily pulling away. 'Frankly, I bloody wish you did, Lisa! You know I really love you,' he went on after glaring at me for a short moment.

'I know you do,' I mumbled.

'But I'm getting fed up with being your punchbag.' Dropping the basket of towels again, he spread his short arms in frustration. 'I've *tried* and I've *tried* to make you happy, but for the last few weeks ... well, I ... Frankly, I just don't know what to *do* any more. I can't seem to do anything right in your eyes.'

'That's not true!'

'Isn't it?'

I looked away from his probing gaze, unable to admit that he was right. How could I tell him that I neither loved nor fancied him, and that I never could? With what well-chosen words could I admit to him that I now loved Robert with a hopeless passion that was driving me mad?

Cecil continued to stare at me. A bead of sweat stood out on his forehead. 'I'm really sorry, Cecil,' I repeated. 'We do need to talk about all of this. But not now. Not here. Not in public. Let's go inside and have a swim.'

I took Cecil's arm, and we passed through the gate and into the Beach Club where the air rang with the sound of animated chatter, and the assorted bleeps of mobile phones. Two middle-aged men, their paunches strung with huge gold medallions, clamoured for service at the Bamboo Bar, cigarettes dangling from their fingers, their tattooed arms wound around two platinum-haired bimbos. Scores of children splashed in the shallow end, or leaped from the diving boards with the enviable abandon of youth. Up on the raised terrace of the Potinière restaurant, waiters in crisp white shirts swung easily between the crowded tables, huge platters of raspberry millefeuilles balanced on their upheld hands.

And there, standing in her usual position slap-bang in the middle of the walkway, a huge straw hat pulled low over her face, the straps of a leopard-skin costume flicked low over her shoulders, bare back to the sun was Zuzu – the last person in the world I felt like seeing just then.

'So there you are, dahlinks!' she cried as we approached her. 'I wondered if you'd be down today. We haven't seen you for ages, have we girls?' she said, turning to Tamara and Marina, who were draped on matching Hermès towels on their sunbeds.

'No,' Marina drawled in her Texan accent. 'Not since that hunky friend of yours was here, Cecil. Oooh,' she added curiously as he stomped on past her after only a cursory greeting, 'Did I say something wrong, Lisa? Did I put my foot in anything?'

'No. Not at all. Why should you have?'

'Ooh, no reason.'

'But look at you, dahlink, you look so washed out and pale!' Zuzu suddenly shrank back, as if afraid she might catch some disease from me. 'Like you might be sickening for something.'

'As it happens, I haven't been feeling very well lately.'

Taking off her sunglasses, Zuzu squinted at me curiously. 'Unwell, huh? You're not by any chance expecting a visit from the stork, are you?' she said in a knowing voice.

It was my turn to recoil from her. 'No, I'm certainly not!' I snapped angrily.

The only thing I was expecting was a telephone call.

The phone call never came.

Neither did my period.

Two weeks, and a great deal of vomiting later, I crept out of bed at dawn, tiptoed out of the bedroom so as not to wake Cecil, and shut myself in the guest bathroom. I'd bought the pregnancy test the day before in a pharmacy at the back of the town. Now I took it out from its hiding place behind the lavatory rolls in the bathroom cabinet and, armed with a French dictionary, attempted to translate the instructions.

I remembered that, somewhere along the line, I'd mentioned the word condom to Robert. I'd even found a used one after his departure, neatly wrapped up in a tissue, underneath the bed. One condom. Was that enough? How many times had he made love to me while my limbs were spread like the hands of a clock on the circular mattress, arms at ten to two, legs at twenty past eight? How many times had his fingers explored my secret places – fingers that, after taking off the aforementioned used prophylactic, hadn't been washed? It only took one sperm to fertilise an egg, and a single drop of semen contained millions of the little bastards. Probably enough to repopulate the whole of France, and certainly enough to plant a little bastard in me.

I threw the dictionary to the floor, tore open the foil wrapper of the plastic dipstick, and held it underneath me in the lavatory bowl while I peed. Less than one minute later, a telltale pink line appeared in the tiny viewing window.

I was pregnant.

Eureka. The thing I'd so longed for when I was single had finally happened. Was I pleased? Did I feel like breaking open the champagne? No, I felt like breaking open my head. Because, after all those years of taking careful contraceptive precautions, I'd allowed myself to get knocked up during a one-night stand with my husband's best friend. Of course I had. It went without saying. Because that was about the level of my luck.

But maybe, just maybe, if Robert knew I was pregnant he'd come to my rescue. I hadn't planned on contacting him, but I realised now that this wasn't something I could face alone. Keeping despair at arm's length, I crept into the living room, closed the door and unearthed Cecil's address book from his briefcase. I knew where Robert's number was written down, because I'd already looked it up a hundred times before. Heart pounding, I now dialled it for the first time.

It rang for ages. Damn it! He was probably back in Australia by now. Then, just as I was about to hang up, the receiver was snatched clumsily off the hook.

'Yeah?' grunted a sleepy voice.

'Robert?'

'Uh?'

'It's me. Lisa.'

'Whah?!'

'Have I woken you?'

'Mmm.' There was a loud yawn. 'What time is it?'

'Just before six. Oh no, I forgot about the time difference! It's an hour earlier for you, isn't it?'

'Doesn't matter.' There was a shuffling noise. I imagined him stretching his tanned, powerful arms, then rolling over and pulling himself up in bed. 'S'wonderful to hear from you. I've been hoping you'd call me.'

'Have you?'

'Mmmm. I wanted to call you so many times.' I bit back the words, *So why didn't you?* and waited for him to speak again. 'Only . . .' His voice trailed off into another yawn.

'Only what?' I prompted.

'Obvious reasons. Or rather reason. I mean, I am supposed to be Cecil's best friend. Best friends don't do that to each other, do they?'

Isn't it a bit late for scruples? I wanted to say. After all, what's so terrible about telephoning your best friend's wife when you've already, in your own words, fucked her senseless? Instead, I said, 'I'm so glad you're still in London.'

'Where else should I be?'

'I thought you might have gone back to Australia by now.'

'Oh, that! No. Well, I put it off. But I'm going in a couple of days.'

I tried to hold down my rising sense of panic. 'How are you?'

'Kind of OK. Only I miss you, darling. Terribly.'

'Do you really?' Annoyed as I was with him, the warm purr of his voice was beginning to melt me.

'What do you think?' I knew very well what to think, but in my present situation, I was prepared to believe anything that weighted the odds in my favour. The triumph of Hope over Experience. 'I think about you all the time, Lisa.'

'What sort of thoughts?'

'Naughty ones,' he whispered. 'Nothing I could possibly say over the telephone.' To my amazement, I found myself giggling. 'And I think . . .'

'Yes?'

'Well – if only we'd met under different circumstances. It seems so cruel that you and I are destined to be ships that pass in the night.'

I took a deep breath. 'Maybe we're not. I mean, we don't have to be.'

'But . . .' There was a long pause. 'You're married to Cecil, darling!'

'Yes, but . . . I don't have to stay married to him, do I? Not if I don't want to. In fact,' I hurried on, gaining courage, 'there's a very good reason why he and I might split up pretty soon.'

'Really?'

'Yes! You see, the thing is . . . the thing is . . . Well, Robert, the thing is, you see, I'm . . . well, actually . . . I'm pregnant.' This news was followed by such profound silence that I thought the line had gone dead. 'Robert? Are you still there?'

'Sure.' Robert cleared his throat. 'I don't understand, Lisa. I mean, if you're pregnant surely . . .?'

I started to laugh. 'I'm sorry, darling. I'm so silly! I should have explained! You see the thing is, the baby isn't Cecil's.'

Another long pause. 'Not Cecil's?' Robert repeated in a numb voice.

'No!'

'Then . . .?'

I laughed again. 'It's yours, of course.'

There was a strange, foreboding silence from London. As each subsequent second passed without a response from

Robert, my heart sank a little further. 'Mine?' he croaked eventually. 'But that's impossible!'

'I'm afraid not.'

'But . . . Are you sure, Lisa?'

'Absolutely. I wouldn't have told you otherwise. You see, Cecil and I haven't . . . I mean, we didn't . . . Well, the timing's right.'

I heard a muffled noise as his hand covered the receiver for a moment – but not before I'd caught the scarcely audible '*Shit!*' on his outbreath.

My stomach sank with leaden disappointment. 'You . . . you don't have to do anything about it,' I stumbled on. 'That is, I'm not expecting you to. I . . . I just thought that you ought to know, that's all.'

'Yes. Yes, of course. Well, Lisa, thanks for telling me.'

What could I say – *It's a pleasure*? 'Do you . . .' I hesitated again. 'Would you still like to see me? I mean, I could come to London for a few days – without Cecil, I mean. We could talk things over.'

He cleared his throat. 'Talk what over?'

He sounded so cold that I began to shiver. I had a feeling that the man I'd been talking to earlier had packed up his emotional baggage, and was already halfway out the door. 'Well, what I'm going to do about it.'

'What do you mean, do about it? Look, Lisa, I don't want you to think I'm trying to wriggle out of anything, but . . . Are you really sure the baby's mine? I mean, you could be wrong, you know. Couldn't you? Don't you think that, before you do anything drastic, you maybe ought to wait till the baby's born and perhaps give it a, well, a sort of paternity test?'

'How dare you!'

'Mistakes do happen, don't they?'

'Not to me!'

'Only . . . I thought I'd used a condom.'

'You *thought* so? Well, I thought so, too. I wasn't exactly in a position to check, was I? Look, I don't mean to sound so angry, but . . . The thing is, I didn't exactly expect this to happen, Robert. And frankly, I . . .' I fought back tears. 'I really don't know what to do.'

'Oh, my poor Lisa!' Suddenly the voice on the other end of the phone took on something of its old warmth. 'Shit! What a fuck-up! I wish I was there to comfort you.'

'So, should I come to London or what?' I asked miserably.

'What? Yes. Sure.' My spirits lifted a fraction, only to be shot down by a crushing, 'But . . . The thing is, darling, there's a certain logistical problem. I'm leaving for Australia first thing tomorrow morning.'

'*Tomorrow*? You said before that you'd be in London for a few more days!'

'Did I? I must have been half asleep. No, it's definitely tomorrow. Besides . . .'

'What?'

He paused. 'Maybe there isn't any point. In us seeing each other.'

'Isn't there?' I replied numbly.

'I mean, I don't think . . . You see, I've got nothing to offer you, Lisa. The baby'll need a good father. And . . . You know, when you've had it, Cecil can afford to give you – and it – all sorts of things I couldn't.'

'I don't want *things*, Robert. I just want to be happy.'

He considered this in silence for a moment. 'But the truth is, darling, I don't think I could make you happy. I've never really wanted children, you see. I guess I'm a bit of a loner at heart. And Woolabongalonga's not a place to bring up a baby. I mean, they don't have nannies or nurseries or any of the other things that babies need. We're talking serious outback here, Lisa. Christ, there isn't a branch of Mothercare for thousands and thousands of miles. Where would you buy the little sod's nappies?'

The Aborigines seem to manage, I thought but didn't say.

'Shit!' Robert's voice had become the very essence of exasperation. 'Look . . . Oh, Christ, I'm sorry Lisa! I . . .

I'm half asleep now. I'm not making sense. I'll ring you later and we can talk it through then.'

'Promise?'

'Promise.'

'Really?'

'God's honour, darling. Goodbye.'

I switched off the telephone and, crouched in an appropriately foetal position on the floor, burst into tears. I'd never felt so miserable in my life. Sandwiched between a husband I loathed and a lover who didn't want to get involved, I had nowhere to go but into the Slough of Despond.

Which is where Cecil found me a few minutes later.

'Lisa? Lisa!' My puffy eyes unscrewed to a view of hairy ankles and the uneven hem of a dressing gown. 'Good God, darling!' Cecil exclaimed, dropping to his knees beside me. 'Whatever's wrong?' I tried to speak, but succeeded only in dribbling down my chin. His mouth split in a horrified expression, and he felt my forehead with the palm of his hand. 'Are you ill? Are you in pain? Is it that gastroenteritis you had the other day?'

His innocent question – how easily I'd fooled him! – made me bawl even louder. I rolled over onto my side on the floor, and curled up like a caterpillar. 'Oh, Cecil!'

'Darling! Whatever's the matter? Tell me.'

'I can't!'

'Of course you can.'

'No, no, I can't!'

'Look, calm down! Calm down, OK? Take a deep breath – go on, you can do it!' For I had begun to hyperventilate, and was gasping for air. 'Go on, breath in deeply. Deeply, darling! Now, breath out. Yes, that's it! Good girl.' He dabbed my wet face with the end of his sleeve. 'Oh dear, look at you! You're nose is running! Hold on, I'll get you some tissues and a warm flannel from the bathroom. You'll feel better when you've freshened up.'

The next second Cecil had leaped to his feet and was out of the door. I waited for him to come back with the passive acceptance of a sick child waiting for its mother to give it medicine.

At long last he reappeared, ashen-faced and, to my horror, clutching the plastic dipstick which, I suddenly remembered, I'd left lying on the side of the sink. 'Lisa,' he whispered, looking down at me through eyes which seemed to have grown to twice their normal size, 'what does this mean?'

I stared mutely up at him, not knowing what to say. I felt as guilty as if I'd just been discovered in the act of committing a murder – which in a way I had: the murder of our odd marriage. As I crouched there in silence, Cecil examined the dipstick closely, and his knobbly brow creased into a deep frown. 'Does this pink line mean you are or you're not p . . .' His stutter caught on the word pregnant.

I hung my head in shame. 'I'm sorry, Cecil,' I sobbed. 'I'm so, so sorry.'

My cuckolded husband knelt on the floor beside me and gently took hold of my hands. 'But . . . I don't understand.'

I looked at him through a curtain of tears. 'I'm sorry. Believe me, I never meant for anything like this to happen.'

Still frowning, he blinked at me slowly. 'So, you are . . .' His voice trailed away. Then he muttered under his breath, 'Oh my God, you're pregnant!' and his face broke into a 100 watt grin.

'Cecil?' I stared at him in alarm. 'Are you all right?'

'Am I all right? *Am – I – all right*?' He waved the dipstick in the air like a magic wand. 'This is the most . . . the most *wonderful* news I've ever heard!'

'*What*?'

He laughed manically. 'A baby!' he repeated, and his grin turned into a full-scale lighthouse beam. 'Do you realise what this means, darling? We're having a baby!'

The only thing I realised, at that point, was that no one had ever taught Cecil the facts of life. *We* were having nothing. And if Robert didn't come up trumps, *I* was probably going to end up having an abortion.

'Oh, you clever, clever darling!' Still grinning, my lunatic husband kissed my tear–drenched cheeks, then sprang to his feet. 'Oh my goodness! I must tell the family!'

'*Are you crazy?*'

Maybe he really was, because the next moment he'd picked up the cordless phone and was dialling his parents' number. When I tried to snatch it away from him, he ran across the room to get away from me, dodging past the huge mahogany coffee table and clambering onto the sofa. 'Stop, Cecil! Give that to me!'

'Hello, Mother? Sorry – did I wake you? No, nothing's wrong. Mother, you'll never guess what!'

I made another grab for the phone, but Cecil was too quick for me. Leaping nimbly over the back of the sofa, he headed for the door. 'Yes! That's right! That's right! Marvellous, isn't it? Oh, early days yet but . . . What? No, not yet. Yes, yes! That'd be marvellous! Bye!' Flushed, victorious and grinning smugly, he came back into the room and sat down in an armchair. 'I said it'd be OK if my mother rang yours and spread the good news. I hope you don't mind.'

Defeated, I collapsed on the floor and buried my face in my hands. 'Oh Cecil!' I yelled. 'You idiot! Why on earth did you do that?'

'I . . . I . . .' he began excitedly.

'You know perfectly well that the baby's not yo . . .'

'Lisa!' he yelled back with a ferocity that shocked me. 'That's enough! I don't want to hear another word about it!'

'But Cecil, the baby's not your . . .'

'Stop it! Just stop it!' He plugged his fingers into his ears. 'I don't want to hear!' When he saw I'd been silenced, he dropped his hands. His chin jutted stubbornly forward and his jowls ballooned out. 'As far as I'm concerned, you're my wife, and this is our baby, and anything you choose to do is all right by me. Understand?'

Suddenly, in a flash, I did understand, and all the unanswered questions that had been floating around in my mind suddenly made sense. 'Oh my God!' I gasped. 'You're gay!'

'*What?*' he screeched.

'You're gay! You're gay, Cecil! This marriage is just a front for you, isn't it? That's why you don't mind about . . .'

'Shut up!' He glared at me furiously, and his face turned the colour of stewed red cabbage. He started to speak, then changed his mind and stomped out into the hall. 'Let's get this straight – I am not gay!' he shouted at me from the corridor. 'Frankly, there have been times lately when I wished I was. But for some stupid reason, I just happen to love you, Lisa!'

Exhausted and confused, I sank down on the sofa. There was no point trying to make sense of any of this now. I'd wait and see what happened when Robert phoned me back later.

But, of course, he never did.

Twelve

And so, by one phone call too many – from Cecil to his parents – and one phone call too few, I was trapped into staying with my husband while I incubated his best friend's baby in my womb; an untenable situation, as I told Elena over the telephone.

To my surprise, Elena didn't understand how I was feeling. 'But you've moaned for ages that you wanted to get preggers,' she said. 'Aren't you pleased?'

'How can I be, under these circumstances?'

'You're going to be a mother, for God's sake! Isn't that the reason why you married poor Cecil in the first place?'

'I wish you'd stop calling him *poor* Cecil. And this isn't his baby.'

'So what?' Elena said. '*He* obviously doesn't mind about that, so why should you?'

Why did I mind? Why did I feel so joyless at the thought of having this baby? I couldn't even think of it as a baby at the moment; it felt more like some kind of parasite which had hooked itself inside my belly and was refusing to let go. Maybe my feelings of hatred towards it had something to do with the fact that its real father had made it clear by default that he didn't want to know. 'Oh, don't be ridiculous, Elena! Do I really have to explain?'

'If you ask me, Cecil's behaving in an extremely civilised manner. I really don't know why're you're always running him down. Frankly, he's turned up trumps.'

'He's being idiotic!'

'There you go again! You should count yourself lucky.

165

For some unfathomable reason, Cecil seems to worship you
no matter how badly you behave. Yes, you're right, he *i*
idiotic.'

Elena guffawed at her own, tasteless joke. 'I wish you'd
be serious,' I snapped at her. 'Look, of course I want to have
a baby – but I can't have this one.'

My friend drew in a long breath, and sounding serious,
said, 'You're not really thinking of having an abortion, are
you, darling?'

'No. Yes. Oh, I don't know!'

'But . . .' she began. Then stopped.

'What?' I prompted her.

'It's not that I'm against abortion or anything,' Elena
continued. 'It's just that . . . well, I think you might regret
it if you do. After all, Lisa, you're nearly thirty-six. If you
want to have kids – and you do, don't you? – when are you
going to have them, if not now? I mean, are you planning
to get rid of this one just so you can get pregnant again
in another year or so by someone else? And what if you
don't meet anyone else? What if you do, but you don't get
pregnant again? I don't mean to be a scaremonger, but you
ought to think about it. You'd be missing out on one of the
most important experiences in life.'

'That's not what you usually say.'

'No, but . . .' When Elena spoke again, it was in a wistful
tone I'd never heard her use before. 'I know I'm always
complaining about Sophie and Rupert. And I'm not saying
that motherhood's not hard work at times. But still, nothing
beats having a family. I wouldn't have missed out on it for
the world.'

I suddenly imagined myself as an old, wrinkled spinster
alone in a depressing bedsitting-room, with no visitors, no
friends and Radio 4 as my only company. Then I pictured
myself as an earth mother figure like Elena – in a kitchen,
frying chips with one hand while sticking a plaster on my
child's cut with the other, at the same time conducting a
business meeting from a telephone tucked under my chin and

simultaneously correcting proofs with a pen stuck between my toes. Yes, the second picture was infinitely more cheerful – until I saw Cecil and our parents standing in the doorway, pointing their accusing fingers at me.

'I hear what you're saying, Elena,' I said firmly. 'But your situation's quite different from mine. Your children are yours and Peter's. Mine wouldn't be Cecil's. How could I possibly deceive both our families for the rest of my life? Everyone thinks that the baby's Cecil's.'

'*He* doesn't, does he? And that's what counts.'

I sighed. 'Frankly, Elena, I don't think Cecil knows how babies are made. No, it's all *wrong*. Everyone's so bloody thrilled about it. Everyone except me. I feel so trapped! How can I go on lying to them all? The thought of it makes me feel quite ill.'

'Goodness, I never knew you were such a conventional creep. Fifty years ago, the aristocracy did that kind of thing all the time.'

'I'm not an aristocrat.'

'No, you're a writer. So think of yourself as a character in a book. In one of your own books. Like that – what the hell was she called? In that horsey novel you wrote?'

'Perdita?'

'Yes. Did she think twice about having a baby which wasn't her husband's?'

'That was completely different. Perdita'd had amnesia ever since she'd fallen off her pony at that gymkhana. She didn't even remember that she had a husband until that second tumble on the bridleway brought her memory flooding back.'

'*On the Bridal Path* – was it really me who thought up that brilliant pun for the title?' Elena mused. 'And, while we're on the subject, how's the new book going?'

'Please! Not now! Do you really expect me to write at the moment, when my life's such a mess?'

There was a short pause. Then Elena snapped, 'Yes, actually, I do expect you to. Look, I had to struggle to

167

convince Simon to push your next book – he's so bound up with Flora MacNalty's next title that he scarcely wanted to know. Actually, between you and me, he's so bound up with Flora MacNalty herself that he's scarcely on this planet any more. Cyberfuck, my foot. Look, speaking as your publisher for a moment, Lisa, it already looks like you'll be late in delivering – sorry about the double entendre. I hope you're going to hand in this manuscript at *some* point. I'd hate to have to sue you for breach of contract.'

'Elena, you wouldn't dare!'

'Wouldn't I? If you want my advice – my friendly advice, darling – I'd get back to work on it right away. Because, believe me, you'll never get down to it after the baby's born.'

Who needed advice? I did, apparently. And, since Cecil had gone public about our 'happy event', I was getting plenty of it. Now that I was pregnant, it was clear that my life was no longer my own. Lorelei and Rita were the worst culprits. So concerned were they about the health and future of 'their' putative grandchild that it was all Cecil and I could do to dissuade them from jumping on the next Nice-bound plane and taking up residence with us until the thing was born, grew up and left home.

Once Zuzu knew I was pregnant, it was only a matter of hours before the entire English-speaking tax-exile community in Monaco knew too. The Spoiled Wives Club plied me with *shoulds* and *shouldn'ts* which ranged from where and how I should have the baby and what model of BMW I needed to buy for my future offspring's nanny to what jewellery I ought to wear for the birth. Acquaintances of Cecil's, people with whom I'd previously only been on nodding terms, now felt at liberty to come up to me in the street, press my stomach as if it were a melon in the market and lecture me about what I ought and ought not to eat.

As for Cecil, he cosseted me as if I was a valuable brood mare about to give birth to a potential Derby winner. Though he was now working late almost every night, and was frequently away from home on business trips, he telephoned me at least three times a day to find out how I was feeling, and whenever he was home he hovered around me bearing cups of hot chocolate and packets of imported McVities Digestive biscuits spread with Nutella – the only solid food I could keep down. His saintly ministerings drove me crazy. I'd far rather he'd stabbed me to death with a kitchen knife in a jealous rage than killed me slowly with kindness, as he obviously intended to do.

In fact, the only person who expressed no interest at all in my pregnancy was the foetus's father. No, he was too absorbed in studying the reproductive habits of termites to answer the letters I intermittently sent to his London address with *Please Forward to Australia* printed at the top . . .

I'd heard it said that some women enjoy being pregnant. I'd even seen some of them at the Beach Club, reclining under parasols in designer bathing costumes, women who only had a neat, elegant football of a bump at seven or eight months. Women of whom it could truly be said that they'd never looked more beautiful in their lives. Within weeks, it became apparent that I wasn't going to be one of them. I wasn't blooming, I was ballooning. It seemed miraculous that one could gain so much weight whilst throwing up so often – obviously a divine punishment for the terrible thing I'd done. Had Robert seen what I now looked like, he might have shown more interest in me, for by the beginning of November, my formerly tanned, size ten body look as pale and bloated as that of a queen termite, distended with eggs.

'Lisa, dear . . .'

'Please don't call me dear, Cecil. It makes me feel like I ought to be wearing carpet slippers.'

'Sorry. Look, de . . . darling. It's nearly midday. Don't you think you ought to get out of bed?'

I sank back in a depressed heap against the mountain of white broderie anglaise pillows, chosen by Alexandre to adorn our new antique wooden bedstead. 'What is there to get up for, Cecil?'

Judith Summers

'Well . . . It's a lovely autumn day and . . . And it's Saturday, and I'm not working and . . . You should get up, Lisa. If not for yourself then for the . . .' His voice caught on the word *baby* – the one word he knew I couldn't bear to hear. I turned my head away with a sigh and stared out of the french windows. Cecil sank down on the foot of the bed. 'You can't stay in all the time.'

'I don't see why not. After all, I feel ill!'

'But you're not ill, darling,' Cecil ventured. 'You're only pregnant.' When he saw my furious expression, he quickly squeezed my hand in an apologetic manner, but it didn't do any good.

'That's easy for you to say! You're not vomiting all over the place. I want to know why they call it morning sickness when it goes on all day long.'

'I know it's horrid. Still, you do need to get some exercise. Dr Semollo told you so, and we must take his advice. Look, why don't you come out with me for the day?'

'Where to?'

'Well . . .' Cecil's amphibian tongue flicked out and moistened his lips. 'We could wander up to the Boulevard des Moulins and see what's in the shops. You used to like buying clothes.'

'Well, I don't any more,' I said ungratefully. 'What's the point, when nothing fits me? And all the other shops are boring. I can't understand why, in a place where there's so much money around, there's nothing interesting to buy.'

Cecil laughed. 'We could phone Zuzu up and arrange to have coffee with her.'

'I can't face anyone, Cecil. Especially not Zuzu. I look too awful.'

He blinked at me with his usual blind adoration. 'You look marvellous to me. Quite Rubenesque. Come on, darling,' he urged as he helped me to my feet as if I were a recuperating invalid. 'Let's go for a ride up to Saint-Paul. We can have lunch at the Columbe d'Or – just something light, if you're up to it – and then drive up to the Fondation Maeght to

170

look at their new exhibition. I could do with some culture and, well, we haven't been there since just after we were married.'

Later that afternoon, the Porsche roared up the steep wooded hill to the secluded car park of the Fondation Maeght. Even before Cecil had turned off the engine, I'd flung open the door, and was desecrating the tranquillity of the forest setting by regurgitating my lunch over the nearest stone wall.

'Oh God, when will this end?' I muttered as, perched on the bonnet, I took sips of mineral water from a bottle held for me by Cecil.

Cecil stroked my forehead. 'You really are having an awful time of it, aren't you? Come on, be brave – let's have a look inside. Maybe seeing something different will take your mind off being sick.'

It did, but not in the way that Cecil had anticipated. Because the moment we walked into the shady, velvet-grassed sculpture garden, I spotted someone I knew. And he was the last person I'd expected to see there.

Though his back was towards me, I recognised Andy immediately. Was it the way his hair curled up at the nape of his neck that was so familiar, or that old, rumpled leather jacket slung casually over one shoulder, or the sexy curve of that neat, denim-clad bottom I knew so well by touch? A clammy sweat broke out all over my body as I noticed that he was holding hands with the woman standing next to him – a slender wisp of a girl with long, lank mousey hair.

I stopped in my tracks, and watched him stroll towards the gallery doors with that slow, loafing step I remembered from countless walks on Hampstead Heath. I knew there was no point in speaking to him, but old addictions die hard. With Cecil trailing behind me, I hurried inside the building, and caught up with my former lover in the first gallery.

'Hello, Andy.'

He swung round. For a moment, he didn't seem to recognise me, then his mouth dropped open. 'Lisa! Shit!'

We stared at each other for a long moment. 'Well, isn't this a coincidence?' I said as Cecil came up beside me and, like a gaoler, linked his arm through mine. I swallowed hard and introduced them to each other. They nodded at each other warily. If I could have had one wish at that moment, it would have been to have changed Cecil into a Hugh Grant lookalike, and to have added a good twenty-four inches onto his height, for I could see Andy sizing Cecil up, and I knew what he was thinking: how could Lisa have married such a small, ugly man?

The pale gazelle standing next to Andy gave his arm a tug. I'd seen pictures of the enemy before, and built her up in my mind as a long-faced monster, spouting tears and hysterics in a way befitting the millstone-round-the-neck which Andy had so often compared her to. In the flesh she looked less like a millstone than a rather pretty china ornament – washed-out and delicate, with a small bow-lipped mouth set in a heart-shaped face. 'Andy? Aren't you going to introduce me to your friends?' she said in an upper-class accent which made Andy's Eton drawl sound like something out of *EastEnders*.

To give him his due, Andy had the decency to look embarrassed. 'What? Sorry. Er, Lisa – Francesca. Fran – Lisa.'

'How do you do?' The enemy offered me her hand – a limp child-sized thing which I dropped as soon as decorum allowed.

'What are you doing here?' I asked as calmly as I could.

The china doll clutched Andy's arm and murmured shyly, 'Actually, we're on our honeymoon.'

I wanted to die. But first I wanted to kill Andy for having the gall to marry Francesca after all the dreadful things he'd said about her in the past. Unable to do either, I merely swallowed hard and croaked my congratulations and, with difficulty, managed to stretch my lips into a smile, which my former lover returned with an embarrassed, lopsided grimace. Maybe Cecil noticed the tension between

172

us for, stepping closer, he shook Francesca warmly by the hand.

'Yes, congratulations!' he stammered effusively. And added with a blush, 'Lisa and I got married quite recently too.' Andy nodded, as if he hadn't known. 'Um – how do you two know each other?' Cecil went on after a short, uneasy pause.

I looked at Andy. He looked at me. Then he said, without a shred of hesitation, 'Lisa was in a film I once made. About the romantic fiction business. Lisa writes romantic novels, Fran, under the pseudonym Mahonia Medmenham.'

'Ah!' Fran's bow lips parted in slight acknowledgement. 'Oh yes! I believe Andy did mention you once.'

Once? Was that all I'd merited? As Andy and Cecil both escaped in the direction of the nearest painting I smiled at Francesca poisonously. 'Oh, that's funny. He never mentioned you.'

The woman I'd once resented more than any other in the world laughed so good-naturedly that it was almost impossible for me to hate her any more. 'That doesn't surprise me! Andy's such an obsessively private person. Almost an emotional agoraphobic, actually – if one can have such a thing.'

I feigned interest in a Miró sculpture made out of a red shop dummy and a Bentwood chair. 'Oh? I'd never have guessed.'

'One doesn't,' Francesca prattled on. 'Not unless one knows Andy very well. People think he's very gregarious and stuff, and wants to be out at parties and things all the time, but actually, he's a real home-bod at heart.'

'A home-bod,' I repeated. 'Really?'

'He's obsessive about work of course, but on the rare occasions when he's not working, he just wants to stay at home watching telly, or cooking, or fiddling about painting walls and things. Sometimes he's so boringly domestic that I wonder why I married him. Andy's idea of having a day out is to drag me down to Sainsbury's Homebase to look at door handles and hinges and things.

173

Sometimes I think I'll die before he ever takes me out to a restaurant.'

Probably because he's too afraid the staff will say something like, *Hello, Mr Hetherington, and where's your other wife today?* 'Have you two been together long?'

'Donkey's years. Though we did break up three or four times.' Not wanting to appear too interested in this bombshell information, I walked away from the millstone, and examined the label of a huge, monochromatic semiabstract painting. Georges Braque. A black bird, flying through a grey sky – just like I felt nowadays. I was dying to pump Francesca for more details, but I had my pride. Luckily, after a short pause, she continued, 'I always left Andy for the same reason – because I couldn't stand his unreasonable jealousy.' *She'd left him?* Was I hearing right? 'Do you know, he once made me give up my job and go freelance because he couldn't bear me going to work? He was frightened I'd run off with a colleague!' Francesca ran her hand through her limp brown hair and sighed. 'But somehow, Andy always talked me into having one more go.' I swung round, in search of a long, sharp pointed object I could plunge through Andy's back, but the only thing remotely that shape was a six-foot-high Giacometti bronze. 'He can be incredibly persuasive,' Francesca continued. Didn't I just know it? 'And so incredibly needy. But, though he always promises he'll change, he never does.' Yes, I'd drink to that. 'He's an awfully possessive person.'

'Is he?'

'He can't bear the thought of losing anyone. So jealous. God knows what he'll be like when the baby's born.'

I froze. 'Does this mean you're . . .?'

A smile lit up her face, transforming her in one fell swoop from a dull country mouse into a stunning, home counties, English rose. 'Three months' pregnant!'

A spurt of acid splashed up in my throat. 'Me, too.' I croaked.

'No! What a coincidence! Andy! Andy, guess what!' The odd twosome discussing the Calder mobile ahead of us swung round in unison as Francesca called out, 'Your friend here . . .' She turned to me, 'Sorry, I didn't catch your name.' I muttered it hoarsely. 'Lisa's pregnant, too!'

I was gratified to see Andy's eyes bulge till they were as large as Cecil's. 'Wow! Congratulations! I thought you'd put on a bit. Congratulations, Cecil.'

Cecil's face split in a fatuous grin. 'Well, it looks like congratulations are due all around.'

The two men turned away and walked on, deep in conversation together, leaving Francesca and I trailing even further behind them. 'Isn't it simply glorious?' Francesca said.

I glanced at the painting she was looking at – a splurge of red and green paint on a huge white canvas. 'Not really my taste.'

'Actually, I meant being pregnant. I suppose it's particularly glorious when, like me, one's been trying for a baby for so long.'

My legs came to a sudden standstill. 'Did . . . did it take you long to conceive, then?'

'Oh, we must've been trying for a couple of years.'

Mental arithmetic had never been my strong point, but even so, it didn't take more than a millisecond for me to work out that Andy had been hard at it with Francesca all the time he'd been hard at it with me. I thought suddenly of his comment on the day I'd broken off with him, when he'd said in a derisory tone, *'In another minute you'll be telling me you want babies and things,'* and my heart ached with an acute pain.

'One feels so very special when one's pregnant, doesn't one?' Francesca went on in a dreamy voice. I smiled at her weakly: if I felt at all special at the moment, it was that I felt like an especially disgusting piece of shit. 'And the funny thing is, I feel so well. I certainly haven't had any morning sickness or anything like that. Have you?'

Why did I feel so competitive about this? 'Oh, I was just a little bit sick. At first, you know. Just *feeling* sick. Now and then.' Like right now, when I felt like spewing up all over the art gallery's undulating terracotta-tiled floor. Or maybe it was jealousy that was threatening to spill out of me, or the burning, murderous anger I felt towards Andy, or the suicidal anger I felt towards myself. As we walked on, down some stairs and into the next gallery, I caught a glimpse through the window of a clear blue pool where mosaic fishes flashed beneath the water, and I had a sudden urge to fling myself through the plate glass and drown myself there and then.

At last, we caught up with our husbands, who had stopped in front of a vast, colourful painting. 'What's this?' I asked dully.

'C'est la vie,' Cecil mused to himself.

'But what's the painting called?' I persisted with some impatience.

'C'est *La Vie*,' he repeated, still staring up at it. 'Marc Chagall painted it in 1964. I think it's one of my favourite paintings here.'

'Really?' I stared up at the huge canvas. It was covered in images of musicians, acrobats and animals, and dominated by a huge bride and groom who rose up on the lefthand side, carrying a child. 'Isn't it all a bit – well, chocolate-boxey? A bit too pretty-pretty?' I said dismissively.

Cecil shrugged. 'You're not alone in thinking that. Chagall was one of the most accessible twentieth-century painters, and in a funny way, his very accessibility makes him unpopular with contemporary critics. But to me ... to me, he was a great artist. Perhaps, the first true post-Modernist.'

I glanced at Andy and laughed. 'Honestly, Cecil, how can you say that?'

Cecil gave me a long, cool look, then turned back to the canvas. 'He borrowed elements from practically every other movement, from Surrealism to Pointillism, and put them all together to create something of his very own.'

'Doesn't that just make him derivative of everyone else?' I sneered.

'I don't think so.'

Francesca slung a possessive arm around Andy's shoulder.

176

'I agree it's a beautiful painting, Cecil. But what do all the different images mean?'

'Well, that's hard to say,' Cecil continued in an earnest voice. 'On one level, it all adds up to a simple celebration – of music, love, marriage, birth, sexuality, religion ... in short, the magic of Life. Hence the title. On another level ... Well, see the vignette of Paris down there? Maybe the whole painting's a homage to Paris. You know, when Chagall first went there in 1910, Paris seemed to symbolise life and freedom to him. As well it might ... Just think about it, he'd grown up in a close, relatively small, Hassidic community in pre-Revolutionary Vitebsk, a community dominated by religion, tradition and superstition. Sudenly he was part of the wider artistic community, and,' Cecil pointed to the artist's palette in the bottom righthand corner, 'working at a studio called La Palette.' Cecil smiled. 'But maybe one shouldn't speculate too much. After all, to Chagall, it was the visual effect of a painting that was important, not its meaning. He said that one could see all the questions and answers on the canvas. It's all there in front of you, to be experienced rather than analysed. You shouldn't have to use words to explain the images. And, after years of minimalism and conceptual art, and the incomprehensible verbal contortionism of groups like Art is Language, that's a viewpoint I'm coming to sympathise with more and more strongly.'

This was by far the longest speech I'd ever heard Cecil make, and certainly the most intelligent, and it left me frankly flabbergasted. 'How do you know all this?' I asked without thinking.

'Art's my passion, Lisa,' he said. There was a reproachful look in his eyes, which seemed to suggest that I ought to have known this. And before I could ask him why he'd never mentioned it to me before, he added, 'Besides, it's my job to know.'

I was about to ask why, when Andy said, 'What line of work are you in, Cecil?'

'Well, Andy, I'm an art dealer.'

I looked at my husband in astonishment. The words *No, you're not!* sprang to my lips, but I was too surprised to speak. My mouth fell open like a goldfish's when Cecil went on, 'I buy and sell contemporary works for a range of private and corporate clients.'

'Do you specialise in any particular area?' Andy said.

Cecil shrugged. 'Whatever I'm offered, to an extent. Whatever's in the salerooms. And, of course, what my clients want. Johns. Hockney. Stella. The occasional Moore and Picasso. The Saatchi school. For my sins, I was one of Carl André's first patrons. I flirt with the idea of Damien Hirst now and then, but the smell of formaldehyde puts me off.'

Andy laughed. 'Do you have a gallery?'

My open jaw dropped another few inches when Cecil answered, 'I used to. In Bell Street, near Lisson Grove. Oh, and I had a branch in New York for a year. Only a tiny place, on the fringes of SoHo.'

'What was it called?' Andy asked.

'Just the Cecil Brown Gallery.' Cecil blushed modestly as he added, 'After me. My total lack of imagination, I'm afraid.'

Andy scratched his head. 'Hey, that wasn't on the corner of Bleeker and 10th, was it?'

'That's right.'

'Do you know, I think I went in there once? About five years ago. There was a terrific exhibition of young Spanish printmakers.'

'Ah, then that must have been seven years ago – in 1990.'

'Yeah, you're right, because I bought a print there for Fran's twenty-fifth birthday.'

'What, that lovely canary yellow one that we've hung over our bed?' she exclaimed.

Cecil rubbed his chin. 'That wouldn't be a small, abstract lithograph, with a slash of cyan across the top?'

'Well, yes!'

'By someone called Clara Soto, wasn't it?'

'Wow! What an amazing memory you have!'

There was general laughter – mine bordering on the hysterical. 'So what happened to your galleries?' Francesca asked at last.

Cecil shrugged. 'They did all right. But the overheads were . . .' He paused for a moment as his stutter got the better of him, then finished off, '. . . ridiculous. It simply wasn't worth all the hassle. So I sold up everything, and came to live down here. Now I deal on a much smaller scale.'

At long last my powers of speech returned and I gasped, '*Do you?*' And then, when I saw the odd way the three of them were looking at me, I added, '. . . happen to know if there's a lavatory near here?'

As I reeled away, I overheard Andy say, 'You know, Cecil, I'm rather glad I ran into you. I've just been commissioned to do a new weekly series on the visual arts for Channel 4.'

'How marvellous!'

'Yeah, it might be, if I could find a decent presenter and get together the right mix of studio guests and interviewees. Would you mind very much if I picked your brains?'

Downstairs, I retched violently into the lavatory bowl, then sat on the seat for a good ten minutes, my elbows on my knees and my face buried in my hands, attempting to digest what I'd just learned. As far as I'd always known, Cecil was in import-export, and whatever it was he imported and exported had been a matter of such indifference to me that I'd never bothered to find out what it was. How could I have lived with him for so long without discovering that he dealt in contemporary art – just the kind of art, in fact, which I myself loved?

Still in a state of shock, I staggered outside into the garden, and sank down on a low stone wall. A few moments later, Andy came out of the building and sat down beside me. 'That was a bit hairy, wasn't it?' he mumbled.

I gave a big shrug, to show that I didn't care. 'Where's your *wife*?'

'Dunno. Out on the terrace at the back, I think, taking

pictures.' Andy took his cigarettes out of his jeans pocket, and lit one. The poignantly familiar, acrid smell of his Gauloise tobacco wafted up my nose.

'What have you done with Cecil?' I asked.

'I left him in the bookshop. Buying up everything in sight. Hey, are you supposed to do that?' he added as I snatched the cigarette from between his fingers, and put it between my lips. 'Isn't it bad for the foetus?'

'What business is it of yours what I do?'

'Sorry, Puss.'

'And don't call me that.'

'OK! Don't bite my head off!' he snapped back.

After several drags, I handed the cigarette back to him, and he took another drag. A perfect smoke ring hung like a halo above his head before slowly drifting away.

'You never told me you were marrying an art dealer,' Andy said at last.

I choked back the words, 'I never knew,' and instead hissed, 'And you never told me that Francesca left you. Or that she's been trying to conceive for the last two years.'

Andy's face paled again. With a gesture I remembered so well from every time he'd been cornered, he raked his hair into untidy clumps. 'Fran didn't really want to leave me. She only thought she did. For a day or so. She changed her mind pretty sharpish every time I got the suitcase out.'

'Here we go again, Andy!' I said bitterly. '*Plus ça change.* You're so full of bullshit, it isn't true.'

He threw his cigarette onto the tarmac path, and ground it underfoot. 'What does it matter any more? It's all water under the bridge now, isn't it? You're the one who decided to up and get married, for Christ's sake!' I looked away. 'Cecil's an interesting bloke, as it happens. I can see why you shacked up with him.'

'Can you?' I retorted.

'I don't know that I've ever met anyone with such original opinions about the contemporary art scene.'

'Really?' I gave a bored sigh. 'I wish he'd hurry up in there. I want to go home.'

Andy sniffed. 'How *is* life in Monte-Carlo?'

'Fine,' I said shortly. 'How's your famous one-bedroom flat in sunny Shepherd's Bush? Still hanging your clothes on the lavatory cistern, or have you knocked up a set of louvred-door wardrobes from B&Q?'

Andy flashed me a wistful, lopsided smile. 'You know, I do miss you, Puss,' he said rather wearily. 'Life's not much fun without you. If only . . .'

'Yes?'

He shrugged. 'If only we'd managed to work things out . . .'

His hand slid up my spine and squeezed my shoulder through its new padding of fat. The old power was still there. Despite all my anger towards him, I felt myself begin to melt . . .

But, just then, a squat shape squeezed through the doors of the gallery and loped towards us, his pudgy palm raised in greeting. With a lump in my throat, I stood up and walked away from Andy. There was no point in thinking about what might have been. It was all too sad.

'Cecil?' I said as we drove back home along the *moyenne corniche*.

'Yes?'

'Why didn't you ever tell me that you were an art dealer?'

His fingers tightened on the steering wheel. 'But I did, Lisa.'

'No. I'm sure you didn't.'

'Yes. I did. On our first date, as it happens.' At length, with a hint of grievance in his voice – the first I'd ever detected – he remarked, 'I don't think you could have been listening.'

'I was!'

We drove on for another mile or so without speaking. Then Cecil suddenly said, 'What on earth did you think I

181

did? Imported plastic Eiffel Towers from Hong Kong for the French tourist industry?'

'I . . . I don't know.'

There was another long pause. Cecil cleared his throat. 'Well, now that you do know, does it make any difference? I mean, to how you feel about me?'

I gulped guiltily. 'What on earth are you talking about, Cecil?'

'I'm still the same person, aren't I?' he said, without taking his eyes off the road. 'No matter what I do for a living?'

'Of course you are,' I insisted.

But somewhere deep inside me, I had an odd feeling that he was not.

Thirteen

———◆———

I thought that'd be the last I'd ever hear of Andy. But one week later, as I was polishing off a packet of Digestives in bed, the telephone rang and a familiar voice crooned, 'Hello, Puss.'

The biscuit crumbs caught in my throat. 'Andy!' I choked. Delighted as I was that he'd phoned me up, I feigned indignance: 'Really, under the circumstances you should know better than to call me up like this!'

Andy hesitated for a moment. 'Actually, er, it wasn't you I wanted.'

'Sorry?'

'I was looking for your old man. Is he at home?'

'No, he isn't! He's at work. Why on earth do you want to speak to him?'

'Oh, it's a kind of business matter,' was his vague explanation.

'What business can you possibly have to discuss with Cecil?'

'Don't sound so suspicious, Lisa. I've got a sort of proposition to put to him.' Andy hesitated again. 'You know, I really think I ought to talk to him about it before I tell you.'

For the first time in my life, I retaliated with the *w* word. 'I'm Cecil's *wife*, for God's sake! I've got a right to know!'

An uneasy silence echoed across the satellite link. 'What's happened to you, Lisa?' Andy said at last. 'You never used to be like this.'

'Like what?'

183

'So prickly, and so fucking snappy.' I was about to respond with some ascerbic comment when I stopped short. Andy was right. 'You used to be so nice. It's almost like you're unhappy. Look, is everything OK?' A lump the size of a golfball suddenly swelled in my throat. 'Because, you know, you can always talk to me about it, darling.'

'Oh, Andy! The thing is . . .' I was about to confess everything, but stopped myself just in time. If Andy didn't gloat over the mess I'd made of my marriage, he'd be horribly sympathetic; either way, his reaction would leave me distraught. 'I'm fine, really.'

'Look, about Cecil,' he said reluctantly. 'I've had this idea . . . It's a long shot, but . . . You see, I'm still desperately looking for someone to front this new arts programme. If I don't find someone soon, I'm going to lose the commission. Anyway, I wondered whether Cecil would be interested. What do you think?'

'Sorry, I don't quite understand.'

'Do you think Cecil might be interested in auditioning for the job?'

'What job?'

'The presenter's job, of course.'

'The presenter's job,' I repeated numbly. Then I gave a short, sharp laugh. 'You're not really suggesting that you'd like Cecil, to present your television programme?'

'Well, as a matter of fact – yes.'

For a moment, I was dumbstruck. Then I hissed, 'If this is your idea of a sick joke . . .'

'Why should I be joking, Lisa?'

'Cecil? Present a television programme?' My voice rose in a strained crescendo. 'Are you completely mad?'

'I don't think so. It's about the visual arts, and he certainly seems to know the subject. And he's just the sort of offbeat person I'm looking for. A new face.'

I screwed up my eyes and tried in vain to picture my husband's sagging jowls, bulging eyeballs and crinkle-cut forehead beamed into millions of British homes. 'But . . .'

'A kind of male rival to Sister Wendy,' Andy interrupted me. 'An ordinary, intelligent person viewers can identify with, with opinions as provocative as, say, Robert Hughes. I've given this a lot of thought, you know, and I've got a strange hunch Cecil'd be a brilliant presenter.'

'But . . . Really! What about his stutter?'

'*Does* he stutter? Hmm. Funny, I never noticed. It can't be very bad. Besides, does it really matter? Think of the late, great Paddy Campbell.'

'Andy, Cecil's stutter is appalling! And besides, he doesn't look anything like a television presenter! He's so small and . . .' And ugly, I thought but didn't say.

'Height doesn't matter,' Andy said. 'He'll be sitting down most of the time.'

'But he's practically bald, Andy!'

'So's Clive James. I'd have him, only he's tied up elsewhere and I can't afford him. We could always get Cecil a rug, I suppose, if anyone objected. Plenty of male presenters wear them. David Frost. Bruce Forsyth.'

'For goodness' sake, Cecil isn't David Frost or Bruce Forsyth! He hasn't got any personality! I mean,' I added quickly, 'not the kind of personality which'd come over on TV.'

When Andy spoke again, he sounded curiously cold. 'It's strange. You sound like you don't want Cecil to try for the job. I'd have thought you'd be really pleased.'

'I . . . I would be, if I thought he could possibly handle it. But he couldn't. It's just not on.'

'Maybe Cecil ought to be the judge of that,' Andy said with a stubborn snort. 'Look, just give me his work number, will you? I going to ask him myself.'

'Can I get you a drink, madam?' said the air steward, leaning over me.

'A rum and coke, please.'

Cecil sat forward in his seat, and laid a restraining hand on my arm. 'Do you really want rum, darling?'

'Yes, Cecil. Otherwise I wouldn't have asked for it.'

'But the baby . . .?'

I sighed. 'The baby's not going to be born with foetal alcohol syndrome because I drink one rum in nine months. Besides, I'm nearly four months' pregnant. The critical time for brain development's over by now – Dr Semollo told me so the other day. He said a few drinks won't do me any harm at all. In fact, he said a bit of alcohol'd do me good.'

My husband nodded doubtfully. 'I can't imagine an English doctor saying that. Still, I suppose you know what's best.' Cecil turned away and looked out of the window at the snow-covered Alps which rose like a frosted Christmas cake under the path of our Nice–London flight.

'Yes, I do know best, thank you,' I said curtly.

The steward handed me the drink and a packet of peanuts, and turned his attention to Cecil. 'And something for sir?'

'Yes, an . . .'

'You'd better not have anything, Cecil,' I warned, interrupting him. 'You can't turn up at the TV studio reeking of alcohol!'

'An orange juice please. How long have you known me, Lisa?' Cecil said when the steward had moved on.

'I don't know. Six or seven months, I suppose. Why?'

'Haven't you realised yet that I never drink during the day? And rarely at night, either, as it happens.'

'Sorry.'

'Besides, I have no intention of turning up pissed for this screen test.'

'I just thought that, well, you might be nervous.'

'Oh, did you?' Cecil settled back in his seat and buried his head in the *Independent*. Uneasy, I glanced at him through the dark brown veil of my drink. The week before, he'd greeted the news of Andy's job offer with elation but with little surprise – almost like a religious zealot who'd been waiting for 'the call'. Now he was approaching his audition with an eerie calm. Didn't he realise that he was going to be crucified in the studio later that evening? For there was no way he wouldn't make a terrible fool of himself, and, by association, me. Having thought about it all week, I still couldn't understand what had induced Andy to think that Cecil could possibly be a television presenter. I could only imagine that the whole thing was a cruel and elaborate plot designed to humiliate me.

'Are you sure I need to get a haircut today?' Cecil said suddenly, closing his newspaper and tucking it into the pocket of the seat in front. 'There isn't much of it to cut. I'd far rather skip the barber's, and come and have lunch with you.'

'I've already booked an appointment for you.' I glared at the coil of hair piped on top of his head like a swirl of chocolate icing on top of a cup cake, and before I could stop myself, I said, 'Really, you can't possibly go in front of a camera looking like that!'

Cecil frowned up at me over his orange juice. 'Like what?'

I pointed at the offending spiral. 'That.'

'This long bit?' He reached up and patted it. 'But it's the only decent bit of hair I've got left! And it covers my baldest patch.'

'No it doesn't, Cecil. It just draws attention to it. I . . . I hate it,' I admitted.

He looked astonished. '*Do* you?'

A critical demon suddenly took hold of me, and I squinted with open dislike at his navy blue blazer and brown and grey checked trousers. 'And you know, I really think we ought to go shopping this afternoon and buy you some decent clothes to wear tonight, too.'

My husband looked shocked. 'How do you mean, decent?'

'Something smarter, and more stylish,' I said as kindly as I could. And continued, rather less kindly, 'Something that's a little less *fin-de-sixties*, and a little more . . . well, *fin-de-siècle*. Clothes that are less middle-aged.'

'But I am middle-aged, Lisa! Practically. I don't understand. What's wrong with what I'm wearing now?'

I shook my head. 'There's nothing right about it, Cecil. I

187

mean, those trousers – they could have come straight off an American tourist, *circa* 1970. And as for that jacket – well, it looks like you picked it up for £3 in an Oxfam shop.'

He frowned, then said, 'As a matter of fact, it was £5 at a Help the Aged jumble sale. Only joking, Lisa. Actually I bought this in San Remo last year. The man in the shop told me it was the latest fashion.' He gulped down his orange juice thirstily, wiped his mouth and turned his wounded eyes on me. 'So, are you telling me I look terrible?'

The answer was yes, but how could I say so? Yet I knew that if I didn't speak up now I never would. 'Let's just say that you don't exactly make the best of yourself,' I muttered.

'But . . .' Cecil shook his head. 'Why haven't you said any of this before, Lisa? I'd have done something about my appearance if I'd known it mattered to you.'

I took a deep breath. 'I suppose I didn't want to hurt your feelings.'

'Oh!' Inordinately pleased by what he took to be my affection and concern, Cecil picked up my hand and interlocked his fingers with mine. For once, I didn't pull away.

In London, I deposited Cecil at a Mayfair hair salon, with strict instructions that the stylist should do something drastic with him, then I took our taxi on to Selfridges, where I was meeting Lorelei and my mother-in-law for lunch.

'Baby!'

'Lisa, dear!'

I was embraced – warmly by Rita, and briefly by my mother, as though she were afraid of catching something from me – and the hard ball of my pregnant stomach was patted and measured by two pairs of wrinkled hands. 'Ooh, yes! It must be a girl!' Rita pronounced excitedly.

'How can you tell?'

Her dark brown eyes sparkled at me kindly through the misty halo of her cataracts. 'If it's a boy, the weight tends to be all in the front, dear. But – see? – you've put on weight everywhere!' She patted my waist. 'That's a girl for sure, isn't it Lorelei?'

'I never believed that old wives' tale.' My mother passed a palm over her own pancake-flat stomach. 'All I know is, I never put on a single pound with *her*.' She pointed at me with her thumb. 'When I went into labour, the doctors couldn't believe I was nine months gone.'

I squeezed into a chair, while my two mothers sat down on the velvet banquette on the opposite side of the table, where they tilted their heads to one side and examined me as inanely as two demented hens – Lorelei neat and quick with scarlet plumage; Rita plump, grey, and carelessly untidy, like one of those rare breeds which have tufts of feathers sprouting in all directions from their heads.

'Let me look at you, hon!' Lorelei's nose twitched. 'Jesus, you look godawful. Doesn't she just, Rita? Her cheeks are all pasty, and there are zits on her chin.'

Rita reached across the table and squeezed my hand. 'Lisa always looks lovely to me.'

'Her hair's going grey at the top. She needs a rinse. You need a rinse, Lisa.'

'Thanks for telling me, Mummy. Actually I had my colour done last week. Can we order? I'm starving.' I glanced at the menu. 'I haven't had anything since breakfast, and we've been travelling since eight.'

'You know, you really should eat regularly now. You owe it to the baby. How's the morning sickness? Gone yet?'

'It's a little better, thanks.' I picked up the menu and scanned it. 'I think I'll have the cottage cheese salad.'

Rita's face fell. 'Oh, I wouldn't do that dear, if I were you. It might kill the baby.'

'What?'

'Cottage cheese. Soft cheese can have listeria. Especially that smelly French cheese. I hope you haven't been eating that?'

My mother glared at me as if I were a truculent six-year-old. 'Don't worry, Rita. Cecil'll have made sure she hasn't been.

And now, she'll have something else. Have something else, honey. Something safer.'

I scanned the menu again. 'OK, I'll have an omelette and chips.'

There was a short pause. Then Rita said, 'Is that wise, Lisa? I don't want to interfere or anything, but what about salmonella poisoning? I don't think I'd risk eggs, if I were you – not in your present state.'

'But . . .' I gritted my teeth. 'OK.' This time I waited till the waitress was taking the orders, then said, 'I'll have a glass of white wine and a cheeseburger.'

'Are you crazy?' my mother snapped. 'I don't want my grandchild born with Mad Cow Disease!'

Why not? I thought. At least then she'd have something in common with it.

'So,' Rita said after I'd ordered the only uncontentious thing on the menu – a dry roll and a bowl of tomato soup. 'How's the new book coming along? Finished yet?'

'Not quite.'

'Of course not! You must be far too busy redecorating the flat and getting it ready for the baby to bother with any of that.'

My mother smirked at me across the table. 'I always told you that you'd lose interest in that writing crap once you got married. As you can see, I was right. Now, tell us something interesting,' she added. 'What's all this about your wonderful husband going on TV?'

An hour later, I trudged down Bond Street, where I'd arranged to meet Cecil. Lunch with my mother had left me feeling like a wrung-out J-cloth – the kind that's been used to scrub a floor for six weeks then boiled to the point of disintegration. Her verbal joustings, her sly probings, her less-than-subtle digs about my work, my personality and my appearance – why did I let them all get to me? Why couldn't I rise above her criticism? Why couldn't I just let her get on with being horrible to me and not let it destroy that fragile sense of myself which I'd painfully built up over the years?

I crossed Brook Street and entered the portals of Emporio Armani, where the rap version of 'Killing Me Softly' was playing over the loudspeaker system. A flame-haired beauty in a severe black trouser suit smiled at me pityingly. 'Can I help you?' Her voice belied her thoughts – no, she couldn't help me, because someone who looked as bad as I did was beyond help, almost beyond the pale. 'Are you looking for anything in particular?'

'Just my husband. Thanks.' As I stomped across the wooden floor, past the racks of immaculate suits, jackets and shirts, I caught sight of myself in a large mirror, and recoiled in shock. Was that old frump really me? The navy-blue coat that had looked so smart when I'd set off from France that morning was covered in fluff, and the front glistened with fallen strands of my lank, lifeless hair. My skirt was as creased as crumpled tissue paper, and my white blouse was straining at every button over my pneumatic, hormone-enriched breasts. The black khol with which I'd underlined my eyes had smudged onto my cheekbones, and an oil sump was seeping through the pores in my nose. That willowy, Modiglianiesqe beauty I'd once been famed for had completely disappeared; four months of pregnancy had changed me into a lumpy, depressed-looking Lucian Freud portrait, complete with sharp-focus broken veins and technicolour spots. I really must pull myself together. When I got back to Monaco, I'd book in for some beauty treatments. And I'd take the Spoiled Wives Club's advice and buy some designer maternity clothes . . .

'Lisa?' called a disembodied voice. 'Is that you?'

'Cecil?'

A hand appeared over the top of the nearest fitting-room door and waved at me. 'I'm in here, trying some things on. I won't be a tick. No, no,' he continued in a muffled voice, 'this jacket's much too large for me.'

'I'll try and find signor the *smallest* size.'

I sank down on a nearby sofa, stretched out my aching legs, and sunk in a pit of self-loathing, watched as a string of ever-more beautiful people drifted past me. Everyone except me was tall, skinny, and groomed to cat-walk standards, especially the shop assistants. Maybe Armani had some kind of invisible filter on the door, which made sure that only smart, good-looking people entered the premises. In which case it was a miracle that Cecil and I had been allowed in. I looked like a poor relation. I looked old enough to be everyone's mother. And then it hit me – *I was old enough to be their mother!*

Cecil's voice drifted under the fitting-room door, grating on my already shredded nerves. 'Oh yes, that's much better. But are these trousers the right size for me?'

'A little tight in ze waist, perhaps. And far too long. Let me pin them up for you, sir.'

I rubbed the two plump sausages which had once been my slender ankles, and as I stroked my calf, my fingers touched on something raised and hard. A varicose vein, protruding from my skin like one of those tiny wormy, sandy mounds you see on the beach when the tide goes out. My whole body was falling apart . . .

'Well?'

I looked up. Standing in front of me was a rather arresting-looking, stocky stranger dressed in a beige suit.

I did a double-take. 'Cecil!' I gasped.

For Cecil was virtually unrecognisable. The hairdresser had certainly taken the drastic action I'd suggested. Not only had the offending spiral been removed from the crown of his head in a brutal yet merciful act of surgery, but the rest of his hair, which had previously hung in untidy, thin strands, like the *Before* picture in a hair-transplant advertisement, had been clipped to a scant quarter-inch all over, leaving Cecil now practically hairless. Yet, strangely, this hairlessness had the opposite effect one would have expected – it made Cecil look less bald.

It had an extraordinary effect on the shape of his head, too, for his skull no longer looked outlandishly large, and his strong features seemed to fit better on his face, which had taken on the patrician air of a grand, if rather debauched, Roman senator – the heavy lips satirical, the large nose sensual and noble, the knobbly forehead furrowed with knowledge instead of anxiety. His wet, amphibian eyes no longer protruded from their sockets with the pathetic and stupid expression of a kicked dog; they seemed instead to bulge with a profound intelligence. His cheekbones stood out proudly above his jowls, and a strong jawline I'd never noticed before was clearly visible above the folds of his triple chin.

But, wait a minute! It wasn't a triple chin any more, just an ordinary double chin, and not a very large one at that! In fact, it fitted quite respectably into the soft collar of that black jersey Armani shirt. As my eye descended slowly along the softly padded shoulders of the jacket Cecil was wearing and between the crisply cut Armani lapels, I realised with a shock that, while I had been growing steadily fatter since the summer, my husband had been losing weight. Not a lot of weight, true, but enough to stop his pendulous breasts from jutting forward against the clingy shirt fabric like the two soft, over-ripe mangoes they'd once been; and enough to prevent his paunch ballooning over the top of his waistline in an undulating, squidgy wave; as my own now did.

Arms akimbo, Cecil walked towards the nearest mirror, threw back his shoulders and drew himself up several inches in height. Critical, though not damning, he gazed at his altered reflection with the same surprise and amazement with which I did. A slow, proud smile of satisfaction crept across his face.

I shook my head. This was real life, I reminded myself, not a fairy tale. It would take more than an expensive haircut and an Armani suit to change this particular frog into a handsome prince. Still, the transformation of Cecil was extraordinary. Why, he no longer looked repulsive! He still looked ugly, of course, but it was a sort of OK-ugliness. Quite an intelligent ugliness, as a matter of fact. The kind of strong, solid ugliness that made a man look rather interesting and – yes! – almost attractive, if in an ugly kind of way.

As he watched me staring at him, Cecil's smile faded and the toes inside his old black socks curled against the polished wood floor. Leaving the mirror, he walked towards me, rolling his eyes with that old fearful look which made me despise him so much. 'I don't know,' he said hesitantly. 'You're the boss, Lisa, so I want you to be brutally frank about this. It's nice – but is it me?'

Fourteen

'*Run autocue.*'

There was silence in the studio. Cecil's tongue, multiplied six times on the bank of six TV monitors, flicked out and licked his lips. Six pairs of Cecil's eyes rolled in a clockwise circle, and smiled fearfully at the screen. 'Um, sorry, Andy. Do you want me to start reading *now*?' his six mouths said.

'Yes . . . No, hold on a moment.' Standing beside me in the cramped control room of the Soho recording studio, Andy scrutinised the monitors carefully. 'Before we do – can the camera pull in a little?' As the camera operator wheeled her camera forward, Cecil's face loomed even larger on the screens, and the pores of his nose came into sharp focus. 'That's enough,' Andy said. 'Back just a little. Yes, right there. Can we have that top light down a bit, please? That's great. Right, Cecil, are you ready? We'll try to run through now. And relax. We're not recording yet, we just want to test the sound levels. OK? Everyone set? Run autocue.'

I looked through the sound-proofed window and into the next-door studio, where Cecil was sitting behind a desk in a high-backed, swivel leather chair. He caught my eye, and winked at me. Then he looked back at the autocue and began to read. 'Good evening, and welcome to the programme.' Here he paused for a moment to clear his throat. 'Tonight we'll be looking at the way in which . . . in which post . . . post-Modernism has . . .'

Like an organist playing a complicated symphony, the studio director sitting at the control desk pulled and pushed at the bank of levels and keys. 'Can you get him to sit still,

Andy?' he muttered as, squinting short sightedly in front of him, Cecil wriggled forwards and backwards in his seat. 'The sound level's all over the place.'

'Hold on a minute, can you, Cecil?' Andy said into the intercom. Cecil's voice petered out again. 'We've got a small technical hitch in here. Can you go back to the top and start again? And this time, if you can, try not to move about so much when you're reading. OK?'

Cecil blinked anxiously, and adjusted his earpiece. 'Oh, was I . . .? Sorry.' During the short wait while the autocue rewound, he shifted uncomfortably in his chair and coughed several times.

'OK. From the top again. Ready?'

'Ready. Ahem. Good evening and welcome to the pro-gramme. Tonight we'll be looking at . . . at the way that . . . that post-M . . . post-M-Modernism has affected the . . .' The more Cecil stuttered, the deeper the blush that rushed to his cheeks. For a while he battled on against his impediment, then, throwing his hands in the air, he juddered to a complete halt, and turning to the window behind which we were standing, said in a crestfallen voice, 'Sorry, Andy. I've lost it.'

I heard Andy swear under his breath, and I shot him a furious look which said *I told you so*. 'Don't worry, Cecil, that was great,' he said into the mike. 'We've got the sound levels right, and we'll try another run through in a minute. Remember, if it goes wrong we can always do it again.'

Cecil looked dubious. 'But . . . my stammer . . . I . . .'

'Don't worry about it. It doesn't matter. Just relax. And next time, I want you to talk to the camera as if it was a real person. A good friend.'

Though Cecil nodded, he looked crestfallen. He took a sip of water from the glass on the desk in front of him, wiped his mouth, and mopped his brow.

'Where'd you find your new Melvyn Bragg?' the studio director muttered to Andy. 'Local speech therapy centre?'

To my surprise, this remark made me so angry that I

ould have killed the man. 'It's not his fault that he stutters!' hissed.

Andy gnawed on his thumbnail. 'He's probably just ervous, that's all.'

I moved closer to him and whispered, 'Don't say I didn't varn you about it. I wish you'd listened to me!'

He glanced at me in an abstracted fashion. 'Oh, do hut up!'

'I just don't like seeing Cecil humiliated like this,' I persisted. First you get all his hopes up for no reason, then you dash hem down. It's just not fair on him!'

With a furious glance at me, my erstwhile lover bolted rom the control room. Wreathed in reassuring smiles, he eappeared in the next-door studio a moment later and rouched down in front of Cecil, his back towards me. Vhatever it was he was telling Cecil, my husband obviously lisagreed, for he was shaking his head.

'What's he saying to him?' I muttered.

The studio director put his feet up on the mixing desk, lit cigarette, and threw the match into his coffee cup. 'Usual rap pep talk,' he said. 'You know: relax. Forget you're being ideoed. Imagine you're at home, watching TV and having wank.' He laughed. I looked through the sound-proofed vindow again. Cecil had stood up as if to leave but Andy nade him sit down again. A bead of sweat began to trickle nto the crease at the top of Cecil's nose.

A moment later, Andy rejoined us. 'OK, we're going to ave another go.'

'What's the point?' I cried. 'You can see that Cecil can't ope with it!'

'Maybe he can't,' Andy muttered, tapping his fingers. Maybe he can.'

'But, Andy . . .'

Andy's eyes flashed at me like blue fire. 'Look Lisa, you're ot helping matters. I've got a big investment in pulling this ff. I'm sorry, but I just don't need you interfering right now. 'ete,' he went on, turning to the studio director, 'we'll try him

on autocue again, and if that doesn't work this time, we'll d
the interview and see how that goes.'

Unable to watch this process of humiliation any longer,
scribbled a note for Cecil, fled from the studio, and took
taxi back to our hotel. On the way, I ran through the li
of all my past lovers and, seething with self-hatred, I aske
myself again and again why, after going out with all tho
really quite acceptable men, I'd ended up marrying a frog lik
Cecil. What was I *doing* with him? I had to face it: Cecil wa
one of life's losers, a person who had no talent for anything
that was, unless you counted his unerring talent for ruinin
any opportunity that accidentally came his way.

Back in our hotel room, I kicked Cecil's spare shoes fro
my path, plucked his old blazer from the floor where he'
dropped it earlier and, with a furious sweep of my hand
swiped his ghastly old check trousers from the bed. As the
fell to the floor, a mess of coins, broken Polo mints an
screwed-up receipts fell out of the pockets and scattere
across the floor.

'Oh, shit!' I yelled.

I dropped to my knees and began to scoop everything up
Then I stopped and burst into tears. Had I really been reduce
to this – a miserable lump scrabbling around on a hotel-roo
floor, pregnant by a man who didn't love me, picking up th
belongings of a man I loathed? I hurled the old Polos int
the waste paper basket and, gathering up all the little piece
of paper, sat down on the bed to sort them out: this one
Visa receipt from today's shopping trip to Armani; that one
bill from the café at Nice airport; this, an American Expres
receipt from the snack meal we'd had three days before i
Monacoville; that, a torn and rather grubby business car
belonging to someone called Flamberto, in Milan. And wha
was this little scrap here?

I undid the tightly folded square of paper and smoothed
out. For a moment, I gazed blankly down at the sheet of crea
vellum without really seeing it. Then the spidery copperplat
calligraphy and the unusual purple ink swam into focus.

Sniffing back my tears of self-pity, I glanced at the letter with a dullish curiosity. There was no date or address at the top. Instead, the sender had scrawled in huge letters, with a dramatic flourish, *Darling C . . .*

Darling C . . .

Just had to write and thank you for last night. Did the earth move for me? Did Picasso change the face of modern painting?! You were so sweet! (And so sexy!) When I woke up and found you'd gone, I could hardly bear it. To think that you were out of contact! Wanted to ring you, but knew that I couldn't . . . Please come again before too long (unintentional pun – but I mean it – in all ways!)

Good luck in London. I just know you'll be brilliant. I'll be with you in spirit . . . How I wish I was going with you! You deserve a companion who really cares.

Maybe I'll be naughty and turn up anyway! Our usual room, our usual hotel.

Muchest love,

S

PS: Next time, let's make it four *times in a night!!!*

I shook my head, and reread the letter. Then, falling back onto the bed in a state of near paralysis, I read it for a third time.

Dearest C . . . Surely that initial C couldn't possibly be referring to Cecil? But if not Cecil, then whom? And that *Good luck in London* – what else could it allude to other than the screen test? Once more, I ran through the last paragraph, my cheeks red with shame at the unavoidable implications of the last two sentences: *Wish I was going with you. You deserve a companion who really cares.*

As shocked as a mother who'd just discovered a half-empty condom packet in her thirteen-year-old son's bedside drawers, I drew in a horrified breath. What this letter seemed to imply was simply impossible! Because Cecil was sexless – as sexless as one of those plastic children's dolls which, instead of having

199

genitals, have a clean, smooth bump in their groin and an indented Y at the back. Cecil and sex just didn't go together. He wasn't interested in sex! Why, he couldn't be, because since our ill-fated wedding night, he'd never made a single move on me!

Now, suddenly, I understood why.

Cecil was having an affair.

Holding the letter out in front of me as if it was some lethal contaminant, I paced up and down the bedroom. Cecil was having an affair! And not just any old affair: a hot, steamy, torrid affair. I mean, what did that *Let's make it* four *times a night* and those three exclamation marks in the postscript imply if not that Cecil and his lover had already made it up to three? Not that I'd ever put much store on numbers myself: one bonk a night, properly executed with the right mix of genuine affection and passion, had always been enough for me. But still . . . Three times a night? It was embarrassing to think that Cecil – my sexless Cecil – was capable of such a thing. Had done such a thing. With another woman.

For some unaccountable reason, I began to feel shivery and I crawled into bed. Suddenly, a lot of little things I'd never really thought about before began to fall into place: all the evenings when Cecil had worked late at his office; his odd nights away 'on business'; his long lunch meetings which lasted well into the afternoons; those early morning meetings he ran off to so eagerly; those increasingly frequent phone calls from his office in which he told me that 'something had come up' and he was going to be an hour late home. Of course, of course! Cecil was having an affair! How could I have been so blind as not to have realised before?

Had my coldness driven him into the affair, I wondered? That *our usual room, our usual hotel* business at the end implied that their *liaison* had been going on for some time. Or had his fling with the mysterious S-woman started even before Cecil and I had met? As I contemplated this, a huge weight lifted from my shoulders, settling instead in the middle of my forehead. Good God! Maybe the problem with our marriage wasn't that I didn't fancy Cecil. Maybe he didn't fancy me!

If Cecil had been having an affair with S when we'd met, why hadn't he married her instead of me? But perhaps S was married already, and I, who'd thought myself so important to Cecil, was in reality a stoodge chosen to keep his family content, and maybe S's family, too. To think that I'd felt guilty all this time for marrying him under false pretences, when all along it'd been he who'd inveigled me into the unsuitable match.

But I was getting carried away. For all I knew, Cecil had only recently met this . . . this . . . this *bitch*. With a pounding heart, I reread the letter closely, as if by searching between the lines of loopy script I might find clues to his lover's identity. Was she older or younger than I was? More intelligent or more stupid? Was she plain, pretty or devastatingly attractive? Did I know her? Had I met her? Did everyone in Monte-Carlo know about Cecil's affair with her except me?

When the telephone rang, I jumped as if I'd been bitten. 'Yes?'

'Lisa?'

I gulped. 'Oh, Cecil!'

My husband hesitated. Then, 'Are you all right?' he said curiously.

'Of course!' A vision of him in bed with a woman suddenly flashed in front of my eyes, Cecil on top, his naked buttocks pumping away like pistons, with S half-hidden underneath him, her legs wide apart . . .

There was a short pause before Cecil said, 'When I found out you'd gone home, I thought perhaps you weren't feeling well?'

'Didn't you get my note?'

'No.'

'I, er, I felt a bit sick. But I'm OK. I . . . I'm just very tired,' I stammered. As you probably are, too, I thought. I mean, three times a night is good going for anyone, let alone a man in his mid-forties!

There was was another, longer pause. Then Cecil said, 'Well, aren't you going to ask me about it?'

For a horrid moment I thought that he must have installed video surveillance in the hotel room and already knew that I'd found the letter. 'Ask you about what?' I snapped.

'My screen test.' He sounded hurt, almost aggrieved.

'Oh yes! Sorry.' What had S said? *You deserve a companion who really cares.* 'How did it go?'

'Well, actually, it wasn't at all bad.'

'Really?'

'In fact, once I got used to it, I think it went very well.'

'Sure.'

'Your friend Andy seemed extremely pleased with me.'

'*Did he?*' I tried to control the incredulity in my voice, but without success.

'You don't have to sound so surprised.'

'I'm not! It's just that . . . well, I only saw the beginning.'

'Oh, that!' Cecil sounded unusually blasé. 'It took me a few minutes to get used to the autocue. But once I got the hang of it, I was fine. I had to do an interview afterwards. Andy said that went very well, too. As a matter of fact, everyone said that I'm a natural presenter. Whatever that means.'

I conquered my speechlessness enough to breathe, 'Cecil! That's marvellous!'

'And do you know something, Lisa? Once the cameras were rolling I didn't stutter once. I have a feeling that I might well get this job, you know,' he said smugly.

'That's unbelievable news, Cecil!' Judging from what I'd witnessed in the studio, it certainly was. But, as I was only just finding out, my husband was a man of secret talents and hidden parts. 'But Cecil . . .'

'What?'

'Do you think you'd want the job? I mean, did you enjoy doing it?'

'Oh *yes*! Yes, I *loved* it.' He sighed as wistfully as a man recalling an earth-shattering sexual experience – or maybe my imagination was running away with me. I swallowed hard, to try to rid myself of the sudden feeling that everything familiar in my life was about to fall apart.

'W-well done, Cecil!' I stammered. 'I'm so proud of you.'

'Thanks. Actually,' he giggled, 'I'm feeling rather proud of myself. What are you doing now?'

'Me? Oh, just watching television,' I lied, 'in bed.' The very word *bed* made a chili-pepper flush rush to my cheeks. 'Why?'

'It's only that . . . well, Andy asked if I wanted to pick up something to eat on the way home . . . At the Caprice, I'm afraid.' He chuckled. 'Not your favourite restaurant, as I recall. I'm sure he wouldn't mind if you came too.'

A meal with three-times-a-night Cecil and my ex-lover Andy, at our old haunt? Would I be able to look either of them in the face? 'No. No, thanks. You go. I'm sure you've got lots to talk about.'

It seemed meaningful that Cecil didn't try to persuade me to join them. Instead, he said, 'OK, then,' in a tone that implied relief. 'Goodnight, Lisa.'

'Goodnight.'

'Oh, and Lisa?'

'Yes?'

'Don't bother to wait up for me. Andy and I have a lot to talk about. I might be very late back.'

I tossed and turned in bed, convinced that Cecil's lover had come to London, and that after the meal Cecil was going to meet her at their *usual hotel*. My mind spun with a question which I couldn't for the life of me answer: why did I feel so betrayed at the thought of Cecil's infidelity? Since I had no desire whatsoever to have sex with him, why should I give a damn if he had sex with someone else?

The room was dark when I awoke. The digital clock on the front of the TV said half past four. The faint hum of the air conditioning was augmented by the sound of soft, peaceful snoring. Cecil was asleep beside me, in the other twin bed

I propped myself up on an elbow and peered at him through

the darkness. His naked shoulder rose like a pale, softly sloping mountain from the wrinkled glacier of a turned-back sheet. For the first time since our wedding night, Cecil wasn't wearing pyjamas. Strangely disturbed, I slipped out of bed, and went into the bathroom for a pee. As I came out, the shaft of white, fluorescent light behind me lit up his new suit, which he'd hung on the back of a chair.

I checked that Cecil was still asleep, then quietly searched his pockets for fresh evidence of his illicit liaison. Finding nothing, I tiptoed over to the bed and looked down at the sleeper facing me with detached curiosity. Cecil lay on his left side, his shaved head sideways on the pillow, his mouth half-open, his double chin tucked into his massive neck. The semicircles of his closed eyelids lent his face a kind of false innocence which I now knew for a fact that he didn't possess. This was no sexless doll, I reminded myself, this was Mr Three-times-a-night. *So sweet and so sexy.*

As if it had a will of its own, my hand reached out towards him. I snatched it back. Before I could turn away, my arm, as unstoppable as a robotic one on a Toyota production line, reached out again. During the six months we'd been married, I'd never once seen Cecil without clothes on, nor had I had the slightest desire to; even at the Beach Club, when I saw him in his swimming trunks, I'd found the very idea of his nakedness repulsive. Suddenly, that repulsion seemed to have changed into a compulsion. I just had to know what Cecil looked like.

With the stealth of a voyeur creeping up on his victim, I took hold of the corner of the sheet and lifted it a couple of inches. When Cecil didn't stir, I lifted it a little higher. Now I could see his chest, and the shadowy gorge of cleavage between his pectorals. Another few inches and I could see outlined the dark curve of his stomach as it flopped gently onto the mattress.

Cecil snored on. I searched his face for signs of wakefulness, and finding none, lifted the sheet a fraction higher, then a fraction higher still, uncovering his tightly clenched hands, and then his hips, and then his legs: the left one pointing straight down into the darkness, the right bent at the knee and folded over his left thigh, hiding his genitals from my sight.

Cecil gave a loud snort. His hands unclenched, his fingers stretched. With a wild gesture, he flung his right arm above his head, rolled over onto his back and spread his legs.

Now I could see all of him, laid out before me like some mysterious moonlit landscape: the softly curving hillocks of his pectorals bearing large, flower-like nipples; the soft plateau of his stomach in which was set the mysterious pool of his belly button; the narrow copse of dark body hair which gradually thickened over his lower abdomen and spread out into a thick, black forest. And there, deep in the forest's delta, lay the pale caterpillar of his penis – a long, thick, tender creature, flopping flaccidly towards his legs.

Transfixed, I stared at this for a long while, wondering how it might look when erect.

Then, feeling thoroughly confused and disgusted with myself, I dropped the sheet over Cecil's nakedness, and crept back to my cold twin bed.

Fifteen

Dear C –
Before I met you, I thought 'orgasm' was that transparent silky fabric which women wear to the Red Cross Ball.
You have taught me better.

S

*   *   *

C . . .
I hope you don't mind me writing. I promise there are still no strings attached. But there was something I wanted to tell you the other night, and I did not dare. It's just that – well, you're the best lover I've ever had.
There, now I've said it! I promise I'll stop blushing before we next meet.
Don't let this make you too conceited. Remember, you are quite perfect as you are.

S

*   *   *

You wonderful, wonderful man!
What did you do to me yesterday? I only have the vaguest memories – all as delicious as those tartes aux fruits. But do not come to see me again until la semaine prochaine – when I hope you will come and come and come again. My little 'cerise' is quite bruised with over-use and needs a rest . . .

S

*   *   *

Cher C –

Did I ever tell you that the sound of your name has become like an aphrodisiac to me? We were out at Rampoldi's the other night with G, F and B, and one of them – F, I think it was – mentioned you, and I nearly had an 'organza' on the spot.

I don't think anyone guessed, even though I spilled my espresso all down my new, white Chacock dress, which is, as a consequence, completely ruined. I want you to know that I hold you personally responsible for the damage. Expect me to demand reparation in kind.

S

*　　*　　*

Darling . . .

Yesterday was so drôle! I don't think I have ever laughed as much with anybody as I do with you. And in bed, too!

I simply don't understand why a certain person – who shall remain nameless – doesn't appreciate you. Still, there's no accounting for bad taste. Believe me, I'm very, very, very grateful that her lack of it is my gain!

S

*　　*　　*

Dear Chef,

I can hardly wait for next week's meal. I'm a starving woman, craving food. Give me British Toad-in-the-hole again! (and again, and again!)

Please, please, please come to see me sooner than we arranged! I'll find the time somehow, and I'm sure she won't notice if you aren't there. But beware – every time I think of you, I salivate like a wild beast . . .

La Dineuse

Cecil got the presenter's job, and Andy got his commission. And, while Cecil was away in London, having endless discussions and meetings with my ex-lover, I had ample opportunity to rifle through his possessions in search of more letters from his current one.

I found plenty, all written on the same thick creamy vellum in that same, loopy handwriting, penned in the same, affected purple ink. Each letter had been folded into a similar tight, neat square – the paper scored by Cecil's thumbnail and pressed with anal precision into a tiny parcel that could be easily hidden away. In his wardrobe; under a pair of old espadrilles on the back balcony; inside an old suitcase; pushed into the cushions of our new Charles Eames leather chair; behind a box of plasters in Cecil's bathroom cabinet; beneath a pile of Y-fronts in his underwear drawer; there were letters stashed everywhere.

As I unfolded each one, so I unfolded Cecil's secret life and, perhaps, the key to his character. What a revelation! For according to S's letters my dullard of a husband was a brilliant, amusing, over-sexed lover who got his kicks from making love in the most public places in town: behind a palm tree in the Casino gardens; in a doorway in the deserted Metropole shopping mall; under a tarpaulin in a Riva speedboat boat in the harbour; in a car parked in front of Prince Rainier's palace, within earshot of the guards.

Darling C,

I always wondered if anything saucy went on in the cabanas at the Beach Club when it closed at night. Now I know.

That was a very close shave! Do you think that Arnaud spotted us when he walked past? As for what we did afterwards . . . Well! Making love as one swings from a 2.5 metre diving board may only be a little variation on 'swinging from a chandelier', as you insisted, but it was certainly new to me!

S

* * *

My Cecil had done *that*? *There*? Was nowhere sacred? I mean, the thought of him dangling above the swimming pool – the pool in which I swam every day – suspended, I imagined, by his arms, with his legs locked around this mysterious *S* . . . It was ludicrous! It was risible! It was bizarre! It was deeply shocking.

Is it any surprise that my curiosity was aroused?

C . . .

Who would have thought that we could get away with that? I was never aware that a secret corridor existed behind that ancient gilt mirror. Your knowledge of the nooks and crannies of the Hôtel de Paris never fails to amaze me. Likewise, your knowledge of my nooks . . .

You really ought to write a guide book. To what, I shan't say.

S

*   *   *

Who was Cecil's lover, and what was she like? She was certainly no mindless bimbo, that much was clear, for her letters were concise, to the point and annoyingly witty. But what did she look like? Was her hair curly or straight, dark or fair? Was she English, French, Italian, American? Married or single? Merely attractive, or heart-stoppingly beautiful? Had I passed her in the street? Did I sit next to her at the hairdresser's? Was that her, choosing Camembert in the market? Or that woman over there, pushing a loaded trolley around the supermarket in Fontvieille?

The streets of the principality had never been so full of gorgeous, smart, well-dressed women. I suspected them all of being *S*. I saw her everywhere.

The deadline for handing in my manuscript came and went. A fortnight later, Elena phoned me up. 'Please don't give me any more of your excuses, Lisa,' she said in a clipped voice. 'I really don't want to know. I've just phoned to tell you that, at great cost to both our professional credibilities, I've put off publication of the next Mahonia Medmenham novel for a year. So, you've now got till next September to finish it.'

Thoroughly ashamed of myself, I mumbled, 'Thank you, thank you! Oh, Elena, you're such a marvellous friend.'

'Not so, Lisa.' She sighed impatiently. 'Don't expect any more favours from me. If it's not on the table by then, you're on your own.'

Outwardly, life with Cecil went on much as usual. The winter months crawled by. House painters from Menton arrived to paint the flat, Alexandre presented us with an outrageous bill, and the rest of our new furniture arrived. Festooned with chi-chi cushions, Provençal swags, rustic armoires and huge arrangements of dried lavender, my new home looked virtually unrecognisable. By now, so did I.

In public, Cecil and I appeared as a happy couple. He played the part of a dutiful husband, just as I, in turn, played the part of a dutiful wife. In reality, he was playing around behind my back and I . . . Well, I wasn't playing at all. No, I was rotting like one of those limp vegetables that lurks at the bottom of the fridge. I was waiting for something to happen to break the deadlock I found myself in. I was waiting for Robert to have a change of heart and turn up and spirit me away, and I was waiting for the parasite distorting my stomach and my life to disappear. But Christmas came and went without Robert so much as telephoning, and the parasite continued to usurp my belly, making me more bloated by the day.

Since Cecil had clearly found happiness in the arms of another woman, why didn't he leave me? I asked myself time and again as he brushed my now-plump hand with familiarity during dinner at Rampoldi's, or put up a jolly front – every inch (except the six most important ones) the 'expectant father' – when our parents telephoned. Could he really be staying for the sake of the baby – a baby that he knew wasn't his? However emotionally dense he was, he must know that I didn't love him, and I was equally sure that he didn't love me. He'd certainly stopped following me around with that hang-dog, wounded expression that had driven me so mad when I'd met him. In fact, the new, post-haircut Cecil scarcely looked at me at all. He was too busy even to talk to me most of the time. Work, and S, occupied every hour of his day; and S, and work, his nights.

The only conclusion I could come to was that, for some unfathomable reason, the odd status quo suited Cecil. To my chagrin, it seemed to suit him far better than it suited me.

> C . . .
>
> *You are a very naughty boy, and you'll get me into terrible trouble one of these days! What would we have done if someone had walked in on us? You ought to know that I'm not the kind of woman who does that sort of thing – at least, I wasn't, until I met you . . .*
>
> *For your future reference: the time it takes the Europa lift to travel from the rez-de-chaussée to the vingt-cinquième étage and back again is just too short!*
>
> S

There I was, stuck in a foreign country, emotionally down at heel and physically up the spout. By myself, most of the time. I grew quite aggrieved at the lack of attention from Cecil. He'd get up at six and rush off to his office, he'd seldom return for lunch, and he'd work late every other evening; or so he told me; S's letters indicated otherwise. Twice a week, he'd dash off to London for so-called 'meetings'. If that wasn't bad enough, on the increasingly rare occasions when he was actually at home, the portable phone was always nailed to his ear. As he strode from room to room and out onto the terrace, deep in conversation with Andy, his free hand flailing the air like a one-armed windmill, he flung out names like 'Mach', 'Tarentino', 'Howard Hodgkin' and 'Carl André'. 'No, no,

Andy. I really think we ought to include him out – to pinch a phrase. However, if we could get someone like George Steiner to comment on that one? Hmm? Or perhaps you could persuade Germaine to say something? No. Ah, I get your point. Robert Hughes, then? Ye-es. Maybe we ought to talk this through face to face.'

And he'd be off to London again the next day for another crucial lunch meeting at the current most trendy restaurant to persuade whichever hot academic, painter or critic he and Andy were currently pursuing to be interviewed on screen. After lunch, Cecil would invariably manage to find time to stop off for another shopping binge at Armani, or Browns for Men, or the Paul Smith shop in Covent Garden, invariably followed by another session in the hairdresser's chair.

'Never in the field of human vanity was so much charged by so many for cutting so short so little,' he quipped on his return one evening in January, dropping three carrier bags of shirts onto the bed and running his hand over the grey velvet pile of his newly shorn scalp. 'Does my hair look better than it did this morning?'

I parked my boat-size posterior beside his shopping bags. 'It looks exactly the same.'

An expression of profound disappointment furrowed my husband's brow, and he ran to inspect his image in the eagle mirror in the hall with a heartfelt, 'Surely not? They charged me nearly forty quid!' Cocking his head to one side, he smiled at his reflection curiously. 'Do you know, Lisa, I can't understand why I clung on to that old hairstyle for so long. I feel like a new man since I've had it cut.'

'You are a new man – a thoroughly conceited one. Do stop admiring yourself and talk to me. I've been by myself all day.'

'Poor thing! Wasn't Zuzu around at all? I'm not admiring myself, actually. Well, maybe I am, a little. Making up for lost time.'

'I've made supper. I'm starving. Do come and eat.'

The face in the mirror assumed a crestfallen expression. 'What, now? Oh dear! Sorry, but I really must drop into the office first. There's a pile of work waiting for me.'

I bit back the words *I bet that's not all that's waiting for you* and said, 'But, Cecil, you've only just come home! And I've made you chicken chasseur!' Well, I hadn't actually made it, as it happened, I'd bought it from the delicatessen under the Mirabeau Hotel. But the principle was still the same.

'Oh, did you?' Cecil glanced at his watch, then with gritted teeth shook his head. 'I just haven't got time, Lisa. And you really shouldn't have bothered. I picked up something on the plane.'

And so, as usual, within an hour of Cecil's return, I found myself sitting alone at our new, distressed oak dining-room table, eating more than enough food for two. I gulped everything down without tasting anything, and it lodged in my chest like lumps of burning coal.

Afterwards, I put on a coat and, slumped on one of the sunloungers on the terrace, listened to the faint click-click of the in-line skaters as they twirled and leaped athletically along the marble promenade thirty-two storeys below. Motorbikes roared down the Avenue Princesse Grace, going nowhere in particular, then back again. The sounds of other people enjoying themselves made me feel strangely depressed. Not knowing what to do, I scanned the satellite TV magazine to see whether there was anything worth watching on any of our seventy-six channels, but there wasn't a thing.

'Don't wait up for me, darling,' Cecil stuttered down the phone when he rang me at eleven. 'I'm drowning under a sea of paperwork here. And darling?'

'Yes?'

'Look, I completely forgot to tell you but . . . Well, I realise I've got to go to Geneva tomorrow morning.'

'*Why?*'

'For an auction. There's a painting I've got to bid for, for one of my Hong Kong clients. I'm awfully sorry to leave you again but . . .'

I took a deep breath. 'It doesn't matter.'

'Really? I should be back in a couple of days.'

Half an hour later, I rang Cecil's office number, but he didn't answer. Nor did he come home till nearly 3 a.m. I lay wake for ages, wondering where he really was and what, or rather whom, he was drowning under. Not that I needed much imagination to guess.

C . . .
I shall remember that moonlit boat ride on Lac Leman every time I look at my wrist. You are too, too generous, my darling!
When Neeli came today, I asked her to fix that ridiculous cuckoo clock to my dressing-room wall. Every time I'm standing in my underwear and that little man pops out from his little house and bows to me, I shall think of you!
S

At last, my feverish curiosity had something to work on – a tiny, nevertheless tangible, clue. But I would have to step carefully if my quest to find S was not to be discovered.

'Do you know, I really think I ought to get a housekeeper, Zuzu,' I said as casually as I could as she and I swam together in the indoor pool at the Hôtel de Paris.

'And about time, dahlink,' Zuzu said, peering at me from under a fuschia pink, Yves St Laurent swimming hat. 'Frankly, I can't believe that you haven't got someone before now. What were you thinking of?'

'Oh, I don't know. How *does* one find a good cleaner?'

Zuzu's index finger waggled at me firmly from within the sheath of the 4-carat diamond-and-ruby ring she'd bought herself for Christmas. 'Make sure to get a Philippino. The Philippinos are the best. I'll ask Margherita if she knows anyone.'

'Thanks.' As we came to the edge of the pool, I took my feet off the bottom and rolled over onto my back so that my belly bobbed up above the meniscus. After a short pause – I didn't want to seem too eager, but nor did I want to give Zuzu a chance to change the subject – I continued, 'Actually, I do remember someone I met the other day telling me that they knew an excellent cleaner who was looking for extra work. I think her name was . . .' I cleared my throat. '. . . something like Lily. No – it was *Neeli*. The trouble is, I can't remember who it was who told me. You, er, don't happen to know anyone who has a cleaner called Neeli, do you, Zuzu?'

The new silicone implant in my companion's lower lip quivered. 'Really, Lisa! How the hell should I know what other people's cleaners are called? You think I haven't got better things to do with my time? By the way, dahlink,' she added over her shoulder as she began another width in breast stroke, her head held high above the water so as to stop her hair getting wet, 'I bumped into your marvellous husband yesterday.'

I froze. Was it mere coincidence that had made Zuzu mention Cecil the moment I'd mentioned Neeli? There was something sly, almost suggestive, in her tone. 'Where did you see him?' I asked, swimming after her as fast as I could.

'He was just going into P—'s.' Zuzu named a small and discreet restaurant, tucked away at the back of the principality. Strange, Cecil hadn't told me he'd had lunch there yesterday. In fact, he'd told me he'd been at the office all day. Had he been alone or with *S*? 'I thought you might have been with him, dahlink. In fact, I went up to him and I said, *"Cecil? Where's Lisa? Why are you alone? Why is a handsome man like you, who has a beautiful wife like Lisa, lunching by yourself?"* He said he was meeting someone, on business.'

'Yes. Yes, I know.'

Zuzu smiled at me pityingly. 'He looks so different nowadays, doesn't he, dahlink?'

'Mmm.'

'Obviously, this new way of life suits him.' What new way of life? I wondered. 'All this *success*.' Zuzu threw an arm in the air, making her diamond bracelets jangle. 'Cecil seems to exude this glow of happiness. But of course,' she went on, smiling at me innocently, 'I'm sure a lot of that must be to do with you. And he's so much thinner, isn't he? Must be all this . . .' Zuzu paused for a second, 'this rushing around he's been doing. This extra exercise he's taking.'

'Exercise?' I echoed.

'He told me yesterday that he's joined the gym under the Houston Palace.'

I nodded, as if I'd known all about this, too. 'Oh yes.'

Zuzu's nose quivered; she looked like a cat which was planning to pounce. 'You know what I was thinking, dahlink? Maybe you should join this gym, too.'

I'd suspected that something nasty was coming, but even so, I was taken aback. 'What, now? I'm nearly seven months' pregnant, Zuzu!'

'Mmm. I've noticed, dahlink,' Zuzu said. 'Still, that's no reason to lose your muscle tone. Once it goes, you know, you'll never get it back. And you used to have such a lovely figure.' Her eyelids, relifted over the New Year in a clinic outside Denver, narrowed at me slightly, and the corners of her mouth twitched into a tight smile. 'I hope you don't mind me saying this, dahlink, and believe me I only say it because I'm your friend – you're really not looking your best at the moment.' She stopped beside me and, reaching under the water, tweaked a handful of my cellulite thighs. 'You really mustn't let yourself go, just because you're *enceinte*. This is just the time when a woman ought to look her best – if she doesn't want her husband to wander, that is. And, take it from me, this place is full of women on their own who'd give anything for an attractive man like Cecil. My God, if I didn't know you, I wouldn't mind him myself. Yes, you should be looking your best right now, dahlink,' she repeated sternly. 'And if you don't mind me saying so, you don't.'

C,

What a sweet card! I shall try hard to believe all that flattery, but I doubt that I'll succeed. My breasts are simply not 'round as poached peaches', nor my nipples 'sweet as raspberries', whichever way you look at them – and you, my darling, have looked at them every which way.

Now, be honest – am I really as luscious as an overripe mango to enter? Come to that, how do you know? And do

I really taste better than the freshest, most expensive oysters? Well, that is for you alone to say!

Be careful how you praise me in future, or I might think that you are all words, and take myself off the menu.

I take it back. You're not all words!

With love from your dish of the day (and every day!)

In the bathroom that night, I stripped off my clothes and inspected my bloated body in the mirror. My breasts were hard, pendulous and blue-veined, like large scoops of ripe Stilton, tipped with nipples which were as round and brown as oatcakes. My belly looked like an overripe pumpkin – one that the farmer had forgotten to pick. My once-firm thighs hung slack like the flesh of a part-boned chicken; when pressed, they took on the classic, lumpy texture of cottage cheese.

Dismayed at the ruin my body had become, I shrouded it in Cecil's old bathrobe and slumped barefoot into the kitchen, where I searched the fridge for solace in the form of a bar of chocolate and a large triangle of Brie. So, S tasted like the finest oysters, did she? I probably tasted more like a pair of old kippers! Bugger Zuzu! I thought bitterly. And bugger that bastard Robert! And bugger bloody S, with her raspberry nipples!

And then it occurred to me – Cecil probably had.

Darling . . .

Entering someone else's hotel room without permission is criminal. Likewise, entering someone else's wife. Doing both at the same time maybe qualifies you for a dreadful punishment, such as a public flogging, or at least banishment from the principality.

I feel quite sorry for Signor Cantarini from Milan (that was his name, wasn't it?) of room 23 at L'Hermitage. If he accidentally packs those black satin Christian Dior panties I left beside the bed, he'll be in terrible trouble with his wife.

Kisses to you, millions of them, everywhere . . .

S

218

'Surely you don't have to work late *again*, Cecil?' I shouted, hurling my copy of *Nice-Matin* on to our new Italian glass coffee table.

Perched on the arm of the white leather sofa, Cecil blinked at me with infuriating innocence. 'I'm sorry, Lisa. I've got to go to London again on Monday. And, unless I get my desk cleared tonight, I'm never going to catch up.'

'But you worked late last night, Cecil! And the night before that!'

'Yes, yes, I know, I know.' He gave the helpless shrug which seemed to have become his stock-in-trade response to all my reproaches. 'I can't help it. I *am* virtually doing two full-time jobs at the moment.'

I glared at him furiously. 'What's that supposed to imply? That I'm not doing one job?'

'Not at all!' His head on one side, he smiled at me in a kindly fashion. 'Though, come to think of it, you're not working at the moment, are you, darling?' he added. 'Now don't take that as a reproach! I'm sure you'll get down to it eventually. Goodness, you've got enough on your plate right now, and I quite see that you're not in the mood to write. But money has to come from somewhere, Lisa. And we have been spending quite a lot of it on the flat.'

'Is that my fault? It was your idea to redecorate!'

'I'm not complaining, Lisa, really! I'm just trying to say that, well, at the moment, we need every penny we can get. And with all the time I'm having to spend in London, well, I don't want my own business to go kaput.'

'But I never see you any more!' I wailed. Which astonished both of us.

Cecil blinked again, this time more slowly, and said in a curious voice, 'Does that really matter to you, Lisa?'

'Of course it matters! I mean, what's the point of me having spent weeks and weeks choosing all this bloody furniture, and all that wallpaper and stuff, when you're never here to see it? Sometimes, Cecil, I . . . I . . .'

'Yes?'

'Well, sometimes I wonder why you married me!'

Cecil's lips twitched. 'What a funny thing to say!'

'Is it? Anyone would think that . . . that . . .'

'That what?'

I took a deep breath and spat it out: 'That you were having an affair!'

A look of guilt crossed Cecil's face, so fleeting that I almost missed it. Then he remarked flatly, 'Why should I do that?'

'Because . . . because . . .' I spluttered into speechlessness, a stain of embarrassment flooding into my cheeks. 'Oh, never mind! I'm sorry, I'm sorry, I'm sorry!'

'What about, darling?'

'Everything! Nothing! Look, just leave me alone and go to your office, if that's what you want to do!'

C,

I've decided that two days is too long for us to be apart. I cannot sleep. I cannot eat. I ache for you. Once, I cared only for my own wishes. Now, I care only for yours. The happy, selfish narcissist of the past has gone forever. See how you've ruined me!

I thought about your body all last night. Do you know, before, when it was soft and voluptuous, I thought I could never desire it more? But, now, now that your chest is harder, and those lovely breasts of yours have all but disappeared, and now that your stomach is flatter and firmer, I find I desire you even more, after all!

One part, I am glad to say, has not grown smaller, despite your new regime . . . I shall measure it again when I next see you, just to make sure! I must see you soon. When? Tomorrow? Tonight? Today? Name the time, and the place. I will be there . . .

'Is that you, Lisa?'

'Oh, hello, Mother.' Cursing myself for answering the telephone – Lorelei had taken to ringing me every morning at the same time lately – I lay back in bed and resigned myself to suffering through her call. 'What's the weather like in London this morning? Any better than yesterday?'

'Cut the crap, Lisa,' Lorelei barked. 'What I wanna know is, have you done it yet?'

I gritted my teeth. 'Done what?'

'You know damn well what!'

'Do I?'

'We talked about it yesterday. *Have-you-gone-and-bought-the-layette?*'

'The what, Mum?'

An icy silence blasted into my ear. 'The crib,' Lorelei said eventually. 'The buggy. The sheets. The blankets. The diapers. The muslin squares. The baby bath. A changing table. Those things they put babies in nowadays that look like straitjackets, what-the-hell-do-you-call-'ems? Romper suits.' When I sighed with deep boredom, just as I had done the day before, and the day before that, my exasperated mother drew in a long, determined breath. 'OK, Lisa I'm gonna catch the plane to Nice this afternoon. Pick me up at the airport at six.'

'*What?*'

'I told your father this morning, I said, *Horace, if she didn't get organised herself yesterday, I'm gonna go out to Monte-Carlo and take charge!*'

I sat as bolt upright as my stomach would allow. 'You are *not* coming here.'

'Why not? If you don't mind me saying so, dear, you're not coping very well alone. I don't know what's the matter with you! You're behaving like a kid, not like an adult. From what you've told me, nothing's ready at all. For Christ's sake, Lisa, your baby's due in a couple of weeks!'

My *baby*? That's not what the parasite felt like to me. No, it felt like an extension of my mother – furiously punching and kicking at me day and night. The only difference was that the parasite was attacking me from the inside, whereas

221

my mother's punches came via the phone. 'There's still six weeks to go, actually, Mummy. That's plenty of time.'

'Plenty, huh? What if the baby comes early? And have you any idea how long all that shopping will take? It's not as if they have Brent Cross or John Lewis over there.'

'People do have babies in France. I'm sure there are shops which sell things for them. I'm not living in Woolabongalonga.'

'*Where?*'

'It's in Australia,' I muttered miserably.

Lorelei sniffed her despair. 'You know what the matter with you is, honey?' she said. I did, actually, and she didn't – but that was no bar to her telling me. 'You're in denial. You see this baby as a threat. You're clinging to the past, and you're unwilling to let go of your happy, carefree adolescence. What you gotta learn to do is embrace the future, Lisa. Wake up in the morning, look at yourself in the mirror and say to yourself, "I'm glad to be alive!"'

Not for the first time in the last couple of weeks, I wished my mother had stuck to watching daytime soaps, and not graduated to *Rikki Lake* and the *Oprah Winfrey* show. 'Look, just because I haven't bought a crib yet doesn't mean that I'm in denial, for Christ's sake!'

'Lisa, a crib isn't just a crib,' she interrupted. 'A crib's a symbol. A symbol of what you're trying to pretend doesn't exist. Wanna know something?'

'What?'

'It's not too late to change your mind and come home and have the baby here.'

Not that old chestnut again! 'It's all arranged. I'm having it at the Princesse Grace Hospital.'

'Why? What's so special about it, huh? What do French doctors know that British doctors don't? You're English. You should have an English-speaking doctor. Have you thought what'd happen if something went wrong when you're in labour? How'd you let the doctors know?'

'I'd tell them – in French.'

Lorelei's voice hardened. 'If I remember, you failed French "O" Level, and never bothered to retake it. Listen to reason, baby – it's not just the birth. If you were in London now, I could come to all your hospital appointments with you. I could do things for you. Go shopping with you. A daughter needs her mom at a time like this.' I said nothing. 'Won't you change your mind? Or at least, let me come out and stay with you till it's over? Huh? Cecil wouldn't mind. He'd be pleased – specially since he's away so much. Huh, Lisa? I wanna come see you! I . . . I miss you!' she went on more desperately. 'Jesus, you've been living in Monte-Carlo for nearly a year, and I haven't even seen your flat yet! Isn't it time that you and Cecil invited me? Lisa? Answer me!'

I took a deep breath. 'I'm sorry, Mum. But I really don't want to see anyone at the moment.'

A shred of metal rasped in her throat. 'I'm not *anyone*, Lisa, I'm your mother! But I see, as usual, that counts for nothing with you. As usual, you don't want your father and me around!'

At last, the guilt card was down on the table. Idiot that I was, I picked it up. 'It's not that, Mum, it's just . . .'

I could hear her scarlet lips smack together in preparation for a final assault. 'Frankly, Lisa, I'm too hurt to discuss this any more. I've had your excuses up to here. As far as I can see, you always were a goddam selfish child, and you've grown into a goddam selfish adult. You've made your father and I wait long enough for a grandchild – the least you can do is let us be in on the birth!'

Cheri,

I have to tell you that you were wrong: that chocolate sauce will not come off my silk sheets, no matter how many times they are washed. I should throw them away, but every time I see the stains I am reminded of our little bedtime 'snack'. A delicious memory . . .

By the way, that lost champagne truffle turned up at long last. Neeli found it – in the shower. 'Has Madam been eating

bonbons in the bathroom, as well as in bed?' she asked. I di
not like to tell her that, on the contrary, my bonbon had beer
eating me.

Let me know when you are coming next, and I shall prepar
another midnight feast. This time it is I who shall eat
Andouillette avec ... quoi? A little raspberry coulis perhaps
Or a simple garnish of crème Chantilly?

A bientôt, mon amour.

'Cecil? *Cecil*?'

I pushed open the door of the spare room, where my
husband had taken to sleeping so that he wouldn't wake
me when he came home late from the office – or that's the
excuse he'd given me. It didn't matter, because I couldn'
sleep anyway. How could I sleep when I knew who he wa
with, and what he was doing?

It was three in the morning. Cecil must have beer
exhausted, for though he'd only come in ten minutes ago
he was already fast asleep. Picking my way over his clothes
which lay strewn across the white marble floor, I stood ove
the bed and stared down at the ghostly hillocks and valley
of his shrouded body.

'Cecil?' Although my whisper didn't rouse him, he shifted
under the sheet, and the top of his smooth head slid out onto
the pillow. Very gently, I touched his soft, shorn hair, willing
him to wake up, though I hadn't a clue what I'd say to hir
if he did. Some terrible cliché, probably, like, *Cecil, we need
to talk*; or *I can't go on like this any more*. Trite but true. The
situation was making me ill with guilt and anxiety. Much as
I dreaded the upheaval and the shame of leaving him, I knew
I had no choice but to make a clean break, as I should have
done right after the wedding. For both our sakes, I had to put
an end to this untenable situation. The question obsessing me
was not *if* I should make a break from Cecil, only *when*.

What an unknown quantity this man was, I thought, as I
gently lifted the sheet a few inches, and peered down at his
body through the gloom. I'd hardly known a thing about

him when we'd got married and, as I was realising with every passing day, I knew even less about him now. He seemed to change all the time, like a snake shrugging off a series of skins, emerging each time stronger, more confident, more intelligent, more . . . The word was interesting, but I didn't dare admit it, even to myself.

'Cecil! Wake up!' Cecil snored. I lifted the sheet a little higher, and as my eyes became accustomed to the darkness I noticed with surprise that his arms and upper chest had grown quite muscular from his daily workouts in the gym. Why, even his body was changing before my eyes!

Somewhere at the core of this unknown person lay the real Cecil – or rather, all of them: Cecil the businessman; Cecil the intellectual; Cecil, the inventive and passionate lover; and the Cecil who, held back by some inner block, had stuttered his way painfully through life; but these were facets of his personality which had never been revealed to me. If I'd been another person, I might have drawn them out of him. I might have discovered what it was that made him tick. But I hadn't bothered to do that, because I'd never been able to see the point in making the effort. Cecil wasn't a bad person, he just wasn't my type. Things might have been different if I'd found him in the least bit attractive, but the chemistry between us had never been right.

That very afternoon, when his paintings had come out of storage at long last, I'd discovered yet another Cecil – the man of exquisite taste. While the removal men were bringing the paintings in, Cecil had flapped around nervously, warning the men to pay attention to what they were doing and handle the pictures with care. Once he'd peeled off the layers of brown paper and bubble wrap and leaned the framed lithographs and canvases against the living-room wall, I'd begun to understand why he'd been so concerned about them.

'Well, what do you think, Lisa?' he'd said.

I looked at the half-dozen or so early Hockney drawings, the small Picasso etching of a woman's head, the large, thickly encrusted Alan Davie painting, the multicoloured Jim Dine heart lithograph, and the jewel-bright splotches of two Andy Warhol prints, and I felt quite speechless with disbelief.

'They're beautiful, Cecil. Really! Really fantastic.'

He shot me a wary glance, eyebrows raised. 'Do you mean that?'

'Of course I do! How could anyone not like them? And what are those over there?'

Cecil turned over one of the six small canvases which were facing the wall. 'Oh, this is just a little collection I made years ago of early British naive art.'

'They're wonderful!' I breathed. 'Goodness, how long have you been collecting paintings?'

Hands in his pockets, Cecil stood back and smiled at his collection. 'Believe it or not, I bought the Hockneys when I was still at school.'

'You're joking!'

'He was still at the Royal College at the time. I was introduced to him through Kasmin. Of course,' Cecil laughed softly to himself, 'I wish now I'd bought more drawings, and a few paintings, but even though they were dirt cheap then by today's standards, I just didn't have the cash. It took all my savings and two years advance on my pocket money to buy these!' Squinting at one of the drawings, he stroked his chin with a thoughtful gesture. 'I suppose I've always been drawn to beautiful things. The attraction of opposites, I guess.' He smiled at me wryly but, unable to share the joke with him, I turned away.

'I . . .' I faltered for a moment. Why did I suddenly feel so shy with Cecil? Why did I find it so hard to break the barrier of coldness between us and pay him a compliment? 'I . . . I never realised that you had such fantastic taste.'

For a moment, Cecil looked taken aback. Then his lips spread in a sardonic smile. 'To tell you the truth, I was beginning to doubt my own judgement lately, Lisa. But then, again,' he added after a short pause, 'I did marry you.'

What exactly had Cecil meant by that rather double-edged comment? I wondered now as, suddenly weary, I sank down on the bed and stretched out beside him. That marrying me had implied good taste on his part or, on the contrary, a terrible lack of judgement? And what of my own judgement? Why, out of all the many men I'd been out with, had I married one I couldn't stand? Why didn't I like Cecil when he was clearly a person of worth, and when everyone else who met him clearly did?

Most puzzling of all, what did Cecil's lover see in his body that I so obviously missed?

Cautiously, I slipped under the sheet, and reached out a hand towards my husband's body, which was facing away from me. 'Cecil?' I whispered. Unaware of my presence, Cecil remained asleep. Stealthy as a mugger about to pounce on a victim, my hand landed lightly on his back. The feel of his skin was surprisingly sensual: soft, luxurious and springy, like the finest silk Persian carpet underlaid with thick felt.

How good it was to feel the warmth of another human body again! Before I knew what I was doing, my hand slipped down a little further, and my index finger began to explore a small, hot fold of flesh at Cecil's waist. From there, I traced a path down to the promontary of his hipbone and, carefully pressing my pregnant belly closer against him, reached round towards his front.

Cecil sighed in his sleep. A great dry heat, like that in a sauna, emanated from his back, a heat perfumed with a faint smell which I breathed in in much the same way one tests scent in a department store. Hmff! A musky, earthy smell, with a hint of Patchouli oil which seemed to come straight out of my misspent youth. A note of jasmine, undercut by the faintest undertone of – hmff! hmff! – yes, sweat, which wasn't at all unpleasant but, on the contrary, stopped the floral overtones from being cloying. Cecil smelled – hmff! – rather nice. His was the kind of smell one wanted to breathe in more of, the kind of smell which, in other circumstances, might have signalled *sex*.

But this, I reminded myself, was my husband Cecil, the last man on earth I desired. I wasn't aroused by him, I was simply interested in what S saw in him. I was curious, in cold-blooded, cerebral sort of way.

I stroked his soft, hairy belly with the tips of my fingers and began to inch down into the coarser hair in his groin. But here I came up against a certain logistical problem: my eight-months' pregnant bump. So the parasite had thwarted me again! I wouldn't be beaten by it! By moving my shoulder diagonally back across the bed and propping myself up on an elbow, I found I could, if I tried hard enough, reach a little further down towards . . .

Yes! I drew in a sharp breath as I touched his penis – velvet-soft, limp and shrivelled as geriatric flesh. Half revolted, half fascinated, I slid my fingers carefully underneath it, and cupped it in my hand. So, this was the *andouillette* that S planned to cover in raspberry coulis, was it? Why, this was hardly the sturdy country sausage her description had implied, this was a mere cocktail Vienna, and as light as a soufflé!

Very, very cautiously, I slid my fingers down to the tip where I drew the foreskin back a little and gave the cool spongy head a tiny squeeze. Then, as my palm tightened around the flaccid shaft, I had an overwhelming desire to laugh. Why, this little thing wasn't much use to anyone!

The next moment, the little thing gave an involuntary twitch. Pulsing with life, it suddenly swelled within the tight prison of my fist, filling my hand with rock-hard muscle, prising my fingers apart.

'Aah!' Now Cecil moaned loudly in his sleep and rolled over onto his back, nearly squashing me in the process. Letting go of him, I wriggled backwards and jumped off the bed. As I did so, his erect penis jolted into a vertical position, pushing up the thin sheet into a kind of marquee.

Appalled, and at the same time fascinated, I gnawed my fist and waited for something to happen, but nothing did. Cecil remained asleep; and, to my amazement, the marquee's mast remained at ninety degrees, in defiance of the laws of gravity.

Holding my breath, I pulled back the linen. A tall, stiff, purple-petalled, Hockney-esque tulip arose from the forest of Cecil's groin, its heavy tip supported by a thick stem. A single dewdrop of moisture glistened on top of it . . .

Mesmerised by its beauty, I knelt down beside the bed and, leaning forward, parted my lips so I could sip the nectar up.

Then Cecil murmured, 'Oh, Sandra!' in his sleep, and I struggled to my feet and fled.

Sixteen

———≫•≪———

It's late April in Monaco. Buckets of sweet, yellow mimosa dot the Monégasque market, and there are lemons from Menton and Italy piled high on the fruit stalls. The sky is a seamless blue, it's almost as warm as an English summer, and bougainvillea has turned the high wall behind our apartment building a deep, vivid purple. Down by the sea, workmen have arrived to take down the wooden hoardings which have protected the palm trees all winter, and the owners of the private beach concessions have laid out neat rows of sunbeds in hopeful, if premature, expectation of an early start to the season.

Four days ago, Andy's programme went out on British television and, in a small way, Cecil became an overnight media sensation – 'a five-minute wonder' as, with typical modesty, he put it himself. 'The most interesting new voice – and face – to hit British screens for as long as I can remember,' said the *Guardian*'s reviewer. 'A mind to be reckoned with,' wrote the *Daily Telegraph*. According to the *Mail*, which also published a full-page feature on Cecil entitled 'Our Man in Monte-Carlo', my husband possesses 'the mind of Sister Wendy in the body of Clive James'. According to the *Independent*, Cecil's interviewing style combines 'brusqueness, clear-sightedness and a total lack of sycophancy. I know of no other British interviewer who could have drawn so much out of their subject whilst saying so little. Brown's quiet manner hides an incisive mind which provides a welcome blast of fresh air in an area hitherto dominated by Bragg and the *South Bank Show*.'

231

I'd travelled to London with Cecil, and I'd watched from the studio gallery as the programme went out live. Though Cecil hadn't talked to me about how nervous he was, I knew how much it mattered to him that everything went right. When he stumbled on his opening lines, my heart ached for him. But I needn't have worried, for after that opening blunder he didn't put a single foot wrong.

Once the broadcast was over, Cecil re-entered the gallery like a hero coming back from the wars. Everyone clapped him and congratulated him. Andy said he had been 'fucking brilliant', and about six young, beautiful women colleagues threw their arms around him and kissed him as if he was their oldest friend.

As for me, I felt excluded from all this bonhomie. Saying that I wasn't feeling well, I left Cecil to go on to the celebrations by himself, and took a taxi back to our hotel.

When I entered our suite, the telephone was already ringing.

'Hello?'

'Lisa? Hand me over to the star!' my mother yelled ecstatically.

I took a deep breath. 'He's not here yet. He's still at the studio.'

'Huh? So, why aren't you with him?' Lorelei snarled. 'Some supportive wife you are.'

'Look, I was feeling tired! Besides, Cecil's perfectly all right by himself.'

'I bet he is,' my mother sneered.

'What's that supposed to mean, Mummy?'

'Just that you ought to be with him, Lisa. After all, he's your husband. You should look after him. If you don't mind me saying, you're really very lucky to have him.'

But I didn't have Cecil. Not any more. He was Sandra's, in every way which counted. To realise that, you only had to read her latest letter, which, after a short search, I now found at the bottom of his overnight suitcase.

Darling C,

Yes, yes, you are right – I know shouldn't go on about her. How you choose to live your life is not my business. And after all, what does she have to do with us and what we have?

But, but, but . . .! There are times when I feel so angry with her! And angry with you, too, for staying with her. You deserve to live your life with someone who really appreciates you. Someone who loves you for what you are. Someone like me.

Forgive me if I spoke out of turn last night. I did it only because I love you so much. The last thing I wish to do is upset you – this week of all weeks.

As for tomorrow – Bon chance, mon amour! I believe in you, and I know you will be wonderful. Make love to the camera just as you make love to me and you will conquer the hearts of the British public just as you have conquered mine!

S

The day after the broadcast, Cecil and I flew back to Monaco. And the next day, he flew off to Paris for a sale of modern paintings, and from there to New York via Concorde, to interview some bigwig from the Museum of Modern Art.

'You don't mind me going, do you?' he asked on the way to the airport.

'Of course not.' How could I mind when the prospect excited him so? And did it make any difference to me? Even when he was physically with me nowadays, Cecil wasn't really there.

He touched my knee absentmindedly. 'But what if the baby comes while I'm away?'

I shrugged indifferently. 'It's not due for another couple of weeks. Besides, aren't first babies always late?'

Cecil glanced at me doubtfully. 'Are you sure you don't want anyone to come and stay with you?'

'Like who?' I said somewhat impatiently.

'How about your friend Elena?'

'You know she can't come!' I snapped. 'She's far too busy. Besides, I haven't spoken to her in ages. She's been distinctly pissed off with me ever since I failed to deliver my book.'

'Then how about asking your mother to come over for a few days?' Cecil suggested.

I was about to explode when I saw the twinkle in his eyes. 'That's all I need. No, honestly, Cecil, I'll be fine on my own. I've got lots to do. Books I want to read. Things like that. And there's Zuzu's cocktail party tomorrow night.'

'Oh yes!' Cecil smiled. 'The Spoiled Wives Club jamboree.'

'Don't be horrid. Anyway, Zuzu's not a wife, she's a widow.'

'The merriest widow I've ever seen,' Cecil remarked. 'Well, I can't say I'm heartbroken that I'll be missing her party.'

'Don't say that. Zuzu's made such an effort. Did you see that marquee she's had put up beside the swimming pool? Apparently, she's invited hundreds of people.'

'*Are* there hundreds of people here?' Cecil said dryly.

'I have to go, or she'll never speak to me. Besides,' I added, patting my stomach. 'I suppose it's time I got the spare room ready for *this*. Anyway, don't worry about me, I'll be fine by myself. I've always enjoyed being alone.'

Was that still true? Back at the flat, I moped around, not knowing what to do with myself. A depression seemed to have settled over me, as thick and grey as the clouds which cloaked the mountains behind the principality. Determined to torture myself, I telephoned Robert's London number several times, and listened to the message on his answering machine. 'Robert here. I'm afraid I'm unavailable to take your call right now. But do please leave your name and number, and I'll get back to you as soon as I can.' The last time I phoned, I muttered, 'You bastard!' after the bleep before I could stop myself, but the moment I'd done it, I wished I hadn't. If only there was some way of erasing it! When he next came back from Australia, my angry, bitter voice would still be there . . .

By the following afternoon, I was desperate to talk to

someone – so desperate that I rang up Elena at her office.

'Hello, it's me!' I said as cheerfully as I could.

'Ah, Lisa,' she said frostily. 'Do you have any news for me?'

'Well, if you mean, is it a boy or a girl, I haven't had it baby yet.'

'Actually, what I meant was, have you finished the book?'

'Not quite,' I lied.

'So, what do you want?'

'Oh, just to say hello. How are you?'

'Busy,' she said curtly, shuffling papers in an ostentatious manner.

'Sorry.' I attempted to keep the disappointment out of my voice. 'I'll ring back later.'

'Later'll be no good either,' Elena barked. 'I've got meetings. Then I've got to dash – it's Sophie's school play. The murder of Julius Caesar. Performed in fucking Latin, would you believe? By nine-year-old girls. I'm dreading it. I wish to God I'd sent her to the local primary instead of that poncy prep school. They ought to sack the sadist who dreamed up the idea for this play.' She sighed with resignation. 'You'd better tell me what's wrong now. I'll give you two minutes.'

'Oh, no, no, it's nothing.'

'Lisa!' There was a warning note in her voice which, for some reason, made me burst into tears.

'Oh Elena! I'm so terribly depressed! I don't know what's wrong with me.'

'Frankly, neither do I,' Elena replied. 'It seems to me that you've got everything!'

'Everything except the one thing I really want!'

'Which is?'

'A real relationship!' I sobbed.

There was a short silence. 'Well, as I've told you before, real relationships don't grow on trees. If you want one, you have to put some effort into it.'

'But who with? Robert's in Australia and . . .'

My friend sighed. 'Have you thought of having a relation-ship with your husband? Believe me, if you don't, someone else will.'

I was about to tell her about Sandra's letters, but decided against it. 'I can't, Elena! I've tried and tried, but the spark's just not there! Oh God, what am I going to do?'

I heard Elena slam something down on her desk. 'Just stop being so bloody passive and do *something*! Leave Cecil if you don't like him! You're not doing him any favours by staying with him under sufferance.'

'But I'm about to have a baby!'

'So you'll join the hundreds of thousands of other single mothers in Britain. There are worse fates. Besides, the baby's not even his.'

'That's beside the point,' I grumbled. 'For some reason, he seems to want it. More than I do.'

There was a short but ominous silence. 'Lisa,' Elena said eventually in a clipped voice, 'I don't understand you. Frankly, there's nothing at all wrong with Cecil. Quite the opposite. You know, I was literally glued to the TV set when he was on the other night. You never told me how clever or interesting he is – in fact, all you've ever done is run him down. It seems to me that you're just a dissatisfied person. First you want to get married, then the moment you're married you want to get divorced. You want a baby, then the moment you get pregnant you change your mind! You're so bloody perverse, I don't know what to say to you any more. I can't help you through this.'

'But I . . .'

'Look, I've got two children, a husband and a job to do, and I'm under pressure everywhere. To be honest, I can't afford the time to listen to all your endless whingeing.'

'How dare you!' I shouted. 'I do not whinge!'

I slammed the receiver down with a resounding thwack, then threw an old coat over the maternity tracksuit I'd been wearing all day and went out for a walk to cool off. By the time I'd plodded down to the beach, I'd realised that Elena was right. I was whingeing. Determined to apologise, I came straight back to the Bellavista and, on my way upstairs, stopped to check the postbox in the lobby. It was empty - save for a cream vellum envelope, addressed to Cecil in that familiar purple ink. So, Sandra was writing openly to Cecil now at our address! I was about to open the letter, when I realised that a large furry animal was breathing down my neck.

'Anything interesting?' Zuzu lifted her sunglasses and peered at the envelope out of thick swathes of white Dior mink.

I clutched the envelope to my chest. 'Not really. You look nice,' I said to change the subject.

'I've just come back from the hairdresser's.' She glanced at my own, untidy mop of hair and her nose wrinkled. 'I see you haven't had yours done. I hope you're going to at least wash it before the party. You look so peeky, dahlink. How are you? And were's your famous husband? I've been reading about him in all the English papers. He's making quite a name for himself! You must be very proud.'

'Yes. Actually, he's in New York at the moment.'

Her mouth stretched into a horrified O. 'Does that mean he's not coming tonight? What a nuisance! Another man less! You are coming, aren't you?'

It was the last thing I wanted to do. 'Of course. I mean, if I'm feeling all right . . .' I faltered.

Zuzu raised her eyebrows. 'I want you there, Lisa!' she said in a voice which brooked no argument. 'In the absence of Cecil, I'm relying on you to amuse all my friends!'

The moment I'd shut the front door of the apartment I tore open the cream vellum envelope and read the unsigned note inside it.

Darling C,
  What a wonderful, wonderful idea! See you at the Plaza. I cannot wait!

There was a sharp kick inside me, and for once it didn'
come from the parasite in my belly. I glanced at my watch
then calculated the time difference: it was lunchtime in New
York. Cecil would probably be out, at some meeting. Still
. . . With trembling fingers, I dialled the Plaza and asked to
be put through to Cecil's room. To my surprise, he picked
up the phone.

'Mmm?' he said sleepily.

'Cecil?'

'Lisa!' He sounded astonished to hear from me. I could
almost see him frowning. 'Is everything all right?'

'Fine.'

'Has anything started?'

'The baby? No. I, um . . . well, I just wanted to say
hello.'

'That's nice of you. Look, hold on a second, will you?'
My heart lurched as I heard him cover the mouthpiece and
mutter something to someone at the other end. I tried to
picture Sandra, lying naked next to him in the bed. 'Sorry
Lisa,' Cecil said.

'Who's with you?' I croaked with a throat as dry as
sandpaper.

'Oh . . . Just some people. From PBS.'

Oh yes? 'Sorry. I'm disturbing you, aren't I?'

'Well . . .' He hesitated. Why didn't he at least have
the decency to lie? 'Sorry, but I am in the middle of a
meeting. Could I possibly ring you back in – what? – about
an hour's time?'

After I'd put down the phone, I sank down on the bed
feeling bleaker and lonelier than I'd ever felt in my life. The
situation between Cecil and I was so sad, and at the same
time so horribly sordid. And the worst thing was, it was all
my own fault.

I threw off my clothes and took a long, steamy shower.
The water ran over my head, down my blue-veined breasts
and onto my protruding belly before cascading to the tiled
floor. I soaped myself again and again, but I felt no cleaner.

All my life, I'd been blessed with a body I was at ease with. Now, I couldn't stand to look at it or touch it. Anxious to avoid seeing myself in the mirror, I unhooked Cecil's bathrobe from the back of the bathroom door, and quickly slipped it on before going into the kitchen and pouring myself a drink. If a glass of white wine was harmful to the parasite, it was just too bad – it was what I needed right now.

Out on the balcony, I stood at the railing, gazing out across the sea. The night was cheerless, like my mood. Thick clouds scudded across the moon, casting a ghostly, flickering light on the oil-black water. Far below me, the marquee beside the swimming pool glowed like a yellow paper lantern. From inside it came the faint sound of clinking glasses, talking and laughing. Zuzu's cocktail party was warming up. I knew I ought to get dressed, go downstairs and put in an appearance but I had no heart for the endless, empty chit-chat about clothes and holidays, and the exploits of the Grimaldis, and who in Monte-Carlo (apart from Cecil) was screwing whom. The people I knew here weren't my friends, they were no more than aquaintances. I didn't really care about any of them and none of them really cared about me.

In fact, when I thought about it, no one cared about me any more. Andy had forgotten me. Robert probably didn't remember me. Elena was angry and impatient with me. As for my mother, she'd never really loved anyone but herself. If Cecil had once cared for me, I'd successfully killed off his feelings. How could I blame him for not liking me any more, when I didn't even like myself?

What a failure I was, in every way! As Mahonia Medmenham, I'd let my readers down by giving up writing. I'd let my father down, and I'd let down Cecil. And soon there'd be someone else with whom to fuck up a relationship – the parasite. The heartburn it was currently giving me would soon give way to heartbreak. How could I ever love it, knowing whose child it was? How could Cecil love it when he was in love with Sandra? And the baby, when it was born, would be a constant reminder of how I'd betrayed him . . .

I looked down over the balcony railing. The dizzying drop beckoned me to welcome oblivion. Never before had I felt suicidal, but now I was suddenly tempted by the idea. One minute of terror, followed by nothingness. How bad could that moment of terror be?

I dragged a chair over to the railing. As I climbed onto the seat, the thing in my belly gave me a sharp warning kick. I laid my hand on it to calm it down. What it didn't know couldn't hurt it . . .

I put one foot up on the top of the rail. My head swam. Now, all I had to do was topple forward and, like Zuzu's husband, I'd crash to my death. No more problems. No more worries. No more angsting about what to do. No more me.

Trembling violently, I transferred my weight forwards.

And then the doorbell rang.

I held my breath and hesitated. When the bell rang again, I climbed down from the chair.

A tall, dark Adonis in worn jeans and a sweatshirt was standing outside the apartment door, his arms spread in readiness to embrace me. An unseasonal Panama hat was perched on his head, and a long black leather trenchcoat swung from his shoulders.

'Darling!' he said, grinning at me as if he'd only seen me yesterday.

I had a sudden sense of *déjà vu*. I couldn't help feeling that I'd been here before about a year ago, but with someone else.

'Robert,' I said flatly. 'What are you doing here?'

'You left a message on my answering machine yesterday, so I dropped everything and came to see you!' Before I could slam the door in his face, he had me in his arms and was hugging me to him as closely as the airbag of my eight-and-a-half months' pregnancy would allow. When he felt me push against him, he drew back and looked me up and down. 'God, look at you! So very preggers!' His right hand slipped inside my dressing gown and caressed the taut bump. 'Mmm! What a wonderful, fruitful shape! It really turns me on!'

Words failed me. I felt like I was being embraced by an alien from outer space. Still hugging me, Robert kicked the front door closed behind him, shrugged his coat onto the floor and hurled his hat across the hall like a frisbee. Then, taking my hand, he drew me into the living room. 'Why, it's all transformed!' he exclaimed. 'Very smart. Very chic. Very *House Beautiful*. Very South of France. What happened to all that marvellously kitschy furniture you used to have? I liked all that. And . . . Hey!' He squinted at one of Cecil's Hockney drawings, now hung above our new sofa. 'Is that a real Picasso? Must have cost Cecil a bomb!' Without waiting for an answer, he sank down onto the cushions, pulled me onto his lap and began to nuzzle the nape of my neck.

I wrenched free and struggled to my feet. 'What the hell do you think you're doing?'

Robert sucked in a long breath and looked up at me through his thick dark eyelashes. 'You're angry with me, aren't you?' he said through gritted teeth.

I straightened my bathrobe. 'What do you think?'

'You are. I can tell by that glorious glint in your eyes. And, do you know something, Lisa? You're quite right to be angry with me. Because, darling, it must seem to you that I've behaved extremely badly.'

'You could say that.'

'When the fact is,' Robert continued, 'the fact is, Lisa – and when I tell you the truth, you'll understand perfectly – the fact is, I've actually behaved extremely well.' Seeing my stony expression, his mouth drooped. 'This business has hurt you a lot, hasn't it? Well, I'm very, very sorry about all of this.'

'Are you?'

'How could you doubt it? I couldn't tell you at the time, but there were reasons – perfectly good, honourable reasons – why I had to stay away.'

'What reasons?'

'That's what I've come here for – to explain. You see, darling, the trouble was . . . the trouble is . . . You see, it was work. It was . . .' He waved an airy hand. 'Christ, this is hard! Look, can't you just accept that I wasn't able to get in touch with you?'

'Don't tell me – the termites ate your only pencil? Or have you been stuck up a eucalyptus tree for the last eight months, out of reach of a phone?'

Robert burst out laughing. 'God, I've missed your sense of humour, you funny face! No, it was nothing like that! Actually, I've been in London all the time, but . . .'

'London? LONDON? In that case, why didn't you ever ring me up? Why didn't you come and see me? Why didn't you at least answer my letters?'

Robert flung his hands above his head. 'Darling, I'm sorry! I just *couldn't*. God knows, I wanted to! But, you see, I felt so guilty about Cecil . . .'

'What about *me*?' I shouted. 'I'm the one who landed in the shit, for God's sake!' I laid my hands on the parasite. 'I'm the one who's got to cope with *this*!'

'Yes but . . .' Robert rubbed his forehead. 'That wasn't exactly my fault, darling.'

I gave an exasperated laugh. 'Look, I'm not saying it wasn't mutual attraction. I mean, we both got carried away. But you could have been more careful with that condom!'

His shoulders hunched in a helpless shrug. 'Lisa, believe me, my hands were tied!'

'As I remember, it was my hands which were tied.'

In a dramatic gesture, Robert fell to his knees and attempted to encircle my gargantuan waist. 'Wait till I explain! Don't condemn me out of hand, darling.'

Freeing myself, I turned away and stalked out onto the balcony. 'Don't call me *darling*, Robert. Don't call me anything. And don't try to explain anything because I'm not interested. Just go away!'

Still on his knees, he shuffled out after me, arms outstretched in supplication. 'Please hear me out!'

'Get up! You look ridiculous.'

'I beg you – listen to me! I adore you, Lisa! If you only

knew how I've been suffering! God, it's been torture! Believe me, I've tried my best to forget you . . .'

'Thanks a lot!'

'. . . but I just can't do it. I realised that when I heard your voice on the answering machine yesterday. It made me see that we have to be together, Lisa. For ever and ever. I need you. You're the most important thing in my life.'

'More important than termites?' I snapped.

He laughed bitterly. 'I don't give a monkey's for termites. I never did. Truly, darling, I only care about you.'

'That's tough, Robert. Because I don't care about you any more.'

This silenced him for a moment. His jaw dropped, and his eyes widened in astonishment. Eventually he gasped, 'I just don't believe that!'

'Well, you'd better.'

'No, no, no!' Robert got to his feet and walked towards me. 'I *know* that you love me.'

'Oh? How?'

'Remember that day?' He put one hand on either side of me, pinioning me against the balcony rail. 'Our picnic in Cap Ferrat? The moonlit walk along the beach down there? The magic of our first kiss? And, oh God, the fireworks! I'll never forget those fireworks as long as I live!'

'You know what they call them in French?' I hissed as his face drew closer. '*Feux d'artifice.*'

He moistened his lips with the tip of his tongue. 'That wasn't artifice for either of us, my love! Don't tell me that wasn't as real for you as it was for me.'

I bit my lip. I couldn't deny what he was saying. 'That was then, Robert. This is now.'

He kissed my forehead. 'What difference does a few months make with a love like ours?'

'A hell of a lot in this case. Hey, you're squashing me!' In vain, I attempted to push him away. 'Look, Robert, frankly I don't believe a word you're saying. You sound like an actor reading lines in a play.'

243

He looked genuinely put out. 'Do I?'

'Don't you understand? All this is about nine months too late!'

His voice dropped an octave: 'It's never too late for love,' he purred as his lips moved to within kissing distance. 'So don't fight it any more. Admit it, Lisa – you're in love with me.'

'No, Robert, I don't love you at all. In fact, I . . . I hate you!'

His eyes lit up, and he tilted my chin towards him. 'God, I love you when you're like this, you little vixen! Kiss me! Ow!' For I had taken my hand off the balcony rail and slapped him hard across the face. 'That hurt!' he said as he backed away, rubbing his cheek with his palm. 'It might even bruise!'

'I hope it does. Now, listen to me – I don't want to kiss you. I don't even want you near me. OK?'

A look of frank incredulity came over his face. 'Why?'

'For God's sake! I . . . I'm Cecil's wife!'

He smiled as if this was totally irrelevant. 'Sweetie, you can't possibly find Cecil attractive! He looks like a bloody frog!'

I narrowed my eyes. 'Why are you being so horrible about him? I thought you were supposed to be his friend?'

'Come off it! What could Cecil and I possibly have in common?'

I looked at the gorgeous-looking man I'd once lusted after, and suddenly I remembered a saying of my father's: Handsome is as handsome does. 'At least Cecil's stuck by me through all this, Robert. Which is more than I can say for you. Cecil's worth a million of you.'

'If you ask me, he's worth a cool million, and that's what you see in him. Whereas I . . .' He spread his arms wide. 'I have nothing. You take me as I am, for richer, for poorer . . .'

'Or not at all. Forget it.'

'How can I forget? If only you knew what pain I've been through! If only you knew how I feel about you!' I backed away as he came towards me again. '*My bounty is as boundless as the sea, my love as deep: the more I give to thee, the more I have, for both are infinite.* Romeo and Juliet, Act Two, Scene Two.'

My back crashed against the balcony railing. 'Very erudite. Very touching. In the right context.'

He raised an eyebrow, and pressed closer. 'It's the balcony scene, Lisa. What could be more appropriate than that? *With love's light wings did I o'er-perch these walls; For stony limits cannot hold love out, And what love can do that dares love attempt; Therefore thy kinsmen are no stop to me . . . There lies more peril in thine eye than twenty of their swords . . .*'

The next moment, he put his hands under my arms and, with superhuman effort, hoisted me onto the balcony rail. Behind me was nothing – just a 100-metre drop.

The hairs on the back of my neck bristled. 'What the hell are you doing, Robert?' I whispered, gripping the rail hard.

His mouth curved into an adoring smile as he slipped into a perfect Bogart imitation: *'Just looking at you, kid.'*

'Well, take me off here!'

'Not until you promise to divorce Cecil and marry me.'

There was a short silence in which I wondered whether the best thing to do would be play along with him. 'Look . . .'

'She speaks,' he interrupted. *'O! speak again, bright angel; for thou art as glorious to this night, being o'er my head, as is a winged messenger of heaven Unto the white-upturned wond'ring eyes Of mortals, that fall back to gaze on him When he bestrides the lazy-pacing clouds, And sails upon the bosom of the air!'*

Boy, when I made a mistake I really made one! Robert's major fault wasn't insincerity, it was insanity. He was barmy. Bonkers. Bingo! My choice in men had never been good, but this time I'd really hit the jackpot.

'Don't worry, Lisa – you're quite safe,' he said, as if sensing what I was thinking. 'I'm holding you. And I'll never let you go, never! Trust me.' Hadn't I heard that expression once before from Robert? And where had it got me last time?

'Please, Robert!' I begged. 'Let me down from here.'

He laid his cheek against my belly, which was now pushing

uncomfortably up into my ribs. 'Not until you've promised to marry me.'

'Robert, *I'm frightened*!'

'Of me?' He laughed, as if this was a huge joke. 'But I love you, darling!'

'I'm frightened of *falling*!' I hissed between my chattering teeth. Just then, the telephone rang inside the flat. Some sixth sense told me it was Cecil. My knight in armour had telephoned long-distance to save me. Unfortunately, Robert seemed deaf to anything but the sound of his own voice.

'The telephone's ringing, Robert.'

'Is it?' He continued to beam at me as if in a trance. 'So?'

'It's probably Cecil.'

'Who cares?'

'I . . . I must speak to him! He's phoning from New York.'

'Damn it, Lisa, let it ring! He's had you all this time – now it's my turn.'

'But I must answer it! He'll . . . he'll think there's something wrong. He . . .' I cast around desperately for a reason. 'He'll send round the police.'

'Then stay where you are, sweetie! I'll get it!'

'No!'

'I'm going to tell him everything!'

'Robert, *don't*!'

But it was too late: Robert let go of me, and turned away, leaving me perched precariously on the balcony railing. As he stepped through the french windows and into the living room, I felt my body start to tip backwards. '*Robert!*' I shrieked as I overbalanced in slow motion. But by now, Robert was out of sight and out of earshot. '*Robert!*'

The fingers of both my hands tightened around the metal rail, with the result that I ended up in a half-somersault position, with my body jutting horizontally out over the abyss, and my legs sticking up in the air. But with my huge stomach pushing into my ribs, and gravity pulling me down, I knew there was no way I could hold on for long.

In the living room, Robert must have picked up the phone because I could hear him talking. '*Cecil? Hello, old chap! What do you mean, who is it? It's me! Yes! Surprised? Well . . .*'

My left hand gave way. As I fell, I twisted sideways and my legs plummeted downwards so I hung from one arm. There was a wrenching sound as my right shoulder took all my weight. 'Robert!' I screamed. 'Help me!'

'*What do you mean, what am I doing here? No, no! Now hold on, Cess, I can explain . . .*'

A searing pain shot down my right side. I felt the muscles in my armpit stretch and tear. The metal rail cut into my hand like a cheese wire. I moved my left hand across, and grabbed hold of one of the vertical bars, but I couldn't get a proper grip on it. 'Robert! Help! Help!'

At last he must have heard me because I heard him call out in a reassuring voice, 'Don't worry, darling, I'll make him understand! *Now look here, Cecil . . .*'

I had to hold on. I mustn't look down. Far below, I could hear the clinking of glasses and the clash of crockery. I pictured Zuzu's guests in the marquee: the men in their Valentino blazers and Cartier cufflinks; the women in their Christian Dior dresses, Ferragamo shoes, Van Cleef & Arpels diamonds and Prada bags; all of them sipping champagne delivered by a bevy of white-coated waiters, and eating canapés provided by the Hôtel de Paris. All of them talking with great seriousness about nothing of importance, unaware of the drama taking place thirty-two floors above them. If only someone would step outside the marquee, look up and see me . . . But they'd never spot me in the dark, and even if they did, what could they do? By the time they'd worked out which floor I was dangling from, taken the lift up and banged on the door, it'd be too late and I'd have fallen . . .

Oh God! I was going to die! Half an hour before, I'd been about to take my own life. Now that it was about to be taken from me, I wanted to live. Elena was right – I was perverse. I wanted to live, but I wasn't going to. And no one, not even Cecil, would ever know what had really happened to me.

'Robert! ROBERT! HELP ME!'

'*What? No! Yes, I know I did but . . . Look, wait a minute, will you? I think Lisa's calling.*'

At last! His footsteps ambled slowly across the marble floor. Hadn't he heard the urgency in my voice? Why didn't he hurry? My palm was on fire, and my arm was coming out of its socket. 'ROBERT!' I watched through the railing as he stepped out onto the balcony, glanced around the empty terrace with a puzzled frown and went back inside. 'ROBERT! COME BACK!'

His head popped out again. 'Lisa?'

'OVER HERE!'

Robert started in my direction, but painfully slowly. 'Where? Stop playing . . .'

I was on the rack. Every muscle and bone in my body was tearing. I could scarcely breathe now. One by one, my burning fingers began to slip from the rail. 'HURRY! I'M . . . Aaah!' Something seemed to give way in my shoulderblade. I jolted down, and as I did so, my left hand slipped down the vertical rail. A split second later I came to a halt, this time hanging only by my left arm. I felt like a joint of Parma ham strung up in a delicatessen. Pain spread through my whole body. My legs thrashed the empty air in a desperate search for a foothold.

'Jesus Christ!' Eyes bulging with horror, Robert's face stared down at me from above the railing. 'Lisa! What are you *doing* there?'

What did he think I was doing? Practising a new form of aerobic exercise? Trying to clean the windows of the flat below with my feet? 'Help me!' I gasped.

'Yes. Yes of course!' Crouching down, he stuck a hand through the bars and grabbed hold of my wrist. 'Can you get your other hand up? Go on! Try! Try harder, Lisa!'

I tried to lift my right arm, but whatever strength it had once possessed had been spent. 'I can't!' I sobbed.

'You must!' His eyes wild with terror, Robert stuck his other hand through the bars, so that he had my left wrist in a double grasp. 'Stay calm!' he commanded in a voice that was anything but. 'I'll try and pull you up and lift you over the rail.' Squatting on his haunches, he attempted to drag me upwards. 'Loosen your grip!'

'No! I daren't!'

'Loosen your fingers! Go on, I'm holding you! Jesus,' he spat through gritted teeth as he failed to budge me. 'How much do you weigh?'

Did he want the answer in stones or kilos? I didn't have a chance to ask. Because just then, I did as he'd asked and loosened my grip, and at the same time Robert said, 'I think I'll try to reach you from above . . .' and let go of my wrists, and the iron bar slipped out of my grasp.

I reached up towards him, but Robert's face was shrinking like a deflating balloon. 'Don't go, Lisa!' he screamed, as if I had a choice in the matter.

But I was going. Faster and faster. Robert had disappeared, and the floodlit swimming pool and the marquee were flying up to meet me like a floating carpet and a hovering jewel . . .

Seventeen

❖

Just before my death, a last moment of clarity:

I brace myself for the big smash, but, instead of violent obliteration, there's a dull blow to my back.

Winded, fighting for breath, I open my eyes to find that I'm surrounded by whiteness – not pure, snowy whiteness but a kind of blank, creamy whiteness such as I always imagined blind people might see.

Am I dead? Can I feel anything? I reach out a hand, and find that the whiteness is a tangible thing, taut as a hammock and rough as a cat's tongue.

Suddenly, with a terrible rip, the whiteness gives way underneath me and I plummet down again, this time into a fairyland of candles and lanterns. With a loud yell, I crash-land onto something cold, wet and very slippery.

I'm lying stark naked on a giant silver platter of caviar canapés. Humanoid monsters with black-rimmed eyes stand around, horror-struck, gawping at me.

Then, 'Dahlink!' grates a gravelly, sarcastic voice nearby. 'I'm so glad you decided to drop in!'

After that, it's pain, blackness and silence. So, this is death, is it? What a let-down! Even though I'm not a religious person, I'd expected something a little more awesome and profound than this. Some feeling of physical liberation, perhaps, or a brief instant of psychic enlightenment. You know – a long, dark tunnel with a light at the end of it, and as you gradually reach the light, you realise that, in death, you're suddenly happier than you ever were in life.

Sadly, the mystical near-death experience that people who've almost died recount in such detail bears no resemblance at all to the real thing. In truth, I just wish I had a bottle of double-strength aspirin, and that someone else would come into this darkness and switch on a light.

I wander on through the blackout. Then something changes: the silence stays the same, but a light comes on overhead and the pain gets worse. Hell exists, and I'm in the midst of it. It's all here, laid out like a Breughel painting: the clanking iron instruments of torture, the masked, gaping ghouls, the fire which threatens to consume me from the inside out.

Pain ripples through me in great waves. The last shreds of Life are being torn from my body like teeth.

Bloody hell! I know it's too late for regrets, but I can't help thinking that if only I'd kept my hands off Robert and been a bit nicer to Cecil, I might have gone to Heaven instead.

I'm swimming through a thick cloud of nothingness. And getting nowhere. But wait! I can see a light in the distance after all! I float towards it, body aching, mind drifting in and out of consciousness. Unconsciousness is actually my preferred mode of being, because when I'm unconscious I don't have to face reality. But the powers that be here in Hell are determined that I should suffer. Gently but firmly, they shake me by the shoulder, and slap me on the cheeks.

'Madame? Madame Brown! Reveillez!'

'Levmealone' I say in a slurred voice.

'Madame Brown! Ouvrez les yeux! Madame Brown!'

'Goway! Wannnagobaktersleep.'

'Regardez, Madame! Regardez votre fille!'

The shutters of my heavily drugged eyelids unroll just long enough to see two red blobby images swimming in front of me. I attempt to focus, and for a brief moment the images collide. Is this really what they want me to look at – this blotchy, spotty, bald little rat with screwed-up piggy eyes?

I realise with alarm that the parasite is alive and kicking.

Come to that, so am I.

I may have ruined Zuzu's party by squashing flat the caviar
canapés and destroying the marquee, but here in the hospital
I'm considered something of a heroine. Doctors and nurses
come from all departments to peer at me through the door,
because, in this Catholic country, for an eight-and-a-half-
months' pregnant woman to emerge from a 32-storey fall
virtually unscathed but for a broken ankle and a premature
start to labour is declared to be nothing short of a miracle.

I'm the talk not just of the town, but of the whole
principality. In fact, of the entire Côte d'Azur. 'Drama –
Mortal Plunge in Monaco!' screams the front-page headline
of *Nice-Matin*. 'Tragedy Averted by Hors d'œuvres!'

Cecil has been summoned back from America. Meanwhile,
my parents have arrived from London, with Cecil's mother
Rita in tow. Rita seems set to stay for a while: she's brought
her own crochet-covered, wedge-shaped cushion – just like
the one in the Ford Escort – and even her knitting. 'Look,
Lisa, dear!' she purrs, thrusting her sharp needless at me
none too kindly. 'Now isn't that the prettiest matinée coat
you've ever seen?'

Since turning up at the hospital this morning, my three visitors have taken up permanent residence on three chairs beside
my bed. There they sit, moaning with relentless cheerfulness
about the weather in England, the scurrilousness of the tab-
loids they're reading, and the weakness of foreign tea. Strange
how none of them has yet mentioned my accident . . .

During the rare moments when it isn't being picked up, cud-
dled and cooed over by its three doting grandparents or having
its nappy changed, the parasite lies quietly in a see-through
plastic fish tank near the window. From time to time its lips
part as if it's about to cry, but then it shoots me a wary glance
and, seeing my cold expression, changes its little mind.

The nurses declare this silent, miracle baby to be an angel.
The truth is that the parasite is intelligent: it knows better
than to chance its luck by annoying me.

As I doze off all remaining traces of pethedine, my parents confer in a stage whisper.

'She's just not natural.'

'What're you talking about, Lorelei?'

'Haven't you noticed? She never smiles at her. She doesn't talk about her. She doesn't even seem to want to pick her up. You should see the way she looks at her when she's feeding – as if she hates her.'

'No!'

'Horace! I know what I'm talking about!'

'Mmm. God knows, you may be right.' My father digests this for a moment. 'But remember, Lisa's had a terrible shock, poor love. That was quite a fall she took. She's incredibly lucky to be alive!'

'You got no sense at all,' Lorelei hisses. 'It wasn't a *fall*.'

'Of course it was.'

'How can a woman in her condition *fall* off a balcony?' There was a loud smack as my mother's lips came together. 'I'm afraid we've got to face it, Horace – she tried to commit suicide!'

So, that's it! Perhaps they're worried that I'll try to do it again – I can think of no other reason why they won't leave me alone for a single moment. I'm going mad, trapped here in this hospital bed, listening to their mindless chit-chat. If only I could escape! But if escape wasn't impossible enough last night, what with the heavy, itchy cast on my broken ankle and the soreness of my episiotomy stitches, it's even more impossible this morning, because two concrete-hard, lumpy barrels have appeared overnight on my chest.

Where have these barrels come from? And what are they doing there? Surely these monstrosities weren't once human breasts? Incredibly, I'm expected to feed the parasite from them. Every hour, on the hour, it is removed from its fish tank, swaddled in a pink blanket to keep its arms from flailing, and placed upon a bared feeding tap. Its little gums clamp to my sore nipples like vices, and as it sucks steadily, my stomach muscles contract with pain.

I hope that the parasite will suck me dry before the day is out. But no such luck: the more milk it wolfs down, the more milk I produce. By afternoon, milk spurts from my nipples like water from a baroque fountain, wetting my nightdress, soaking the bed. The nurses tell me I have enough milk to feed every baby on the post-natal ward. An electric pump is brought in, to which I am soon hooked up like a cow.

Former profession: novelist. Present job: one-woman Express Dairy. Maybe I should try suicide.

'Lower, hon!'

'Higher!'

'Move the baby to the left!'

'No, move her to the right!'

It's feeding time at the dairy again. Lorelei and Rita stand guard on either side of me, issuing step-by-step instructions which contradict each other and contradict the nurse.

'Don't listen to what she said! Press your finger in above the nipple. Otherwise you'll suffocate the baby.'

'No, not like that! Like *this*!'

The parasite's gummy gums clamp together on my sore nipple. 'Ouch! It bit me!' I scream.

'She's just trying to latch on, dear,' says Rita soothingly. 'Tickle her under her chin and she'll let go.'

'Not like that, hon, like this!'

'Yes, dear, that's it. Now push the nipple into her mouth.' Despairing of me, Rita shakes her head and picks up her knitting again. 'In my day,' she tuts, 'we believed in the bottle. Every four hours. And that was that.'

I soldier on for another minute. 'For Chrissake, Lisa, are you trying to gag her?' my mother yells.

Fed up and furious, I thrust the parasite at my mother. 'If you're such a bloody expert, do it yourself!'

Denied the source of sustenance, the parasite suddenly decides to break its hitherto unbroken record and scream.

Afraid it'll be sick on her red M&S jumper, my mother joggles it at arm's length until Rita yells at her that she's not supporting its neck. At which my father leaps up from his chair and snatches the parasite from my mother, who bursts into tears . . .

At that minute, the door swings open, and into this chaos walks Cecil, looking unusually dapper in a new Donna Karan raincoat. All three parents stop screaming at each other and leap to their feet, smiling beatifically, as if in the presence of some kind of superman.

Ignoring them, Cecil dashes straight over to my bed, flings down a small, book-shaped parcel beside me and, taking my hands, gazes into my eyes with devotion and relief. 'Lisa, darling,' he says. 'Thank God you're all right!' His voice, like his expression, oozes with emotion – emotion which I know is insincere. For the truth is that it would have been extremely convenient for Cecil, and certainly for his lover Sandra, if I hadn't survived after all.

Unable to look him in the face, I turn away. Maybe Rita has noticed this, for she grabs Cecil and throws her arms around him. 'Congratulations, Daddy!'

'Where is she?' Cecil says, unnecessarily, for with that much noise coming from the parasite, he could hardly miss it. 'Here, Horace, give her to me! There, there!' He takes the parasite from my father, puts her straight on his shoulder and gently rubs her back. The parasite sobs pitifully three or four times, then, forgetting that the origin of its anger was, in fact, frustrated hunger, closes its eyes and falls straight asleep. Horace, Lorelei and Rita look on in wonder as, cradling its neck with the expertise of a Norland Nanny, Cecil lays it back in the fish tank.

'Why, she's beautiful!' he murmurs as he gazes down at it. He grins at me across the room. 'It's a good thing she's inherited your looks, darling!'

Rita clucks like a proud mother hen. 'There's nothing wrong with her father's looks, either!' she declares. How right she is! Although, of course, she doesn't realise why. 'You look tired, darling.'

'I'm OK, Mum.' He shrugs off his coat to reveal a splendid new, if rather crumpled, suit. 'I came here straight from the airport. The flight was interminable. I tried my best to get a seat on Concorde, but both the London and the Paris flights were fully booked.' He sighs. 'But I'm back now, thank God. And look, darling,' he adds, picking up the parcel and thrusting it at me, 'I've brought you a little present.'

'Thank you, Cecil.' I nod towards the bedside table. 'Put it over there.'

'What's the matter with you?' my mother snaps. 'Aren't you going to open it?'

'I'll do it later.'

'What's wrong with now? If Cecil's bothered to bring it all this way . . .'

'Oh, for God's sake!' I grab the parcel ungratefully, and tear off the paper. Inside is a small line drawing set in a wide, expensive-looking gilt frame. I glance at it quickly. The subject – mother and child. This choice is not merely insensitive of Cecil, it's actually downright sick. 'Very nice,' I mutter, and put the drawing face down on the bed.

Cecil picks it up. 'It's a Matisse,' he says in a quiet, disappointed voice. Like spectators watching an impressive firework display, our parents let out a collective gasp. 'I bought it at a sale yesterday.'

Three pairs of hands reach out for this exquisite treasure, but none of them are mine.

'Let's see!'

'Marvellous! Must have cost a packet!'

'Aren't you a lucky girl?' says Rita, handing it back to me.

'Aren't you going to thank Cecil?'

Cecil protests that there's no need for me to thank him. But, obedient to my mother's command, I force the words out of myself. Inside, my anger is building up like floodwater behind a cracked dam. Any minute now it's going to burst through and bring the entire teetering edifice of our marriage crashing down.

There is a long, uneasy silence, at the end of which my father, who is now sitting down again, says, innocently, 'Well, Cecil, you must be glad to be home with Lisa and the baby. Your new family.'

Cecil swallows. 'Oh yes, I am.'

At this seemingly innocuous remark, the dam inside me breaks. 'Oh, for God's sake, shut up!' I yell. 'Shut up, all of you!'

'Hush, Lisa!' Cecil murmurs.

My father jumps to his feet and spreads his hands. 'What have I said?'

'Nothing, Horace!'

'*Nothing?*' I stare at Cecil in despair. 'What's the matter with you?' I shout at him. 'Why are you carrying on this ridiculous pretence? Are you mad, or just stupid?'

Cecil stares at me with pleading eyes. 'Lisa, please . . .'

'How long do you think we can carry on like this? Why don't you *tell* them?'

Cecil's mother frowns, and her lower lip – so like Cecil's, I note – juts forward and quivers. 'Tell us what, Cecil?'

Cecil hesitates on the brink of confessing all. Should he? Shouldn't he? He decides not to, and waves a dismissive hand. 'It's nothing. Nothing at all.'

I glare at him. 'How can you say that? It's not nothing, it's the truth – the one thing you can't stand!'

'Lisa, don't shout at Cecil!'

'He's my husband, Mum, and I'll shout at him if I like! And if you don't like it, get out of here!'

Cecil glances at them desperately. 'Maybe it'd be better if you all left for a little while.'

'So, we're being thrown out, are we?' my mother gasps in full melodramatic flight. 'After all we've done for her? I've never been so insulted in my life!'

'Get her out! Get her out of here!' I begin to scream.

Cecil's short arms flap impotently. 'Please, Lorelei! All of

ou! I don't mean to be rude but ... Can't you see this is
ll too much for Lisa?'

'Lisa, Lisa! Why does everything always have to revolve
round her?' Lorelei sobs.

'She's the one whose had the baby, darling,' my father
croons in his mild, gentle voice as he stands up, ready to
go. His hand reaches for the door knob. 'Come on, love.
Come, Rita. Everybody out. Cecil's right. The kids need
some time alone.'

Lorelei stands up, smooths down her rucked skirt and grabs
the shield of her black patent handbag. 'I know when I'm not
wanted!'

Horace places a comforting arm around Rita's now heaving
shoulder, and marshalls her, and my grumbling mother, out
into the corridor. Once they've gone, silence fills the room,
broken only by my whooping sobs as I cry into my hands.
Miraculously, despite all the brouhaha, the parasite has
remained sound asleep. Through my half-closed fingers, I
watch Cecil inch towards it and peer down at it with a
simpering smile upon his face.

'Don't look at it like that!' I snap.

'Like what?' he says, turning towards me.

'Like a proud father.'

Cecil frowns with concern. He sits down on the bed beside
me, and takes my hand. 'Lisa ...'

I yank my hand away with a violence which makes him
recoil. 'No, don't try to be nice to me! I just can't bear it!
I can't stand this pretence any longer! I can't go on like this
any more!'

'Calm down, darling.' Cecil doesn't look at me angrily,
as he should, but with a mixture of sadness and concern.
'Everything's all right! I mean, it will be soon. I promise you
it will.'

I laugh hysterically. 'Yes? How? Look at the mess we're
in! What do you plan to do – just carry on pretending that
that ... that *thing* over there is your child!'

Cecil's chin juts forward stubbornly. 'She *is* my child.'

'Sure! Our whole marriage has been a sham, so I suppos you see no reason why the bloody charade shouldn't continu forever! Oh, Cecil!' I collapse in tears of shame. 'If only yo knew how I've deceived you!'

'No, no, darling, you haven't!'

'I have! Surely you realise that the baby's not yours? Haven you guessed that it . . . it's Robert's?' Cecil doesn't look a shocked as I'd imagined he would, but he does draw in a long sharp breath. Maybe, at long last, I'm getting through to him 'And . . . there's more. I . . . I didn't even love you when w got married,' I blunder on in an avalanche of confession. 'I fact I . . . oh, God, it's so awful . . . I despised you!'

Cecil nods. 'I know,' he says with perfect calm. 'I knev it then.'

This so shocks me that my tears instantly dry up. 'Bu . . . How?'

His eyes roll in a way that used to remind me of a frightene dog. Now, for the first time, I see the irony in his expression 'I'd have been a complete idiot not to know, wouldn't I?'

'But then . . . How could you . . . I mean, why on eartl did you . . .?'

'Why did I marry you?' He laughs ruefully. 'Why do yo think? Because I was madly in love with you. From the firs moment I saw you sitting in the gutter in the Haymarket, thought you were the most beautiful, the most elegant, th most intelligent and the most attractive woman I'd ever me in my life. I couldn't believe my luck when you agreed t go out with me. And when I asked you to marry me, an you said yes . . .' He shakes his head. 'I realised you mus be desperate to get married, though I couldn't for the life o me understand why. I mean, a woman like you – so gorgeou and talented . . . I knew you couldn't possibly want me, but was so much in love with you that I just couldn't believe tha everything I felt wouldn't, some day, be returned. If it wasn' – well, I guess I felt that having you under sufferance woulc be better than not having you at all.' His long mouth twist: into a lopsided smile. 'Though I'm not so sure about that any nore. I suppose I hoped against hope that once you saw past my fabulous face and divine physique and got to know me, you'd grow to love me, too. But . . .' His smile dries up like a trickle of water in sand. 'I see now that I was being just a little over-optimistic. I owe you a big apology, Lisa.'

'*You* owe *me* an apology?'

He takes a deep breath. 'You're not the only one who's been deceitful.'

'I wish you wouldn't talk in riddles.'

Cecil's mouth opens silently, and his hand passes over his forehead in a despairing gesture. I haven't seen him this distressed for months. 'Do you remember when I proposed to you?' he says at last. 'I promised then that I'd do anything – anything at all – to make you love me. Well, darling, you have no idea – no idea at all – what lengths I've been to. Oh dear, oh dear!' He turns away from me. 'I'm so ashamed!'

'Ashamed? Why?'

'You see, I wanted . . . You see, you were . . . When Robert came . . .'

'Robert? What's he got to do with this? Cecil, what on earth are you talking about? Hey, wait!'

For, red-faced and lips a-quiver, Cecil stands up and lunges for the door. He returns two minutes later, pulling Robert by the hand. But this is a Robert who is almost unrecognisable. He's still wearing the clothes he wore when I last saw him, but his hair is filthy and matted, his eyes are haunted and underscored by shadows, and his black leather trenchcoat is a crumpled wreck. Two days' beard growth pricks through his cheeks, and there's a pea-sized blob of dried tomato ketchup on his stubbly chin. There both men stand, hand in hand and side by side like a mismatched comedy duo at the end of my hospital bed.

Robert smiles sheepishly at me, and attempts a cheerful wink. 'Hello, darling. Um, sorry about what happened the other night.'

With dropped jaw, I stare at him for a moment, then turn to Cecil. 'What the hell is he doing here?'

'He has to be here,' Cecil replies. 'I think it's best if we explain this together.'

I look from Cecil back to Robert, then back to Cecil again. 'Explain what?'

'You see, Lisa . . .' Cecil clears his throat. 'The thing is Robert isn't really my best friend.'

This statement is so ridiculous under the circumstances that I almost laugh. 'Do you think I'm not aware of that by now? And, look, I'm very sorry about it. And I want you to know that what happened was just as much my fault as his.'

Cecil lets go of Robert's hand, and wrings his own. 'You don't understand. When I say he's not my best friend, what I mean is, he never *was* my best friend. Or any friend. I hired him.'

'You did what?'

'I hired him. I hired him to pretend that he was my friend. I brought him into our relationship because . . . because . . . well . . .' Unable to say more, Cecil resorts to his penguin flap.

'Because *what*, Cecil?'

He swallows hard. 'You see, Lisa, I had this plan, this stupid no . . .' Stuttering for the first time in ages, Cecil paces towards the window and starts his sentence again. 'I had this notion that if I could break the awful physical barrier between us . . . if I could make love to you just once . . . well, that you might stop hating me and fall in love with me after all. But the trouble was, I couldn't get near you. It was strange, because, well, to be honest, I'd never had any problems with women before. But with you, it was different. As if you'd erected some invisible electric fence. So I . . . well, I hired Robert to help me. I wanted him to . . . well, to put it bluntly, I wanted him to get you in the mood for sex.'

Incredulous, I turn to Robert. 'This isn't true, is it?'

Robert nods, and has the good manners to look ashamed. 'Every word of it.'

'So . . .' I say as I try to make sense of this, 'you're really not an old friend of Cecil's?'

''Fraid not.'

'But what about all that stuff you both talked about – all
those stories about your old school?'

Robert shrugs. 'All lies. We cooked them up over the phone
before I came.'

'You're telling me you flew all the way here from Australia
just to pretend . . .'

Robert raises a finger to interrupt me. 'Er, there was
no Australia. No Woolabongalonga. And before you ask,
there weren't any termites either. The truth is, Lisa, I live
permanently in London. The nearest I've ever come to the
Australian outback was doing a voice-over for Castlemaine
XXXX.'

I stare at him in horror. 'Who exactly are you?'

'I'm an actor,' he announces. 'With the RSC. Well, I say
with the RSC, but I'm not exactly with them any more. I did
a couple of seasons for them, a few years ago. Since then . . .'
He shrugs. 'It's a tough profession. You take what you can get.
Pantos. Provincial rep. The occasional walk-on spear-holder
at the National. I was once an understudy for Ratty in *Wind
in the Willows*.'

'So, let's get this straight – this was just a job to you?'

He shrugs helplessly. 'Darling, I needed the money. Besides,
if I'm honest – and I am honest in real life, believe it or not –
I suppose that I was intrigued. I mean, it's not every day one
gets offered a part like that.'

A part. Was that all it had been to him? I think back to the
magic between us in Cap Ferrat, and our kiss on the beach,
and I realise with horror just how thoroughly I've been had.
'So, let me get this straight: Cecil paid you to tie me up and
make love to me,' I state angrily.

'Uhhuh!' Robert raises his finger again to correct me. '*I* tied
you up,' he says. 'But it wasn't me who made love to you.'

'Sorry? What on earth do you mean?'

After a long, unhappy pause, Robert jerks his stubbly chin
in Cecil's direction. Cecil's head is lowered, and a tear is
trickling down his cheek. Slowly, darkly, the terrible truth
began to dawn on me. At first I can't believe it. Who could?

263

I shake my head wildly, because what Robert seems to be implying just isn't possible.

'No!' I breathe. Cecil and Robert both nod. 'But you were in Paris, Cecil! Robert and I took you to the airport!'

Cecil clears his throat. 'That's as far as I got. Once you'd driven off, I caught a bus into Nice and spent the day going round the galleries. Then, while you and Robert were out on the beach that night, I secretly came home and hid. It was I who switched off the electricity, because, I . . . well I was afraid the blindfold would fall off and you'd see me.'

A pit opens up in my sore, deflated stomach, and a cauldron of anger and confusion and embarrassment bubbles inside it as I think back to those wonderful hours of abandonment and ecstacy, when I was tied up in the dark bedroom, believing that Robert was making love to me. And all the time, it had been Cecil. How could I not have known it? How could this awful thing be true?

'How could you both do that to me?'

Cecil takes a deep breath. 'Please, don't blame Robert. It was all my idea. I . . . I was desperate, Lisa! I don't know what possessed me to be such an idiot. I see now how unforgivable the whole thing was. Criminal. I deceived you. I made love to you against your will. I was planning to tell you immediately afterwards, but, well, I lost my nerve. It was the way you kept crying out Robert's name when I was making love to you . . . It was only then that I began to realise what a terrible thing I'd done.'

I look accusingly at Robert. 'And you . . . you colluded with him. Just for the money! How much was it, Robert? Mmm?'

Robert is about to speak, but Cecil touches his arm, and says, 'That's irrelevant, Lisa.'

'Not to me. I want to know. How much, Robert?'

'Twenty grand.' Robert spreads his hands as if to show how helpless he was in the face of financial necessity. 'That's a lot of dough for a week's work. Besides, until I met you I didn't realise what I was letting myself in for. It all seemed like a bit of a joke.' He takes a deep breath. 'It never occurred to me that I might really fall in love with you.'

This new revelation is as ludicrous as it is bitter. 'Are you really asking me to believe that?'

'It's true, Lisa.' Cecil paces back and forth at the end of the bed. 'Robert told me so when I took him to the airport. He said he didn't want the money, he only wanted you. I told him to get lost, of course. I said that you were my wife, and that I wasn't going to let you go.' His right hand forms a tight, angry fist and punches hard into his left palm. 'I , . . I told him I'd kill him if he ever so much as tried to see you again. I couldn't bear the thought of anyone else loving you. But then . . . then . . .' Like a punctured tyre, Cecil deflates onto the visitor's chair. 'After he'd left, I saw how miserable you were. I knew that you were pining for him, and the thought of it tore me up. I couldn't bear to see you suffer like that, because of me. So, I decided to do something about it. I was about to ring Robert up, and tell him how you felt, but then . . .'

'Then you found out that I was pregnant,' I say matter-of-factly after his voice trails away.

Slowly, with great sadness, Cecil nods. 'That changed everything, of course. I was so excited. I fooled myself into thinking that once the baby was born you'd forget Robert and everything would settle down between us and turn out all right. But, as usual, I was wrong.'

Cecil looks so miserable that, despite my fury, I reach out and squeeze his hand. At which Robert sits down on the other side of the bed and grabs my other hand. 'And as for me, darling,' he booms, 'I realised immediately that I couldn't run off with you when you were expecting Cecil's child. I mean, think what you like of me, but I'm not that much of a cad. Besides, how could I have ever explained the real situation to you without making you hate me? But, believe me, Lisa, not a day went by when I didn't stand in front of my bathroom mirror and say to myself, *Robert, you poor bastard, you've brought this on yourself!* When I heard your voice on my answering machine the other day, I realised I couldn't stand it any longer. So I came to see you. To tell you how I felt. And fuck the consequences. I was on the point of confessing everything when you . . .' His voice rises in a crescendo. '. . . you disappeared.' There follows a long, dramatic pause in which Robert stares into the distance. Then his head gives a quick shake and he continues, 'My first instinct was to jump off the balcony after you, but then I thought to myself, *What good would that do?* It wasn't as if I'd have been able to save you. I'd only have spoiled your dramatic exit by muscling in on the act. By the time I got down to the marquee, you were surrounded by people who knew you, and there was nothing I could do except stay out of the way. I ran after the ambulance, of course, all the way here. The nurses jabbered at me in French, and wouldn't let me in to see you. I've been sitting on a bench in the car park, ever since, just waiting for Cecil to get here. Which is why you'll have to forgive me if I look a little wrecked.'

There is a faint whimper from the fish tank in the corner. Cecil gets up and joggles it around a bit, and the whimpering stops. He looks across at the bed, where Robert's sitting beside me, still holding my hand, and then he turns away and stares out of the window. After a long while, he unhooks his overcoat from the back of the door and picks up his briefcase.

'Where are you going?' I ask.

'Home,' Cecil says quietly. 'To pack some things. I'm going away for a while, so that you two can have some time together to sort things out. You both deserve it, after what I've put you through.' His face contorts into a painful smile. 'I really do want you to be happy, Lisa. I couldn't bear to think that you were suffering because of me.'

'But . . .' I call out as he opens the door.

He turns back. 'Yes?'

'Well . . .' I realise that there's nothing left to say; the whole sordid drama is over. 'What about the baby?'

He stares at me blankly for a moment, then says in a flat voice, 'That's up to you, Lisa. Whatever you decide, I won't interfere.' Then, lowering his head as if to fend off the onslaught of parental interrogation, Cecil walks out of the door, and out of my life.

Robert and I sit in silence for several minutes and listen to the raised voices jabbering outside. 'Well, well!' he says eventually. 'It looks like you and I are on our own at last.'

I take my hand out of his, and point to the parasite in the corner. 'Not quite.'

He gives a short laugh. 'Well, at least we're shot of Cecil.' Something about the way he says this annoys me intensely. 'We're free, love, free to be with one another.'

Politely, I grunt my agreement. But, strangely, I don't feel free. Freedom implies a lightness of being. Whereas, at the moment, I feel like I'm being crushed by an unbearably heavy weight.

'I must say, Cecil did that very well, didn't he?' Robert burbles on. 'Bowing out and all that. I couldn't have done that speech better myself if I'd rehearsed it for a month.'

I surprise myself by leaping to Cecil's defence: 'It wasn't a speech to him, Robert! Cecil meant every word of it. Anyone could see how hard it was for him.'

'Sure!'

'He's a very sincere person,' I snap. 'And extremely honourable. He . . .' My voice fades as I remember my night of bondage. There was nothing particularly honourable about Cecil's behaviour then! Quite the contrary. I mean, to double-cross your wife by making love to her when she thought she was being made love to by her lover!

A tremor passes down my spine as I recall, as clearly as if it had happened an hour ago, the pleasure of dissolving under that shower-bath of kisses, the mind-blowing thrill of Robert's soft fingers dabbling between my legs . . . No, not Robert's fingers, Cecil's fingers. Oh, I feel sick and confused! So that's what I've been missing out on during my marriage when, every night, I've turned my back on my husband and feigned sleep! No wonder his lover Sandra's so crazy about Cecil. Because, apart from being honourable and sincere and all that, Cecil, I realise, *knows how to give a woman pleasure in bed*.

Does Robert sense what I'm thinking? He's looking at me oddly, as if I'm a stranger in a bar. And I look back at him like . . . yes, like he's a stranger, too. Well, he is a stranger. I don't know a thing about him. I don't know *him*. The Robert I fell in love with is as fictitious as a Mahonia Medmenham hero, and, I suddenly realise, bears many similarities, starting with his exotic profession, and up to and including his cleft chin. The Robert I fell in love with is an invention. Whereas the Robert sitting beside me is real.

Oh well, I'm sure I'll fall in love with the real Robert, too. How could I fail to fall for him? I mean, just look at him! His bone structure's quite perfect – so perfect, in fact, that there's almost something offputting about it. And he's so very interesting – well, he must be interesting because he's an actor, and actors are creative people, and creative people are interesting *per se*. In fact, Robert's just the kind of partner I've always dreamed of. If he's not a success yet, so what? He will be one day. The RSC may not have found him sufficiently talented to keep in their company, but he certainly succeeded in convincing me.

The voices in the corridor have died down. I realise that Cecil must have made some excuse to our parents, then gone home. A strange, hollow feeling opens up inside me, but I've no idea what it is.

'. . . We can live in my flat for a bit while I . . . Lisa?' Robert squeezes my hand. 'Darling? Are you listening?'

'Sorry. What were you saying?'

'Just that we can stay in my old flat until I get some work. It's not really suitable for the little sprog, but we'll manage somehow. And the moment I've paid Cecil back the money, we'll buy a bigger flat where . . .'

'What money?' I interrupt sharply.

Robert hesitates. 'You know, the twenty grand.'

'But I thought you didn't take it?'

'I didn't.' He raises his chin proudly and tosses back his

hair. 'Not at first. But then, when you phoned to tell me you were pregnant, and I knew I had to give you up, that I'd never see you again . . . There didn't seem any harm in it then. After all, I thought, Cecil had you, so why shouldn't I take the cash? At least I'd be able to go away for a few weeks and try to get over things.'

What *is* this hollow feeling inside me? I struggle like mad to put my finger on it, and suddenly I locate it.

It's loss.

I've lost all my feeling for Robert.

Much worse than that, I've lost Cecil.

But I don't want Cecil. I never liked him, not even in the beginning. Stupid me, here I go again, being perverse. I try to focus my mind on all the pluses of my potential future with Robert, but all I can think is, *I might never see Cecil again*.

'Lisa? What's the matter?'

I sit up in a panic and, clutching the milk-barrels with one hand, swing my broken ankle onto the floor. Out of bed, I throw on my dressing gown then hobble over to the fish tank and pick up the sleeping parasite.

'Where are you going?' Robert calls out as I limp from the room.

Out in the hospital corridor, my parents and my mother-in-law crowd around me, all yelling questions at once. 'Where do you think you're taking that baby?' 'You should be in bed!' 'Who's that man in there?' 'Is something wrong between you and Cecil?' 'Lisa, I don't understand – what's happening?'

'Where's Cecil?' I demand.

'He's gone back to the flat. And why . . .?'

'Lisa, what's going on?' my mother yells after me as I flee down the corridor towards the lift.

Downstairs, ignoring the curious stare of the hospital receptionist, I stumble out into the car park. Shoulders hunched, head lowered, Cecil is making his way over to his car. When I call out his name, and he swings around in surprise, I see that his eyes are red.

'What about Sandra?' I pant breathlessly as he walks towards me.

Cecil freezes. 'Who?'

'Sandra!' I repeat. 'You know – S!'

Cecil frowns. After a moment, he takes a handkerchief from his coat pocket and blows his nose noisily. 'There is no Sandra,' he says.

'Yes, there is! You're having an affair with her!'

Cecil smiles unhappily. 'That's not true.'

'For God's sake, what's the point in denying it now, Cecil? I know all about it. I have for ages. You even said her name once, in your sleep. And I . . . I read her letters!' I admit.

Cecil smiles faintly. 'Yes. Yes, I know you did. Don't look so guilty, Lisa. I'm glad you have at least one vice – even if it's only going through my suit pockets.'

'But I don't understand . . . If you knew I was reading them, why did you leave them lying around?' This time Cecil says nothing, he merely shrugs and turns away again. 'Cecil?'

'You're a novelist, Lisa,' he says over his shoulder as he walks back to his car. 'Use your imagination.'

Despite the pain in my ankle, I hobble after him as fast as I can, and tug at his sleeve like a nagging child who refuses to be fobbed off. 'I know that Sandra was in New York with you this week. I don't blame you for having an affair with her. After all, I drove you to it. Do you . . . do you love her very much, Cecil?' Something twists inside me when I asked this. 'Are you going to see her now?'

Cecil turns towards me and sighs. 'No, no.' He looks utterly defeated. 'Look, Lisa, you may as well know – Sandra doesn't exist. She never existed. I invented her, just like I invented Robert.'

'That's not so! What about her letters?'

'I wrote them myself. I mean, I composed them. I paid a woman in Villefranche to write them down.'

'I don't understand!'

'God, you're making this difficult for me!' He takes a deep breath. 'The letters were my last-ditch attempt to win you.

I left them around because I wanted you to find them. Idiot that I was, I hoped that if you thought someone else wanted me, you might want me, too.'

For some reason, a great weight lifts from my shoulders. I feel like a condemned woman who's suddenly been granted a reprieve: *Mrs Brown, your HIV test was not positive after all* . . . 'So does that mean you're not in love with her?'

'There is no *her* to be in love with,' Cecil smiles sadly. 'My darling, this may not be to my credit, but I've never loved anyone but you.'

He walks over to his car and opens the door, but then I say, 'Good,' and he does a 360 degree turn and walks back towards me.

'Why good?' he whispers, frowning at me as earnestly as if his life depended on my answer. 'What do you mean?'

I force the words out of me: 'Just that . . . I love you, Cecil.'

Cecil's face bleaches to white. '*What?*'

'I love you.'

His mouth opens slowly. 'I thought you loved Robert?'

I shrug. 'I thought I did too. I mean, I suppose I did for a while. As a fantasy figure. I'm afraid the reality is much less appealing. Anyway, that's all in the past. It's you I love now.'

Cecil passes his hand over his closely shaved head. 'Again,' he says urgently. 'Say it again, Lisa. Once more with feeling.'

'I love you, Cecil,' I repeat. 'I really love you. I think I've loved you for a long time, without knowing it. I mean, I still feel furious with you for doing what you did but . . . well, I think I can forgive you.' I smile shyly. 'After all, it's not many men who are prepared to pay £20,000 for one bonk with their wife. And anyway, I still think you're the most extraordinary man in the world. You're unselfish, and original, and intelligent, and generous. And you really care about me. I mean, I don't know about now, but I know that you did care once. And I was wondering . . . I mean, despite

271

everything that's happened, do you think we've left it too late for a happy ending?'

Just as I say this, the bundle in my arms wakes up and begins to squirm in a violent worm-like fashion. Within seconds, its face turns the colour of sun-dried tomatoes, and it gives a toothless, frenzied wail. 'Oh God!' I cry, holding it at arm's length. 'What's wrong with it?'

Tenderly and carefully, Cecil takes it from me and, with a gentleness and skill which provoke a sense of envious wonderment in me, joggles it up and down on his shoulder. 'It can't be too late, Lisa,' he says above its screams. 'This is our child. Our daughter. Her happiness depends on us. Look at her! Isn't she beautiful?' he whispers, gazing down in awe as she stops screaming and begins to gurgle. 'The most beautiful baby there's ever been!'

I look at her doubtfully. 'Do you think so?'

'Of course! Look at that tiny nose! And these little bitty fingers!' He strokes the baby's cheek with his thumb-tip. 'Oh, and feel how soft her skin is, darling! Like the finest rose petals in the world.' Lightly, he plants a kiss on the parasite's wrinkled forehead, then hands her back to me with a sly smile. 'I hope you won't get jealous because I love her so much.'

I look down at the tiny creature in my arms, and for the first time it registers on me that it's not a parasite; there's a real human being lying there, and I'm its mother. I have a child. A daughter. My daughter. At the age of thirty-six I've joined that hitherto exclusive club where the annual fee is permanent exhaustion and the membership card sick stains on the shoulders of all your clothes.

Something new stirs inside me – a desire to protect my daughter from harm, to be there for her whenever she needs me, and to be a better mother to her than my own has been to me. A flood of emotion gushes up from some deep reservoir I'd never suspected existed in me. Ten minutes ago, I hadn't even wanted to pick my daughter up. Now, I never want to let go of her.

Great hot tears of love begin to spill from my eyes onto my daughter's head. 'Don't cry, darling!' Cecil whispers as he puts his arm around my waist. 'We're just beginning, just starting out. A little late in the day, perhaps, but . . . well . . .'

'*C'est la vie*,' I sniff, finishing the sentence off for him.

'Yes. *C'est notre vie*. Ours, and little Molly's here . . .'

'Molly?' I gasp. 'Who said anything about calling her Molly?'

'OK. Lolita, then.'

'*What?*'

'Didn't I ever tell you that Nabakov was my favourite writer? Mahonia Medmenham excepted, that is.'

'No! What a coincidence! He's mine, too! Still, this baby is Lolita over my dead body. We'll have to think of another name. Anything will do. At least,' I add, glancing at him slyly, 'anything except Sandra.'

'Or Roberta.'

We look at each other nervously, then we both burst out laughing. Cecil's mouth – his heavy, rich, sensuous mouth, how could I ever have compared it with a frog's? – reaches up to mine. Maybe the pethidine hasn't quite worn off yet, because my head begins swimming even before our lips touch, and my sore, swollen nipples prick with pleasure – or is it milk?

I close my eyes and breathe in the wonderful elusive scent I once searched for in vain in Robert's sheets, a scent more sweet and musky than the most expensive men's perfume . . .

'Ouch!'

'What's wrong?'

'I think it's my stitches.'

Cecil draws in a sharp breath. 'Poor darling! When I think what you've been through because of me!'

'Snap!'

We giggle together, but our daughter doesn't seem to enjoy the joke as much as we do. Her tiny mouth stretches into a wet cavern, and she lets out a piercing wail. 'Maybe she's hungry,' Cecil suggests. 'Should we take her back inside and feed her?'

Despite my stitches and my broken ankle, I waltz back into the hospital on Cecil's arm. My feet are floating above the tarmac, the birds are singing, and the sunshine seems unnaturally bright. How can it be possible that I'm suddenly so happy? It feels like a miracle. When I come to think of it, it is a miracle – the miracle of falling in love. The day before yesterday I felt suicidal. Now I'm cock-a-hoop. And why shouldn't I be, when I have a beautiful baby daughter, and a wonderful husband with whom I can never imagine having an unpleasant word?

OK, maybe that *never* is an exaggeration. No doubt Cecil will annoy me to distraction one day soon, and I'll annoy him, too. Inevitably, there'll come a time when we'll be at each other's throats again. He'll criticise my untidiness, and I'll tell him off for not pulling his weight in the kitchen. He'll interrupt me when I'm writing, and I'll accuse him of always being on the phone. He'll become an impossibly conceited media celebrity who's never around when I need him, and I'll be an incredibly boring stay-at-home mother and wife.

When I come to think about it, we'll probably argue about everything: how much money we spend; and where to go on holiday; and which slob was it who forgot to rinse out the bath; and at what age – if any – our precious little daughter should be allowed to go out alone with boys.

I suppose it's even possible that, one day in the far distant future, I might find another man attractive, or that Cecil might run off with a real live Sandra. Perhaps I ought to warn him right now that I'll kill him if he does . . .

I remind myself that this moment is just a beginning, and that there's no guaranteed happy-ever-after. But, right now, I don't really care what the future has in store for us. So what if I'm living in a fool's paradise? I'm happy to stay here for as long as it lasts.